White Shark

A JIM HAWKINS MYSTERY

White Shark

Ross Gresham

FIVE STAR
A part of Gale, Cengage Learning

GALE
CENGAGE Learning

Farmington Hills, Mich • San Francisco • New York • Waterville, Maine
Meriden, Conn • Mason, Ohio • Chicago

LIBRARY OF CONGRESS CATALOGING-IN-PUBLICATION DATA

Names: Gresham, Ross, author.
Title: White shark / Ross Gresham.
Description: Waterville, Maine : Five Star Publishing, a part of Cengage Learning, Inc. 2016. | Series: A Jim Hawkins mystery
Identifiers: LCCN 2015050626 (print) | LCCN 2016003828 (ebook) | ISBN 9781432831813 (hardcover) | ISBN 143283181X (hardcover) | ISBN 9781432831745 (ebook) | ISBN 1432831747 (ebook)
Subjects: LCSH: Police—Massachusetts—Fiction. | Missing persons—Investigation—Fiction. | BISAC: FICTION / Thrillers. | FICTION / Mystery & Detective / General. | GSAFD: Black humor (Literature) | Suspense fiction. | Mystery fiction.
Classification: LCC PS3607.R49865 W48 2016 (print) | LCC PS3607.R49865 (ebook) | DDC 813/.6—dc23
LC record available at http://lccn.loc.gov/2015050626

First Edition. First Printing: May 2016
Find us on Facebook– https://www.facebook.com/FiveStarCengage
Visit our website– http://www.gale.cengage.com/fivestar/
Contact Five Star™ Publishing at FiveStar@cengage.com

Printed in the United States of America
1 2 3 4 5 6 7 20 19 18 17 16

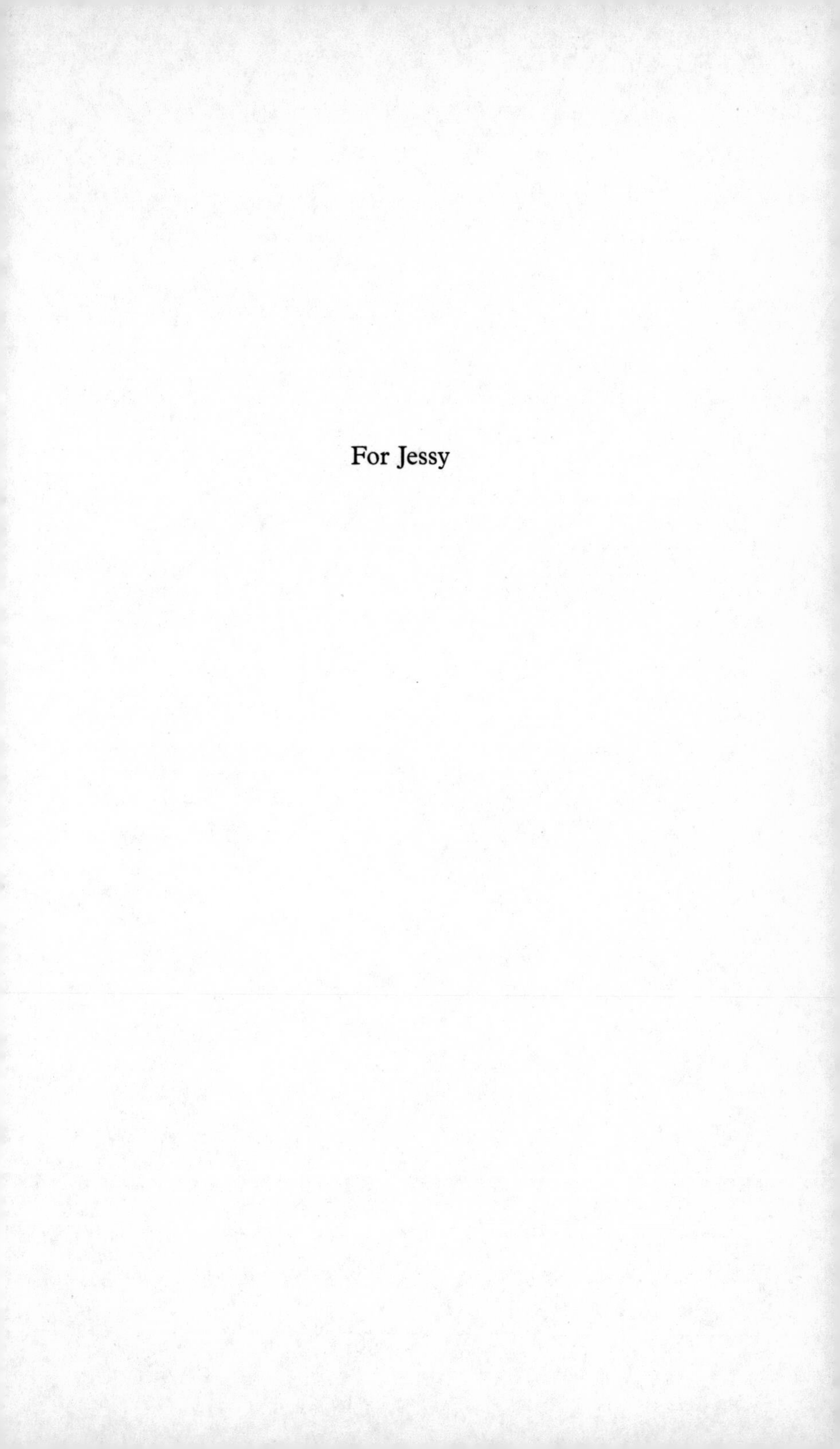

For Jessy

Chapter 1

My wristwatch beeped. *First, do no harm. Second, do no harm. Third, do no harm.* It didn't keep accurate time—gave its best guess—but if you knew how to listen, it talked like a seashell.

It was the early season, mid-morning, and I was out there with my cop whistle in the suicide intersection with no traffic to direct, just looking stupid.

The new warning signs were bloody. Tourists nudged in at five mph, gripping the wheel, looking left and right for the promised collision. Then their thought was: What's that cop doing in the road? One-man checkpoint? They passed so slowly that we found it only polite to sustain conversation. Weather? Plans for their day?

Sometimes the wife had her purse open. They figured I was out there to collect some new fee. They'd learned how the island works. Some new pleasure tax we imposed on visitors.

Mid-May. For island tourists, these were the poor ones. They were packing their lunches, making do, picnic on the breakwater. Europeans on bikes. Young couple with a baffled baby harnessed to the backseat. They knew they were supposed to vacation out here, and they could just afford a week at 2K. High summer and it would be double or more.

Already hot. The morning sun had softened the blacktop road, so that my footsteps fell as quiet as on the forest floor. Already I was plucking my pants away from the back of my knees.

I wasn't in a fine mood. I rarely was those days. My housing situation had gone bad and I was bivouacked on the beach, showering in the public place with the pull-string. Hated my boss. That was just the general day-to-day situation. Then not five minutes before I'd been matadored by a black Audi that came off the pier at highway speeds. I thought I recognized the car. There was a storage garage I patrolled most evenings.

First, do no harm. Second, do no harm. Third, do no harm. Still echoed in my head.

Over at the fish stand, the Jamaican kid beckoned. I got there and the manager was outside trying to quell the situation with his arms. "We're all set, we're all set," the manager said, meaning I should go away. The Jamaican kid hadn't yet realized that he was a slave in all matters, and he was still complaining, still indignant. And of course my heart was with the summer help. They ship these kids in, big promises, then as soon as they step off the boat the deal starts to get worse.

"That man run off on his food!" the kid said. The manager shook his head, to say the kid was crazy.

"The Audi?" I said. "Fancy black car?"

"He ordered ninety dollars in food, and then he's off. We never have time to prepare it. Back there we're preparing it as fast as can be."

"That dick." For some reason the kid handed me the bag of lobster rolls. The manager had never quit talking but he did now, throwing up his hands like the kid and I were both crazy. I told the Jamaican kid, "I'll make a special delivery."

"You be the pizza man for that guy," he said. "Show up with your lights turning and tell him to come back here."

So the whole thing started with a bag of lobster rolls. What a joke. Out there on the island, I was a joke too, a cop hired for the summer rush, no different than the Jamaican kid. In the ancient town charter, the budget line designated me as "the Parking Warden." The Parking Warden. Yes, should have been laughs all around.

My memories of what happened next are mostly crap. Who pays attention to their day? You don't know it's going to be important. Of course, now, when I look back, the whole morning glows with significance.

I never knew the back roads on the island. No one could. Unlabeled intersections, branching off at angles like the arms of a starfish. But that drive, that morning, was maybe the only time I didn't wander lost and give up. Instead, there I was, floating along in the cruiser, making all the turns like an island native.

Maybe the dust in the air guided me. The standard dirt on Nausset Island is sand. It doesn't hold water, and that was a dry, dry summer. Maybe a haze of sand still hung in the air from the passing Audi and led me like a thread in a maze.

I ate lobster roll after lobster roll. Later I counted the wrappers and the guy, Cunningham, had ordered seven lobster rolls, food for his whole family.

Turns out I knew his house. I'd seen it from my island, where I camped out. He had the mansion with its own cove.

From the road the house was even bigger. There was no end to it, like a grand hotel. Gray Nantucket shingles and a private dock. A little boathouse. A little crafted harbor. The ocean. To the side, the view, as far as you could see, was acres of salt-grass marsh.

Something was wrong. Wooden posts were torn off, right beside the gravel drive. The posts were broken at different heights, low and high. The fractures were fresh, bright pine. They were a wrecked structure.

And the Audi was parked wrong. It was parked sideways across a sizeable gravel strip, and the driver's door was open. Door open, but no driver. It was the only car.

The mansion itself looked abandoned. It was still closed for the winter. The porch chairs were bunched in the corner of the deck. The front windows displayed the police papers that announced that it was unoccupied. All the island houses wore these papers until the owners returned.

I got out of the cruiser, just from momentum. I didn't have much reason to be there. I had nothing to show. On the seat, the food sack was empty except for wax papers, salt packets, and a tub of lemon wedges. "Hey?" I called.

The wreckage wasn't a shed or anything. It had been a sign, a huge sign, like a highway billboard. Something had smashed it. You'd say the wind caught it like a sail, but the flat part of the sign was marked by tire tracks. A vehicle with knobby tires had run it over again and again.

LAST LIGHTHOUSE. CONDOS FROM 250.
MULTIFAMILY. SECTION 8. SUBSTANCE ABUSE
COUNSELLING ON SITE. DOG PARK.

My anger and energy drained away. Like the island rain drained through the island sand. I was overcome with pity.

The man was losing his house to developers. With a place so beautiful, you couldn't stand to lose it.

A little sloop sailed out toward the mouth of the cove.

I could have called down. It wasn't far, a hundred yards—I could have thrown him a baseball. Instead I stood mute. Something was changing in my day, and I hadn't figured out what.

The boat's sails were badly set. Main and jib shivered. The man in the cockpit was resting with his head over the side. He was looking for ropes trailing in the water. There was a blur and sparkle to the whole picture, which was clear flame, the clear flame of burning alcohol.

I always liked the sense of humor in that. Giving yourself a Viking funeral. Flaming ship in the morning. You decide you've had enough, but hey, that's your private decision and you don't want to be a nuisance. You set your sailboat on fire and point it for the high seas. Blow your brains out.

It's a likeable suicide. No inconvenience. It's got wit and showmanship. You wouldn't know some bored cop would show up and spoil it. A cop shows up in a cloud of dust and in an instant he strips down. He swims out to stop you right at the mouth of the cove. You would have made it anyway but that shore wind shifts—always shifty where the land meets the water—and your boat needed to bang on the rip-rap a few more times before it was going around. Two more knocks on the rock, then straight on to Valhalla.

Sure, you make some mistakes. Suicide isn't something you practice. With your brains blown out you have to put your trust in the autopilot, and no autopilot can account for the fickle wind. Instead of gasoline, you use the alcohol fuel for the boat stove, which barely burns hot enough to ignite paper. And you forget that flames burn upwards. They're not going to do much to your fat disaster of a body—barely crisp your clothes—and they're not going to magically travel down into the can of lawn-mower gas, just because you leave it uncapped. So, no farewell fireball.

But the ultimate bad luck is the cop. You get the one frustrated cop whose life is going nowhere. Under-employed, or thinks he is. Even the US Army cut this guy from its payroll! That says a lot. And then his girl apparently discovered the same flaws, because she cut him loose, kicked him out of her place, so that now he has to swim a mile each night to camp on the deserted barrier island.

The idiot cop collects your bobbing shoe on his swim out—hey, thanks! Useful! And he pulls himself over the side only to slip in a puddle of alcohol and plunk back in. Hits the gunnel like a bull sea lion—what a clown!—almost breaks his hip.

Well, at least he doesn't feel very good about stopping you, once he sees the blood, once he realizes what you were trying to do. And if it's any consolation, he doesn't get a lot of thanks.

Chapter 2

A week later I waved down a junk Buick that was going 38.

I admit it was a speed trap. Two miles before you came into town, suddenly you were down to twenty on an open road.

The danger came from a line of squat, ancient trees that grew within a yard of traffic. Their limbs made no pretense of straightness but twisted like arms of a fairy-tale forest, and these limbs had been brutally cut back into a tunnel for cars and trucks. We also cut three perfect pull-outs, then generated revenue by concealing a cop with a radar gun.

The speed trap was a trap for tourists, tourists only. Chief sold "island" stickers to all the locals, and if the car displayed one of those, we let it go.

That was Chief's policy, anyway. Instead I gave out warnings to all customers. Those poor tourists. I carried free maps to distribute, to try to give them some idea what was ahead.

This guy, when I asked for the license, the guy instead held up his private investigator license. Simon Boco, Private Investigator.

"What's this?"

He was a local. The window had a run of stickers back into faded history. Boco was an older guy with frizzy hair and the summer island squint. He squinted ahead now, his lips working a murmur monologue. He held the P.I. card in two bent fingers as though he might flick it in my face. Read it and weep.

"Step out of the car. Bring your license and registration back to the cruiser."

This private investigator, Boco, had caught me at a bad time.

There was my tension with the Chief.

The Chief hired me to come out to the island. When I got the call, I'd been scrambling for anything, so I could follow my girl, Marsha. I thought Marsha was my girl. I would have taken any job whatsoever. I had honestly applied to scoop ice cream. So real police work? *Yow,* jackpot, that's what I wanted to be.

The Chief and I faxed the papers back and forth. Maybe said a word on the phone. Done deal. Going great. Then he and I finally met face to face. Ten minutes off the boat, he and I struck sparks.

He was an old prune in a cowboy hat. His mouth hung open to show a full set of amber teeth. "You're the Chief?" I asked.

He looked me up and down with hatred and disbelief, like he'd been expecting a girl and I'd arrived as his dinner date, bait and switch.

Another officer was there to show me around the station—Detective Wakin—and the Chief actually trotted behind the two of us on this tour, like he couldn't believe what he was seeing. By his expression you would think I had an obscene face tattoo, or contact lenses that made my eyes glow green.

At this point I should take a minute . . . There's nothing wrong with me. I'm a big guy, have white hair and pale eyes, but I'm not an actual albino. In every way I am normal, but I do have this power that you witness here: I induce instant animosity. It's only with some people, but by no means is the Chief alone. It's hate at first sight. I just prompt it with some percentage of strangers. You find something similar between certain dogs.

So I arrived. My guide guided me. Detective Wakin. He didn't like me either, but only because he was too important to do this menial duty, and he was too fat to walk except in emergencies, like to escape a fire. Wakin showed me my police belt and my locker. No pistol—not for a six-month contract.

The locker had old uniforms. They were uniforms from the kid hired the previous summers. I lifted one on its hanger and burst out laughing. I couldn't fit my hand in the sleeve. My size goes up and down, but never under 200 pounds. I mean, some cars don't fit me. These uniforms were for a doll. "Maybe have to get them altered," muttered Detective Wakin.

"What?" I laughed. " 'Altered'? You need twice the fabric. Maybe if you sewed two of them together. Believe me, you have to order a fresh set."

"Yaargh"—the Chief made a death rattle, so that Detective Wakin and I looked back in alarm. My demand turned the Chief an unhealthy color, where he lost both blood and eye focus.

The Chief was at a stage of his life where he could not be told anything. Being told a fact meant he didn't know it already, so that he couldn't abide, and being told he must do something . . . He'd been police chief for decades. Maybe for twenty years, no one had spoken to him other than to fawn or beg.

Tactics! My problem is that I have no tactics. So I've been told, and it's true. Tactics could have gotten me new uniforms. I could have twisted the matter until it sounded as though the Chief were granting me a favor, my one birthday wish. Tactics! It would have been nice to have decent shirts, because once a week I blew out those things. I'd stretch or reach for something and *Kapow!* I'd jog back to the car in shredded rags, like the Frankenstein creature hounded by villagers.

By the end of my time as Parking Warden I was down to just one miracle shirt, older than the others, sewn with ancient thread that held like parachute cord. That shirt did solo duty almost the whole last month. You'll see. I started May 1 with a locker full of shirts but by the end I wore that last one for twenty consecutive days. Then it got wiped out in the most dramatic fashion. You'll see. Completely wiped out, and I liked that shirt. It was a tough little number.

Whatever other sickness the Chief suffered from (bad lungs, heart, organs—all that summer he knocked at death's door) . . . whatever else, the Chief had boss sickness. He saw himself as a Southern sheriff. Boss Hog. He loved favors, especially. The Favor Economy. He loved to tear up tickets while people were watching, all the while fixing you with a bright eye. Give him a wink and comp him an ice cream, he would be happy to let the party go on another hour, whatever the noise ordinances might read. As long as everyone knew who made the dispensation. Hey, thanks Chief!

When a local drove drunk, one of these wash-outs he went to high school with, we weren't allowed to arrest the man. Instead we had to park his car, like the hotel valet—"will this suit, sir?"—"very good, my man"—park his car and give him a ride home.

At least that was the stated policy. When this situation actually arose, a better solution suggested itself immediately, which was to take the drunk's keys. Confiscate the keys and lock them inside the vehicle. The trick was to leave the keys dangling in plain sight. Then, after I drove off, the drunk could choose to bang out his own window, if he nerved himself up to it, or he could accept the situation and walk home. A healthy night stroll—nothing better to clear the head—his choice.

As the officer on scene, that was your safe play, because if you took the drunk's keys and just whipped them off into the darkness . . . I tried *that* and the fucking fool skulked around for hours, searching on his knees, to be mistaken for both a prowler and a Sasquatch. Nine-one-one calls lit up the switchboard.

Anyway, the Chief hated me right away, and right away I knew he was a clown, and this was before we'd exchanged one word. So at least on this one matter, our mutual feelings, we had a sort of handshake agreement.

Then, my first week on the job, there was the incident at the Wharf House.

The Wharf House was a restaurant so pricey you imagine laughter at the session where they write up the menu. Plate of clams at $30, 40, 50, can we dare ask $60? Let's do it! $60! Everyone hated it. It was terrible. Nice view, overlooked the main harbor, but tourists only.

So one morning, almost my first day, I heard that the place had been vandalized. I'd been on island two days, writing parking tickets for the Chief to rip up later, barely knew where the Wharf House was. I had just fit myself into a uniform shirt when the Chief came through the lockers. "Jimbo, time to put all that fancy schooling to work. Take care of this." He said this so it had the Godfather echo: "Take care of this." Like before I departed I was supposed to kneel and kiss his big Catholic jewel ring.

I asked directions and drove to the restaurant. At this point no one had told me a thing.

Right inside, the restaurant foyer smelled like the dumpster behind the dog shelter. The whole room was a gas of dog shit, so thick it browned the air and filtered the available light like the glass of a beer bottle.

"Christ!" I let out, breathing through my sleeve.

The carpet! The carpet had been shellacked with dog shit, in major quantities. You've never seen anything like it. Not the entry carpet, because that could be removed. That was untouched. But the seating area was totally smeared. Painted. Someone had used a push broom.

A summer kid knelt there scraping with a cedar shingle and a beach bucket. He was smeared brown—knees, apron, and even smudges on his little paper hat. A week over the deep fryer had already given the kid a complexion like a bug attack. When he saw me, he slumped off mutely.

Out came the owner. Mr. Trent. He looked me up and down with the island squint, which became more pronounced in his disappointment. The Chief had sent him the summer hire? He didn't articulate this complaint, however. He didn't say anything to me because for fifteen minutes he was on his phone.

He talked to cleaners on the mainland. He kept using his first name as well. Malcolm Trent. He mentioned "the Wharf House" as though that would seal the deal. On the national register, maybe. "That's right, this is Malcolm Trent." Been written up in *Food and Wine*. Whoever first answered the phone, he would get their name. Then he'd demand to talk to the manager, and he would use that name: "Mike, Mike, I was talking with Candice there and she said you guys could hook me up."

I was pleased to see, however, that the cleaning companies didn't seem to be responding. They offered him bookings a few weeks down the road. They didn't want to waste their day taking the ferry.

Long story short, Malcolm Trent was a dick, a major dick. Let me be clear. This wasn't one phone call he took while I stood there. He was dialing company after company. Rather, he made the Information girl connect him. "April, you're not doing it for me here. April, I'm talking professionals." Then suddenly Trent came off the phone with urgency. "What the fuck?" he said to me. He shrugged as though he couldn't believe: "Don't you got to get this guy? You got to call the boat, stop the boat."

"The 9:15 ferry? I can make the 9:15," I said. "You already know who did this?"

"Je-sus," he said, disgusted at this waste of time. He hurried me out the door with a name. *"Just pick him up."*

I didn't get any real information until I was on the ferry itself. There was Dr. Harris, as described, at the rail, making no attempt to hide. He stood beside a bicycle with a milk crate lashed on back. He saw my uniform coming up the gangplank, and he looked down bashfully.

"Dr. Harris?"

Dr. Harris nodded, gave me a shy smile, but didn't speak. He either wouldn't speak or couldn't. Dr. Harris was a seventy-year-old doctor, bald and formidable, muscle and bone. Looked like he oiled his stubbly head.

"So, ah, the Wharf House . . . ?" I ventured. By no means was I an experienced interrogator. Truth be told, even some of the credentials I'd faxed the Chief were more my plans than actual accomplishments, some of the coursework and whatnot.

The doctor held up a single finger, as if to say, hold that thought. Doc's attention was on the ferry crew. They cast off the enormous cables, one by one, calling out. This was a process the doctor wanted to study, or it was the sort of performance he didn't feel was appropriate to talk over.

Fine. I watched and waited along with him. When they threw the last rope, the doctor immediately turned to me with all his attention. He was a doctor now, could be asking questions for his clipboard. "What is your name, officer?"

"Jim Hawkins."

"Yes," he said. "You're new."

Have I told you how inbred the island is? Any fresh set of facial features sets them a-tizzy. I cleared my throat. "Sure. I'm the summer temp. Parking Warden."

"And you would like to discuss the history of the Wharf House supper club. Specifically, as it pertains to me. All right. I'm agreeable. Would you like to take notes? No?"

Believe me, Dr. Harris didn't need to be prompted. With the ferry under way, he became a doctor explaining your cancers. His hands moved, lost, searching for his props, searching for the plastic doctor's office models of your organs. His story had a calm, practiced pacing.

Here it is: End of last season, Dr. Harris and his wife had come over to the island from Boston. It was their 50th wedding anniversary and, for some reason, his wife wanted to go to the Wharf House. They had been coming to the island for years and she wanted to try it. They both ate bad clams and spent the night as you can imagine, firing both ends. Between bouts, Dr. Harris walked over to the Wharf House and told them that the clams were bad. Mr. Malcolm Trent handled the matter himself. Came out of the office. Apologized. Multiple handshakes. The meal was going to be free—credit card charges wiped. The clam supplier disciplined. The bad clams destroyed.

The "bad clam scam." The Wharf House was a tourist restaurant. Why would they throw out clams when instead they could sell them for money? Why would they wipe a check just because they said they would? On Dr. Harris's homeward boat the next day, a half-dozen people were lining up outside the ferry restroom. All victims of the Wharf House. Dr. Harris ministered to the sick. When he received his credit card statement, the charges for the poison meal hadn't been wiped.

There were follow-up phone calls. American Express got involved, in some impotent way. Hostilities escalated.

"So you really came back here to pour shit all over the carpet?" I asked him, impressed. "You imported dog shit on that bike?"

Dr. Harris studied me. "What shit? Whose carpets? Did I

suggest that at any point, young man? With the information I provided to you? I ask you, if I were seeking appropriate revenge, wouldn't I have vomited on the carpets also?"

Then he brought out a telephone and wanted to show me something. A number was there on the screen, ready to go. "Shall I call Saul?"

"Who's Saul?" I asked.

"My personal attorney." He showed me the screen more closely.

"Only if you want to talk to him," I said. I told Dr. Harris to have a nice day, bought him a hot dog.

All of which is a long way of saying that Simon Boco's speeding ticket was part of a larger picture.

"Let me see the radar. What kind of radar you guys using? Some of these older ones . . ." The monologue of Simon Boco, PI, had grown more audible. The radar gun was right there on the dash for his inspection so I said nothing. "Some of these older ones . . . Believe me, I did my time behind a radar gun."

"Yeah? Makes hash of your sperm count."

"Oh sure, I was on the beat, believe me. Oh, yeah. Believe me." He shook his head to indicate that it would be impossible to articulate the extent of his service. "You a vet?" he asked.

I grunted and finished his ticket.

"Whoa, we got the highway patrol out here. Texas highway patrol."

"What was that?" I said.

"I asked if you were a vet."

"Sure," I said. "Army. You?"

"Oh yeah, oh yeah. Navy."

"Now do we suck face?"

"Hey, okay, Jesus. I mean, because I did my time on the big ships, I mean the carriers, the USS . . ."

An island bus passed, moving so fast that the cruiser rocked on its struts. Going at least 50 through the trees. It couldn't help but undermine my righteousness, though Boco didn't say anything for a while, squinting at my handwriting on his ticket. Then he said, "They doing a memorial service out here for Cunningham?"

"Cunningham? Out here? I'm sure it's in New York City, not some summer island."

"Summer island? Oh man. He was big out here. Big? Real big. The biggest. Oh, man, you have no idea . . ."

Boco went on breathlessly. It didn't matter that I wasn't paying any attention, that I was watching the road in my side mirror. Boco left short pauses for me to express wonder or admiration. Finally during one of these I raised a finger to indicate his Buick. "You're all set. Keep it slow, partner, for the children."

Then I looked over, and Boco was hunched as though I'd just clubbed him. This speeding ticket was the worst thing that had ever befallen him in his life. He turned it in his fingers like a telegram notifying him of family tragedy—looking, looking away, looking again. He'd put on little half-glasses, such as might be worn by a Christmas gnome. It was hard to guess the age of those island guys, with their beat-up faces and their ratty cutoffs.

I sighed. "It's just a couple hundred bucks. Write it off on your taxes."

"Cunningham died owing me some hours. Yeah, big time."

"Really?"

"Oh yeah, I can't tell you how many hours, lots of hours. And because there was mileage, oh yeah, all over the place . . ."

"That poor man," I said, and I felt it. I hated to imagine what those "hours" would be. Cunningham, a real professional, was probably used to New York, dealing with professional people, and somehow he is stuck listening to Boco, and paying for the time. I said, "Anybody can go broke. Lose your house. They cut it up into cheap condominiums. When poverty happens to these guys, the numbers are inconceivable. Unstoppable poverty, in the millions."

"Broke?" This caused Boco to take off his glasses and smile, a strangely still smile, directed at me and unwavering. Finally I shrugged. Boco said, "Marcus Cunningham could have taken out his checkbook and written you a check for one million dollars. Any time since he was sixteen. One million, five million, twenty-five million . . ."

"He was in properties, right? I figured with the market—"

"He owned a third of the island! Broke! If you think that guy is ever going broke, was ever going to go broke . . . There could be a nuclear war and who would survive is Marcus Cunningham, doing just fine, thank you, with some attractive options to buy . . ." Boco went on, general theme, Cunningham's wealth; secondary theme, my ignorance of Cunningham's wealth.

I noticed that the muffler on Boco's car was attached with a coat hanger. I said, "Well, that shit bucket you're driving . . . Apparently he couldn't pay you."

Boco cawed like a parrot. Just as before, one minute he was a loud mouth, then I said one thing in response and he was ready to weep. I had honestly hurt his feelings. It wasn't fair, this Boco conversation rhythm. He'd pitch hardballs. You hit one back, he dissolved in tears.

"Man," I said, "if Cunningham had money, his estate will settle the debt. Just talk to his widow."

"The widow!" Boco cawed again. I'd chosen the right thing to say, because immediately all despair was forgotten. He hooted. "Oh right. Sarah Palsinger. That's exactly who I can't talk to, if you know what I mean. I'm going to bill Sarah Palsinger for some photographs? Let me remind you of who you're speaking to. Think about it. I'm a licensed private dick."

"You're what? Man . . . I get it, but just quit saying things, for one minute."

Boco allowed me a breath or two before resuming. "Cunningham came out here for Sarah, because this was her place. It was her thing, but he liked what he saw and you know he started buying, you know he's going to buy . . ."

"His wife was leaving him?"

"I didn't say leaving him. Check this out. You got to see this." Boco went through a purse-bag. He produced a camera with a picture screen. "That's Cunningham's own place. He has a dozen properties, maybe two dozen. That's his wife going in, you see. Now look. Eh?"

It was all too tawdry. Imagine Mr. Cunningham's position . . . He builds a mansion home for his family. The man dreamed big, you can see that. But then suddenly his pretty wife changes her mind. Women change their minds like the weather, and they don't have to explain the reasons. So the wife starts straying, and Cunningham flails around for anything, any kind of help. He hires what passes for a private investigator. He gets Boco here . . .

In the first photo, a classy lady went into a purple cottage. In the center of the town there was an extensive village of dollhouse cottages. The village was a famous site. It sold its own postcards. Each cottage was primped with its own design and arrangement of flowers.

In the picture the lady smiled self-consciously at her feet. She knew someone was watching. If you had her shape, probably someone was always watching. She had the figure of a pinup girl, and her modest blouse just made it worse. Across her chest the fabric was tight as a spinnaker.

A dozen photos of her. I took the camera from Boco and flipped through. The series of photos animated her movie-star walk.

The next photo stopped me. A man went into the same house. Same house. Same daylight.

"You altered the picture?"

Boco threw his head back in scorn. "What? Get out of here! I altered the photo? You give me one single—"

The man was so pretty, there was something wrong with him. I couldn't say what. He turned his face. His cheekbones were prominent knobs. The look wasn't real. He was part human and part something else. Cat. Leprechaun.

"Yeah, you see now," said Boco.

The man is the wrong shape or size. "You didn't alter this?"

A creep is a creep. I clicked the camera back to the woman, Cunningham's wife. In the last photo, she had an expression as she closed the door. I could only guess at it. Resolved? She was tough.

When I looked up again, Boco's face was right in mine. He eyed me hungrily. I shut him down. "*Pfft,* what bullshit. They're not together. This doesn't prove anything."

"It's a job! He hires me to snap photos. I snap photos. I have hours invested, and those are billable hours."

"All garbage. Christ, the man is dead. There's no proof here. Trash for the tabloids. Stir up bad feeling."

"I'm hired, and I do my job, the same—"

I ejected the chip out the side of the camera. "Is this everything?" The little screen went blue in protest. "All right. Let me keep this and I'll rip your ticket."

"What are you talking about?"

So that was the deal. I owed Cunningham. I had wrecked his Viking suicide. Now in return I ripped one bullshit ticket, a nothing price. Of course, I also had to endure ten more minutes of Boco's mosquito whine. To escape that I went under his car and re-did the coat-hanger wire that held his exhaust system off the road. At least his muffler wouldn't spark fire to the dry grasses of the island.

On my side of the trade I got some crap, gossip pictures that no one would ever have to see. I pushed the little memory chip deep into the solid wad of trash and wrappers that jammed the ashtray.

Boco made constant protest noise but essentially the exchange excited him. He loved it. But he worried I couldn't deliver. He said that I couldn't rip his ticket. I didn't have the authority. He repeated this old rumor: Once the cop begins to write a ticket, that's it, he can't stop.

I'd heard that rumor, too, but frankly couldn't see why. We used the old-style ticket books, with carbon paper. With my fingernail I just tore out the carbon. Gave Boco that as well. The last I saw of Boco, he sat at the wheel of his Buick trying to un-crumple it, for reasons best known to himself. Already his hands looked like he'd been playing in a bag of charcoal.

CHAPTER 3

Brand Frobisher led his young lady companion to the water's edge. Not for the timeless dance with the incoming surf, but rather because there the wet sand was firmer and he could bring her along at a more business-like pace. The boathouse was an exhausting mile, and there was nothing to do but cover the distance.

"Oh my God. I could live here forever," the girl said.

She was a heavy-boned young woman, apologizing for her broad shoulders by bending them forward, hoping to conceal and remediate her sturdy shape with a viciously tight dress. She was going barefoot but not enjoying it, not at this pace. The coarse sand. This wasn't California. This was Massachusetts. She'd seen party beaches on television and didn't understand the difference. The tide went out, half-heartedly lapping as though someone had switched off the machine.

"My girlfriend Irie has a cabin, but nothing like . . ." She spoke constantly, at the same pitch of praise and amazement, though now, in the dark, she had run out of fresh things to admire. She began to hear the tiresome pattern of her own birdsong.

Brand, a slight man, was always a step ahead. She couldn't see very much of him. The night was unpleasantly, rather than romantically, dark. And cold. It was early spring. He did not offer her his jacket.

She finished describing her friend's inferior lake cabin. "This is literally the nicest place I've ever been."

She reminded herself that this man was dreamy. When she and her girlfriends had come into the party, he was already there, staring openly. No drink. No cigarette. His hands at his sides. Immediately she and her friends went red under his unmistakable attention. They tightened their formation and talked at random. To three relatively plain girls, literally holding onto each other in their insecurity, Brand had appeared otherworldly. How could they have the attention of a man so beautiful?

And there *was* an elfin beauty in Brand's thin face, if the night had allowed her to see it. As always, he came immaculately dressed—tonight in a crisp, linen suit. His black hair swooped like a curl of butter frosting.

Yet the same face had something terribly wrong with it. The slight bone work, and the prominent jaw hinge, misplaced high under the ears . . . What was striking about Brand Frobisher's face and head would, upon further consideration, begin to appear alien, and then freakish. When he spoke, his expressions called attention to these alien dimensions. After beauty, the next impression he gave was of being infantile, or unfinished.

Brand knew the effect he had on women better than anyone. In a crowd a certain size, girls looked once, twice, three times. They winked, they flushed, and they giggled. But the clock had started.

Tonight, in the sand, he slowed a moment and caught her wrist. He did it to insist on the pace, but she misunderstood and took his hand. "This is so perfect."

She stopped to face the ocean. It was no view but the ocean was there. She bounced on her toes, anxious and uncertain.

Brand understood her better than she did. She didn't want to go farther into the unfamiliar dark.

"Not yet," he said. "Honey. Not here."

He certainly recognized the steps of this cooling. For two decades they had governed his seductions. And the next development? Next, she would begin to hint that she wanted to go home. Whatever excuse the two of them had used to leave the party, now the girl would pretend was real. They *did* just come out for the air, for a cigarette, to gaze at the water.

At this stage, in Brand's experience, American girls lasted longer. They had been taught to overcome their natural revulsions, or at least to hide them. Don't stare at the burned man's melted features, they had learned, and don't look away, either. Don't point at the cripple. When Brand got her to the boathouse, she would pretend that Brand's rough games excited her, too.

She could not see him, but realization had begun to set in nonetheless. The hand that she had taken was unpleasantly tender. She dropped it again. It felt like a hand that had just come out of a year in a plaster cast.

She rubbed her own bare arms. "I've always been, like, thin-blooded. My mom is the same, so we have sweaters just . . ."

A hot pin of anger slid between Brand's eyes. He would beat the bitch silly. Except that didn't work. Here in the sand, it became endless chasing and wrestling. The grit ruined the sex.

He played the next card: "We keep a car . . ." He walked ahead.

She followed. What else could she do? She had come to a private island. To get here Brand put his car onto a tiny, sputtering ferry. The ferryman had been waiting for them.

The boathouse appeared as a black sketch against the dark ocean. The loom of it calmed Brand, and put him in mind of other times. There was lust, yes: the memory of another girl's naked back, as she tottered away like a broken crab. Stupid bitch, tripping over her own panties. Yet at the same time, a vein of pollution ran through the memory. The endless scolding and mess . . . whole days of legal tedium . . . Brand couldn't shake the sensation.

"So you are in school where?" he asked suddenly. He had forgotten her name. He heard only the broader patterns of what she said, and so far no trouble. She was ideal. With constant glances, she checked to be sure she was doing her part correctly. She didn't even know how to walk beside a man—she was an untrained puppy.

"School? I'm doing that program. In broadcast radio. I want . . ."

She had to concentrate to answer Brand's sudden barrage of questions, boring questions, questions that made him seem like an old man: her age, her situation, her plans for the future. He sounded like a guidance counselor with a printed list.

What she mistook for clumsy interest was really Brand's business-like probing of her connections, and she didn't know how lucky she was. She couldn't have answered better. In the fall she was leaving for an obscure religious college in Iowa. To Brand, this meant her people had money. Her answers told him that she had a father and brothers. She spoke to her mother.

Each reply clubbed his enthusiasm. Each settled on him like a weight, pressing him into the damp sand. It was too much.

Then a breeze came across the water. The boathouse was close, and the breeze brought the smell of its boards. "Oh, this old place," he said, as though surprised to find it. "You have to step in here. Just take a look. A moment."

"Sorry," she said. Talk of family connections made her stop and check her telephone. The screen lit the night. "Just a sec."

A phone. Brand had never gotten used to this complication. Time was, a girl that had come this far was alone. Now a major carrier had come to the main island and set up its towers, clumsily disguised as forty-foot pine trees. These pushed their coverage over Brand's island, his family's island. It was an outrageous intrusion, but no law would stop it.

Her plain, unhappy face was lit by the screen light. Suddenly Brand's legs seemed to weigh a hundred pounds apiece, like sacks of lead shot.

"Mfff." Brand's complaint was like the mewing of a cat, a noise he'd made since before he knew language. He felt no pity—he did not know the emotion—but the bother! Suddenly it was too much. She was spared the boathouse. What trouble was it worth, after all, for a teary half hour? He couldn't put her through much. Why did he even bother with these local girls?

"Sorry?" She closed her phone. "Sorry."

His face still tight with frustration, Brand moved to kiss her. She turned her mouth away.

Beyond belief! Brand's rage was immediate and volcanic. He reached for her collar bone. He would grip this like a handle, so that his first blow would break her teeth.

"Sorry." She had turned away to take out her chewing gum. The gum was a white daub on her finger, and she looked at him puzzled. She was ready to follow his lead but didn't understand this dance.

He took firm hold and kissed her, sloppily, excited by the near violence. She obliged. She broke away to murmur, "That's so nice."

He pressed down on her bare shoulders. For a moment they shuffled until she understood and dropped to her knees. He unzipped his pants.

"Okay," she giggled with nerves. She still held her gum in one hand. The air stunk of fruit candy. She said something coy and nuzzled his inner thigh.

"Come on." He shuffled.

She was so silly and young that she presumed she had consented to something. For the girl this was a bad deal, not what she wanted to be doing, but it was not as bad as it could be.

Somehow she understood that. Her instincts ran ahead of her thoughts, and like a flash of lightning, she was surprised to find herself overjoyed. Her guts, her spinal cord, understood that she had almost been hurt, and now she wouldn't be.

Little enough time had passed that in the dark the girl could still work with her first impression of this man, Brand. He was dashing, like no one she'd ever seen, with a last name that she had heard before. Almost like a movie star. She held onto that vision now, and hoped she might be able to call it up later, for the sake of sanitizing this memory, while she took him into her mouth, this strange thin monster whose hands twisted her hair like dials, the very smell and taste of him like nothing human.

CHAPTER 4

Michael Coburn stood at the handrail of the tiny ferry. Fifty-five years old but still athletic, his hair and life kept in neat pieces. "Did you get her name? Anything? A license plate?"

Jack, the ferryman, pretended not to hear. Or maybe he didn't hear. He steered from his little weather booth. It was an old, four-car ferry, the private ferry to Donald Frobisher's private island. Coburn and his Cadillac were the only passengers.

Coburn said, "She stood up okay? She was walking okay? She looked okay to me."

Jack raised his eyebrows, to acknowledge he was being spoken to. He had unsnapped the canvas side panels, in accommodation of the spring air, but otherwise this scene hadn't changed for two decades. Every day, all seasons, all hours, Jack was here. When he wasn't driving the boat back and forth, he watched a primitive TV or tinkered with one of the two outboard engines.

Coburn found himself wondering how much Jack was paid. When he was paid. If he was paid.

Jack barked, "Blues are running." He jerked his head toward the water.

Coburn took a look. Fish? Bluefish? No fish could live there. The water was a nightmare of turbulence. This channel between Nausset Island and Frobisher's private island was only a few hundred yards. When the tide changed, the entire Atlantic Ocean tried to scream through. The water twisted and folded over itself entirely. It cut back in deep seams. Beneath Coburn's feet, the beams of the deck dipped unpredictably, as whirlpools sucked at the hull.

It was a mistake to look. Coburn had never liked the sensation of the deck under his feet, and would rather have stayed in his car. Now he fixed his eyes on the land ahead, where placid asphalt waited, buzzing with lazy insects.

When he had his bearings, he stepped over to Jack's booth. He pointed at the dirty fuel gauge, and used the gesture to drop a rolled tube of money, a roll of twenty-dollar bills the size of a cigarette. "I appreciate the call," he said.

The money scared Jack. He didn't touch it, and the roll tottered with the boat's vibrations.

"What? It's your tip," Coburn said. "A tip for a tip."

Jack mumbled, "Nothing, nothing."

"What happened?"

"Nothing." Jack meant every kind of no. No deal. No history. No talking.

Coburn rubbed his face. He'd sensed Jack was nervous. Another old arrangement had changed.

In order to ignore the jittering money, Jack put all his attention on the water ahead, and Coburn realized how old the man was. Decades outdoors had marked his neck with actual pits and scars. It was the skin of a turkey where the feathers had been yanked.

The old arrangements. Whenever Brand Frobisher, the crazy son, went off the island, Jack would phone Coburn. And Jack would phone again, with a more urgent code, if Brand lured a girl back with him. For eighteen years this had been the deal, more or less. And now?

Coburn didn't retreat. "Don't kid yourself, Jack. You know that freak doesn't have a driver's license. You know that? Bottom line, don't fool yourself, he can't be trusted out on his own."

As Coburn rolled his Cadillac off onto the asphalt, he paused to call out his window, "Where do I find the old man?"

Jack ducked and made his nervous smile. "Cleaning his boat?"

"Yeah? Cleaning his boat?"

Ugh. Everything about the boat ride was unsettling, and here was more, another cold pack to Coburn's stomach. Cleaning his boat. Did Jack know the significance of what he said? Probably. His eyes went skittish, left and right, as though the ancient currents were giving him trouble.

Cleaning a boat was a job for a day laborer. Not a job for a former congressman of the United States. Multi-millionaire. President of his own bank. The man who should have been president of the United States.

The island was twelve acres, two complexes, several cabins, and minor buildings. Good roads and beaches. There was a partially-dismantled lighthouse. The island used to be a federal property dedicated to maintaining and operating the lighthouse. Now it was a private playground.

Once on the island, Coburn drove east, to the smaller house. Instead of dramatic ocean views, this one overlooked the island's tiny harbor.

Into his thirties, Coburn had worked for the United States Secret Service. He met Frobisher when he protected the congressman on a trip to Southeast Asia. The two men found that they understood one another. When Frobisher left Congress, Coburn left the secret service.

Over the years Coburn had told people that he quit the secret service because he refused to take a bullet for the newly-elected president, Bill Clinton. This wasn't accurate—Coburn had never protected a president—was too junior. But that story took shape when Clinton's shenanigans with an intern sent half of the country into a cycle of hot flashes. Coburn claimed he had known the man's failings from the start, from first glance. He began to see himself as having a gauge for moral character. He refined the Bill Clinton story until it became the first thing he told strangers about himself.

In fact Coburn had left the secret service for his perfect job. A perfect fit, Frobisher and Coburn, employer and employee. For eighteen years, Coburn had served as Old Frobisher's right hand, indispensable, almost equal partners.

And now? Over the last year, that relationship had changed. For a while it looked like good timing. The old man didn't see the need for a professional fixer, while at the same time Coburn had decided to pursue a new career. They could part, naturally and amicably.

The problem arose when Coburn wanted to cash out. Over the years Coburn collected very little of his salary. To avoid all the red tape of fees and taxes, Frobisher simply invested most of it for him, in various ventures. Frobisher always had irons in the fire.

Now Old Frobisher seemed surprised by the figure. He owed nine hundred thousand dollars? Coburn wanted all of it at once? The funds were invested. What did he presume? That the money was lying around in suitcases? No, it was in the world. It was buildings and projects and businesses. There certainly would be a delay. Assets had to be liquidated. Losses incurred.

At the back harbor there was Old Frobisher, alone, working. From his motor dinghy, the old man lifted a garbage bag onto the small floating dock. Failed. The bag was nearly empty but awkward for an old man sitting. He slung it by the neck. Succeeded.

Moored out in the harbor, where it had been moored all year, was Frobisher's stately motor yacht. The *Danube.* It was a wooden beauty from the 1930s. Twelve meters? Fifteen meters? These days it looked shabby and neglected, with blooms of salt along the hull. No crew was allowed aboard to oil and wax.

But the inside—Coburn knew—the inside . . . by this point Frobisher had cleaned it one hundred times. He had scrubbed it. He had scoured it. He had bleached it with every chemical until his gloves melted, pair after pair, and until his ancient, lotioned hands would never heal back to their normal color. Still he moored the *Danube* out. He refused to bring it to a dock.

Frobisher saw Coburn approaching. "October first!"

"October first," Coburn agreed quietly. He looked around to see if anyone else might have heard. Frobisher covered secrets by shouting them. Nothing to hide.

Though the two men hadn't seen each other for weeks, Coburn stepped into the project as though he'd been away only a moment. He took the garbage sack and walked it up the dock. It reeked of fumes.

Frobisher got his knee onto the dock and then himself. He called loudly after Coburn. "Tell me, tell me why I didn't give up all that nonsense twenty years ago. This is retirement! This is what I always dreamed of. Working with my hands. I'm the happiest I've ever been, and the proudest. A day's work, a day's sweat."

On the beach was a city dumpster and a can of gasoline. Coburn added the sack. The neck opened, revealing scraps of foam and upholstery. The dumpster was already full of foam and fabric scraps. The material was soaked with ammonia, whole jugs of it. Vapors rose and bent the air like heat waves.

Frobisher came up behind Coburn, still extolling the gratification he felt in working with his own hands.

Coburn faced away to ignore this embarrassing blather. He wished he could stop Frobisher from watching detective shows on television. The latest crop was programs about forensics science. An ancient blood stain would tell the story of a pharaoh, or of a regiment missing in the Revolutionary War. The genius investigator would convict everyone on the evidence of a single human hair. And there would go Frobisher again, buzzing out in his dinghy, to slosh concrete deglazer onto pitted teak. Coburn said, "October first, sir?"

"The start of the year. Rebirth."

"Sir, you'll always be on the government calendar." He steeled himself and spoke as directly as he could. "So on October first, or, say, that Friday, I can make transfers? Bottom line, I guess. I established an account. To be ready to receive."

He offered the bank slip, but Frobisher didn't seem to see it. The question settled into the old man, like rain into invisible cracks in the pavement. A change came over him. One minute he was a cheery granddad, full of platitudes—yessir—the virtues of ice-cold lemonade. Now his face drew up into an expression of cold reserve. The years fell away along with the smile.

Old Uncle Frobisher became Congressman Frobisher, minority whip circa 1975, in the private chambers of a new congressman who didn't yet understand the system and had gone to the newspapers, publically dithering about how he would vote. Now away from the aides, wives, picnics, and reporters, Frobisher laid out the case in quiet tones: Get in line immediately or be utterly destroyed. Already you're going to be punished, Frobisher's manner said—this isn't an offer of amnesty. You crossed me, and for that you'll never be the same. But do as I tell you or you'll hear the crack of your own spine breaking.

The two men stood beside the reeking dumpster. Fumes rose and twisted in such intense waves that it served as a campfire of sorts, something to look at. The fumes rubbed like they might ignite.

Frobisher glared and breathed through his tonsils. Coburn withstood it as best he could. He had known it would be this bad or worse.

Finally Frobisher said, "We can manage a payment."

He did not look at the account information in Coburn's hand. Instead his eyes focused in the distance, and all at once his face changed again. The laugh lines returned, those imbecile crinkles. In puzzlement, Coburn followed his gaze. A woman was outside on the deck of the house.

The house was a quarter mile away. The woman moved strangely, fast to one part of the deck, then languid, swaying her arms. Catching a butterfly? Practicing dance with an imaginary partner? On the deck were barrel planters, and she may have been attending to these. If there was music, the sound didn't reach the men.

Beside Coburn, Frobisher was waving. No response. She didn't look. Frobisher chuckled as though he'd been blown a private kiss. "Goodness, is she beautiful," he said.

"Yes," Coburn agreed. He had seen her up close. He cleared his throat. There was no possible transition so he didn't make one. "Brand had a girl out. Last night. I phoned."

"Aww. He's not seeing Laurie?"

"Laurie?" Coburn failed to keep the astonishment out of his voice. "Laurie left Nausset. She married the purser on a cruise ship. Filipino man."

"Shucks. And she just doesn't love Brand anymore?" Frobisher asked, with sincere regret.

"Laurie? Sir. Laurie doesn't live here."

Laurie was two years ago. She was a solution too good to be true. An addled local widow, forty or forty-five, who retained a certain high-tension glamour, and who pursued and doted on Brand. For one good summer, every time there might be trouble, Coburn got in his Cadillac and brought Laurie over on the ferry, breathless to see her Romeo. Brand hated her, but hate was a necessary flavor for him. She slaked his impulses.

For his part, he never killed her or fractured her skull. In the dark morning Coburn would collect Laurie, wrap her up in a coverlet, and take her back to Nausset. He kept replacement clothes in the trunk of his car. He knew her sizes. At least some of her weeping was the breathless excitement of love.

For that one summer they had no legal incidents. No payouts—no teary contracts in the paneled law office of Rex and Hayworth. But that was two years ago.

Coburn had been hired to keep Frobisher's son, Brand, out of prison. For years that had been his primary responsibility. He and Frobisher had always been able to discuss their strategies frankly, though with their own language. "Rape" was never mentioned—instead "Brand might have gotten rough with her." Broken noses and broken arms were "injuries." Even "broken arm" would have been easy, inaccurate shorthand. What Brand seemed to like to do with his girls was to pop the elbow capsule—to dislocate an elbow with a sudden twist. Abortions had their own euphemisms, which evolved over two decades.

The two older men kept the discussions practical. When Frobisher retired from Congress, he sought out young Coburn and asked him to come along because the young agent had demonstrated not only ability (untangling Frobisher from two Thai pimps on the scent of blackmail) but also discretion (afterward the incident simply did not exist). Frobisher found the right man. When handling the scandals of young Brand, Coburn never took an interest in the larger patterns—questions of sanity or moral judgment—but merely the facts at hand.

Discreet to the bone: Coburn never asked the story of why Old Frobisher had cut the bridge. When the federal government owned the island, a steel bridge had linked it to Nausset Island proper. The structure had not been elegant—a corps of engineers special—one traffic lane—but it served to span the wild channel.

Then it was gone. To this day the roads at either end were still in place, cracked and pierced with sizeable trees. The year Coburn was hired, the year young Brand turned sixteen, that bridge had been closed for upgrades and repairs. The repairs were never made. Instead a Massachusetts state dredge had come and pulled the pilings. The roads on both sides of the water were rerouted for a ferry landing.

What had triggered this? In one year, Brand Frobisher had turned sixteen, Old Frobisher left Congress and cut the bridge to his island. He had hired a man away from the secret service. To mind his son. To wait and watch on the other side of the vicious, impassable water.

"Well, Brand will find his someone special," Old Frobisher said.

Coburn studied the old man. Was he lying or delusional? "His 'someone special' "? The boy was a sadist. Surely Frobisher couldn't think to deceive Coburn, who had mopped up Brand's bloody messes for almost twenty years.

Who *was* this new version of Frobisher? At times Coburn wondered if the old man hadn't lost his wits, suffered a stroke. But then the dementia would pass, and his old boss would return.

Everything had changed in the past ten months. Up until last May, Coburn and Frobisher had been partners. Friends of a sort. Unspoken, of course. In June, Frobisher informed Coburn that Brand would now become "Head of Security" on the family island. Okay, fine, wink wink, it seemed a silly title. Every father wants his son to hold a job at some point in his life, build a record and a resume. Old Frobisher never gave up on Brand; you could say that for him.

But then things really began to slip. Old Frobisher began to treat this title as real. "Head of Island Security" wasn't a fake job. Frobisher consulted with Brand in the same manner he used to consult with Coburn. The two had their plans and their secrets. And of course at the same time—all at once—Brand himself was no longer a subject to be discussed. Brand wasn't handled anymore; instead he handled things. He delivered money and threats. He took the private ferry when he chose, gone all night . . .

Recently they had done something together. Brand and Frobisher, son and father. Something serious. Coburn couldn't figure out what, but Frobisher was a beaming proud papa. Ferryman Jack didn't know or wasn't telling. Coburn was reduced to scanning the newspaper. He monitored the emergency radio bands.

"Anyway," Coburn concluded, "it was a false alarm. Brand didn't even scare her. She tried to hold his hand, walking back, and I got some video of it. In case, you know, you get any calls. We're covered. No payout anticipated. Nothing we have to account for."

Coburn left off to silence. Since he'd mentioned Brand and the girl, Frobisher's face hadn't moved. He heard nothing bad about his boy. To him, literally nothing had been said.

This was the effect of euphemisms on a fading mind. Coburn used euphemisms to be discreet. ("She wasn't happy with his kissing.") Always someone might be listening.

But now old Frobisher used these euphemisms in his head, where they had become actual. Over time his son's vaguely-described sins had faded into uncertainty ("back in '96 wasn't there a chippy who thought suing Brand was her meal ticket?"), and then into doubt. Perhaps under divine oath, at the gates of Saint Peter, old Frobisher might have shaken the clouds out of his skull and acknowledged that his boy had hurt women. But then, he would have added, who didn't sow their wild oats?

Coburn grunted. "So that's acceptable, money-wise. Cash

flow." He stopped. This was as much as he dared. What he had planned to say—what he had repeated over and over in the privacy of his car—was this: "Keep Brand here. Take his car keys. Tell Jack not to bring him across. Bottom line: Until the deal goes through, until you can pay me, you keep your boy on a leash. Bottom line. You can't pay off another of these girls that he knocks silly before he screws them."

Frobisher's lips thinned as though he chewed a bitter stick. He wasn't going to prolong conversation with this fellow. Why did Coburn keep showing up, without invitation? Didn't he realize? He had made himself an expense, not an asset. For some reason the man had decided to make himself into an expense!

Frobisher might not have said another word, except that the Coburn situation put him in mind of a juicy tidbit. "One fellow won't be costing me a dime. Chief Hanson."

"Hanson? Is he sick again?"

Frobisher's eyes twinkled with their superior knowledge. "He doesn't earn a dime from me, lying on his back. In a public hospital."

"Hospital? How long is he going to be out?"

Frobisher shook his head as though Coburn were trying to sneak something past him—oh, no, no, no. "Uh-uh. He's done." Frobisher was gleeful.

"That's bad. Chief Hanson . . ." Coburn stopped, unsure how much to articulate. Chief Hanson had helped them any number of times. The chief of the island police. Chief Hanson understood that when a girl showed up at the hospital, the first thing to do was to clean her up, shower *and* bath, physical evidence whirling down the drain. The chief of police was their surest, most important ally on the island. "Hanson understands business. Always has understood business."

Frobisher snapped. "You're the one who wants money. Well,

now there's some money for you. I'm not paying him, so if *you* want to, make whatever arrangement you like. Go into business together."

Coburn blinked. He settled on the practical question: "Who's going to step in? Do we have any idea? Detective Wakin?"

Frobisher shook his head again, not at Coburn's guess but at the very idea that this was his concern. He refused to be the victim of sharp practice. He moved his finger to emphasize each word. "I pay my tax dollars. You have no idea how they tax a man who earns."

The protective move was complete and astonishing. One minute the old man scoured his yacht for evidence of a murder. The next he was no more concerned with the police than any private citizen. For Frobisher, his crimes were expensive, and didn't bear thinking about, so when possible he expunged them from his memory and his conscience like a complete remission from the Pope.

To complete this transformation, Frobisher's face returned to the expression he had worn earlier–placid joy, an old man's fascination with a restored Studebaker, or his own amateur handiwork aboard his yacht. He waved with a slow, open hand, like polishing a mirror. Coburn turned. The girl was back on the deck. Maybe she had always been there.

Coburn realized that she was naked. She was as tiny as a girl. She didn't have breasts. It was Oxana, Frobisher's fourth wife. From Poland or somewhere close. She didn't know English. Either that or she didn't know how to speak at all.

Chapter 5

If you're a tourist, come off the ferry, you see the giant houses, the Grande Old Dames of the city park, and you think, wow, two hundred years these things have stood there in their painted colors. Amazing!

But you only think that because you missed the month of May. In May, windowless vans crowded off the ferries, delivering a combat brigade of workers come to repaint, re-shingle, and rebuild. Twelve hours a day, like a shipyard, the park was a roar of compressors, generators, and power saws. Guys would monkey up there on aluminum ladders and tear off whole sections of a house with a crowbar, rip off whole turrets where the salt air had eaten the heart out of the wood and transformed it into worthless balsa. Boards tore away like Styrofoam.

Salt air is hungry. It dissolved nails under paint, so that everywhere on island, painted walls bled dots of rust. And the paint itself? In a few months the salt air bubbled and stripped it off like a chemical rub. The corrosive air got into things like your wristwatch and coated the workings with salt gum. It wrecked cars—ate the rubber and flecked the metal.

What I learned—it turns out that no one should even live on an ocean island. You could *visit* the sea coast, have a swim and a nap in the sand, but don't stay. Don't put up houses. If you did, in six months they started to come apart. Everywhere on the island, every time you went into a restroom to take a leak, there was black dust on the rear rim of the toilet, grains of black on the porcelain. The screws that held the seat to the bowl were turning to powder. You leaned your hand on a wall and it shrieked. If you owned a place, after a few years, nothing for it but to cut down a Canadian forest, truck the pine out here, and rebuild the same floor plan.

The first night after my girl kicked me out, I camped on the barrier island. The next morning I swam in. The fog was down hard. I was at the beach hut trying to pull a sleeve over my damp arm, and the fabric just gave way. "What the . . . ?" The salt air had eaten the fabric! One minute I had a collar shirt, the next I was holding three tatters like I was ready to juggle handkerchiefs, as a topless street act. Add to this, under my feet, the boards for the beach shower squished in and out, in and out. The wood was turning to dirt, and it was already some flaky half-product. Thick, crusty nails worked up from the planks like earthworms.

I understood then that this whole enterprise was unnatural. This world was deteriorating before my eyes, like stop-motion science photography.

In May my job brought me round the park ten times a day. I saw. Every place was partly rebuilt. Instead of being original construction from the time of the whale captains, these houses were like the human body, rebuilt wall by wall, so that after seven years they were entirely new material.

For all that, though—the money!—the waste!—these places cast their spell. No argument. These were American castles. The park was ringed with a row of stately, three-story houses. Some were only two stories, but those didn't draw the eye. The mansions formed a crescent around the wide park. They were all from the same Victorian era but each had its own colors and parts—turrets and wings and sometimes modern elements, like an entire wall of windows. Somehow you didn't just want to sit there. Somehow you needed to *own* one of them. If you did, the rest of your life was peace.

There's got to be a name for this particular delusion. When I was in the army, one of my comrades would talk about the false allure of farmland. His family owned a thousand acres of gorgeous farmland, which passed from generation to generation. The Red River valley, which I guess is the supreme farmland of the world. Super lush. Land so fine, you could grow whatever you like, wine grapes or saffron. But this guy said the acreage was just a trap. All you really acquire is work and heartache, and all the land does is grow crates of decomposing shit that you sell away for pennies a truckload. In the history of his family, the beautiful land wiped out man after man. Fathers, brothers.

My squad mate recognized the trap and ran. Every time we encountered some farmer out in the color—Africa, Asia—this would be his theme. He'd laugh. "Don't put your money down. Listen to me. Don't sign the banker's papers. That farmer looks sixty, but in fact he's younger than you are. So pretty? That's because we're passing through. Stay for a season and then tell me about the charm. When I turned eighteen, I would have walked to Canada to join the service. I would have walked fifty miles on my knees."

A little guy from North Dakota. Wanted to be called "Swede" but general misunderstanding evolved this to "Sweet." Which fit because he was maybe the only happy soldier in the army, crowing like the Saved.

One day we were in eastern Africa, convoying through these miracle banana orchards. Each leaf was the beautiful fan. Again we heard about the thousand acres Sweet renounced in the Red River valley. My sergeant shook his head in wonder. "Nothing in Dakota ever looked like this." He said he wanted proof. North

Dakota Sweet had none, no photos. He had pictures of his parents and pretty sister but no outdoor photographs. From that time forward, he would incorporate this fact into his monologue. He hated farms so much that he wouldn't even allow a picture of farmland on his phone.

I was no bowl-cut farm boy, but I was new to the island, and in my life I hadn't seen money. It was probably inevitable that the gorgeous houses caught me in their spell. There I was among them, twelve hours a day. Part of my circuit was to patrol the park for bums that might be getting off the ferry. (Never happened—why would it? how could it?) I walked in the shade of those wooden towers.

Then I began to visit the park during breaks, to eat my lunch on a bench. Then I moved onto the porches. Each day I'd choose a different place. Try it out. I'd dust off a big porch chair, sit there, and eat. I chose places that still had their police notices, and places that workers weren't rebuilding.

"Excuse. Will you rent me a clean room?"

I was up on the porch of maybe the biggest place—the place I would have chosen—four-story turrets capped with cones—and a young man approached. Back on the sidewalk he left an oversized duffel with wheels. He was pale and serious, and neatly dressed. "I want a clean room without pets or sharing."

"Me? A room?" I said. "*Pfft.* I sleep on the beach like a crab."

The young man nodded once. He didn't know English so he misunderstood and thought I had refused him. He leaned to look along the side of the house. It went back and back the length of a city block. Gables, windows, a whole floor even above the garage. "Okay. No room anywhere?" His little smile politely forgave my lie. He looked a true Russian—his skin white as mayonnaise, with black stubble in exact lines as though drawn with an eyebrow pencil.

"Here? This isn't my place." I laughed at the idea.

The Russian didn't understand or didn't believe. He accepted that he had been refused. He turned deliberately, walked back to the sidewalk, and hauled his bag to where he could turn for the next front door. Another mansion but with no turrets. Inferior porch arrangement. This pilgrim went up and knocked, waited, knocked, waited. Apparently he couldn't read the police notice in the door window. No one was home, and no one had been home for six months. No one had arrived for the summer yet. But construction was going on, off to the side. Apparently our pilgrim mistook the Jamaican workers for the home owners, Jamaicans in pirate doo-rags.

"No, no, no," I called to him. I left my sack of oranges and orange peels. Went over and tried to explain. Pointed out the notices. Told him about the boarding houses for summer workers—slummy places inland. You had to take the bus. But we were destined not to communicate, this pilgrim and I. When I talked, he looked beside my head, no comprehension. I was no friend of his, after refusing him, keeping all twenty beds to myself. He knew his role in life, which was to wander and suffer, and he was calm about that.

All right, I gave up. Tourists! Or I guess not in this case—some Russian kid imported as a dishwasher or fry cook. But it was the tourist phenomenon. How do they get so stupid? How could I not feel superior? I was up there on the porch, part of the postcard scene. He could only look and dream. I'm on the cedar throne and the Russian peasant went house to house with his formal clothes and his duffel like a peddler. Tut, tut, what a fool.

My watch alarm interrupted the scene. *First, do no harm. Second, do no harm. Third, do no harm.*

I probably didn't even need the reminder. The tremors—I was already feeling the tremors. My face went cold. I stumbled up and got off that porch. My legs took me so fast that I had to return in the night for my sack of orange peels.

This kind of encounter corrupts. Certain sensations—artificial distance from your fellow man—you have to guard against. Otherwise, what happens? The very worst kind of things. I've seen it. In the army. Everywhere else. You become a prison guard, hurting people as you'd never imagine. You wake up one day and you've become the Chief.

So that was two lessons I told you about the Grande Old Dames. The deterioration. The facade. The unignorable majesty. The trap. I hadn't been two weeks on island and I resolved never to set foot near them again. But of course I still didn't know anything. Number one of what I didn't know was that these people would be important to my summer. The Russian would turn out to be named Sasha. And then Mrs. Yellow—

The day after the Russian, I was back to the park, sent to deal with a noise complaint.

It was late afternoon when I approached the address that made the call. Three ladies sat in a screened section of the porch. I walked right up but got no notice. I took another step. Stopped. Took another. Three ladies. All had seen me. All ignored.

"She said, she told him, I lost my virginity to my horse!"

"That is why they rode side-saddle in the nineteenth century. You know, we have a side-saddle, at our—"

"No, no, she said it, she told him, I lost my virginity to my horse!"

"And he said, he probably asked her, well was he from good stock?"

Squalls of giggling.

At this point I was all the way up on the porch. I cast my

shadow on their drinks, which forced one of the ladies to rise, with a sigh of exasperation. "Over there. I told you, over there. Over there." She chopped a motion with both hands, like ground crew directing a jet liner.

Yes, music noise came from the neighboring property. A full painting team was out, four black men with tarps and ladders, and they had a boom box on the grass. The music was something loud like Led Zeppelin. (Don't trust me on music identification. I don't listen. Music gets in your head, and clings whether you want it or not.)

I asked the lady how long the music had been playing. She answered something. Neither of us could hear, over the scream of a power saw. The saw was in her backyard. Work was being done.

"*I* am not looking for a gigolo," the lady told me clearly.

She retreated. She had never opened her screen door, and now I lost her in the shadow of her foyer. "That's Mrs. Yellow you should apply to. But you're the wrong color. She only takes these Haitians to her bed."

To me, no response suggested itself. The lady's friends watched, their faces calm, nothing out of the ordinary. Beside me, on the porch, was a bicycle, notable because it was made entirely out of wicker. Not the tires and chain—it was a functioning bicycle—but the frame was woven like a basket.

"Ah . . . and did you try to talk to those fellows?" I stammered.

"What did you just ask me?" The lady reappeared in a hurry. She unlatched her door and came out a step. She was an older lady, slim and elegant, but with a hard, square face. She wore a white evening dress, very bright, like the fabric of a tablecloth. "I called the police. I'm tired of listening to their noise, and I called the police."

She threatened with a hand slice. This phrase, "Call the

police," came easily to her, polished ten times a day.

"Right," I said. Clearly this conversation was untenable. I thanked her (habit, training), and backed down the porch stairs. Probably looked like I was bowing at each step, and that she was the Sun King. The women resumed their conversation, clucking with indignation.

I wandered over to see if the painters would be more manageable.

This neighbor house was perfect yellow, yellow like a rubber duck. Up high, one of these painters was busy with his brush, laying perfect yellow on perfect yellow. From the sidewalk I couldn't see how he could keep track of where he'd already painted.

The police notices were gone from the windows. The owner was back for the summer. So, two adjacent mansions occupied, enough to begin a feud.

On the porch, a man painted scrollwork with an artist's brush. I'm pretty sure he was Jamaican, not Haitian. I watched until he noticed me. "Oh, she's upstairs, upstairs, yeah," he said.

"Hey, could you turn the music down?"

"Oh, yeah, yeah," he said, sympathetically. He shrugged—what can you do?—and said, "You go talk to her."

"I should go in?"

"Go in, go in. Of course. It's a pretty place."

"But I need you to turn down—"

"It's a nice house. You never been inside one of the Grand Dames?" He gave a toneless chuckle. "Sure. Go on up the stairs to her."

Inside was about what you would expect, like the lobby of a grand hotel. The sofas showed their wood. Instead of a normal light fixture, you had your chandelier. "Hello?"

Antique fanciness, just as I imagined. What surprised me was the evidence of people. There was a mussed newspaper folded to the crossword . . . sandals kicked off in the corner, several pair . . . crayon drawings on the wall—children's drawings that only a mother could love. You don't expect *people* to be living in the museum.

"Hello?" I called. No response. "Hello?" This wild talk—gigolos—"entering" grande dames—the painter smirked—I didn't want any surprise scenes. "Hey there?" I called out every few steps like a hiker in bear country.

Nothing and no one. Curtains moved in the breeze.

I took the stairs. They ended in a long, crooked hallway. Up there the walls were plain painted wood. The ground floor might be a public ballroom, but the party didn't continue upstairs.

All these doors were open. "Hey there," I said. "Hello?" I didn't need to announce myself. With each step I took the wood floor complained—*aeiy! aeiy!*—as though a 220-pound man was beyond any conceivable design limits, the final indignity.

The rooms I passed were bedrooms or sitting rooms that led to bedrooms. In all of them, the furniture was draped with colorless cloths. Painters' drop cloths? No, this furniture was draped for dust. Up here, no one had moved in. No one had opened a window. Old dust hung in the air, the rot of winter, which smelled like the sulfur from the head of a match.

The last room wasn't a bedroom but instead a junk pile of antiques. You couldn't walk two paces. A dozen tiny tables crowded the floor, rickety as TV trays, loaded with knickknacks of porcelain and tarnished brass. Antiques for the whole house were stored away. Scrimshaw bones. Jars of shells. There was a diorama featuring dusty birds the size of prairie chickens, mounted in a wild dance with their wings perpendicular.

Against every wall lay framed pictures. Most of the pictures were sea maps. There was a larger table like a work bench and that was piled with still more maps. Island maps. You make it out to Nausset Island and what do you post on your walls? Reminders that you're on Nausset Island.

That was it. That was the last room. I was at the end of the hallway. "Hey hey?" At some point the music had stopped completely. So enough, I thought, my job was done. No reason for me to be sniffing around Tut's tomb. I retreated, experimenting with different gaits to reduce the floor complaint—heel/toe, flat-foot, shuffle—

"Did you injure yourself?"

At the straight of the hallway there was a lady. An old lady watched me from the doorway of the very first room, the room over the porch. She sat primly upright, and rested her hands on a thin cane topped with a glass ball. She hadn't been there before. Had she been hiding? Then she dashed over, dragging her stool?

"Mrs. Pale complained, did she? Well. She would like to be called Mrs. White, but we have a Mrs. White. We've had a Mrs. White for fourteen years. You can't expect internet money will buy you everything."

"Ahh," I said wisely. When she had surprised me, I popped the neck seam of my shirt. Air poured in, and I rubbed the seam to assess the damage, trying not to call attention.

"She feels 'Mrs. Pale' is a slight, but what color has a positive connotation? True blue, I suppose. Mrs. Scarlett—but you can imagine the expectations Mrs. Scarlett feels she must live up to. It can end a marriage. More than once I believe the name was responsible."

This lady was maybe eighty, at least a generation older than grim-jaw with the wicker bicycle. This one had gone fragile, ninety pounds, perched with the reed cane to help balance. Her eyes fixed me, unblinking. Age had hardened these eyes into blue glass gems. Age or salt air had stripped the gel coat off, and left you looking directly in on the coil. "Ms. Pale," I said.

"Oh, and you're Ms. Yellow. I see. I get it."

"*Mrs.* Yellow. A little game among ourselves. My legal name is Mrs. Palsinger. She is Mrs. Pale, which I have been known to misspell: P A I L. Ha ha ha."

"I'm sure that galls her." To reach the stairs I had to approach. Unless I wanted to vault the rail, or call to the painters for a ladder at a window. "I came to talk to your workers. Their rock 'n' roll music. But their boss sent me upstairs. The man on the porch."

"I have a police matter. But not, I suspect, one for you."

"Okay. You wanted the Chief," I said. "He's getting dialysis today, or some kind of pump-out. Out of commission."

"You wear no pistol," she observed. "So I must be speaking to the Parking Warden." This novelty delighted her.

"A famous position, is it?"

"Position? The Parking Warden is required to leave an illegitimate child behind, when he takes the November boat." She laughed. "Though you look a little more mature than our usual. Most of them were only students."

She turned and gestured. This porch room had full windows on three sides. The ocean, the park, the neighbors. "Mrs. Pale wasn't always so preemptory," she said, and then she cackled again, which wasn't a sound I had ever heard in real life. "Two of her daughters have illegitimate children. In one case, no one has any idea of the father. Did she tell you?"

Mrs. Yellow turned back to me, her lips pursed in quiet triumph. Some card players wore this expression when they played their ace. Pounce! But my reaction disappointed, and her attention returned to her window. Perched on one of the window sills was a pair of binoculars. First-rate, motion-stabilized binoculars. Commando technology.

"We like our traditions, here on the park. There's Mrs. Pale," she nodded in that direction. "Mrs. Lavender, who will arrive the second week of June. Mrs. Gold, whose family name is Gold. Her husband obliged her with a repainting. This is neither the first time nor the second time that has happened."

Mrs. Yellow went through the houses. For each, she offered a drop of gossip. Like most old ladies she focused on illicit sex. Wrong pairing, wrong place. More outdoor encounters than you'd expect, in a close dollhouse of a city. Made you want to look twice where you set down your sandwich, I can tell you. Mrs. Yellow's full spread of windows allowed her to keep up on developments.

Mrs. Yellow started out as a gloating gossip. After a fair list, though, she became sad. "It's a difficult place to grow up. All these boys come and go. Some of them are so gorgeous, and you're only a girl, while they've got the musk of the world on them, my God, my God."

She paused long enough that I felt I should respond. "Tight neighborhood. You certainly know each other." I cleared my throat.

She turned her gem eyes on me. "Am I right that you used to vacation here?"

I shook my head. "You're remembering someone else."

"I wouldn't mistake those shoulders. Most of our new people grow up dreaming about this place. They spend a week's vacation, and this grows in their heart, and finally, finally they make it back." The way Mrs. Yellow spoke, she didn't think this ambition was foolish. Instead it was natural and inevitable. She nodded across the park. "I don't mistake gentlemen. You've been sitting on Mrs. Green's porch, noontimes, making yourself quite at home in fact."

So, a very useful lesson. People on vacation islands don't work during the day. They sit at their windows.

"You may always come and sit on my porch, which has cushioned chairs, now that I've put them out for the season. I extend the invitation. Between the hours of nine thirty and four o'clock, you are welcome to take your lunch there. And you may help yourself to one drink. By going inside, you will scandalize Mrs. Pale. She will think that you are visiting my boudoir."

I thanked Mrs. Yellow, of course, nervous laughter between my teeth, but was never coming back. I flew out of there. Didn't touch a step on my way off the porch. The scrollwork Jamaican dropped his brush in fright, as though I were coming for a banzai tackle.

But plans change. It's not just old ladies who are starved for human contact. My thing with my girl Marsha fell through, and then it fell through worse, until for days I didn't talk to another human. So I was driving by at lunch and took my sandwich up onto Mrs. Yellow's porch. She brought me a plate and a soda. She phoned friends that she was entertaining the Parking Warden. Whatever they had to say in response to that, she cackled.

Not much was required of me, in those conversations. Mrs. Yellow gossiped about the colors of the houses, the people who would arrive soon to spend the summers in them, and their fucked-up kids.

Power tools buzzed. That was May.

Chapter 6

Of course of all people Marsha had no trouble getting to my beach island.

With nowhere to stay, I had set up camp on Squab Island. Squab Island was the sister island of Nausset—long, low, and empty, about three quarters of a mile from the main Nausset harbor. It had been uninhabited since the federal fort had been hauled away, block by block, in the sixties. Now all that remained were frantic signs.

The signs competed in message. Some of them shouted how the stonework left behind was deadly dangerous. Proceed farther and you'll be lucky to crawl home on crushed limbs. A second danger was the unexploded ordnance expected to wash up on the beach. Five decades in salt water but now it would be ready to blow! In Korea, the DMZ, I'd seen less fuss over a field of land mines.

The competing set of signs spoke their message with equal force: If the stonework and artillery didn't kill me, then the feds would, in their effort to keep me off the deadly stonework. Jesus. They were very specific about the consequences to my trespassing self. The signs went into detail and dollar amounts. It wasn't "shoot on sight," but between the fines and jail time, my family line was going to be on the hook for generations.

In the recent past Squab Island had been swept bare by fire. A layer of black ash lay just under the sand, and any forest was young and scrubby. Other than mice and seabirds, the island was bare of life, but there were old, burnt-up signs telling me that my very presence endangered the existence of "heath hens," which from the drawing on the signs resembled a kind of grouse.

Out there alone, when I ran across these signs, I'd talk to them. Calm yourself, man, I'd say. No grouse out here, doing their elaborate tail dance. No harm done. Just me, a tarp, and bug net . . . a few candy bars . . . a scarf to blindfold myself when the night sky would play its full organ chord of stars, a sight which had always left me weak. I'd tell the sign, *you* try to sleep on the main island. Those beaches! With the drunks and the four-wheelers, it was like being in a residential street. Out here I had a little territory.

To visit me on Squab Island, Marsha took her sea kayak. Across the channel I caught sight of her blue jeep. There was a slip of beach east of where Cunningham used to live in his mansion. Marsha unloaded the boat and waved, but she was waving to no one. She was stretching her rib muscles. She was out on the water when the sun finally dropped. The last quarter mile I was guessing at shadows. Jets shone in the sky, bound for Boston. It was still daylight up there.

Before I saw her I heard the pacing of her stroke timer, which was a wooden piano metronome. Stroke, stroke, stroke. I didn't show a light but Marsha paddled straight in and touched sand ten yards from my feet. Straight in, and I'd sort of imagined my camp was secret.

"So the rumors are true," she said. "Ghost soldiers have returned to their fort." Marsha was ten years older than I, maybe too much tan if you saw her indoors, an exerciser to the last elastic ounce. She ate very little that could be called food, subsisting instead on weighed powders and bars. Yet she brought me a sack of groceries. In the dark I went through it with laughter and affection. Yes, I liked to eat meals rather than drink them, but never when we shared a kitchen did I eat a can of Vienna sausages. Besides the groceries Marsha had all sorts of jokes prepared about my camp. I was Robinson Crusoe, sewing clothes out of goat hides.

She felt responsible because our summer together didn't last a week. She should have made it clear just how tentative we were before I signed up for the summer under Boss Hog.

"Are you still communing with the spirit of your property developer?"

"Ho ho," I said. "I'm not the only one who hasn't forgotten his name. Listen to what happened this morning. I really shouldn't tell you," I said. I shouldn't, but I liked to hear her laugh. "Because I was wrong. But this is an isolated occurrence. I don't want this used to support some larger point about my character." I told her about Simon Boco, P.I. "So where I was wrong was in guessing Mr. Cunningham's motivations. He wasn't broke, with someone turning his house into condos. Maybe it was part that, but he also thought that his wife was fooling around. In a lot of ways that makes more sense, as a motivation for suicide. You're a professional, but through no fault of your own suddenly your life is full of lawyers and losers."

Marsha confined herself to one quip: "Strange that you jumped to conclusions. I mean in this one isolated case." She slapped a bug in the dark. "You still don't have bug spray, even out here?"

"Mud works. Washes off on the morning swim."

"What about the food Cunningham ordered? I don't see that a grieving man would be so rude."

"It wasn't that he couldn't pay. He ordered his usual, maybe for the whole family, then he realized the family was gone."

"I see. So was this private investigator an idiot or not? You don't like him but apparently he changed your theory."

"Thank you for that insight. Yes, Boco is an idiot. He was showing me the fruit of his investigation, and it was pictures on his little camera, like a novelty camera. To find them he scrolled through a thousand pictures of his dog chasing ducks.

"But I went over to the realtor's office. The lady who calls herself the Island Queen. I told you there was a huge sign by the house offering condos.

"She was surprised I knew about the listing, surprised to learn the sign was still there. Typical island shit, she asked if I'd take it down next time I went out. Presumably rope it to the roof of the patrol car and drive it over, because she was busy sitting there at her desk.

"The condo project may or may not happen. She was coy about that, as an island realtor might well be. If she *could* get me in, I'd better not count on the sign price. Two fifty? Any units at that price level had been snapped up. Or there had been a change of plans. Now the entry unit was one point two million. But she didn't want to be held to these figures, you understand.

"One point two million. All this time, I'm standing there in my cop uniform."

Marsha sighed in the dark. Strange to say, real estate had been part of our fight. When Marsha got her job here (school teacher), she went about the relocation in her usual high-energy way, posting papers around town that said, "Island girl coming home and needs housing. Island references." I asked, Island girl? Who cares if you're an island girl? What is this place, Appalachia? How come you don't mention me? The sea air and suddenly you're a "girl"?

It's not that I don't understand the local tensions. You grew up here taking outdoor showers and portaging the family canoe. You graduated with the same class of ten, at some point you've all kissed each other. Then in the early nineteen eighties the island got fashionable, in came the crowds, and now you have to buy a ticket to watch the sunset.

Change has occurred, I grant. My argument is that the islanders don't consider the gains as well as the losses. The old family hangout, wired with lamp cord, with your childhood bikes rusting under the porch, now sells for 2.8 million. You rent it out for the month of July and live the rest of the year on the profit. You lose the fishermen, sure, because there's less money in lobster than in subletting the dock slip. But at least they have that option.

These island people won the lottery. Anyone who owned anything out there was worth a million. A parking space was worth a million. After Marsha made me move out, I entered into negotiations with an herb farmer to rent a rotting trailer he'd abandoned in his septic field. We got to the point I was ready to sign the papers, it turned out the price he was quoting me was for the *week*.

Marsha asked, "The detective had pictures of Sarah cheating?"

"Sarah?"

"Cunningham's wife."

"No. It was nothing. It was pictures of those Methodist cottages."

She laughed richly. "The campground?"

"You couldn't fit a double bed inside without lifting off the roof. Of course the pictures proved nothing. Boco took them from a mile away, with his toy camera. It's Cunningham's own place. His wife is going in and out. There's a weird dude there, at around the same time, supposedly. Hardly pornography."

"A 'weird dude'?"

"Guy can't help how he looks. Very young and very old at the same time." My God, it must have broken Cunningham's heart.

Marsha was quiet in the dark. When she noticed the quiet,

she said, "Maybe your detective has better ones. A professional detective would be discreet."

"Discreet? You really don't trust anything I say. I tell you he's an asshole. I give you an example of asshole behavior. You take that particular example and try to cast it in a better light, being charitable. But that wasn't the sole basis of me saying he was an asshole. Instead, that was an example to invite you to share my understanding."

"Jesus, you're like a lit fuse."

"If you meet Boco and like him, then we can talk. Maybe *he* can move in with you."

I breathed like an old dog. Sometimes I went on like this and left us both speechless. My temper was a third person we had invited along and he would astonish us with his bad manners. I swallowed and said, "Anyway, I got the pictures off him."

"He gave you copies?"

"Nah, I took the chip. You don't want the family to have to deal with that."

"I'm sure he saved some."

"No, I got them. And if the photos were indiscreet he'd have sold them on the internet." There was my breath again, *houk, houk.* "I'm sorry. I need to shut up for a full minute. I'm sorry."

I said no more about it to Marsha. She wanted to talk about love, anyway. I'm sure that was her plan when she paddled out here. I wasn't making it easy. She still loved me even though I was apparently impossible, and my impossibility grew worse, like rabies. She had no problem having sex, out rough like this.

With Marsha, sex was easy to understand. She was cruel to her body, always prodding and measuring. She was an elastic cord stretched to its limit. With a little care she would forget and relax. The darkness helped. It helped that out on the beach everything began imperfect.

All that was welcome enough, but what lingered in my mind

was the scene at the campground photos. Pretty lady. Weird dude. Her unreadable expression.

"I had a fight with the Chief," I said. We were lying there afterward. "One speeding ticket missing from my book. *Pfft.* One ticket and he sings a whole tragic aria, impromptu. 'The Missing Ticket.' "

Again Marsha sighed. After sex she allowed herself to smoke half a cigarette. Probably she once had someone who smoked the other half. In the light of the coals I could see her face closely for the first time, looking lined and worried, though she was only thirty-five. "You don't have a talent for making people like you."

"There may be something in what you say." After however many counted puffs, Marsha offered me the other half. I pushed it into the sand between us, carefully upright like a birthday candle. The smell drove away the twilight bugs. "But it's not my fault. I don't have anything to work with."

Marsha said, "Jim, name me ten people you like. Full names, first and last. That you like without reserve."

"Ten, eh?"

"I think you're going crazy. Five people."

"I like plenty of people. Mr. Cunningham. What's his first name? Marcus?"

"He's dead, and you never met him."

"I like the suicide." I hear the ocean, and the echo of what I've said. "Not suicide in general. Killing yourself is pathetic. It's a weepy thing to do. But in this case, Cunningham shows he's thoughtful of others. He leaves no mess for the maid. Blow your brains out, but you're careful so your brains go overboard."

"Oh my God."

"No, there was a guy who committed suicide out front of Mass General because he heard it was a major transplant hospital, and he thought someone might make use of his organs.

He had all his donor paperwork prominent on his lap. Then, *blam!* Right outside the ER lane."

Marsha got up. As she put them on, her clothes stretched and snapped angrily. "You need to grow your hair out and calm down."

"No, no, I don't mean anything by it. Even the hospital case, it wasn't a complete success. The trauma of the gunshot ruined his eyeballs."

Marsha was furious. After sex she wouldn't put up with much. Tonight she wouldn't even talk while she launched her kayak.

She was doing that, and my words were still floating around, what I'd said. *Mistake!* Obvious omission. Marsha asked me people I liked. I should have told her that *she* was one. That was all she meant. That was what she wanted. I missed my chance, and she paddled away in a lonely fury.

But five people . . . this challenge of hers . . . five people I liked. . . .

To look at Nausset Island was to look at Cunningham's cove. In his abandoned palace, a few lights were on. The same forgotten lights were always on. They would burn until the bulbs burned out. So I stood on my island looking at Cunningham's house, and in the same way, if Cunningham looked out his windows, he'd see my island. When he killed himself, he was sailing here.

Not the sort of thought I could tell Marsha. That was a given. The one person I thought I could tell, I'd met that evening. She was a woman, so when Marsha asked for people I liked, well I'm not stupid. You don't tell one woman about another, no matter how harmless. Anyway, I didn't know her name.

Here's what happened earlier. My shift ended at eleven, and I faced the cold ocean. But right on the hour, Betsy, the dispatcher, called me, with a request to shut down a party. "Eh? Sure," I said.

Betsy was one of these ladies who, once she saw me, she felt an impulse to help. Much like the people who hate me, it's a certain subset, and also has nothing to do with my behavior. Often ladies like Betsy present me with baked goods for no particular occasion.

Anyway, when I first arrived on Nausset Island, the Chief assumed I had a cell phone and wanted my number for his master board. He would use it for a certain kind of dispatch. I told Chief I didn't carry a phone. He said I'd better hurry and remedy that shortfall, and that there was one particular carrier he preferred because of island coverage. Right, I told him, thanks for the coupon but I couldn't see that happening.

At that point Betsy intervened, and now I carried her spare phone. So she was burning her own minutes, telling me about this party. She gave me all kinds of complicated directions, using the color of houses, and features of architecture—"you pass the cupola, okay, but keep going off to your left, until you're cattycorner to a teal house; it used to be teal, but now that's the garage . . ." She laid out my route with architectural features because she knew my feelings about all these street names, two or three hundred cutsie street names with very poor signage. For a six-month gig I simply refused to try to learn any of them.

"Cupola?" I cut her off. "Don't sweat it. I can hear the noise."

One party laid claim to the whole town that night. The sound! The music! An hour earlier, Chet, my fellow summer hire, heard it and wandered off in search, mumbling about girls. Now I paid attention. There were ripping sounds—*blat blat blat!*—music broken and distorted by travel and echo.

I walked and walked and *walked.* And the music still sounded far away. This party's noise carried like a stock-car race.

Noise led me toward the water, onto the peninsula that sheltered the ferry terminal. Here were the sprawling wooden "inns," the hotels for the tourists foolish enough to have booked their accommodations as part of a larger waterfront package. Here their "honeymoon" balcony overhung the main road for off-loading ferry traffic. They paid three hundred, three-fifty for a night to swelter on a thin mattress, the window propped with lengths of broomstick, while scooters and diesel delivery trucks revved below. (That price I quote is before the island hospitality tax, which by itself would be a comical nightly rate.)

I would have said the entire peninsula was given over to these rickety firetraps, until I came upon the Party House. This mansion overlooked the town beach, and was too big to be a private home. Party House was three stories tall, and its yard occupied most of the block.

Though the house was enormous, party goers spilled out over the porch onto a side street and the narrow beach road. How many people, total, were milling about? Seventy? Ninety? In the dark it was like trying to count a forest by the shadows of the trees.

I approached and the terrible noise was just as terrible. It never got any better. Some fool had the sound system blasting so loud it had ripped the paper on the speakers. Why?

Rude public behavior . . . I tell you . . . forcing others to accommodate your fun . . . The nuisance isn't an accident, either, or a side effect. Certain parties delight in their transgression. These shrieks and screams aren't for the person standing across from you. This party wouldn't be fun if it weren't bothering the neighborhood. This party wouldn't move to the moon if it could.

In my pocket Betsy's phone rang and vibrated and did its thing. It went off like that every few minutes. No obvious switches, in the dark, so I popped the back and removed the battery.

★ ★ ★ ★ ★

Betsy had sent *me*, not Chet or Mason. Chet especially, because he was a party boy. Betsy didn't want this party to "tone it down." She didn't want them to move the festivities inside. She wanted it done, over, finished. She wanted dispersal.

This particular event had made the misstep of bothering Betsy's friends. This party had located itself not two blocks off the park I mentioned—the big park—the postcard park—and in this way it was bringing downtown nightlife to the quiet, stately homes. Two worlds collided.

Now don't ask me for every detail. All these cliques. Island politics. Wheels within wheels, my friend. Really, unless you were born on-island, who cares, right? Not me. (Though everyone wanted to tell me about it, endlessly.)

But here are the basics: Betsy was from a certain crowd. While she herself wasn't super rich, she took tea with ladies who were. Mrs. Pale. Mrs. Yellow. That was the grand side of life on the island. History and preservation. Old houses around the giant ocean park. This world was lace and doily, both inside and outside. They'd carve the doily right into the trim of their houses.

The giant houses on the park—I've told you about them—the smallest had maybe ten bedrooms. Towers and turrets, "the Grande Old Dames." Old dames lived there. And in town these same ladies had their side of things: Antiques and crafts. Sprouts restaurants. The ladies kept small dogs to pamper. No joke, up at the cash register, these restaurants offered treats specially baked for small dogs. These cookies were colored and shaped like gingerbread treats. More people than me ate one by mistake, I'm sure, thinking it was a complimentary sugar cookie.

As I say, this crowd was older ladies. The male half of this tribe was lost or missing, nowhere around. Sometimes they could be seen at a distance—they hadn't all been murdered or sent away to the same camp or something like that—but, in general, if they existed they kept out of sight in their back garages.

So that's one side of island life. That's one population. Then there was the other side. To get some sense of it, think blender drinks, or a house party like this affair, with speakers dragged onto the lawn. This other side is a harder picture for me to draw. It's more a mixed bag of people. As I said, I don't really care, so I'm probably throwing all kinds of types in there together. But let me tell you the crowd as I finally walked up to the fence. There were men in their forties or fifties, bodies so heavy you could tell them just by their pelvic stance, wearing old shorts and open shirts. They shouted right in each other's faces, but in a friendly way. If you stood back, you would think they were having a contest in who could laugh the loudest and fakest, right in the other man's face.

They either wore these open shirts or they wore tee shirts with comic sayings, like were sold by shops in town. About drinks or getting laid or something. Sometimes fishing—you get the sense they thought of themselves as fishermen.

As I approached, I bypassed this jolly pack and came up along the dark side of the house. One big guy was stumbling alone, feeling his way along a row of shingles. If I had to guess, I'd say he was returning from pissing on the bricks. He was preoccupied with his zipper. "Whoa," he said, as he saw my uniform.

"Yeah," I laughed, like it was too bad I had to wear a uniform to such a fun party. I nodded to his cup. "Can I get one of those?"

My man might have been surprised, but of course he said yes, or something like it. So as I turned away, in all this noise, I said, "Inside?" And then I had permission to go inside the house, because to me this guy seemed like the host, or close enough for my purposes.

Inside, the rooms were furnished like an elegant tea parlor—legged sofas and shaded lamps—but it was a jam of people. I had to step and slide between groups. A few of them said, "Uh oh" or something when they saw me as a cop but then I was past, and I still wore a friendly smile. Quieter in the house than on the lawn. I found a little speaker on a plastic stand and followed the cord. It led off into a second area with a food table and a grand piano.

Follow the speaker cord. To shut down a big party, that's how to do it. I hate to explain anything while there's a lot of noise. You can get wrapped up just trying to find out basic information. (Where's the host? Over here? No, over there. Find him. He's gone. Here's his cousin. Explain. Endless negotiation. Can't understand. Can't hear.) So instead, first thing, the music goes off.

For a party so ridiculous—one of these parties that knows it's got to stop—when you find the stereo, just yank the plug out of the wall. This action lays out your starting position, and then, you know, the property owner will make himself available and you can go from there.

At the stereo cabinet, impeding me, there was a lady trying to read the little displays. She didn't know the system, but she tried buttons, and the sound changed, and it started coming down. She cut the volume down by half.

She didn't do this to impress me. She did this on her own. When she stood, she was surprised I was there.

This lady was a certain type also. Summer dress, boom-boom cleavage, really fresh tan overlying a thousand old ones. Tan to a thousand layers. She was sweaty and flush. Everyone in the house was like this, with the humid heat and the drink. It was baking hot.

The lady kept being confused by me. Finally she asked, "Do you smell like seafood?"

"Could be," I said.

"I mean fresh seafood. I don't mean an insult. I smell fish."

"It's true. I was out earlier, out swimming."

I saw that she was a pretty lady, a little older than I was, in her thirties. I had mistaken her age because of the summer dress. The expression on her face was knowing and playful. It could go any number of ways, but I didn't think this was a game of "mock the cop." She smiled ruefully: "You had a noise complaint."

"Several. Better drink up."

She discovered the cup in her hand. She returned to studying me intensely. "You're really with the police?"

I shrugged. I was the Parking Warden. Everyone else could tell. I assume she could, too.

"Really? But where do you come from?"

She looked so genuinely puzzled. I checked my shirt to see whether I'd blown out a seam. My uniform seemed intact. "That's your police question, lady?" I laughed. "That's how you'll prolong this happy gathering?"

She shook her head, frustrated at being misunderstood, but then returned to studying my face. So serious. "Please."

Where did I come from? The way she asked, I came from planet Mars. "Nowhere," I said. "I didn't grow up in any one place. I had a crazy dad. Itinerant childhood. Van with a mattress, you know, and little curtains."

"Yes." She nodded somberly. "Okay then. I have to ask you. When the police offer a reward, is that serious?"

"Rewards for tips and information, that kind of thing?"

"In the newspaper, it said a reward was offered. Does that

mean that the police really care? Or is it one of these things where I tell them and suddenly I'm the one in trouble?"

"Good question. To tell you the truth, I'm the most rookie cop you can imagine. I'm not even a real cop. But my guess is that you would have to negotiate immunity, if you were involved in the crime. You know, get a lawyer for that. But otherwise I bet they pay the money. I think most rewards are offered privately. It's not like we have a big cash box at the station, behind the desk."

She didn't listen. "If I told you what I know, would you pretend you got the information by yourself?"

"You mean would I steal your reward?"

"No, I mean I could stay away from it all." Her hands stiffened at the wrists, a shudder of disgust.

This wasn't a party game. This wasn't going to end up being a joke where she gave me the wrong phone number. Her face around her mouth looked slack and flat, as though now she expected to be punished.

"Sure, I'll do it. Unless it's some pissant thing. Some of these complaints we get, you know, it's outrage because the caretaker is growing pot in a window box, or a grandma is keeping an extra cat or two on the property—"

"I can't—" She made another shuddering motion.

I glanced around, but no one was watching her. I said, "I can handle it, whatever it is. I don't mind pissing people off." Shame or disgust caused her to look at the floor. If only she would look at me, I thought, I could reassure her. There was no reason for her to be upset. "Please," I said. I even reached out to raise her chin, but stopped myself. That kind of comforting is beyond my abilities, the comforting touch. I'd scare her, or accidentally gouge an eye.

"You really don't mind at all?" she said.

"That sounds like I'm bragging. One way or another, I piss

everyone off."

She raised her eyes and assessed me frankly. She didn't seem drunk at all. She took a breath. She said, "The reward is for who is shooting those seals."

"Somebody shot seals?"

"They said there's a reward for information."

She stopped, and private considerations moved across her face, in creases. One minute she felt bad keeping her secret. Now she felt bad because she told it. And of course I didn't have any idea what she was talking about.

"I was face to face with a seal last night," I told her quietly. "We were swimming to different places."

My heart fell, because suddenly the lady lifted her chin and moved away. First she looked around to navigate the crowd—chose her path—and then she set off.

But I misread. Instead of leaving, she stepped beside me. She assessed who was watching and now stood against me, not touching except the heat off her bare skin, her heat mingling with my heat. To anyone in the room it looked as though we stood together to consider the stereo. "That's why you smell like the ocean," she said. She was smelling me. "I need to swim again."

"My name is Jim," I said. "What's yours?"

The first time I looked at her, I didn't see anything. I mean, she was one of those women who hung around the guys outside, the high-volume guys. Shriek! Shriek! She went with that whole group, with that party package. And there was no way to explain why any woman would do that.

Really, that's the truth, okay? Don't trust me to describe any of those people, because to me they made no sense. All that noisy laughter—so desperate to show somebody something. It reminded me of myself when I was a boy, whistling loudly through a crowded schoolyard, to show I didn't care that I had no friends. I was a whistling machine. To me, their raucous laughter meant that something was terribly wrong or ugly, like a maimed face. So obviously I didn't understand that whole picture.

The second time I looked at this lady, I saw I had been totally wrong. My mouth was beside her freckled neck. Her beauty shone out, and it was classy beauty. She had nothing to cover up or hide. On my first pass I hadn't seen anything at all. This was the prettiest woman in a crowded house. But she only knew how to be a girl. She was still trying to keep tan, like a teenager on a beach towel. She wasn't overripe or anything but she had grown up and her little dress was wrong. The string dug into the soft, adult flesh of her shoulder.

We stood there. I got to see her a third time, as we faced the stereo. She could have been in my arms. I saw all kinds of things. She was smart. She was unhappy. Her eyes never stopped moving, in little moves, just little drifts. Her eyes had gotten in this habit and moved constantly without her even paying attention, like a reader skimming a book for a passage she half-remembered, but without much hope or even a clear memory of what it was. The skin beside her eyes was set to laugh or smile. She just needed a decent reason, and the search was not going well.

"Hey, it's the law!" All this time, my uniform had been attracting some comment. Now a big man came in. Malcolm Trent. Proprietor of the Wharf House. Trent's arms were out wide, like an opera singer stepping to the front of the stage for his solo. He was the host. All right. I probably underestimated him, too. A heavy man with a snarled mustache. Trent wasn't just a fatty, and he had let his black mustache turn to white and gray. He wore the clothes: shirt open to his belly. I'd probably passed him outside in the yard.

He came right up. He put his enormous head on my lady's bare shoulder. In his big public voice he said, "He don't like the music, baby?"

"Noise complaints." I said it in a normal way, which couldn't be heard, and I made no special effort to move my lips.

"What was that?" He moved his rough stubble on the skin of her shoulder.

"Noise complaints," I repeated quietly.

Trent had brought others behind him, not as a gang or reinforcements but rather they trailed him because they anticipated a scene. Everyone. Including all the older guys I would see again and again at the bar. I may have to tell you about them individually at some point, all their names and relationships, but maybe I can spare you. At that point—early summer—*I* sure didn't know who any of them were. And at no point did I care. Basically, they were all blood brothers.

In this crowd, the general look was anticipation. A sea of these big pan faces. Right there, right then, that was the center of the party. Even my girl was curious to see what would develop.

Me too. What could they imagine would happen? Me too. With all this curiosity, I found myself as curious as everyone else. "Just a sec," I mouthed. I knelt and found the stereo plug, yanked it. Silence. I rose quickly so I wouldn't miss developments.

Look, there's always more to tell. But compared to what happened afterward, who cares? This was nothing. What followed was just your basic scene. Who cares. Who cares about Malcolm Trent. All the posturing, all the fake hostility these guys gin up . . . Whatever their game, I don't play. I don't oblige. No need to bump chests with Mr. Man-Tits. Instead, I just stood there for a while, letting his rant pass like a shore breeze.

Trent's whole role was a trap, something from the movies.

Let him figure that out on his own. He's expected to play outlaw biker, but he's in his nine-million-dollar house. When things start to break, they'll be his things, all right? In his life, the Law is the best friend he ever had. I understand his situation, and even sympathize—a guy gets in a certain mood, night and music, and finds himself trapped in a certain pose. But the sun is coming up, man. You've kept the old ladies awake long enough. You're the one who has to greet them in the morning, as they're picking plastic cups off their lawn.

Trent produced a little cell phone. He tried to phone my boss, the Chief. Maybe last summer that would have done something. But the Chief was dying on a reclining bed in a hospital. By nine o'clock every night he was drugged to the world. He was hooked to a half-dozen machines. The Chief's private number rang and rang. If Trent tried the station number, he got Betsy.

Phone threats, how dramatic! *Pink, pink, pink,* Trent's fat fingers on the little numbers. He raised a meaningful eyebrow to me: Wait until this call goes through, ho boy!

The gathered crowd watched, they tried to get a good view, and gradually deflated. Add to this, Chet suddenly appeared. Chet, my fellow cop, the other summer hire. He popped out of a closet or something, holding the wrist of a flushed-face beauty. Chet wore his excited smile. He was like an action figure of a fraternity boy. Chet ruled parties and could tame them effortlessly, with his Texas smile. "Let's head over to the Duck!" he called, and immediately the call was taken up. The party broke up like river ice.

The seal lady was gone. I couldn't find her. I swam home to Squab Island. Marsha visited. I thought about the girl.

The next day I was directing traffic off the ferry, and there were five or six news vans from the mainland—news vans with cameras that can rise up from their roofs on hydraulics. The vans shot off the ferry in a hurry. They were running for the compounds up-island. For the first time in twenty-eight years, there'd been a fatal shark attack on Nausset Island. It was a woman. She was a local woman. Her name was Megan Palsinger. Then I saw the picture.

Chapter 7

Coburn sat in his Cadillac, parked in front of the Wharf House, the flagship restaurant for this Malcolm Trent character. He ran the engine for the air-conditioning and listened while a moron caller wasted two, three, four minutes of Marko Mac's time on his mid-morning show.

Marko Mac was Coburn's favorite political shock-jock. He saw right through the politically correct baloney and talked straight. His only problem was that he babied his callers. Why didn't Marko just hang up on these fellows? If they didn't listen regularly, they shouldn't be allowed to speak on the broadcast.

Last Wednesday Marko had done a whole show on President Obama's connections to organized crime. Now this man called up to point out the president's debt to the Chicago mob, hinting that he knew more than he was saying. But he didn't even know all the facts that Marko himself had revealed! And his voice! He hemmed and hawed like a hillbilly lying to the judge, twisting together new lies on the spot as new evidence rolled in.

If Coburn got his own radio show, that's the first thing he would tell his producer. Screen out the uneducated. Bottom line: Screen out the uneducated. Coburn's radio show was going to be called *Bottom Line Time.*

Coburn seethed. The call had gone on too long. Marko's program ran all morning, and Coburn knew the timing in his blood, the way a stomach knows its meals. Now Marko wouldn't take another call before commercial. "No one wants to hear *you,*" Coburn exploded. He said the same thing again, using a different voice. He gripped the air theatrically, so for a moment Coburn looked like a bit actor—tall, gray, and wholesome, if a little wooden. In a different era he could have played a straitlaced TV cowboy.

"Bottom line, that's enough from you. That's the bottom line. It's bottom line time."

Coburn practiced for the day when he had his own radio show. That was his new career after Frobisher paid him off. He practiced throughout the day, in the privacy of his car, and had developed a nice low burr to the words "bottom line."

"Bottom line," he said to the window. "Bottom line, I hate amateurs."

Malcolm Trent was out the side door. He came back and forth, supervising the repair of a frozen-food truck. Two kids were on top of the truck taking apart the freezer unit. Every few minutes, Trent would come out, scold, then huff back inside. The kids on top of the delivery truck didn't know how to hold their tools. They dropped them over the side. Sooner or later one of them would slip and fall himself.

Malcolm Trent was a money man, though he wasn't like any money man that Coburn was accustomed to. He was big, sloppy, and loud. How could a man like that write big checks? One check for two million dollars. In addition to his restaurants, he sold frozen seafood up and down the Cape—packed stuff, clam shells stuffed with bread crumbs and flavor powder.

On the car radio, the commercial came on, Marko himself doing the advertising. Funeral insurance. "Fuck," Coburn said, quietly. He heard himself, bit his lip, and practiced radio synonyms. "Ah, baloney. Shoot. Shucks." *Bottom Line Time* would be a family program, and Coburn worked to purge bad language from his vocabulary

"Shucks, aw shucks, aw shucks." He checked his phones. He

had four different telephones, laid out beside him on the passenger's seat. He gave out different numbers to different types of people in different situations. To keep them straight, Coburn marked the back of the case with different postage stamps. Phone "Love" was never allowed to ring. But it had been seeing a lot of traffic. Coburn went through the caller ID. Nineteen calls in one hour, all from this Simon Boco character.

He'd read his man right. Simon Boco. Nineteen calls.

Boco was a nobody. But somehow this nobody had managed to spook Old Congressman Frobisher. Boco had an old-school fax machine, and was maybe one of the last men to use such a device. He'd type and send out documents, so these would appear at all hours, like legal papers being served by surprise. Boco faxed the Massachusetts state police an official request for "the report" on Marcus Cunningham's death.

Frobisher heard this and panicked. "Private investigator!" He instructed Coburn to "handle" it. In that way it was like old times, handling scandal for Frobisher or his psychotic son. Coburn's bread and butter. But this was such a table crumb.

Wait him out, Coburn advised. Simon Boco? Who was he? A private investigator without an office. A nobody.

But that term—"private investigator"—"P.I."—it excited people. Put that on a document, and it got their blood racing. Old Frobisher pictured Boco as a grizzled, chiseled detective who would stop at nothing, with a sexy secretary and a ragtag surveillance team he could call upon. Coburn had tried to tamp down this panic. Bottom line, all that "private investigator" actually meant, as a job title, was that no one would pay the man a salary. That's why he was private. On your loan application, "private investigator" meant the same as "self-employed."

In any case, who cared what this Boco guy wanted? Cunningham decided to kill himself, and he probably had his reasons, but Frobisher wasn't tied closely to his affairs. Their only history was recent.

This current land deal, for the new island, was the first time Coburn had even heard Cunningham's name. And the deal itself seemed fine, unaffected by Cunningham's suicide. No danger. Everybody just had to wait and sit on their hands for the government new year, October first.

When Coburn had tried to talk sense, Old Frobisher became more upset. He didn't hear well anymore. Conversation frustrated him, any two-way conversation. Soon the two men were arguing. Coburn said, "Sir, I made the call. At the state office, no one even knew what Boco meant. The report? There is no report. Bottom line, no one cares about Cunningham. Maybe the family will read the will in, what, thirty days? Another thirty days the suits go through his portfolio. If the man committed suicide, it's going to be a mess."

Frobisher had said nothing. He winced and breathed like a boss with incompetent employees. He rubbed his raw old hands. Coburn ignored the expression and pushed home his thinking: "So, sixty days. Sixty days is a lifetime. Sir, can you remember what you were doing, sixty days ago?"

Bad luck on this question. Coburn had selected the dates at random, but Frobisher's expression had become suddenly lucid, as he counted backward. He reached sixty days on his mental calendar. His eyes widened, and he regarded Coburn with astonishment. "Yes, all right. I understand you. I began to renovate the *Danube.*"

"No, I meant Boco will have given up in two weeks. A man like that. Bottom line—if some report *does* come out, bottom line—"

"If you can't bring me reassurance, on the matter of this single gadfly, then tell me what your role is as my employee?" The memory galled Coburn. This single gadfly? Old Frobisher went on: "I will tell you, Michael, I'm ready to handle this myself. If you can't do it, my other resources . . ."

Coburn sighed at the memory. October 1, this land deal would get signed and he'd receive his check. Then he could see about getting behind a microphone.

All Coburn's professional life, he had served as a kind of soldier of the private sector. But now it was time to take his fight public. Coburn was the old breed, an unapologetic American patriot. His radio show might wake his dying country. Once properly explained, liberal ideas were not ideas at all.

So, reluctantly, Coburn had "handled" Boco. First, he confirmed who he was dealing with. Simon Boco. Took a glance at his finances. Confirmed, Boco was a one-man operation. No secretary or answering service. This kind of "investigator" was one step up from a repo man, or a bail bondsman. Likely as not, he also sold spas and burglar-alarm systems on commission. He'd be in and out of business in six months, his business cards still wet from the printer's. If form held, he would already spend most of his day trying to collect the petty debts owed to him by his own clients, and, any day now, the whole "P.I." idea would have shriveled beyond resuscitation. Boco would be on to his next gold mine—farming llamas, on the sales force for a miracle vacuum or new investment product, something to be offered exclusively door-to-door.

A man like that, how do you get a handle on him? Due to the hustling nature of his work, never use the carrot. Coburn carried twenty thousand dollars in a duffel bag in the trunk, but the worst thing you could do with an independent PI would be to bribe. Right away Boco would know he had something of value, maybe for the first time in his life. The man would try to soak. He'd hint. He'd insinuate. It would be full-time with him. Calling the newspapers, peddling his story to each of them for five . . . four . . . one hundred dollars?

So, threats? That's what Old Frobisher wanted, of course. "Handle him. Send him a message." Which meant what? Mail him a dead rat? Break his knee with a pipe? Never. A threat was as bad as a bribe. Same message. It would tell this man that he was *near* something. A payday. A scene. This man, his whole life, no one paid attention to what he said, not even a wife and kids. Now, suddenly, someone cared? Suddenly the loser was a player? He called nineteen times in an hour. If threatened, he would call nineteen times an hour to negotiate: "Let's set up a meeting. Not a meeting but a sit-down . . ." Coburn shuddered.

No, Coburn was an old hand. He knew that the best way to handle Boco, to handle almost any small-timer, was by inquiry. Inquiry. That murderous friend with the forgettable, bland name. Inquiry—that invisible car that could stay outside your window, all day and night. You weren't in trouble. Inquiry wasn't saying that. Not going that far, not yet. Inquiry was just curious. Just wanted to set up a time to walk through your taxes, side by side. After all, you signed at the bottom. We just want copies of receipts. An *inquiry* about your private investigator's license. I wouldn't say there's been a complaint—not exactly . . .

If Boco were a rich man, his lawyer could handle this. But a poor man was doomed. A poor man was in the soup. With all the rules, all the potential violations, no licensed private investigator could run completely clean. And who would know best where he had cut corners? He would. By now Boco would be out of his mind with worry. Nineteen calls in one hour!

Sitting in his car, Coburn hummed tunelessly at his success. He thumbed through Boco's voicemails, erasing without listening. Like all practiced torturers, Coburn knew the value of empty time. For Boco, two or three days would be about right.

As Coburn completed this housekeeping, the car radio delivered the sound of a semi-truck: *Err! Err!* Mack truck.

Marco Mac was back on. Perfect timing. Now for the best part. Marko Mac would sort through the news of the day. The country was going insane and Marko Mac wasn't going to let these news items pass unnoticed.

A phone rang aloud. "Fuck. Shoot. Shoot." That ring tone. The phone with the George Washington stamp. With reluctance, Coburn leaned forward, adjusted the volume on Marko Mac, up and down, until he was still just audible. He answered on the fourth ring. "Yes, sir."

Frobisher wanted to go over it all again. He was agitated.

Coburn listened and made sounds of sympathy and agreement, with one ear on the radio. Coburn had actually written Marko Mac a letter in which he had described *Bottom Line Time*. He proposed that Marko Mac take him on as an apprentice, or understudy, before eventually forming a partnership. No response yet.

"What do I pay you for?" Frobisher asked, having listed his complaints. "I'm deeply upset. I've been upset all night. Deeply upset. Your job is to make me sleep easy. You failed in your job."

Time, the great torture tool, was working on Coburn's boss as well. "Sir, sir, sir . . ." With great reluctance, he switched off the radio. "You *can* sleep easy. To me, this is adequately handled," he said. "But okay, there are other options on the table."

Coburn's tone of voice told Frobisher that these options were unnecessary. They were bad options. Frobisher wasn't receptive to this hint. He sighed with exasperation, that he had to micromanage everything. "Brief me."

"Well, next step, if you're still concerned. I hire him away."

Coburn explained the process. He would invent work for Boco. In Maine. In South Dakota. Some useless job—basically to track down overdue library books. Get the "whole story" on a random inmate at the local jail. A fake employer would wave real cash in Boco's face. Not a bribe (God forbid) but the irresistible distraction of steady work. Paid expenses. "Coop him up at a Holiday Inn with some drink vouchers . . ."

Frobisher hated the idea. He groaned at every chance. The noises meant, has everybody gone crazy except me? Finally, in a pause, he asked, "And how much does this cost? Real dollar amount, please."

Coburn tapped his front teeth. Like any professional, he had an instinct against being specific over a telephone. "Between fifteen and eighteen thousand dollars a month."

"Coming out of your salary," Frobisher quipped. "Eh, is that right? Coming out of your salary? No, I didn't think so. I don't want to pay this man. I want this man fucked."

"You can't have that. Bottom line. It costs more to screw him. A lot more."

"And it's all money, is it?" Like a nightmare Frobisher's reasonable voice slid into a patronizing laugh. "For thirty thousand maybe I'll engage a kill team. A three-man kill team. What's that, two months of your hotel solution?"

A kill team. *Kill team.* Had Frobisher actually just said that aloud? On a cell phone? This whiff of fatal craziness froze Coburn in his seat. He did not move or react in any way.

"That's a real solution, not paying healthy salaries to dead wood. A one-time payment, fee for service."

Kill team. Always Frobisher had liked to insinuate that he had violent connections, can-do connections—that if any problem got too knotty, he might solve it with a phone call and a brick of cash.

When a girl's father would refuse to drop his lawsuit against Brand, or when a judge ruled that Brand had to appear in court, Frobisher would rail and carry on and at some point suggest assassination. The idea would calm him, that the ultimate power was his. The ultimate mercy was his.

So what was new? The term. "Kill team." Recently Frobisher had been helping an ex-CIA acquaintance. The man had lived fat on Iraq contracts. With Iraq winding down he called every connection in the government. He got Old Frobisher.

It was too easy. It wasn't fair or right. Old Frobisher had always been a sucker for this kind of talk. It was luring a child with candy. Frobisher had always had bad instincts, and instead of wanting to put distance between himself and rough stuff, he wanted to get closer. If he drank a little whiskey, he would start to talk as though he did gunplay himself. He was up for it. Maybe he had done some already. Like a lot of old men, he had whole basements of expensive firearms.

Coburn couldn't find anything to answer, and Frobisher hung up, angry: "That's about enough from you, I guess."

By habit Coburn turned on the radio. It was a minute or two before he listened. Truck sounds. Eleven o'clock. Marko Mac was on repeat, from his seven a.m. program.

He jerked upright, as Malcolm Trent knocked a knuckle on the window. Coburn powered open the glass. Trent said, "It's you Frobisher sent? Ten thirty? You're supposed to help me fuck this vandal doctor?"

Coburn nodded once, reluctantly, like a man stifling a burp.

"You're not billing hours for the morning, I can tell you that. Okay? Take a look at this parking lot. You think it looks like you need to patrol?"

Malcolm Trent pointed and instructed. He had ideas for cameras and ambushes and even mantraps. Coburn said nothing. He followed the gestures with his eyes, so for a few minutes Trent continued to mistake him for a mall cop. For a few minutes Coburn felt what it was like to be a security guard, a by-the-hour security guard, trusted with a long flashlight.

CHAPTER 8

"Shark in there," said Mr. Lee.

"Right," I said. "Millions of them. So, hazard pay, twenty-five a fish."

We looked at the fish in the trunk of my cruiser. I had six monster "stripers"—striped sea bass—that I took with a spear gun not an hour before. My hair was still ocean wet. Mr. Lee laughed and made a rueful sound. "Hazard pay. Okay, okay."

Two at a time I transferred the fish from the contractor bag in the back of the cruiser to the trunk of his Chrysler, which was steaming from blocks of dry ice. Everywhere Mr. Lee drove, on a hot day, steam rose out of his trunk as though it was a mobile science lab.

Mr. Lee bought fish for his restaurants. He had at least three restaurants. I kept discovering that some other restaurant belonged to Mr. Lee. That night, walking my shift on the wharf, the chalkboards for the fancy places would feature preparations of sea bass.

Mr. Lee counted out the bills. He got coy. "One hundred dollar."

"One fifty."

He clucked. Did me this one favor. He showed me that his big roll of cash was only twenties, so I accepted 140. "Owe me ten," I say.

He didn't acknowledge. His poor English meant he would forget this. It would give us a topic for next time.

We stood and considered the fish, now on ice in his car. "Big fish," Mr. Lee said happily.

"That one could be forty inches," I said.

Mr. Lee clucked and pointed where a spear has ripped open its side. "No, no," he complained. "No, no, no." He pointed out better places to target the fish. Not surprising, he wanted me to make head shots. He pointed and jabbed and worked himself into a mood. By gesture he said I should take that one back. He now rejected it. "No, no, no."

Mr. Lee's poor language skills made us comfortable with one another. This was just how we talked. He liked vicious bargaining, and maybe no one else indulged him during his day. He lectured me, in sounds more than in words, and in return I made noises of sympathy and rue. What could I say? I sold him bass that I shot with a spear. They were going to have a hole in them.

"Thursday," he said. "Ten big fish. Bigger."

"Can't," I said, looking away. "I work Thursday morning. Friday morning. For the weekend crowd. Five fish," I said.

"Ten. Two hundred dollars. I pay cash premium."

I just laughed. He had other demands. He wanted crabs and lobsters. Already he wanted to set up delivery for Fourth of July weekend. Bass, bass, bass. I was supposed to slaughter the local bass population for that tourist influx.

Every morning Mr. Lee drove the whole island in his steaming car. He had other regular sources. I opened his trunk and it would be crawling with groggy lobsters. There were nets of the fat, muddy local clams. On the fishing charters for tourists, rules allowed the baitboys to keep a fish for themselves, and they all knew Mr. Lee would pay cash for scup, bluefish, anything he could put in the soup. The first time I opened the trunk, the whole thing was carpeted with an enormous rayfish so fresh I thought it was alive, its skin still pulsing out color. I didn't know you could eat rayfish but I guess you can take a cookie cutter, stamp holes out of the wings, and pass the meat off as scallops. That night I walked by the "specials" board of Lee's Asian fusion place. "Scallops in fiery sauce" was the feature preparation.

Maybe he caught the rayfish himself. He did haul around fishing gear in the Chrysler's backseat, a rod with an ancient trolling reel, incapable of casting, strung with incredibly thick line, like the cord on a weed-whacker.

Any man or woman fishing on the beach, Lee stopped his ice-mobile and made broken conversation. All day, Lee found them. If a fish came in, whatever size or species, out came his roll of cash. "Good fish! Ahh, good fish!"

The first time Lee came up to you, you saw his lousy teeth and the way he was dressed, you thought he was homeless. But that was a costume to go with the act. His English got better depending on how much he needed. It got worse when that was an advantage.

He was sharp. For example, he wanted me to spear more fish. I put him off that I was working, or that the fish were getting clever, and I couldn't find ten. But somehow Lee knew it was just my personal qualms. There were limits of decency in that kind of thing. Really the bass hung around piers and structures like cows around a feed trough. Mr. Lee understood and worked to undermine my sense of decency.

"Fourth of July, you bring me that big shark," he laughed. "Everyone, all weekend, they eat the big damn shark."

The shark. I thought about the girl constantly. Megan Palsinger.

Lee moved from mood to mood. "You are useless." He brought his arm across viciously. "Fourth of July, ten fish, or nothing."

"I'll bring the shark, to stick up your ass." I slammed the

trunk on his Chrysler. I slammed it so hard it bounced open again.

As I walked away, Lee came after me, jabbering this and that, which surprised me. I mean, I was glad he was angry—I couldn't stand sadness—but it was surprising. He was just an old guy and there was no one around to see him being brave.

I tried to drive and he stood in front of the cruiser, still gesticulating, coming over the bumper. Jesus, I thought these moods of Lee's were pretend, for the most part, but he sustained. All I had to meet this was sadness, for some woman who never told me her name. Lee jumped up and down, he was so furious.

Then he switched mode again. He whipped out his cash and rolled off forty dollars. "Friday," he said. He stuck the money under the blade of the windshield wiper. "Friday, five fish."

Chapter 9

Anna Fedorchak awoke from the closeness of her plywood cubby. She was a compact young woman of 17, but might have passed for any age between 13 and 30, her dark, serious features set in a complexion of a pale flower petal.

Blinking, seeing the world afresh, she was surprised to discover how comfortable she had gotten in the United States. She had allowed her things out of arm's reach. There was her purse, where she'd let it fall beside the door. Her second set of underpants dried on the back of the plastic chair.

On the chair were papers, fliers asking for information about her missing sister, Kat. These fliers were the failed first draft. The good ones, on colored paper, were all around town now, pinned to bulletin boards and taped to poles. These fifty failures represented five dollars in wasted money. Anna had printed them before she had a phone number, so they simply listed this street address. They read like something from the nineteenth century: "Ten dollar reward. Please inquire at . . ."

She had recognized the foolishness of this. So she invested in a phone and one hundred minutes of calling time. Thirty days of service.

Now she touched a button on this new phone, to light the tiny screen and confirm that it was working correctly. She had slept with it against her cheek, and during the night had received two calls. Both were from the same robot voice, who so far was her only caller. The first one came yesterday, hours after she activated the phone, demanding an urgent return call. In a panic, Anna had fumbled the number twice, gulping, near tears, her scalp on fire.

But it turned out to be nothing. The robot voice was just a company collecting unpaid debts. Whoever had owned the telephone number before Anna had even less money than she did. Now Anna had eighty-seven minutes of phone time. Anna explained the situation in a recorded message, but the debt company would not stop calling. Anna no longer answered. Instead, she would shut off the power and let the call go to voicemail.

One week in the United States, searching for her sister, and already she'd spread out, she'd moved in. In another week would she be decorating?

In her travels, she had been constantly on guard since leaving Sevastopol. She had never relaxed a moment. She had toted her full bag with her at all times, every daytime errand, and at night had slept atop it like a hen on an egg. The alien, forever-changing world of train stations and hostels had seemed to be watching, waiting for a lapse. One mistake—anything—trusting her bag too close to the door of a bathroom stall—then swoop, gone, panic, and nothing would be saved or found. She would not be able to go to the police. The only people to ask for help would be the same uniformed people whose job was to stop her, a Ukrainian girl, traveling alone without enough money.

A light knock at her door—Margo's shy knock.

"One moment."

Margo was from Croatia. Like everyone to whom Anna told her mission, she was sympathetic. Though if she *truly* believed Anna—that her sister was missing—then she couldn't offer such light friendliness. Her whole world would alter, and Margo's world didn't alter. Instead, she would knock lightly and invite

Anna to accompany the rest of them to an outdoor concert, to the beach. How could you suggest a leisure activity to someone if you truly believed that her sister had disappeared?

Margo came in, smiling hesitantly. She was slim, dark, and pale, and always wore men's black jeans. "You wanted to fix your papers," Margo explained. She had a surprise, and presented Anna with a set of art markers. They were new in their clear packaging, arranged like a rainbow.

Impossible—this was the set—these were the very markers. They had been on display in the window of the stationery store. The sight had stopped Anna on the sidewalk. Fat-bodied art markers—like cans of paint—with caps that screwed into place, and the promise of a fat, sturdy wick. Anna couldn't remember the price—some impossible figure, like gold jewelry, or a meal in one of these darkened restaurants.

"How could you have these?" Anna asked, holding the package.

"They sell . . ." Margo explained. She spoke with a tone of apology.

The very set—Anna had stood there and coveted. She had considered *stealing* them, at a dash.

This country . . . Margo brought the art markers right to her door. This was part of the larger pattern. The United States anticipated your wishes, and delivered them.

In this place food could be had for the asking. Eight young people shared this house, and those who worked in restaurants stocked the house kitchen with endless free, sodden restaurant food. Food here was unwanted. It was a nuisance. It was garbage.

Anna had to adjust. Her first day, she surreptitiously lifted a few packets of crackers from the table basket, and arranged the remaining packets to hide the theft. All day, as she made her inquiries, she guiltily broke and nibbled the fragments out of the pocket of her dress. But that evening, when she returned to the communal kitchen, she found the basket replenished, spilling over. On top of the refrigerator, a box held thousands and thousands of the same soup crackers. There was no need for her to hoard.

In the refrigerator, the styrofoam shells of leftovers were *meant* to be eaten by anyone. Whoever wanted them. Anna only accepted this at last when one of her housemates stormed through, discarding, in a tirade: Would no one else take the initiative to throw all this food away? Why did this chore always fall to her?

From what Anna could see of her housemates, this would be the next step in her own development. She would learn to complain about a free hamburger, because the bun was soggy with bottled sauce.

Margo still waited shyly in her doorway. Anna opened the package of markers, to a jolt of paint fumes. *If this is a trap,* she thought, *I don't see the teeth.* "I won't spoil them," she said quietly.

Margo stayed. They left the door open for ventilation. Instead of knocking down walls for the usual workers' dormitory, the owner of this shambling old house had subdivided into private cubicles of a few meters.

The two women sat on the floor, cross-legged, doctoring the fliers. They wrote Anna's new telephone number with the big smelly markers, and laid out the papers everywhere, for the ink to dry. As they finished, Margo chose one of the drying papers and traced a red border around the picture. The picture of Kat, Anna's sister, was the center of the flier.

The red border bothered Anna. It seemed festive, a party advertisement. But it definitely called the eye. Anna took up a green marker and on one of her papers crosshatched her sister's jacket. She took a yellow marker, another flier, and colored her sister's hair.

"Your sister is tiny, like you," Margo said.

"She doesn't look like this," Anna said.

"She's not blonde?"

"Her hair could be any color. Who knows. It could be any shape."

The picture showed Kat slumped, looking up at the camera. In this distorted version she looked as though she was bent over by pains in her stomach. In fact, she was lacing an ice skate.

Anna had come on her mission to the United States unprepared in the most obvious way, with only three glossy photos of her sister. None photocopied well. The best picture showed Kat, two years ago, in her diving costume. That was inappropriate for a bulletin board. She wore a swimsuit, and stared down the camera, handsome and aggressive, hands back to put her figure on display.

The third photo showed Kat and Anna together, arm in arm. Anna had tried to cut herself out, but the result was terrible, like Kat was embracing a ghost.

Anna and Margo sat together and decorated all the fliers until each had one moment of color: hair, clothes, sky. They chattered, though Margo was shy about something. She held back. At one point, after Anna made her laugh again, Margo stopped. "Last night, Sasha was at the park."

Anna slowly filled and emptied her lungs. "Sasha would have known her? For sure?"

"He was here two whole seasons. He met everybody . . ." Margo spoke reluctantly, and Anna read this reluctance. Margo wanted to talk and be friends, but she didn't want to encourage this crazy search.

At once the fun was over. Anna carefully capped her marker. She considered her moves while Margo chattered on, oblivious. Margo said maybe later they could find Sasha in the park, and anyway there would be a drum band, and ice cream. Everybody would be there.

That is not how it would happen. Anna was sitting cross-legged but rose straight up without a wobble. Her face settled into its cold, determined set. She had been a gymnast on the Ukrainian national team—her event was the vault—and this was the face she put on before sprinting down the runway. Her coach would say, "smile, smile," but he had given up because her painted smile would not hide this determined face but instead amplify it, like bared teeth on an attack dog.

Whatever Margo had in mind about an evening of fun and boys, they would instead leave now. They would find Sasha immediately. They would walk until they did.

With no mirror, Anna looked down to consider her appearance. It was inconvenient that this first lead was a boy. When Anna told her story, Margo and the other girls in the house listened sympathetically. Boys did the same, their faces growing stern and protective. Then at some point they would try to kiss her.

Chapter 10

I was up on the roof of the Cunningham cottage.

"Sir, sir? Are you supposed to be up there?"

The old lady had been walking circles around, working herself up to challenge me.

I had already searched inside. To zero effect—or at least more questions than answers. What I needed now was a patch of lawn to jump down, a patch of lawn without an old lady.

I said, "Yeah, I'm pretty sure. I'm with Total Quality Island Roofing, ma'am. We're an on-island firm. All island labor. Supposed to do a bid out here." I tried to sound unsure and apologetic. "The dispatcher said the place was purple."

A good cover story, except that the shingles on this roof were so new that I could smell the packaging.

The lady seemed partly mollified. To get up here I climbed one of the street trees. Then I jumped roof to roof, across three neighbor cottages. I assumed they were deserted. On my first landing, someone cried out in shock. "Goodness!" It sounded like six inches below my shoe.

Maybe it was this lady, and I woke her from her nap. She shielded her eyes from sun. "You haven't seen a dead cat, have you?" I asked. "Just lying around?"

She put her hand to her mouth.

Honest to God, I was in the campground for a cat. Someone had phoned about a dead cat in the Methodist Campground. And phoned and phoned and phoned. Detective Watkins finally threw up his hands. He sent me to find it, bag it, and drop it in a Dumpster. I searched, but all the animals were either still alive or else they were these little statues, very realistic and very popular in the yards. Maybe these statues had faked out our caller? Or if there had been a dead animal, maybe a little kid gave it a funeral in a shoebox?

No cat, but then I recognized the cottage. This was the place from Boco's pictures. Cunningham's cabin. Purple filigree. I went past it again and again on futile cat search. The door was locked, but the upper window was open a crack.

Cunningham was often on my mind, I confess. He was a private concern. Marsha went nuts if I tried one word on the subject.

Inside . . . what did I expect? Some kind of adultery setup. Candles and light jazz. But it wasn't like that at all. Instead, the top floor was like an impromptu union office. Just one sweaty room, with no beds or couches. There were five or six telephones so ancient that they had mechanical bells, and on the walls were taped-up phone lists, lists handwritten in dull pencil with a hundred illegible revisions.

The only seats were cardboard boxes, and these held posters and handbills, very angry about this and that environmental cause. Case after case of bumper stickers. Cause after cause. YOU "HARVEST" CROPS/YOU "MURDER" FISH. Strident and humorless. A lot of papers about whaling, for example, which I had thought was a settled issue. This wasn't a crowd that would spend time celebrating their victories. These were the born-again, and the end was nigh.

I had given up, my foot out the window, when I read another bumper sticker: SAVE SQUAB ISLAND. Beside this message was a picture of a little seal with its head cocked. The whole box was the same. So was the next one. Thousands of these bumper stickers about my island.

★ ★ ★ ★ ★

"Hey roof guy! What's your bid?" called a man. He was older with gray, curly hair. Then I recognize the squint. Simon Boco, PI.

"Um, I'll have to write it up," I said. I looked around as though I was gauging. I glanced down at some papers I brought away. Boco and the neighbor lady waited. Maybe if I stood there long enough I could get an audience of thousands. "Eh, I guess about four grand."

"Four grand?" Boco exclaimed, with his familiar squeal of disbelief. "You got to come bid on my place. Have I got some contracts for you. You'll be booked out for months. I'm going to hold you to that. Won't cover your materials, son. Four thousand dollars . . ."

"Yes," the woman said. "Come look at my roof, if you're finished." Then, "You don't have a ladder?"

Boco said, "Lady, the kids these days can fly. Look at him."

I hopped down. Boco wore a new smile—sunny, gap-jawed—a maniac's smile—and patted me with such warmth that in total it added up to a back rub. Until we were alone over by his car. Then he dropped the act. He snarled, "You're running her errands now, eh? Is that what this is about?"

He was primed for confrontation. This was a new Boco. He shut up to wait for my answer, which for Boco was as bizarre as an extended mime routine. "What?" I protested. "I never met her until a second ago. The lady who wanted me to put flashing around her chimney?"

"Oh, that's wise, that's a wise-guy answer. I'll tell you what, I'll tell you what." He was too angry to articulate. Up by his eyes he jabbed his finger convulsively, some strokes so wild that they came near to poking me. "How about I call her, then, smart guy? How's that? I'm calling her right now. Ask her." He brought out his phone and poked at it, a little folding phone that looked fragile as a delicately-hinged clam.

I said, "She's still over there. She's doing circles around the house. I don't think she's carrying a phone."

"Oh wise guy. So wise."

Puzzling as all this was, you had to re-evaluate the man. Boco. God knows I was familiar with symptoms of irrational temper. You spun up all morning on some indignity, then let fly at a punk whose only crime was playing his car radio.

Boco snarled, "It's pissant. It's pissant. That's all this is."

"Calm it, brother. I'm not working for anyone."

His call apparently wasn't going through. His blunt fingers punished his phone. "Oh, you're working for Sarah Palsinger."

"Sarah Palsinger? Right. Not me. I know the grandma, Mrs. Yellow. I met her sister Megan once. A shark killed her."

"Oh, so you're up there what, investigating a crime? You're inside the house why?"

I had no answer for that—being nosy—so I changed the subject: "If this Sarah lady hired me, why would she want me to look at her own house? She probably has keys."

"You're running her errands, big strong errand boy, who knows what else, I'll tell you what else. I shouldn't have given you those goddam pictures, that's for starters."

"*Pfft.* Nothing in those. And there's nothing inside, either." Boco fumed, big nasal breaths. I told him, "No adultery setup. For one thing, it's one hundred and twenty degrees Fahrenheit. Not even a box fan. And there's no real bed. Downstairs it's completely gutted. It's being remodeled or something. No beds. There's a little day couch with no sides. The only chairs are little antique things. I'd need one for each half of my ass."

"I *know* she's not doing anything. I know that. I *knew* that when I took the job. I was hired to follow a lady and I followed her. You have your job, I have mine. Perfectly legal. Yes." He continued this line of argument more or less in his head, and at some point his anger began to die, or to become the jitters.

Boco and I sat on the hood of his car. He held himself tight. "I wish to Christ I'd never done an hour of work on that job." He explained. Apparently he had received some menacing phone calls, asking details about his private investigator's license. A complaint had been filed. "Also I got a lawyer who called me. Asked for the name of my legal representation. Can you imagine? A law firm called me up. Some brief from the mainland."

"So? What are they going to do from Boston? Yell into the telephone?"

"I don't take that. You don't put up with that for one minute. Oh, yeah. I used to walk a beat in Quincy. I know that city."

Boco elaborated on his police days. I checked out his face and his car, looking for signs he was crazy. "It's probably from some angry husband," I said. "Spying on people, an investigator must get this night and day. If it's pressure, what are they pressuring you to do?"

"I don't know! That's it! Is it Sarah, the wife? She's pissed? That's all I can figure. I barely saw her. I did a few hours light surveillance, between other things. Suddenly this."

He was silent for a moment, weighing his thoughts, looking over at the purple cottage. "So it's filthy inside." He dismissed that with a wave, a private investigator who had seen more than he wanted to. "You know with these things, if two people want, they can do their business in the garbage can." He shook his head ruefully. "But Sarah Palsinger. No way. She's gorgeous and Cunningham was as ugly as a frog. Why would she cheat if she signed on for that? It doesn't make sense, I know, but it's true. That's how it works."

"Wives don't cheat on ugly husbands?"

"That's the way it works." Boco had a new thought. "He

never said cheating. Cunningham said to look into her. Her schedule. Her meetings. He was loaded, he was flat-out loaded, no matter what you think. He just wanted a thousand pictures. That was his requirement. I was going to bill some hours, oh man . . ."

The guy was truly shaken. I said, "Look, Boco, you can't sweat this kind of nonsense. If they want the name of your lawyer, make something up, tell them it's Santa. Address, the North Pole. That's what I do." Boco didn't listen. Wasn't consoled. I said, "I can tell you why Cunningham was agitated. Poor man. They wanted to turn his sweet house into condos."

"His big place?"

"And get this, he was trying to save his view." I showed Boco the bumper sticker. SAVE SQUAB ISLAND.

"Squab Island. What, the place for those rare birds?"

"There are no rare birds. Just shorebirds and gulls. There was a fort but it's long gone. No one is out there. Probably super dangerous even to walk around. But from what I see inside"—I pointed a thumb back at the cottage—"from what I see inside, Cunningham was trying to make it a home for seals."

I showed Boco some of the environmental papers. Fields of ocean trash, and all the poison these whales had to carry around in their blubber. I showed him the bumper stickers I collected. "There's a seal swimming in the corner, which presumably was going to be the mascot in the campaign. Give him a name, think up something. You know, maybe there aren't any of these birds, but Cunningham just wanted to keep the island as a refuge for seals."

Boco didn't nod along to my theories. He tilted his head like a baffled chicken. Our roles reversed. He thought I was crazy. I raised my voice to explain. "The top floor is more boxes than floor space. The island became his prime cause, toward the end of his life." I offered him a bumper sticker. "My whole day is spent watching cars. Believe me, these never got distributed. I've never seen one. They are sitting up there in cases. Now you and I have the only two ever distributed. We can keep the flame alive."

Boco wouldn't take the seal sticker. I gave him another choice. "Do you know this guy? Watterson? He's the town clerk. I think he's our bad guy on this development. Look." The bumper sticker said, "IMPEACH WATTERSON." "And he's just the town clerk. He probably issues permits for putting up crap."

Boco gently took my forearm. He spoke to me in a quiet voice. "Son, what you're talking about . . . there's no way Marcus Cunningham would be involved in that activity. Environmentalism? No, son."

"Go up and take a look," I said. I fanned out the bumper stickers like a card trick, giving Boco free choice. He wouldn't read them and wouldn't touch them.

Instead he read me. "He's a developer. He was a developer." Boco sighed. "And he didn't know about this place." Boco was calm now. "I thought I'd scored big. Cunningham didn't know he owned this cottage. He never stepped foot across the threshold. Sarah had kept it. His wife paid the note on this."

Chapter 11

"You don't have to eat those," Donald Frobisher said.

Malcolm Trent drew his hand back from the bowl. He recognized the berries for what they were, white strawberries. Perfect strawberries, but done in white. The seeds were prominent ivory pinheads. "Some gourmet thing?" Trent asked.

"She picks them like that, out of the garden."

"They eat white berries, where she comes from? Poland?"

Frobisher shook his head, an old man dismissing half of life as unfathomable.

At the caps, the berries morphed to incomplete green. As strawberries, these were abortions. Trent pushed the dish away, then realized this might seem an insult to his host. So instead he turned his back, leaned with his elbows behind him on the counter.

Right there was the most gorgeous view in Massachusetts. There it was. The green ocean. Not the bay, the ocean. Here at the end of Frobisher's private island they were on the very knife-edge of the continent, the last piece of rock. The Atlantic Ocean did its stormy thing, utterly quiet through three panes of glass.

Normally this kind of rich guy stuff provoked Trent. He'd fart and rub his bare feet. He would get a beer, and set it down to leave cold rings on anything that looked like wood. But not here. Not at Frobisher's place. Because of Frobisher, Trent was going to be Hollywood-rich himself, in another few months.

So out of the corner of his eye Trent watched Frobisher to learn how to behave. Frobisher had been born to money, and Trent watched him like a farm boy at the queen's dinner, trying to copy which spoon to choose for the soup.

The other thing that kept Trent silent was those strawberries. Frobisher's house was a palace, but something was wrong with it. What exactly? It was impossible to say. All the pieces were here. Leather furniture. The picture window. The kitchen was stainless steel and dark stone. Wine rack. But something undermined the perfection, like a bad smell in the air, like baby shit.

Uneasiness made Trent chuckle. "You've always got the hottest slot on the island, every summer. You expect her to whip up cuisine?"

Frobisher smiled with faint distaste. He looked like a handsome college boy of a certain era, neatly combed, except that now he was nearly eighty years old. Age had thinned the skin of his face and drained the color from his hair. His eyes looked where Trent had looked. They traced the same pattern over his furnishings, searching for the same missing thing.

Trent was the opposite of Frobisher. He was heavy, ruddy, and rough. "I brought this." He dropped a magazine onto the table, where it began to uncurl. *Island Life.* On the cover a big man hoisted a bloody swordfish, cigar clamped between his teeth. "I figure we get a spread in here, you know. Free advertising. We got a unique offering."

He quit talking. Frobisher regarded the magazine as a piece of litter.

Neither man was in practice with this kind of conversation. A visit. A serious conference in the kitchen. In their daily lives, both men were bosses. They told people what to do. Aides and secretaries. Employees. But here, who outranked whom? Who was there to ask favors, and who to grant?

Frobisher certainly thought he knew. He regarded Trent with amusement. "It appears that you cut your face this morning, Malcolm." His thumb and finger touched the hinge of his jaw and glided forward to his chin, appreciating his own perfect shave. "You become accustomed to living with pressure. Think of this time as rest, not as waiting."

"Oh, yeah. That." Trent turned away. "Just a little scuffle."

"A fistfight?" Frobisher's smile stayed up a beat longer, forgotten, and then wilted. "Were there police? In four months. I would think that for four months . . ."

Trent got his chance to chuckle reassuringly: "No, no, nothing big. Nothing that won't keep until we're filthy rich."

Frobisher regarded him coldly. "Then let me tell you about a very serious local problem. Something that should concern you. 'No Condos on Squab Island.' That is a bumper sticker."

"No."

"And yet I saw one in town. 'Save Squab Island' was there as well."

"You're pulling my chain. Come on." Frobisher waited. Trent chuckled and groaned. "Seriously? I hope you peeled it off."

"On a police car."

"A police car?"

"So it would appear to me that you need to see to your local responsibilities, as I see to those on a national playing field."

" 'No Condos on Squab Island'? It's got to be a joke, right? Maybe my brother . . ."

"My son was incensed. And he may decide to deal with it personally."

"Brand?"

The word dropped like a cartoon anvil. Both men had been playing a sort of game, doing the acts they had become so expert in throughout their lives: Frobisher with his superior knowledge and superior bearing; Trent rough and ready. Then, *Brand.* Suddenly for both of them the room grew cold. Trent folded his huge arms and chuckled nervously. Frobisher scratched his shave like a rash. His swallows hurt him. They didn't really know how to be or how to look at one another.

Crime was the problem. Murder. Suddenly there were all these crimes between them.

Back when they made their business arrangement, talking had been simple. They were from different worlds, yes, but that was a strength. Frobisher was old money, and brought connections at the highest level. His phone calls were answered in every building in Washington, DC. Trent was new money, cash flow, his arm around the shoulder of every island official. Cunningham had been their third. Some people were born owning skyscrapers, and those were Cunningham's people.

Differences? This deal they had was so sweet, so once-in-a-lifetime sweet, that it would have the Arabs and Jews singing harmony. From the US government, the men would buy the most valuable unoccupied property in the United States, maybe in the world, paying no more for it than a stretch of Wyoming prairie. A genius plan, and legal enough that they wrote down most of the details in a meticulous contract.

Then came the problems. Crunching bone. Body disposal. Cunningham was gone. Brand Frobisher. The written contract now seemed a crazy risk, and it also seemed one hundred years obsolete, like a yellowed document done in cursive with a goose quill.

Crime of a certain sort Frobisher and Trent were familiar with. All their working lives—log-rolling, barter, golf-course bribery—that was just part of business. Cook the books. Negotiate with the tax man later, if he came sniffing around. That wasn't even crime, to a right-thinking mind, just business. If it had been that, Trent and Frobisher would have known how to talk to one another.

After the first murder, they had tried—little jokes, wink wink—but it didn't work. Murder was a crime for the other side of the courthouse, the smelly side, and with a different set of lawyers instead of their lifelong pals.

Even that first murder—their partner Cunningham—would have been simple to come to grips with. The man betrayed them. The deal was golden, and Cunningham wanted to mine that gold all for himself, and in his own creepy way. Sure you're going to sell the property, he said. But first you blackmail the neighbors by threatening to ruin the neighborhood. It was crazy. No argument. Cunningham had to go.

However, killing bred killing, and now to wipe up the mess would be wiping dirt off the earth. What a swamp. That first murder they shared—a sort of pact—but any balance or proportion had long fallen away. New crimes were committed or came to light for which only one of them had bloody hands, crimes certain or suspected, brother and father, old and new, sins as old as the fillings in Frobisher's teeth. Secrets they denied to their own private selves they now shared with a stranger they disliked. These secrets knotted them together at the arteries.

"Not Brand," Frobisher said, finally, a concession. Though in defense of his son he added, "This is his legacy. I'm an old man. Nothing I accomplish is for me."

Trent merely nodded. Both men had time to thaw, and Trent had time to think. "This cop with the bumper sticker. My money says it's this same crazy cat. We'll put your guy on him."

" 'My guy'?" Frobisher sniffed. He almost denied the association. "Bumper-sticker duty, yes, that's about what he's capable of. And yet the man feels I owe him one million dollars."

"He seems okay," Trent said. "He's got ideas for my problem, you know, my vandal."

"He can deal with that, can he?"

"Your guy has ideas." Trent chuckled to himself but Frobisher asked no more. "He's a thinker. So he told me that you got yourself a loose end?"

One moment Frobisher was the lordly father, and the next he was stricken. So rarely did he ask for a favor, his manners reverted to more than a half-century before, and he spoke like a blushing child. "It is more in your local sphere . . . As my attention is on the national picture, my liaison in the local police . . . that connection has fallen away. So, to enforce . . . to deport a troublesome foreigner . . . a matter for Immigration."

Immigration? Old Frobisher was distracted, or he would have seen Trent struck down by the word. Trent's whole posture changed, assaulted by gravity, as his mind jumped to its deepest fears.

Trent spent his life as a boss on Nausset Island. Winter and summer he employed between forty and two hundred people. Words like "deport" and "immigration" jammed a filthy finger into the soft of his brain. He began going through his roster of employees. Sixty . . . eighty? . . . without illegals . . . It wasn't just the wages he would have to offer. At this point in June, getting the bodies would be impossible. He spoke carefully, gruff, from deep in his chest. "No federal presence on the island."

"And I don't desire that. I don't want to cause inconvenience. In one isolated case—"

"One case?" Trent snapped. "Nope. No cases. This is a resort island, not a Mexican meat-packing . . . You should talk about illegals; you married one."

This wasn't genteel—even Trent heard that. But he was huffing. Foremost in his mind was the mortification of having to hire Americans, kids who would quit when you yelled at them or changed their hours. This generation of Americans grew up without fathers, and they didn't know authority. Instead of telling, you had to *ask*. To your face, they might say to fuck off. That had actually happened to Trent. Turn your shoulder and the kitchen boys would be joking to one another on the prep line. You couldn't even sniff the girls . . .

What a nightmare. American kids—having to hire only legal Americans would change everything about Malcolm Trent and his world.

He blinked. Saw that his private concerns had nothing to do with Frobisher. Frobisher was barely there, looking sad and apologetic and very old indeed. His hand sat forward on the stone countertop, and beneath it was a paper folded into quarters.

Trent gently tugged it away. Frobisher's hand was a mess. The knuckles were dull red scabs, the color of a lollipop abandoned on the sidewalk.

Trent unfolded, searching Frobisher's face for permission. Frobisher stared directly ahead, his eyes never dropping to acknowledge the paper's existence.

All this buildup, yet it turned out to be nothing. The paper was a flier that had been taped to a post or a notice board. It wanted information about a girl. Her name was Kat. The photocopy of her snapshot was terrible. It was just blobs of black ink. The gaps between the girl's teeth were so exaggerated it looked like half had been knocked out. There was a phone number. Trent looked up. " 'Ten dollar reward'? Is this a joke?"

Frobisher tried to smile. The skin under his jaw trembled. His purple hand reached to take the paper, but because he still wasn't looking, he missed and clawed at empty air.

Chapter 12

"Sergeant Gilberto Martinez?"

"Yeah."

"I'm calling about your trooper James Hawkins," Coburn said. He sat in his car. Used his phone stamped with Lincoln. His business phone.

"Hawkins?" Sergeant Martinez barked. "Jim Hawkins? Hawkins? Hawkins?" His voice went distant, searching and panicked: Fire? Fire where?

Coburn's heart wasn't in this. He gave the man time to hold his phone properly, then began his routine: "We've been asked to begin an inquiry into the professional status and qualifications of Jim Hawkins, you understand, his professional qualifications, and it's our purview . . ."

But on his end Sergeant Martinez wouldn't shut up. He fumbled his phone again—*bang, bap, bap, bap*—yet still talked incoherently in the background. At last there was heavy breath, the scrape of stubble across the microphone. "How did you get this number? How did you get this number?" Sergeant Martinez asked, angrily.

Anger?—bullying?—Coburn roused a little. "This number is now a matter of official record. Do you understand that? I'm calling to talk to you about one of your soldiers. One of *your* soldiers. Former soldiers. James Hawkins." Silence, and Coburn was mollified. "You're the right guy for him?"

"Jim Hawkins?"

"You supervised him. Now you understand that I may not reveal the specific allegations, and that this is merely an inquiry into certain professional qualifications . . ."

Martinez mumbled something wheezy. "Hawkins put down my name? He don't have this number."

"Sergeant Martinez, we were given this number by a congressional office. Believe me, way higher up than you're accustomed to dealing with. All right? These are the people who give you orders. Who give orders to the people who give you orders. Now the specific nature of the inquiry . . ."

It was doubtful Martinez heard any of this. He repeated "Wha? Wha?" as though he were drunk or high or the phone call had awoken him out of a dead sleep. "Wha, you're asking for like a job recommendation?" Martinez said. "For Hawkins? Don't hire him. Love of Christ." He wheezed and mumbled words in Spanish and even chuckled a little bit. "Don't hire Hawkins."

Coburn didn't like chuckles. "So you would say that James Hawkins has a poor record as an employee?"

Martinez didn't hear or ignored. His mumbling took its own path. Took him down his own road. "Jim Hawkins . . . ?" he came back. "He put my name down? He don't have this number. How would he? Don't you give it to him, either. Jim Hawkins don't know a single thing about who I am . . ."

Sergeant Martinez hung up on Coburn. It wasn't aggressive but instead as if he'd wandered away.

Chapter 13

It was a muggy night. Marsha rubbed her forehead. "That shark attack is going to murder us."

I nodded and nodded. I thought about the dead girl and my jaw went numb. But what was the point in reacting? I sat with Marsha on a crumbling surf wall beside the harbor. The new plan was for me and Marsha to meet ten minutes each evening. She would walk and find me, and I took my break from herding the crowds. We chose secluded spots. If our scheduled ten minutes went well, the next evening we would try twenty. Build up. Repair. That sort of thing. We'd tried for three evenings and we were still at our original ten minutes.

For Marsha, to grumble about the shark attack was a neutral topic, like the weather. Ten times a day I heard about the shark attack. The talk was not about Megan Palsinger. Instead the concern was that fewer tourists were coming to the island. June numbers were down enough that the Steamship Authority was talking about scheduling fewer ferries.

She said, "It could become a true catastrophe."

Best behavior—I reminded myself—best behavior. "Could be." I hissed air in and out like a tire valve. Peace in Our Time.

We had tried everything. For a week she let me sleep over. Circumstances forced that. After the shark attack, every boat on the island roved the night sea, out for vengeance for the human race.

What a clown show. Cabin cruisers and stink-pots. Guys

dragging volleyball nets through the ocean. It was like the miracle of Dunkirk, done for parody. One of Trent's many pals ran a sailboat camp. At dusk he could be seen perched on the bow of one of the training sloops, armed with a fiberglass bow and arrow from his sports shed. Next to deploy would be the pedal boats they rented by the half hour.

Anyway, you may imagine the direct effect on my life. I couldn't swim through this fleet to get to my island camp. I'd get harpooned by Sea Scouts.

Marsha realized this and offered me her bed. However, after we made love, she would start to negotiate a checkout time. Four a.m., five a.m. She didn't want me seen walking out in the morning. And if I talked too much, I would say the wrong thing, making her sad or angry, so she would evict me right on the spot.

Luckily, after a week the home defense fleet gradually lost interest. The shark attack had been on the other side of the island, twenty-five miles away, and biologists guessed it was a random roving shark, not one likely to hang around.

"August rentals are still healthy," Marsha said. Because she gazed sorrowfully at the wharf, I did too. The wharf was jammed, as always. Big groups roved to purchase their alcoholic slushy. A standard Friday night, except that now they avoided the water's edge as though held back by an invisible cordon. Strange to see. You couldn't walk the wharf, people jammed together like a rock concert—bump, jostle, negotiate—except this bare edge strip of about a meter, which they left for the shark.

"Seems plenty crowded," I said.

When I talked, Marsha tried not to wince. I did it for her, she did it for me.

★ ★ ★ ★ ★

As I said, this same shark complaint came from all sides. Oh, oh, the June numbers!

The irony of this—you couldn't map all the ironies. The island mascot was a shark. The high school selected one student to rove the stands in a foam shark costume, which must have been boiling to wear, and the cheerleaders were the "sharkies" or the "sharkettes" or some such. Half the crap in the tourist shops showed comic sharks baring their teeth. These were tee shirts and can coolers printed months ago in China, before a beautiful local lady was completely eaten except for her hand and part of her torso.

Nausset Island's biggest single claim to fame was a shark movie filmed on site, using local extras and local beaches. The movie was about how a tourist town dies because a giant shark comes and eats some of the visitors off the beach. Posters for this movie hung in every business. Famous quotations were engraved on plaques and door lintels. And now, suddenly, the movie was really happening. Now—for real—nobody wanted to take a boat out to Nausset to buy taffy. No one came to drop three hundred dollars for a night in a sweltering attic.

Here's another place where you want a second opinion. My bias is strong. You want to seek balance from an outside point of view. To me, tourists staying home just meant that people were finally showing sense.

In all my life, I'd never taken a vacation. My dad raised me mostly in a van, on a sort of permanent vacation, and to me the whole phenomenon of the vacation spots was an irrational one, like the gathering of salmon or sea birds in some random geographical coordinate. It was instinctual swarming, with no reason behind it.

Why come together on an island? Huge pain in the ass to get

the tee shirts and tartar sauce over by boat, and huge pain in the ass to haul the garbage back across the water. Most tourists never went into the ocean, even before the shark, so in fact they might have been vacationing anywhere. They might have been in Kansas. Everything they bought here—the drinks and frozen clam rolls—most of that was available at their local Applebees, for half the money.

I sat there beside Marsha on the sea wall. I watched the tourists bumping into each other. Now and then a daring soul would duck out and use the shark's zone as a passing lane. Jump back in. Ugh. In two minutes, I'd be back in that scrum. "It's like ants harvesting dew off aphids," I said.

"You're obnoxious to your bones. You can't help it, I know that."

Marsha rose to leave. Her chin trembled. She sought for something to say, but we were already broken up. There was no lower point she could take the relationship. She left with a terrible stiff walk, as fast as she could make it.

But then she turned back. I thought she would cancel our ten minutes. She would lower me to five minutes. Instead she came back calmer and puzzled. "Did you put bumper stickers on the police car?"

The cruiser was at the curb. If nothing else, being police makes it easy to park. "It's a good cause," I assured her. "Squab Island could be a seal sanctuary. It was Cunningham's dream, I think. I can't get that poor guy out of my mind."

"Poor Cunningham?"

"I see his place, every night. In the same way he used to look across at my island."

"So, in fact, you moved your camp around so that you could see his home." To Marsha this seemed as unbelievable as if I'd dug up his corpse.

"Cunningham was like me, you see? Every time I mention

his name. He provoked strong reactions." Marsha had already started to shake her head. I didn't even speak but she kept doing it, trying to shake loose a bad picture. "Come on. What did I do?"

"You put bumper stickers on your police car? You don't understand anything, do you?"

"That's not true. I'm as smart as anyone I've ever met. You know I'm smart."

"But you do everything wrong. You just can't get a feel. For anything. Not one single thing." This realization twisted her.

"Look, I admit it. But no reason for you to be sad." I glanced over to the crowds. "Meet me tomorrow. I've got to get back. Chet's directing traffic. We'll have midnight gridlock."

"He really doesn't know how, does he?"

"His system is highly aware of girls in jeeps. I can't tell if he gives them right of way or detains them. But it's not efficient. Please meet me tomorrow. Same time tomorrow."

"You have to borrow my kayak, if you're going out to your island."

"I'll be all right."

"Borrow my kayak. First you have to knock and see me."

This is how we were. She would hit the sack with me, but then I had to go away. "It will be late," I said. "I have to check the 10:30 ferry, see if that crazy doctor is on it. Apparently he still takes the 10:30 on Thursdays and tries to fuck up the Wharf House.

"Also," I said, "I have to check the Duck."

On weekdays, 12:00 was when I checked "the Duck." The Gooey Duck was a local bar. Who owned it? Malcolm Trent, though I didn't know that at the time. I could have guessed.

An actual creature exists called a geoduck, which looks like a giant clam. I'm not sure it even lives on the Atlantic coast. It is a gross creature, with a slimy neck three feet long. You mince geoducks and hide the pieces in clam chowder.

On its sign and tee shirts, the Gooey Duck bar used a cartoon of a standard bird duck, with gonzo eyes to indicate it was blasted out of its mind. The duck had both a long neck and huge erection. I suppose it was a power thing, these shirts that made sex seem as disgusting as possible—"Taste the Goo!"—"Long and Slimy!"—you wore something like that, and for whatever reason the woman still had to touch you.

Like everywhere on Slocum Avenue, the Duck did really good business, though it had an awkward location. You had to squeeze up a narrow staircase, past a fat bouncer, to a single door. Among the Duck's dedicated clients were a handful of the older guys I told you about, guys who felt some need to play outlaw. Trent and his blood brothers. At the Gooey Duck, the method they chose to play outlaw was to stay and keep drinking past legal closing time.

Normally closing a bar is an easy police situation, because you make the bar handle it. You say, on May 18th, you served a beer at 12:01, so we are going to pull your liquor license for a ten-day review. Ten days, starting July 4th.

That's what I would have done. But the Chief wouldn't go for it. The Gooey Duck held a special place in his heart. It was open year-round, one of the few places that were, and so fell under the Chief's personal protection. Maybe the customers applauded him, if he made it up the steps, dragging his oxygen tent. Maybe back in the day he squired his bride under the "Duck Fuck" ceiling pennant.

Every night, a police officer had the job to walk up the little stairs, squeeze past the fat bouncer, and tell the bartender he needed to shut down. The customers would shout and carry on, and this was a ritual scene. The bartender would take his time. It was like he listened to both sides and needed to be convinced.

He would put a hand to his ear to demand louder applause: You can do better than that! Okay, ladies, let's hear from you! With the rest of the bars in town already closed, the real drunks collected here for one more, so the crowd could grow ugly. I mean, they *were* ugly. I mean that their behavior could become unruly.

No one wanted this duty, so it largely fell to the summer hires, me and Chet. Also taking a turn was an old local cop named Mason, who often worked the graveyard shift.

As I've said, normally Chet was good with crowds. Party crowds wanted to please him. Normally. And Mason had similar talents. He would tame huge groups, up and down Slocum Avenue.

Mason's method was the opposite of Chet's. Chet was everybody's pal. No need to hassle the cool guy. Maybe he'll hook you up. Mason had an older cop vibe, which worked like magic, especially for college-aged groups. With Mason, kids always seemed to be explaining the circumstances—"I told him not to throw it. I told him I . . ." A block away, you could hear groups of kids trying to apologize and explain. Mason induced these extended explanations but then didn't pay attention, and the kids got more and more desperate. With Mason, your dad and your boss were already involved, the world of consequences, the kids suddenly sober, hearing how thin it all sounded. Just ten minutes ago they were kings and life was fun . . . In this state, Mason could make the kids do anything. Seriously, I'd seen party boys, three a.m., trying to scrub vomit off sidewalks. Mason could herd them.

You'd think closing the Gooey Duck would be Mason's cup of tea. He'd be friends with these guys, softball leagues, their families inbred. Instead he got the worst of it. Chet's magic didn't work. So they left it to me.

★ ★ ★ ★ ★

One night, mid-May, not long after the Cunningham suicide, I'd gotten a phone call, 1:20 at night. I was stripping down for my swim home. I got dressed again, got over there. Chet and Mason stood outside the Duck. Chet was really nervous, his face rising and falling like a set of lungs: euphoric, frightened, euphoric, frightened.

"What's up?"

Chet and I were the same age but had nothing in common, except that we both understood that we had nothing in common. Chet was like guys I'd known in the service, in that day and night, all hours, he strove to get laid. He assumed that this was all any other man thought about, and the rest of life was just pretend.

Once you understood this about Chet, you understood why he didn't pay attention when you spoke to him. His attention was elsewhere, and, in fairness, he assumed yours was, too. I asked him once, when he kept going back to the same pizza place five times a shift: "You like the counter girl? You're trying to get her number?"

"Get her number?" For that moment I had Chet's complete attention. For the only time, he looked directly into my face. "I'm going to take her back and bend her over the chest freezer. Get her number? Do you think I'm going to talk with her on the telephone?" Usually I seemed much older than Chet, but now he had the steady hand. "Close the deal, Jim, on site. Fuck her, and if she doesn't want to fuck, fuck the one with the bad skin, and if she doesn't want to fuck, wait around and fuck the mom, okay? Or get a blow job. Don't get wrapped up in that phone-number scam."

I assured him I wouldn't, and at that he nodded and turned away. So at least Chet and I had achieved clear communication. He paid no attention to men in the world, other than the unconscious attention you paid to people in order to navigate around them, to make your way through a crowd. He mostly didn't know we were there except as obstacles to walking.

Anyway, that night, Chet phoned me. I arrived. He and Mason were on the street outside the Gooey Duck, with the fat bouncer looking down smug, arms folded across his chest. Chet had told them to shut down, but they hadn't, and no one knew what to do.

"Just tell everyone to get out," I said.

Mason and Chet looked back and forth, mumbled. It was hard to understand. There had been a scene. They were traumatized.

"Is it too crowded or something?" I asked. "No children in there, are there? Just cut the power. They'll figure out the rest, or sweat together in the dark. The circuit box is around back, almost always. You can clip the lock with my bolt cutters."

Mason stopped me with his hand. "The Chief."

"He's inside?"

"No." Neither man explained well. Finally, I went up the stairs to try and figure it out. As I squeezed by the fat bouncer, he said something I didn't catch. Then he didn't allow the door to shut. He wanted to follow me inside.

The Duck was terrible, of course. A smelly, low-ceilinged place. Already low ceiling, but then cloths and fishing nets hung down, touching your hair like bug threads in a basement. Everything was loud, but that was just music, just fake atmosphere. No one was really excited to be there. How could they be? Only twenty or twenty-five customers remained, and they'd shuffled the tables together like they were all friends. Right, friends forever.

The jukebox was on the other side of the bar. I went to locate the plug, but on the way a big, sunburned fellow on a stool talked to me so I stopped. Big, bearded fisherman, too big for his clothes. The impossible thing was, I couldn't hear him. He talked, but then when I got close he turned and talked to the wall behind the bar, or to the bartender. Without seeing the man's mouth, I couldn't understand him.

I took the fisherman's head and turned it around so we could be forehead to forehead. "What did you say?" He had bushy, ocean-scented hair. I had to take tight hold of his skull, to control it. "Speak again. I missed every word."

He struggled a little but wouldn't look at me. The bartender was no help. I asked him, "What did this guy want to tell me? This music is too loud . . ."

The bartender shook his head, frightened to death. I asked him point blank, "Why aren't you closed? It is time for you to be done."

My bearded fisherman kept trying to push off my hands. He was drunk and soft, and because he was sideways on his stool he didn't have his legs. I spoke right into his head: "Stop it. Stop moving."

Suddenly tug, tug, Malcolm Trent pulled my shoulder around. I didn't know he had come up. Made me drop my guy, who toppled with his arms out, *kablosh!* Big, soft drunk went to the floor like a foam pad.

Trent shoved me with two hands. He literally shoved me like a school boy.

I watched his face. He couldn't be serious. But he was drunk or something and I swear to God, the man punched me across the cheek.

I ducked in close and took hold of his throat. I cleared out room against the bar in a crash of stools and glasses. "You're turning white," I said in Trent's ear. "Aren't you? You're turning white."

The music died—*Rupt*! Chet and Mason called out loudly, jocular. Chet spoke at my back. He tried to be soothing but his voice was strangled. Trent turned whiter and whiter in my hands. Meanwhile the big fisherman had risen off the floor. He stood with his fist cocked back to his ear. Who was he threatening? He still wouldn't look at me, and he was far, far away.

I tossed Trent aside. He tangled in the fisherman's legs so that they tumbled and lay in a heap.

The lights came on bright. The fat bouncer blinked them on and off with the switch. He thought that he was in charge of the scene. Mason whistled loudly. "Rides, fellas. We'll take you home. Let's go."

My blood was up, however. "No rides," I said to Mason, quietly. I corrected the official position: "There are no rides on offer."

At that point I discovered my club in my hand. I had my club out. As the Parking Warden, instead of a gun I had a karate club, a tonfa. The scene was all so unbelievable. Had that old fat man really struck me?

Wham! All that energy pent up . . . I brought my tonfa down on the bar. The bar exploded. I didn't know it was glass. It looked like shiny wood. It was a wooden bar with a glass top, and I exploded it.

Glass rained. Right, that was satisfying. That's what I wanted. I moved and smashed again. I smashed any large, intact section, my eyes closed against the spray of shards.

Then all the good pieces were smashed. I had to stop and take stock.

The fisherman nuzzled the floor, his hands knit behind his head. He tried to worm away but Trent was still across his legs, face up. At my glare he shrank in groggy terror. His cheek bled. Glass dust was in the air. Glass had settled in his hair and eyebrows like glitter. His eyes were on the tonfa, and he rose on one arm in order to shield his head with the other.

We all paused, for a pulse or two. I recognized this moment.

My club arm was rigid. It rose out of my cuff, fixed and rigid as a marble statue with each muscle carved.

We play at violence. It's astonishing how large a role it plays in our talk and games. You would think life was a pit fight.

In fact the real thing was far away. It was a silent, sparkling world, and even I had to be re-introduced. One temptation is not to stop. Instead, keep going, push through, and defer the moment of reckoning. The bar glass was finished, but I could blast it to finer powder, smashing again and again like timpani. There were also bottles and mirrors and forearms.

The first move was a lady. Everyone stood still as though we were playing a freeze game, but she rose from her chair and approached. "Sorry," I mumbled. I thought she came to confront me but she didn't even look. Her skirt brushed in passing.

Instead she went to the display of shattered glass. She picked shards aside and retrieved a photograph. The glass on the bar had covered clippings and snapshots, and this woman retrieved a snapshot of a lady screaming and lifting her shirt to show her tits to the camera.

She moved other shards and retrieved other photographs. She knew the ones she wanted.

The bartender watched this, his Adam's apple slowly bouncing up and down. He disapproved of this theft. He wanted permission to stop it. I had his eye so I explained to him, "Don't cause me to come here again."

The lady would remember another picture and pluck it out. Peel back the glass. The shards didn't nip her hands. She had a light touch.

I recognized her. Sarah Palsinger. Right out of Boco's photos. Wife of poor old Cunningham. Sister to dead Megan. Granddaughter of Mrs. Yellow.

★ ★ ★ ★ ★

The Gooey Duck was closed the next night. Then for a week it was dark and quiet by 11:45. Chet and Mason and I sat out there watching on the hood of a cruiser.

Summer went on, though, and the time began to creep later and later.

CHAPTER 14

"Sergeant Martinez. This is Michael Coburn. I spoke to you at an earlier date on the subject of James Hawkins."

"Hawkins? Who are you, man?"

"My reason for contacting you today is more as a professional consultant. My company would like you to use your professional influence and leadership . . . to rein him in, as it were. To communicate with him. To facilitate the opening of lines of communication. We would be in a position to offer you a substantial consultant payment, depending on the extent of your success."

"Rein him in? Jim Hawkins?"

"You can tell me what your own professional experience has been, but sometimes the most effective method, through your privileged lines of communication, is to make an offer to him, with then an identical payment to yourself. That we match. The same as he's receiving."

This offer was greeted by silence. Coburn winced at his own clumsiness. He'd missed the right note and shown a soft underbelly. To some extent this couldn't be helped. To offer a bribe, you waved money. But he'd both rambled and been too bald. Now Sergeant Martinez could kill him in negotiations. What was important was to control the starting figure. Everything depended on the first figure mentioned.

"Why? Why you want to antagonize . . . ? Hawkins? Man, don't offer him money."

"For you as well. A payment."

"Leave the man be, is all you can do. You don't want . . . if you sit him down and converse, he listens. Sometimes." Martinez recalled instances where he had employed this method. These memories were discouraging. "Leave the man be. Don't try to offer him money, man. He doesn't like money, is one thing for sure. You just set him off."

Many a time Coburn had waved cash in people's faces. Some people pretended not to care. Give them a moment, though. It's a handicap, talking on the telephone. The sight of cash would hypnotize a nun.

Coburn looked to his note pad. "We could also compensate any effort to put us in touch . . . Generous compensation. Any particular friends, anybody. I understand there's a father?"

"Hawkins never made a morale call. I don't know why I'm talking with you. I don't have to talk to you about a discharged soldier. I didn't tell you nothing, and don't you go telling Hawkins I did. The army was satisfied, discharged him. Safest is just leave the man be. The only safe thing." Sergeant Martinez disconnected.

With the distance, all the lines to unplug and click, it was twenty seconds before a dial tone came over the speakers of Coburn's car. He hadn't moved.

What Coburn felt was deep disappointment. Almost twenty years as a fixer, and he had come to believe in his fix, like a car salesman genuinely astonished to see anyone drive another make. Who wouldn't want what Coburn offered? He wanted it himself.

Over the years Brand Frobisher had done harm to dozens of young women and girls. Some of them sought redress. Frobisher dealt with these, and it became a system. The victim would eventually come to be sitting in the beautiful paneled offices of Rex and Hayworth. She would be crying or not. Sometimes bandaged or smelling of antiseptic. Often there was a parent, a boyfriend, a lawyer, a college roommate. That didn't affect what was about to happen.

Hayworth himself would emerge and sit not across from them but beside them. He was a careful, quiet man, who presented as the wisest prophet in the Bible. He billed four hundred dollars an hour for his conversation, and it was cheap at the price.

If the girl or her party wanted to begin with recrimination, Hayworth would listen—never had there been such a listener. But when *he* spoke it was not of the past but instead of what was to come. The future. How can we now ensure the best happens? He rarely said "we" or "us" yet that was implied. Consensus had been reached.

If circumstances required that Hayworth talk about Brand, he would: The boy she accuses is ill, and has been sent away for treatment. (This was true—everything Hayworth said was basically true—by this point Brand would be out of state or out of the country.) But Hayworth steered the subject to the girl. She needed to get the best medical care in the world. Not merely a good public hospital; what was on offer was the best doctor. The perfumed hands of the Chief of Gynecology at Massachusetts General Hospital, arriving on a house call. Rex and Hayworth had doctors that Coburn had never known existed, doctors who lived so far removed from fees and forms and airless offices that they had become like country doctors of old. They didn't even know about money. They lived to help. They didn't just go to Harvard; they taught Harvard, as their father's father before them. With their care and kindness, you wanted them to be *your* father.

Also on offer—the rest of that "we" consensus: College. Internships. Jobs. Travel. Even a little money, perhaps, a trust fund. Never for much. Always amazing at how little, in fact,

Brand's indiscretions ended up costing. These bribes were not presented as bribes but as the opportunities the world held for the girl all along. Hadn't she known? Astonishing. Here they were. Here they had always been.

Few victims gave in so easily. When they raged, Hayworth met it with silence, understanding, and just the right touch of puzzlement. He had already won that battle. *He* hadn't hurt anyone—he was nothing but a gentleman. Rage away if it helped you, but few could sustain.

If the girl was pregnant, and wanted to have the child, well, Hayworth would be sad to hear it. He produced medical documents (the only false note). The choice was hers, of course, but she should know that Brand's seed was not the best. The top paper in the medical file was an X ray of an infant's skull elongated like that of a movie alien. Hayworth's secretary would schedule the termination. This would be no vacuum in a strip-mall clinic; this would be a room with drapes.

And when she still wanted to bring the matter to court, criminal or civil, well, Hayworth would call out Rex. They would work together. These same reasonable old men didn't quite understand what *had* happened on the night in question. Doubt creased their foreheads. They yearned to believe her, but could not quite. Could they beg her to take them through her story one more time? What they didn't understand was this discrepancy or that. She reported to police that she had drunk nothing. Now she said, in fact, that Brand met her in a bar, where records show that he paid a substantial tab. And what these caring lawyers would really like to understand is how her story fit with other facts on the table. The man who drove the car ferry reported that she and Brand kissed passionately. What was her motive in omitting that from her story?

The lawyers—sometimes now even her parents, if they were in the room—just didn't know what to believe. Regrettably.

Meanwhile, unsaid, the tray of goodies was getting wheeled out of sight. The implications were clear: You could be here, and your life could get better, or you could go to the police station, where the fresh puke had just been mopped with chemicals that smelled worse. Your daughter could be gently handled by our gentleman doctor with his leather bag, or she could get herself to the lout police for them to administer their "rape kit" in the public toilet, with a plastic dipstick for their daughter's vagina.

In his Cadillac, Coburn sighed. This Hawkins, this troublesome cop, would not choose correctly. Coburn took out a list. He crossed out the top item: "Incentive." Three tactics remained to try. Coburn sighed again as he read them. How few tools he had, and how clumsy—or how clumsy two of them were. One was elegant. While there were three options remaining, there was no reason to walk through them like a grocery list. Instead, all at once. "How's that for the bottom line?" He picked up one of his phones.

CHAPTER 15

Every time I spent two minutes at the station I got into an argument with one of the full-time cops. They laid ambush at my locker. At some point I had posited that our police force did more harm than good—in aggregate—and that we should shut down, close shop, auction the caps and pistols, etc. I said it one time but the remark was immediately infamous. Guys took it personally and needed to report their day's heroism. This and that—they'd collared a shoplifter. They oversimplified my position. Refused to look big picture.

I was in an argument with this young buck. His repeated claim was that we were "the thin blue line."

"Between what? Between whom?" I asked. "Come on. We're a sham. We milk the tourists so we can pay our salaries. Rent them cars with nowhere to park, hand out sixty-dollar tickets. I'm not saying there aren't scumbags out here, but they're all rich guys, and them we leave alone."

Young buck blew air, blew veins. Looked behind for someone near enough to restrain him in his anger. He didn't need that. I wasn't going to hurt him. But suddenly he calmed. Inspector Wakin was behind me. He'd heard and looked puzzled.

Wakin. He was a fatso, but could be I undersold the man. He had a presence. When he was in the room, you were not looking at him, he was looking at you. You know? It prevented comprehensive observation. "Jim. Let's talk, Jim."

The hothead cleared out. Wakin and I stayed by the lockers.

It's not like we were going to walk down the hall together, side by side, unless they widened the thoroughfare. I was puzzled because Wakin consulted some papers. "You have no home address?"

"Sure I do," I said. "I gave you one. Kind of staying with a local girl. Island girl. Six, seven generations on the island. Anyway, you can send mail there."

"We really aren't paying you anything," he said, apparently reading the number for the first time.

"Nah, that's okay."

"I'm not offering you a raise."

"I don't need one."

He sweat—giant beads of sweat like bath pearls. Wakin was a full participant in the planet's water cycle. "Uh. You're a college student during the year."

"Sure." In truth, the transcript I'd provided for my job application was more future goals than my current accomplishments. It wasn't an official transcript with watermark but instead a typed list of classes. All kinds of classes sounded interesting to me. I'd always wanted to learn French, for example.

Wakin switched papers, then again. "I'm not even sure . . . You're the Parking Warden. How did you get a car? Haven't I seen you driving an official car?"

I laughed. "How would I get around without a vehicle? You've got me ten places a day."

"I mean, the duties listed here are limited, very limited. So the Chief . . . ?"

Wakin had other papers. He consulted a yellow paper. "Your father is, or was, a college professor?"

"What? My dad? He liked to think so." I had to laugh again, the idea that Wakin knew about my dad. It wasn't on my job application.

Amazing how the people on Nausset cared about personal

details. It was like they planned to surprise me with cake on important anniversaries. My first shave. The first time I rode a bike without training wheels.

"You have a criminal record." Wakin blinked. You can imagine the amount of flesh involved, like a rolling pin up and down. "Of course it's sealed. It's juvenile. It's not important."

He kept his eyes on the paperwork. He was embarrassed.

"A record?" A juvenile record? I suppose I did have one, sure. I hadn't thought about it. Who knew? The Army didn't know. At least it didn't come up at my hearing.

It's kind of a warm bath, to realize that people are aware of your life. Surveillance can be a warm bath. Someone is paying attention. Otherwise, who cares? Your mom? A loving Jesus? Apparently Wakin had commissioned a whole research project on me, Jim Hawkins. My name was known. It lived on, at least in a filing cabinet in Syracuse, where they kept files on the juvenile delinquents of New York State.

"Not important," Wakin repeated. "So we're going to forget all about it." This whole interview was uncomfortable to him. It was a duty he didn't like. So why did he do it? A lot of people are strange in this particular way. They feel bad but keep going.

Wakin had one final question before he could let himself off the hook. He read it directly from a paper. "What is the nature of your discharge from the army?" He was done so he rolled all the papers together. "It's a standard inquiry. It's a fair thing to ask."

"Eh? Don't fret. I don't care." I told him. "Kind of a rare type, actually, my discharge. It's not dishonorable. Some people might think it's dishonorable, but not technically. There's no prejudice or anything."

He didn't like this answer. "I think I may need to hear more." He was ready to move off but instead readjusted his pants (they were a perfect cone, waistline to ankles, like a sea anchor for a cruise ship). "I think I may need to hear about that."

As with a lot of people, Wakin perceived the US Army as a great and righteous authority. This was a strange phenomenon because at the same time most people understood that the army was a refuge for fuckups, and also that it regularly made howler mistakes, like issuing snow parkas to troops in the desert. Somehow citizens can hold these perceptions at the same time without processing the contradictions. In this case, the term "dishonorable discharge" twisted Wakin's cables. It was a mistake for me to use the term.

"Don't trouble yourself," I said. "At another point the army pinned me with a Silver Star. They were confused. I was confused. We had an amicable parting, amicable enough. For all parties."

"Jim. I don't appreciate how you're being evasive with me. I feel that you're being evasive—"

"Hey. No. Whoa whoa whoa." I stopped him. "Enough questions. You're falling into a trap here. Okay? What's in your papers, these trivia bits, they're comforting but don't take false comfort. Beware false comfort."

"Jim—"

"Past events explain nothing. If my dad were here, he would explain. My dad, the great existentialist professor. You hope to know someone from their crumb trail. But that's all it is, a crumb trail. And squirrels and birds have been through, you know? Scattering and selecting. My army days. My gym grades. The motto at my high school. These are not history but detritus. They form no coherent pattern."

Wakin wasn't following my point. His face was a tired slab. So I tied things up: "I'm your Parking Warden. For a few months. I fill a book with juicy tickets."

CHAPTER 16

Margery, a middle-aged woman, moved up the rise of Squab Island, pushing her own knees with her hands. Long boat rides didn't get you in shape for climbing. She found the first feeder and called back to Allison, her partner in life and business. "A lot of the corn is gone. It's like the pellets are here, but the corn is gone."

"Maybe the mice like it."

"They eat the pellets first. Well. Better bring up some more."

Allison pulled their Boston Whaler well up onto the beach. To be doubly sure it wouldn't float off, she was now wrapping the painter around every rock and weed the beach provided.

She finished and came up behind Margery, using the same heavy walk, pushing her own thighs. "Could the nutrition pellets spoil? Maybe this batch was spoiled."

Margery knelt, turning the plastic feeder tube so Allison could witness the phenomenon for herself. "There were sunflower seeds here, too, weren't there?"

"Of course," Allison answered.

The feeder was a feeder for birds. It was raised above a water pan to discourage mice, but the pan was dry. The spring had been ferociously dry. The feed trough was surrounded by rough wire, which would collect feathers from any large bird who dined there. Margery sifted the gull feathers without comment and let the down fall.

Allison rolled the plastic cylinder in her hands. "*Every* grain of corn is gone."

"Could a mouse get inside the tube?"

"Or ants?"

Allison froze. Her heart expanded but did not explode. A still figure watched them, ten yards away at the top of the rise. He was an enormous man. Allison had seen someone like him before, in a film of *Great Expectations,* the convict who had escaped from the prison hulks. This man before her on Squab Island was huge, almost naked, and painted completely with dark mud. He would club them to death with manacles.

He spoke: "You didn't put anything on the corn, did you? Like poison?"

"It's for birds." Margery looked up, squinting, and explained. She was not surprised at all to be suddenly questioned on an uninhabited island. "There were heath hens out here, once upon a time. Now they're probably extinct. But we've got to check and make sure." She did not regard the savage man as anything out of the ordinary. If anything, her tone suggested that this was yet another tiresome interruption.

Right this minute Allison loved Margery more fiercely than she had ever loved anything. Allison and Margery had visited Squab Island forty times and never seen another soul. The island was not only uninhabited but incredibly dangerous. It was littered with discarded military ordnance.

"A heath hen," the man said. "What does a heath hen look like?"

"Oh, kind of like a grouse."

"They don't live here. I saw some, once, in a rich lady's house. But they were dead and mounted in a diorama."

"If they're not here, they're not anywhere," Margery said. She took the sack of feed from Allison's nerveless hands and began to refill the dish. At no point had the man distracted her from her duty. "This was their last habitat, but then a fire got them. It wasn't even as dry as it is this year." She slid the feeder tube back into place.

Allison finally could speak. "We're here for the Environmental Protection Agency. We are private contractors with the federal government."

"Oh," the man said. "I'm with the government, too. On Nausset. Over there." He pointed.

"How come you're so dirty?" Margery asked. She had finally examined the man.

He noticed himself for the first time. "I try different mud to keep off the mosquitoes. It doesn't work as well as I thought."

"We have mosquito spray in the boat," Allison offered, weakly. "They're bad out here, because there's fresh water."

The other two paused as though this offer were inappropriate, so Allison didn't say anything else. She didn't ask where his boat was, or why he roamed naked. He wasn't the convict from *Great Expectations* after all. He was a performer for the Blue Man Group. The mud made his eyes appear silver. The man asked, "If the last heath hen is dead, why do you put out the feeders?"

"Oh, we have to be sure. Can't have bulldozers coming in and squash the last nest. We can't find out we were wrong. But this may do it." She marked a clipboard with a sense of finality.

"Bulldozers?"

"Who knows? After about ten years, they start to remove the protections. It could take ten more. It could be done in a month, if the government can agree on anything."

"So you'll stay out here and hunt for the birds?"

"Nope. We've got three feeders, in the different life zones. We'll check for feathers and tracks." She lowered her ball cap. "They're gone all right. We've been coming for ten years after the fire."

The man seemed deflated. Allison decided again who he was.

He was a First Nation native. She and Allison were Pilgrim maidens, and this was the First Encounter. He stood close now, but clearly harmless. He eyed the feeder hungrily. "What would happen if you found heath hen feathers?"

Chapter 17

On the evening of July 2, I stepped in to close the Duck. Ten minutes until midnight.

It was a weekday night, quiet, as the island rested and fasted for the blowout Fourth of July. The town crouched nervously for this two-month fiesta, the season that set it apart from other places in the world where the people had to labor and pick. Tomorrow ferries would begin to loop nonstop, their rails packed with summer color. The chamber of commerce had a figure: every man, woman, and child walking off that boat would leave behind two hundred dollars a day. Enough pretend, the island was saying. Now we'll see. Now the real money would arrive. Or it wouldn't, if that shark loomed large enough in people's minds.

So July 2, the mood in the Duck was unsure. No loud music, just background radio that was all talk and weather. Maybe eight or nine of the local boys sat in the far corner, miserable. They watched the mirror clock over the bar as though they watched the shift clock at a turpentine factory. They were desperate. They had trapped themselves with this tradition that they had to stay until we cops threw them out.

I entered—must have been like spring rain for those poor fools—I must have seemed a delivering angel.

Trent roused himself to make a scene.

★ ★ ★ ★ ★

Remember old Lee, the fishmonger, and his misjudged joke about serving up the killer shark at his restaurants? As a Fourth of July feast? Instead, ironically, shark had disappeared from island menus. Shark was the one seafood no one sold or ate. Out of respect for Megan. (It feels strange to use her name; she never gave it to me.) All across the island, professional laminated menus would have one item lined-out with permanent marker.

On the evening of July 2, Trent began to complain that he wanted an order of "shark bites."

"I know it's not on the motherfucking board. I'm saying to go in the fucking freezer and fry them up! Do I own this place?"

With an eye on me, the bartender told him that the kitchen was closed. The cook had gone home. On the counter beside him was a donation can to bring inner-city kids out to the island for the sailing camp. Trent allowed the can in his bar but had relabeled it: "Feed a Darkie to the Sharkie." So far nobody had complained.

Trent said, "If you give me a plate of them, I can tell you if it's the right shark. I can tell you if it tastes like her."

Some chuckles. Trent's tablemates shushed him a little, pats on the shoulder, which just made him louder. "What? Anyone here who didn't taste her?" He ate something from an abandoned plate, maybe a cold French fry. "That doesn't taste like her." He ate another one. "That doesn't taste like her. A little bit. Not fishy enough. I tell you. They're going back on the menu at the Wharf House, tomorrow. I can buy shark for a dollar a pound."

You won't believe, but I was the center of this show. The room watched me. The men tried to hide it. Under their hands. Looking off into space.

That's right. In rumor I was connected with Megan Palsinger, like I was her boyfriend. That beautiful woman had talked to me only the one time, at the party. She smelled the ocean in my hair. Then that night she went out swimming.

Sharks are such dumb brute creatures that in essence they aren't alive. They aren't conscious—prehistoric brains like amoebas pulsing around a dish. If I was down fishing and a shark cruised by, I shot it, and it couldn't even feel sorry for itself, my spear protruding from its pebbled-glass skin. It would squirm and twist but remain essentially unaware. In fact it got turned on by its own blood. If it could bend enough, it would bite its own wound.

Brainless sleeves of meat. So one of these was drifting in its year-round darkness and mistook that exceptional woman for a seal.

". . . swimming with her bloody tampon, of course the thing is going to smell her pussy like hot dish . . ."

The bar clock matched my watch. 11:56. Four minutes. The watch face gave its constant reminder to do no harm in this world. No more harm.

Trent did his act because I was in the room. He kept on. Who cares what. His hostility existed only because of my presence. Without me, it would go away. It would never have existed. It didn't exist. Whatever Trent said, it was rain and weather in a place I would never visit.

I won't lie and say that this was always easy for me, to maintain a correct vision of existence, or that I was always successful. All around us, day to day, rises a shantytown of constructs. Of these, the most insistent are the trappings of wealth and status. All such constructs have one power only, which is to seem real. These constructs can build up and restrict your vision, if you allow it. They blind you. They crowd your breathing. However, these are illusory powers.

This island and this terrible bar were not much different or much worse than other places.

Trent got the other men excited. For such a flat night. After four hours in a chair, they were dying for something. They chortled and also lazily tried to settle him down. "All right. All right," Trent agreed. He rose to his feet with an empty mug. "Here's to one half of the best sisters act on the island! (Just a fucking toast. Leave me alone. I can make a fucking toast.) Raise a glass. Best fuck of my life. Her or her sister. Whichever one. I forget. Or both."

"Inappropriate. Inappropriate. No, we won't have that. I won't have that. No sir, no sir, no sir . . ."

Eh? That voice—Boco. That whiny voice. It bubbled up, and bubbled on. Unstoppable. It was Boco. I hadn't seen him, but there he was back behind the others. For some reason he looked straight up at the ceiling. "I'm saying that's inappropriate, that kind of language."

"If I want to toast the fallen . . . I'm trying to . . ." Trent tried to talk over Boco, but how is that done? Boco wasn't standing or threatening. He just uncorked his supply of Boco comment, and that supply was endless. May as well battle an ocean tide.

The bartender was at my arm. "Excuse me, sir, officer, is it all right if I dim the lights?"

I'd missed my time mark. 12:06. The bartender took a step back, eyeing my belt. It's true I held the handle of my tonfa club. My hand glowed white from my grip. The belly of the club was scarred from when I'd hammered his bar to fragments. "Yes, sure, of course," I said, embarrassed.

Trent was gone like a ghost. The whole place cleared out fast, fleeing Boco's monologue. "An apology is in order. Apologize. Apologize. Because that kind of talk lessens him who says it. It lessens him who says it, and him who hears it. Apologize."

No one tried to shut Boco up. Instead they ignored him.

When the homeless guy rants, you keep walking, you don't stop to correct him on particular facts. Boco's voice was weirdly flat.

The bartender's trained eye certainly marked Boco as trouble. He spoke to his crew, and when they dashed around to put the chairs on the tables so they could sweep the floor, they ignored Boco's section.

"All right." I went over. "The party moved on."

Boco's weight settled across every inch of the chair. His whole body was drunk, not just his brain. But when I knelt to lift him on my shoulder, I saw that his glass was full to the rim. The ice had melted to fill it to the rim and over, in a fragile dome. Drunks don't leave drinks untasted. "Are you sick or something?"

"Just tell me the truth, son. Just be open. You're looking at me, right? For Cunningham. You're looking to pin that on me."

Boco's voice was weak and congested. This was a man deeply upset. The flesh of his face was worn-out, too tired to hold expressions.

"Get up, drunk. I'll phone you a taxi."

"Taxi? A taxi? Are you kidding me? At twelve twenty? You'll get me a taxi? How far in advance would you have to set that up? Two days in advance? A taxi? You think? Ask the bartender. How far in advance, would you say . . . ?"

So Boco roused. He was intact in his essence. Correcting me on taxis got him to his feet and out the door. (He was right, by the way: There would be no unclaimed taxis at midnight in July. Even an ambulance would be an hour wait.)

Once Boco and I were outside, he ran dry on the subject of my ignorance and started to fail again. He slumped against the filthy siding of the Duck. "I know this much. The police sent you over to that cottage. That's not a deniable statement. Please do me the honor, to my intelligence, of granting that. Start with that—"

"No, man," I said, "No. Exactly wrong." I told Boco the truth. The Chief didn't know anything. If the Chief heard I was poking around, he'd probably blow his last heart valve.

It was personal, I told Boco. I admired Cunningham. To achieve so much, when the world was lined up against the man. I felt bad for him, and our connection started when I hoisted myself over the gunnel of his little sloop. He was laid out there, his head over the rail as though seasick, his skull cracked and misaligned because of the bullet. "I ruined his suicide."

"Cunningham. Marcus Cunningham." Boco made a new sound, *eh eh eh.* A nervous laugh, nervous sob. His head lowered while he did it, his whole body ratcheting down, so that he ended up sitting on the sidewalk. "That man ruined everything he touched. Ruined every place. Ruined every person. Ruined me."

"I'm no fan of suicide, but it showed wit and class."

"No suicide. That weren't no suicide. Son. Marcus Cunningham was no suicide. Wit and class?" Boco studied me from under his snarled, gray brow. It was the way that Megan Palsinger had studied me, in the heart of that wretched party, like I was something totally new, and that any minute I would reveal that I came from the invisible planet.

Boco talked and cried. Again I lifted him on my shoulder. I helped him through the side alley and helped him to the center of the park. Kids on benches were kissing, but the sight of us approaching cleared them out faster than a siren.

Boco and I had the park to ourselves, with an acre of primped lawn on every side. Hundreds of dark windows could see us—it was not impossible that Mrs. Yellow had night lenses as well—but even Boco's voice wouldn't carry to the paper walls.

He was ruined. He was wiped out. His health was wrecked by anxiety. A lot of his ramble was about his telephone. "I lost my phone. Okay, it turns out maybe someone stole my phone.

That's not on me. I'm the victim in that case. I called the company, as soon as I realized." As a prop Boco tried to show me his replacement phone, but he was slumped again now, his back against the gazebo, his pants pockets sealed tight as a vault. Eventually he shut up and took a breath. "My stolen phone was used only once. And it was that day, you know. It was that call."

"Wait. What? Calling Cunningham?"

"It wasn't a phone call. It was a text. Yeah, it was to Cunningham."

"Do they know the message?"

"No. One text. And then Cunningham dashes out there. Next thing, he's dead on his boat. The timing was—the timing was right on the money."

We both sat there in the night park. I imagined various crude, cruel messages one could send to a man who thinks his wife is stepping out. I said, "What kind of prick . . . ? So they sent him something ugly, and he thought the message was from you, his detective? It made him kill himself, poor guy."

Boco made one of his more extreme Boco noises, which sounded as though he took in air through a hole in the throat. It indicated that I was wrong about something. This time, however, he didn't jump all over me. Instead he led me through his reasoning: "Cunningham rushes to the scene, am I right?"

"Sure. I was ten minutes behind the man."

"Something was said. Maybe he wanted to catch her, you know, in the act."

"Pretty sick."

"Someone is out there and kills him."

Until that moment, murder had never crossed my mind. "Kills him? Kills Cunningham. No way. He was all by himself in the boat. And why? There's no reason."

Boco said, "Jim, sometimes, I got to tell you . . . I want to check if you're wearing a diaper. Seriously. You don't know anything. Let me say it again slowly, for your records. Okay? Of all the dicks on this planet, okay? Not number two. Not number three. Marcus Cunningham was dick number one. Okay? Cunningham was a major, major dick."

"Nah."

"He was into a hundred deals, but for murder, try to think big. Oh yeah. I've got my ideas. Imagine if one day you could buy an uninhabited island. Okay, can you imagine?

"It's placed right in the center of top-dollar real estate, top-dollar on this entire planet. Like suddenly if you could own Nantucket. Right now. Starting fresh. You're out marking the lots with stakes and string. Do you know the place I'm talking about, Jim?"

Chapter 18

"You hired him, didn't you? Hawkins?"

"What?" Coburn checked the screen on his phone. In the dim of his car he had answered the phone with the Lincoln stamp. No one called that phone. No one even had the number. He remembered the voice. "Sergeant Martinez. You're calling me?"

"Hawkins, man. I bet you hired him. What time is it over there?"

"You have access to this number?" he said. "But no. I wouldn't hire anyone with that lack of professionalism."

"He's a good man in his heart," Martinez said, but there was no argument in his voice. Then, "I'm deployed, it's such a shit hole."

Coburn and Martinez talked over one another. It was a bad line—always a bad line between these two. Seven thousand miles, a half dozen relays. One man sitting behind the wheel of his Cadillac parked out on a coastal island. One man in a mountain valley in Afghanistan. That they could even recognize the other's voice was a technological miracle. Even if they both listened and cared, they could be only pretty sure of what the other said. *Pretty* sure, *half* the time.

Anyway, they weren't listening. Both threads of conversation had started in other places, long ago. Rather than talking, this was more shouting between a couple of open boats. Maybe all you could really do was wave and make clear your goodwill, if goodwill was what you were feeling.

To add to the technical difficulties, Martinez was drunk on smuggled hooch, lying flat on his back in a tent. The international delay was a full half second, which didn't fit Coburn's stilted, fistfight phone style. All day long he practiced dealing with callers who just couldn't get to the bottom line.

"Hawkins. Oh man. That guy. The army don't give us schooling in people management. That kind of guy . . . I read this book for managing, but it's not like the army provides them." This was Martinez, with pent-up thoughts to release and revise. "If you're in the congressman's office or whatever, get some of these books out to the NCOs.

"You don't always want the best qualified employee. Isn't that true. That's the answer. Your own private business, whatever. Hawkins was a number one soldier, but he just got bored easy. Boredom is one of the major factors, you know, you have to keep in mind with the troops. Hawkins was from intellectual people. I respect the intellect side, but you can't stand out from the team."

Coburn met this tipsy rambling with bluster. Who was Martinez, to phone him out of the blue? Who was Hawkins, that anyone cared whether his dad wrote books? Bottom line, if Hawkins had such brains, he would shape up, and in a fucking hurry. Martinez should pass that along to him. For all concerned. There was an inquiry, an inquiry, and so far it wasn't looking promising.

Martinez wasn't offended. He didn't hear or understand much. He was drunk and waxing philosophical. Given this, why didn't Coburn hang up? His thumb sat on the disconnect button. But he was in the dark. In his Cadillac. In the parking lot of the Wharf House. Watching, because he had been told to, for some supposed vandal . . . Coburn, the trained professional, guardian of senators and presidents, and here he was given a mission like a minimum-wage mall cop.

This was a surprise call, on a phone that never rang. It opened a line to an entire, mumbling alien world, because Martinez wasn't alone. All around him, other voices spoke into other phones. Soldiers. It was some kind of phone tent, set up for the army, in the wilds of Afghanistan.

". . . so I testified," Martinez said, defensively. "Same thing I said to you. I wouldn't hire him, because I wouldn't. But that don't mean . . . You don't get a choice to give testimony or not give testimony. I didn't tell everything, because you don't just sit up there and say everything, whatever is on your mind. I answered the questions they asked me . . ."

"Testimony?" Coburn picked this one word out of the ramble. "Testimony?"

". . . Some guy gave him a watch. It was one of those Allah watches. You know. They pray five times a day, and the watch has the alarm to remind you, get down and pray.

"I didn't get asked about none of that. This one *maricon* was in the prison there. As visitors of the country, we don't know why any one individual is in that particular prison."

Coburn said, "Hawkins was in jail?"

A moment of silence, shared across seven thousand miles. "No, man," Martinez said, dismissively. "He's an American. But he went into the jail and cleaned it out. They didn't want it to be news. It got to be a big, big story, though, eh?"

"You know he has a juvenile record. I can get that opened."

Martinez paused, then caught his old thread out of the air: "The prisons there, man, have completely different facilities. If you look at them, you're going to think something is bad, because what do you know about that world? See? Coming out of New York or Washington or wherever? Hawkins, I think, is from New York, he said. Probably to them, probably to the Africans our prisons would seem crazy."

At this point Sergeant Martinez had most of Coburn's attention. The subject of prison.

". . . Some guy give him a wristwatch, maybe Hawkins gives him something to eat first, you know. I can't see all my guys all the time. You look away one minute, Hawkins is off talking to the indigenous . . . This wasn't the first incident.

"This *maricon* tells Hawkins a story. How cruel it is, you know. He's a prisoner, so I don't know how he gets to keep his watch, because in that place . . . It's not a real gold watch or anything . . ." Martinez faded in and out.

"The prison, it was a shit hole, but that's a local concern. We're not the world's policeman, you know. Everywhere you go, there's going to be something. Hungry kids and everything. But you got to eat your own rations. We got to ensure that our men eat their own rations, you know? Not give them away."

Sergeant Martinez thought that over. Coburn said, "Bottom line, Hawkins is a legitimate criminal?"

"Man, you didn't hear? You don't know?" Then came something like panic: "I'm not talking to no one."

Click. This voice was gone, the impossible, unexpected human voice. The tether drew back across seven thousand miles, and Coburn felt the loss. He sat subdued but another phone erupted: the Washington stamp.

He said, "Calm down, sir. Come on, Donald.

"Shit. Shucks, shucks. The private detective? Talking to who?

"Okay. Tell Brand to wait. Make him wait.

"Oh, no. I'm ten minutes to the ferry," Coburn said to the caller. He listened. This call was just as unbelievable as the call to Sergeant Martinez, in its own way. He said, "Bottom line. Bottom line time. Your son? Your son can't clean himself, after using the toilet. No, you listen. Bottom line, I don't need any team. I'll take care of business. The same as I always have. This stops tonight."

★ ★ ★ ★ ★

Half an hour later, Coburn piloted a Cessna 172 off a rough strip of lawn. The plane ran no lights, and flew low and east over the Atlantic Ocean.

After ten minutes, Coburn could no longer find excuses to stay at the controls. The autopilot had the stick. There was nothing to monitor. He steeled himself and went back to deal with Brand's mess.

Brand's mess was a broken man. A large man, the private investigator Boco. In the dim light of the instruments, the man was a shadow and a hulking wreck. Parts of him were taped like a mummy. There was no logic or process to the tape. It was everywhere. Tape was wrapped around the man's head like a bandage. He lay still. He leaked blood and fluids, which spread darkened fingers on the floormat.

"No duct tape. I told you," Coburn told Brand. He needed to focus on the practical. "It tears out the arm hair. It's unmistakable."

Brand had no apology. He blinked. This was the best Coburn could expect. Brand would blink, to skip a moment, and you could imagine what was skipped was an apology. "My dad told me to take care of him. He was talking with the cops." Brand sat in the door seat. His little pistol, a .25-caliber pistol, flashed its chrome in the dim. For some reason he was holding it.

A waft of smell came to Coburn. Human waste and cleaning chemicals, the combination of a portable outhouse. The man was slowly farting. He was broken, but he wasn't a corpse. He was alive but damaged, so damaged that there was no question, only one path ahead. Like a dog you half run over.

This was Brand's way. He got excited to hurt, but at some point the damaged body would show its stink and worms. Disgust would overwhelm pleasure and halt the party. Brand would break these girls but then at some point suddenly be repelled by the mess he'd made, so that he never finished. He left that chore for Coburn. So easy to insult a body; so hard to kill it.

Especially with this much flesh. This man Boco was a pile of flesh. His feet were bent at angles. Old man's shoes.

"We start with the tape. It all has to come off," Coburn said.

"*I* am not touching him." Brand shuddered in revulsion.

Coburn saw to the practicalities. Duct tape pulled hair and also left its sloppy crosshatch of glue, which didn't dissolve in water. Coburn had to consider that and all the other consequences of dumping a body in the ocean. The impact from the fall. Whether or not to sink the body with weights. What about clothing? At what stage might the body be found? What signs would remain, and how might they be read? Coburn had done this before, but probably no one had ever done it enough to be confident.

"Did you interrogate him for information?"

"Oh, the cops are definitely interested," Brand threatened.

"In what?"

"Everything. He was talking with a cop."

Brand was sullen that he even had to be here. Like a teenager obliged to go on a family trip, when instead he wanted to hang with his friends.

Meanwhile Coburn prepared the body. The tape came off the bushy hair because the hair was bloody to start with.

The man kicked, weakly. Awake?

"How much junk do you have?" Coburn asked Brand.

Brand blinked again. His apology. He was supposed to bring the heroin and the syringe. "Oh, just drop him out," he said, "It's not that fucking complicated. My God. He's not going to live in the ocean."

Boco spoke. Mumbled. Inaudible. Air blew about the cabin, and the plane engine made noise like a saw.

Coburn saw that Boco's eyes were open. They showed Boco to be a sizeable creature. His eyes moved slowly, and without surprise. The man judged his surroundings and pursed his lips in contempt. Even in the dark the expression was unmistakable—the big lips pressed together and rising in contempt. "No police are interested," Boco said. "I can assure you of that."

Brand flew at him, to be contradicted. He crouched over Boco and jabbed at his face. He had a pen or a little screwdriver. He was trying to stab out an eye.

"Leave it!" Coburn pushed him back. Brand was stabbing with the barrel of the little automatic pistol. Coburn took it. Jesus, if he had pulled the trigger . . .

"I fucking saw them! Him and that fucking cop!"

"No. No police. Nah. Just the parking kid, you know. He's just a kid."

Boco watched Coburn, and Coburn returned the study. In his head, he sought for a hold over Boco. Threats? Promises? There was nothing. No one could have any illusions that this trip could end well.

Boco bled from a fresh puncture in his cheek. "I know about you." He said this to Brand, taunting. "Everyone knows Frobisher's evil little imp."

Coburn still pinned Brand to his seat, though Brand ceased to struggle. His feelings were hurt. From that position, the two older men contemplated one another. Boco looked at Coburn, and his look said, *You, I didn't know. But now I do. It doesn't take a moment to see who you are.* "No one cares about Marcus Cunningham."

"What about Cunningham?" Coburn asked. "Why should anyone care?" As soon as he said it, he guessed. Brand and his father had done some deed. They had been preening. Now he knew.

Brand flew up again, or tried to. He appealed his case to

Coburn, in tears, "But he was talking to that cop!"

"Don't worry about me, that's for sure . . ." Boco started talking. He talked the rest of the trip. Coburn didn't listen. Boco's purpose was clear enough. He wanted to keep living. Coburn recognized that, and he was finished with conversation. He had planned to take this body farther than he ever had before. He would travel twenty minutes out into the Atlantic Ocean. And because that was Coburn's plan, he would travel twenty minutes, even if it meant listening to the dying man. He would forget about the duct tape and other complications. The ocean would do its job.

Because Coburn still leaned over Brand, to keep him sitting, he missed a change in Boco's expression. Boco stopped his talk midstream. The look on his face was fully aware. It was resolved, knowing, even cunning. Then he resumed his patter: "But leave him alone. Hawkins, for Christ's sake. He's no harm to anyone. He's a sweet kid. Have a talk with him, at most. Don't you be rough with that kid. He's a good kid. Doesn't deserve rough treatment. Not him. No. He's a sweetheart. I mean, in his heart. Doesn't deserve . . ."

He went on like that until the end.

Chapter 19

I waited forty minutes for my tide. It came, and I waited some more.

My Russian buddy, the one who tried to rent a room in my mansion, he ran an internet service at night. Downtown, in an attic over Slocum Avenue. He didn't pay for the lines. He hijacked unused wireless signal with an antenna device he'd crafted. It was large as a cabinet, with domes and scoops. It looked like a model of a future moon base.

All night, foreign workers came and used pirated signal to write home. Their young faces shone in the light of their screens, their teary eyes and cheeks.

The Russian may not have charged anything for this service. I didn't understand his business model. I never saw money change hands, and no one was on a timer. Somehow the kids took turns. If the stations were full, you waited in an upright chair. Pretty soon one of the computer users would quietly rise. Without a word, Russian handed off to Venezuelan handed off to Dutch. Who handed off to me.

Up so high, the computer room was always as hot as a kitchen. It was so hot that the ancient rafter beams gave off a scent like a cedar linen chest.

Marcus Cunningham had a surprisingly large footprint on the internet. He made his first real money on a tract of land abutted to a national forest in northern California, an irregularly-shaped strip between a national forest and a national park. By some oversight there was a 78-acre patch that wasn't protected. Cunningham bought it and demanded road permits for access. He was going to develop it, and develop it mightily. He resold this forest land to the government for 18 million dollars, plus some unspecified legal fees that he had incurred. The government bought it so there wouldn't be a highway through the last stand of giant redwoods. What could they do? Cunningham gave them a good twist of the arm.

This deal might have passed unnoticed, except that he made similar money leveraging a bird sanctuary in South Dakota, the last home of this or that rare wading bird. This bird had its own postage stamp and was mentioned in folk tunes from the time of Lewis and Clark. Cunningham got the water rights upstream from the sanctuary, an old beet farm, and leveraged eight million dollars out of the Nature Conservancy and private donors. Otherwise it was going to be multifamily development. The only thing coming downstream was going to be strips of nail-gun plastic.

There were more deals of this sort. One website, an exclusively online publication, late to the game and having only the old facts to recycle, yet still wanting to make its mark, entitled its article about Marcus Cunningham "The Worst Man in America."

The sea was cold. I did the swim with a dry bag harnessed to my shoulders. It held my clothes and some candy bars. Some days I tethered the bag to my heel and towed it, but tonight it seemed crazy to want more drag, to want to make anything in life more difficult than it already was.

Three in the morning is a cold, terrible hour. The only good thing about swimming the ocean at three a.m. was that I had the water to myself. The local fishermen weren't awake except for the rare boat speeding out for deep water, going after swordfish or shark.

But tonight I didn't get even this benefit. A small craft with one light crawled the channel, at fishing speed. This was some fool tourist, a July amateur. He wouldn't catch anything in the channel. He was dragging his flashers through empty water.

However, his presence was a thorn in my side. I had to keep my head up. I had to watch for him instead of him watching for me. I didn't carry a beacon light. Imagine a little bicycle light bobbing across the water. It would just sow confusion.

After twenty minutes, distance swimming is enough like sleep that I had to wake up and pay attention. The little boat wasn't fishing anymore. It was moving too fast. It sped around the channel like it was stupid, like there were drunks aboard. It went this way and that, jumping its own wake, a maneuver popular among those who rented jet skis. *Vvvf! Vvvf!* The props screamed as they came out and spun in the air.

I treaded water and watched. The boat got closer. Full speed, full speed, full speed, sprinting spastic distances. I unclipped the chest strap and let the dry bag float to the tether on my heel. The boat wasn't going to see or hear me. If I had the bad luck to get in its way, I'd have to go underwater.

When it came, it leapt with sudden purpose. I thought it would change its mind and turn again, but this time it sprinted two hundred yards directly at my head. "Yo boys!" I shouted weakly. I panted one quick breath and went under.

The tether jerked so hard I thought my foot was gone. My air was gone. I came up and gasped but couldn't make a sound.

The boat turned back. It knew it had hit something. Putter, putter, and men's voices. There was a spotlight going. The beam flickered over my face. I got my hand up, too late. Then the boat charged again. Straight line. I went under. Again I didn't take the breath I should have.

The twin props tore the surface. They went crazy. Back and forth. Zigzags. Trying to plow every bit of surface. They were definitely hunting, but they had the wrong place. Anyway, I was two meters down.

Underwater, I began to calm. My bag was gone. My foot was still attached. It didn't even hurt anymore. What did they think they had hit? A seal? A turtle? The prize shark? Whatever their mistake, I was done trying to correct it. Up top was amateur night. Their spotlight was three-hundred-thousand-candlepower beaming straight down on a mirror. Good luck to you! They churned and churned, but they had no sense for the motion of water. Their patch of surface slid on, while I stayed where I was.

I'd spent a good deal of time underwater. I'd even had beams come down searching for me. For a while the army had me slotted to be one of their Special Operations soldiers. That didn't work out, but it wasn't because I couldn't swim.

I had more air to release, and I did, a few innocuous bubbles. Another forty seconds under wouldn't do me any harm. The boat got farther and farther, just puttering now, tricked by the movement of the surface waves. Their light would stab in and jag around.

Naked, hiding underwater . . . it's about as alone as you can get. I was naked except for flippers, underpants, and my wristwatch. No sight or sound down there. Nothing to do but to suspend yourself with the lightest motion, merely shaping the water. And reflect on your day—I reflected that this was among my worst. It certainly made the list.

I had been badly wrong about Cunningham. Discovering his body set me off on the wrong track. Then I misread everything. The environmental stickers. Loudmouth Boco, the divorce detective, with his pictures of a pretty girl and some creep.

Instead of changing my mind, I had clung to my first idea like a dog that locked its jaw. When people tried to steer me right, I didn't listen. I'd seen a pit bull dog hoisted twelve feet in the air, on a crane, because he was too stupid to let go of the ball he was chewing.

Gently I floated to the surface of the ocean and took a breath, then another, just my mouth, as casually as you might sip from a drinking fountain: You don't really need it, but as long as you're there . . . I let my forehead break the surface.

I couldn't see details on the boat. The only light was their Las Vegas spotlight. If they aimed it close to themselves, the water reflected the scene. Two men or more. If it was just two, they sure were busy monkeys, scrambling around.

I watched for a minute and got a real glimpse. The light was mounted on a deck swivel. The man aiming it let go, and the light swung down and flickered off the fiberglass deck. Two men lay on their bellies. They scooted fore and aft, frantically searching the water nearby. They leaned over the side and felt under there, as though something were stuck under the hull.

If I were closer, it would be easy to come underneath and yank them into the water. That would certainly sober them up! I chuckled but it didn't catch. My mood was too leaden.

"Off! Off!" one shouted. That was the end of a longer argument. The light went off.

Huh. I let myself sink. In a few minutes, the boatmen's eyes would begin to adjust, and my head would appear as a shadow among the sparkle of the waves in the starlight. "Off! Off!"—the tone surprised me. The man wasn't drunk. The voice was charged with emotion, but it wasn't fear ("we've had a terrible accident!—woe!")—and it wasn't glee ("we nailed the shark"). I didn't know what it was. Command?

I stayed underwater two full minutes. I came up and oriented myself. The boat was drifting. I gently tapped the water from my ears.

"Just fucking shit!" a man despaired. "I mean goddang it." He threw wet fabric overboard, furious. Without the spotlight I could make out shapes from the glow of their gauges and instruments. Two figures, but far distant now.

"How was the strap done?"

"It's just coconut candy bars!" the other answered, quite upset, weeping.

They had found my bag. They were throwing pieces of it overboard. "Was it cut, or did he undo it? Oh shit. Oh shoot. You felt it, right?" His voice went loud because his face turned toward me. As it turned, his profile showed a grotesque mask. Night-vision gear. It was the old Russian night-vision goggles, which glowed green.

I sank gently, and spent another two minutes at six feet under. It's simple. You lift your hands to keep from floating up. I've seen twenty soldiers do it at the same time, in full kit. It makes these war machines look like gentle sea plants lifting with the current. I counted the minutes by heartbeats. The last minute was extra. The boat was gone. It was speeding back toward the harbor.

Instead of going on to my island, I decided to cut my losses and swim straight to the mainland. The mainland was easy to see, to the west, with its constant-colored stars. Boston was further along, a glow, an all-night sunset.

I'd always wanted to try that swim, and this was the time. I had embarrassed myself on Nausset Island. Lost my girl. Made a mess of the job. The place itself had made its dislike clear—it's not often one gets run down by a pleasure craft. No one would notice my absence for days.

The devil inside said, try it, try the swim. The mileage wasn't unprecedented. People swim the English Channel. People swim to Cuba.

Chapter 20

It was an ugly Wednesday night. I have no proof of this ugliness other than no one would deny it. No kid fights or bad weather, but it was not even eleven o'clock and you could hear, *bang bang,* the plywood shutters coming down on the bars.

Still some crowds were trying to push through the mood, you know, ignore the obvious. These kids had paid their money down and taken the ferry boat. Tomorrow was the Fourth of July. What could they do now but try to pretend that life was a party?

There was a particular crowd of boys. I'm not even sure they were in college. Most had the same shirt, a sports team . . .

I passed one of Mr. Lee's places, where they put palm fronds over the canvas umbrellas. Maybe that qualifies it as a tiki bar. As I passed I somehow caught the attention of these boys. They knew it and I knew it. We didn't say a word. We didn't get close enough to speak.

They faced the harbor, the narrow walkway, and before I realized it, this particular kid and I had exchanged a glance. That's right, it could have been lyrics to a love song, except that it was the opposite. It was me, my particular talent: that I induce animosity in a certain number of people.

It was also the uniform. The police uniform only provoked. I made that case to Detective Wakin. Wakin was stuck handling the whole police station, with the Chief on death's door but of course refusing to abdicate. My first advice to Wakin—I went in and said look, just stop having police. Put out a sign and lock the door. Closed for business. There's no crime on the island.

I explained it to him. Everybody out here on Nausset, they already had all their items—the rich people. There *were* some poor people, who were allowed to stay and work the shops, but they knew the score. They knew to be on good behavior. They were mostly foreign kids. Either foreign kids were just more naturally polite, or they realized the obvious, which is that in two hours they could make more money scooping ice cream than they could if they stole a TV and tried to locate a pawn shop. There wasn't a pawn shop on island.

Imagine if you came to Nausset and you did have crime in mind, maybe stealing beach bags while the tourists were paddling around in the waves, which is something to watch out for on every other beach on earth. However, on Nausset Island, for your high-speed getaway, you would be looking to board the blunt-nosed *Island Queen,* which would honk its departure horn for ten minutes, then steam away at the pace of a bicycle.

Detective Wakin heard me out, then sighed with weariness. The job was already wearing him down, deteriorating his mind, organs, and moral center.

He answered me, which is more than the Chief would have done. Wakin said that we were out there for vandalism, litter, and drunkenness. Really? Let's face it—look at the tee shirts in the shop windows—vandalism, litter, drunkenness—that's what we're *selling*! All right? Vandalism, litter, drunkenness. Maybe all we did was try to keep them within decent limits, or to make sure the visitors *paid* for the indulgence.

So—Wednesday night—as usual, I found myself walking into the quiet area at the end of the pier. I gravitated toward the empty streets, away from where I should have been, which is among all the drunken people. If I let my own feet decide, I would keep walking until the pavement ended, and then I'd walk into the ocean and swim. Instead I awarded myself the usual compromise, thirty more paces before turning back into the noise.

Suddenly there were voices and running. I looked around for the fun and I was right in among them, that group of boys. There we go, suddenly my hair was cold. They took my hat.

End of the pier. End of the evening. No one else. A man fished at the end of the riprap, turned away.

"Deputy Dog, Deputy Dog, Deputy Dog."

Ah, the hat game. You make a start for it and they pass it to the man behind. Then they stand there shrugging with innocence—"I don't have it!" They shift your attention like a herd of zebras.

What might surprise you, were you to play the hat game for the first time, was that groups like this didn't form in a circle. It wasn't bear-baiting. Instead the pack kept moving. The game wasn't even their full-time job. This group was eight boys, with half not even paying attention. My hat headed toward the water.

What maddens me, in my long experience, I've always sensed the hat game has a solution. It's a puzzle with an answer somewhere on the back pages, some move I could make. The boys would laugh, pat the hat back onto my head, and walk off as my friends.

Whatever this answer was, it never came to me at the moment. To make matters worse, I chose the wrong kid. Obviously, this kind of game, you don't go for the hat, you go for the man. You go for the man who can stop the game.

I looked for the boy who met my eyes earlier. Dark hair. High, bony cheeks like a jester in a stage play. In the shuffle I didn't find him. He'd changed his face. Instead I somehow got the smallest boy. He tried to jump backward but his friend was there behind him. Just like that, I had his neck and shirt, but I chose wrong. What was he, fourteen years old? If he was college age there was something wrong. His bones were like a bird's. But the others danced off out of reach, and it was too late to throw this one back for a bigger fish.

His shirt was flimsy nothing so I decided to use these handcuffs of mine, which I'd never bothered with. Snap! I got one cuff on. Then this boy flipped out! He spun. He became a wild animal with his foot in a trap. He twisted and dropped so quickly I didn't have time to release him. He dropped right to the concrete, his arm straight back. His shoulder must have unhinged, to drop like that. He squawked and screamed.

"Jesus. Stay still."

Somehow I had captured the runt. The others surrounded me, two or three steps out, at what they thought was a safe distance. They had plenty to say, so indignant, but my hands were full. For two or three breaths my boy would lie still, and then he would explode into twists, like a fish on the dock. "Whoa, whoa," I said. "Let me get the key."

He was drugged with fear. I couldn't remove the handcuffs but I couldn't let him run off with them. If I held his wrist steady, the way he exploded, he would twist his arm completely off.

A light shone. One of the other boys—it was bizarre—held his phone up at arm's length, as though he wanted me to take a call. Speak to his mom? He narrated, "This police took Mikey. This police took Mikey, we're here in Nausset, trying to go home . . ." Ah, a camera. He used the phone to record the scene. Collecting evidence. Any trouble would be mine, of course. How did they know this? I mean, they were right, but how did they know?

Someone else screamed. More like a rodeo shout. It was far away, a completely different scene, down the back of the pier. The boys quieted. The scream was so insistent. "HEY!

PEANUTS! HEY!"

Along the back of the pier was a line of shops that rented scooters and bicycles. These businesses were completely dark now. The street was dark except for broken light from the wharf side. Out front of one of the shops, two women shouted at us and carried on. They slumped on one another, so drunk that they couldn't walk. One screamed "PEANUTS!" again, or maybe "PENIS!" Then "LOVE! LOVE!" It could have meant anything, including bloody murder. This woman saw that she had our attention. She let go of her friend, shimmied, and hiked her skirt. Honest to God. Showed us her underpants, if she was wearing any.

You would think the college boys would go crazy. There was a drunk woman lifting her skirt. But the whole scene was too much. She was more than a block away, and the motion was not sexy. She was sort of front-mooning us, doing some witchy thing, or getting ready to piss in the open street. Her shape was definitely a woman, not a girl.

In a flash I uncuffed my prisoner. He didn't freak out anymore, he was so fixated on the women, frightened they would approach. He rubbed his wrist. "How's your wing?" I asked. He nodded mutely, to thank a stranger for his concern.

One of the boys handed me my hat. The jester boy, his skin ivory. Other than that, the mob was confused. Stay or go. One of them jogged for the water. With that example, they all took off. They escaped whatever weird thing was happening here.

By the time I got over to the women, there was only one. Sarah Palsinger. Megan's sister. Cunningham's widow. Her skirt was back to normal. "What did you think you were doing?" she said, very critical. The air carried a whiff of animal wool.

"I know. They got me when I wasn't paying attention. My name is Jim Hawkins, by the way."

"I'm Sarah." Sarah wasn't drunk at all. "Just Jim, eh? You

know, you have other names."

"Sure. I'm the Parking Warden. To those kids I was Deputy Dog. You've got to consider any nickname a compliment."

She thought. "That's not true at all."

"It indicates you made your mark on the world. Your presence in the world has been noted."

"I hate every nickname I've ever been given."

Sarah wasn't hurt or in distress. As I said, she wasn't even drunk. Her scream had been to extricate me from my situation. On the dark street, she was a clone of her sister, done in slightly larger size. The difference between the sisters was that Megan had been looking around, and worried what her place should be. Sarah was more certain. She had already seen everything there was to see. Except for me, maybe. She said, "You're finished. It's way after eleven."

"I have to wait a little. Before I leave," I said. "I close the Duck."

We knew the subject to be a sensitive one. In a moment, she waved. "It's dead tonight." She appraised my reaction: "In the Duck you're known as 'Rainman.' "

I nod. "Sure, I see the justice in that. I know it's a movie. I'm not a gifted talker in the public venue. But believe me . . . have you ever been a cop, or a guard, or something?"

"Never, I can assure you." She was amused by the question.

"If it happens, you learn to avoid conversation." I showed her. "Position your body to the side of people instead of facing them. Because if you start talking, forget it, there's no escape. It's a phenomenon. I write a man a ticket and out come all the circumstances of his night. Everything. The home situation . . . What am I, his judge? His confessor?"

Sarah's mouth drew back and snapped a yawn, natural as a lion. Her shape, her movement, her walk—even this shift in her jaw—showed how a woman was a completely different creature.

Women have different points of balance. Obviously, no secret there. But some women embrace the difference, some don't, and some are unsure. I imply no judgment. Sarah embraced the difference. She moved so differently that she threw doubt into men's hearts, and left *them* self-conscious of their own basic motions. "They whine a lot, then," she said.

"No. Of course they do, but they also want me to judge them kindly. It's so inappropriate. We're strangers. It's not the purpose of human conversation."

"For your nicknames, there's also 'Terminator.' "

"Another movie, right? I agree with them. I have no talent for crowds. Did you see that kid? He was trying to twist himself to pieces. People are nuts, or at least they behave that way around me."

In speaking, I displayed those untrustworthy hands of mine, where a minute before I held the boy. I had to spin like a square dance to keep him from snapping his own twiggy bones. Sarah studied these clumsy mitts. Something passed over her face.

"What's wrong with your hat? It's wet." She took it.

"They poured liquid in there." I reached for it, but she spun and held it low. She knew the hat game. "Just a blender drink or something."

"You can't wear this."

"It's just a uniform. Come on."

"Aren't you going to wash it?"

"It's all right. It'll be all right. I'll dip it in the ocean."

Whenever a woman has anything to do with me, it starts with this same expression I see on Sarah's face, which is like pity, amazed pity.

Which is such a misreading of the situation. I don't need help. Of all the people in the world. My body is a miracle. Basically I've never been sick. Other guys talk about sprains and breaks, while I don't even know how those would feel. I get banged up or cut, my skin heals itself in an hour. I mean, since I was fifteen years old, nothing has marked me. And if I put force on something, it breaks. People and things. Bodies come to pieces in my hands.

She led me along with the hat, the punch-soaked hat, just out of reach.

Chapter 21

With Sarah I woke up and right away my life was better. She puttered about, watering dead plants, and reminding herself where things where in this neglected apartment. All the while she wore only her underwear, plain underwear, as though we'd been married a decade.

She had taken me to a studio apartment above the stationery store on Slocum Ave. Sarah didn't use it much. The place was not high on her housing rotation.

She put her head in her refrigerator and playfully listed its contents, anything that might tempt me for breakfast. She was discovering things herself in there, tossing crusty jars, apologizing and laughing all the while. With the properties she owned, it was a challenge just to keep any kind of rolls or bread. I did a finger count, one time, and came up with eight refrigerators, minimum, among all her homes. Eight refrigerators to keep track of.

Imagine that in your head. The contents of eight refrigerators. You tell me the world is not a trap.

Her head in the fridge, she said, "You don't have tattoos."

I was lying in bed. Like a moron I checked my shoulder and chest. She looked out and caught me at it. "You don't have army tattoos. I thought you were in the army."

I nodded. Sure, I came out unmarked. On my calves there was a scattering of bumps where my skin healed back slightly raised from the surrounded skin, but they were hardly proof of service.

"What did you do?"

"Soldiering," I said. "The most basic. I carried guns around."

"Were you in Iraq, then?"

"Some."

"You don't like to talk about it?"

"It would kill you with boredom. I'd feel responsible for your death."

"It wouldn't," she said. After a while she resumed her puttering. She called, "Are you mad that I'm nosy?"

"No. To tell the truth, I'm just enjoying these bed sheets. Are they made of something special? Parachute silk?"

"Parachutes? No. So you quit the army to become a policeman?"

"Uh. I got fired, is probably more accurate."

"I didn't know you could get fired. From the army?"

"Well," I said. Sarah in the bed was something. Obviously. But the bed alone, in the morning . . . I kept stretching and stretching out my limbs until I was at all four corners. I stretched to distances my joints had forgotten. "You could say I have a bare handful of talents. Getting fired is certainly among them."

Sarah tried on some clothes until she had the right ones. Then she left.

My relationships with women take their own shape. Rarely did I get to offer guidance. I should ask questions—basic things—when do I have to leave? How am I going to lock the door? It's a deadbolt. But I can never articulate. It seems so presumptuous. ("Okay, we slept together . . .") It's embarrassing.

Instead of having a hand in our future plans, I watch and see what I get. Like with Marsha, it developed, she liked to have me around in bed. Everywhere else, her head was on a swivel. She didn't want my presence to spoil her chances for a real husband, in case one walked by, holding his Martini with an underhand grip, the tan man of easy culture and poise. For Marsha this became a habit or even an obsession. We'd be alone behind locked doors, lights out, and still her attention would stray off, like she had to continue to work the crowd, planning her next conversation. It was just a habit. Believe me, no Kennedys were near unless they watched from the ductwork.

Because I never get up the nerve to ask—to ask Sarah if I'll see her again—instead I have to rely on the feel of the thing. You'd think I was a mystic. I mean, I'm there in a silent apartment. What are the signs? What kind of silence did she leave behind?

Sarah hadn't been to this apartment all season. Whatever her claims, the only food items to be trusted were the heel ends of some French cheese. They were loosely wrapped in their original store cellophane, remnants of an ancient party. I found a knife and pared off any textured growth, then melted the creamy centers in a brass pot designed to brew Turkish coffee. In my search I'd spied a box of crackers. I shook it—reassuring heft. But when I got in, the crackers were spoiled. They had settled to the bottom of their bag and mildewed into a brick of gritty paste.

The cardboard box itself was moist and spongy in my hand. The box was growing into the crackers and vice-versa. Nothing lasted on this island. The first law was deterioration.

These were just the facts. The most lovely woman in my life stood beside me at a party. She needed my help somehow, but a shark ate her before she could even give me her name. Now, not a month later, her sister saved me from an ugly scene on the pier. She rescued me and took me into her bed.

I drank the fondue, a couple of pounds of it, carrying the pot and sipping like tea. In the bathroom, a dried vine reached across the tub for the window.

The next night Sarah found me on the pier. She knew that I could quit at eight, and there she was, in substantial summer jewelry, as though we'd arranged a date. I went with her.

As soon as I awoke this time, however, I slid out of the bed. My skin crawled. The sheets could ruin me. Silk sheets, better than your own skin, they could hold you forever.

"You're leaving?" Sarah asked.

"I should. I have to."

She stretched. There was no limit to what she did to my blood. Heretofore lust had been a cycle—ebb and flow, aroused and satiated—but not with Sarah. She changed my chemistry. Her scent and shape were the primal forms.

She purred. "Were you even going to leave me a note on the pillow?"

"That's nuts," I said. The carpet reached into the arches of my feet—massaged arches I didn't even know about. I tried to explain: "This is all too fine."

In the dim Sarah watched me struggle into my uniform. This provided a certain amount of entertainment and suspense, as I nursed my shirt buttons one by one, careful, careful, like setting a mouse trap. She said, "There's a shirt that will fit you. In that drawer."

"I'm on traffic this morning."

"You can bring a few things here. If you like."

"Okay. Great," I said. What kind of possessions might she expect? Maybe I'd buy something. I had a few clothes in my work locker. When I wasn't in uniform my wardrobe was free tee shirts I picked up at the fire station. The shark attack had spoiled their charity boat race, so they had a box of a hundred shirts.

Sarah said, "You're wild. But not as wild as I expected."

"Wild?" Moment of horror, I thought she was critiquing my bed work. But no, she studied me. Sarah became her sister. These pensive episodes never lasted long. Curiosity would bubble up to the surface, and maybe for twenty seconds at a time she would look around wondering.

Well, I wished her luck, figuring me out. I would certainly be interested to hear any conclusions she might reach on that subject. I finished my shirt buttons, and instead of firing out of there, rude, I sat and held her bare foot. "*You're* the wild one. At the Gooey Duck when I smashed the glass, you came and removed pictures. They were pictures of you, right?"

For an answer Sarah chuckled with nervous energy. She said, "Oh my God, oh my God," at the memory. Lit up with electricity of connections, across people, space, and time.

This was a pattern we had: We would connect across our secret histories on the island.

Imagine you got involved with a movie star, and all her life you'd seen the updates. You already knew about her kids and her boyfriends, her acting legacy, her blockbusters and heartbreaks. You'd read interviews. Well, this was a similar situation. I knew Sarah was the widow of Cunningham, with all that entailed. But *she* hadn't told me, so how much was right to say? I had first seen her in Boco's "adultery" pictures with some creep. I had met her grandmother before I met her—seen her childhood drawings humanizing the walls of Castle Yellow. I knew she was the sister of Megan. A million things like that.

She knew less about me, but you'd be surprised. She knew the army. She knew my work schedule, though that shifted day to day. She kept track of it better than I ever could. For two months I'd been blundering around on her island, and she had observed a certain amount.

Then *Shazam!* We'd reach across the old paths. She had been there, and I had been there, too. We'd been orbiting each other. It may sound mundane, but the moments were so charged that I felt raw voltage, and afterward it would hang around in the air. It was more than a first touch of skin. The sensation was probably why people fantasized they had lived past lives.

I held Sarah's toes. We enjoyed our moment, and I tried for another: "I'm heading to the Methodist campground to set up traffic cones." Sarah's eyes were closed. Reassured of my attraction to her, she was going back to sleep. "I saw your place there. The purple cottage."

"That was Megan's," she said. "Ugh. It's full of trash. I have to get it cleaned."

"Cleaned?"

"My sister used it as her 'headquarters.' " Sarah didn't approve. "My sister wanted to refashion herself as an environmentalist. As I guess you know."

With the fizz in my head, I found it advisable to say nothing. I fitted my shoes. Sarah went on sleepily. "Megan's seal sanctuary." Sarah delivered a worn punch line: "And not even any seals."

"There are seals in these waters."

"Not here."

"Sure there are. I've seen them a half dozen times. I ran into one the other night."

It was three nights ago. I tried to swim to the Cape. Remember? After my encounter with the drunken speedboat?

I ran into a seal. Not literally, but we were close. She surprised me and I surprised her. Neither one of us belonged in the open water, and we circled each other. It wasn't a communion or anything like that. I didn't grow up as a friend to the animals.

She was big as a dolphin, with black, bulbous features. She

looked into my face and bleated. Maybe there were more seals around and she was warning them. Or maybe she was complaining to me. By no means do I speak the secret language of the seals. However, it was clear that I bothered her. This was her space and ocean.

I treaded water and took stock. My arms were weak to the point where I could isolate the strain to particular muscle cords. The Cape lights didn't look any closer than when I started. I was not even a quarter of the way across to my destination. And when I got there, what did I think I would do, naked except for briefs, rubber swim fins, and a malfunctioning wristwatch?

What I did is turn back. The seal didn't trust this. She followed me a few hundred yards before I lost track.

I wonder if she didn't save my life, because that night my swim stroke was broken. The swim just wasn't in me. It was almost dawn when I washed up on Squab Island, collapsing in the surf. My body felt like it had absorbed forty pounds of water, and I was squishy and waterlogged all the next day, not thirsty for anything.

"Ironic," Sarah said.

"What is?"

"She was always on Marcus, my late husband, because he was a developer. She wanted a seal sanctuary on Squab Island. But nobody else did. Think about it. Why would a fishing town want seals?"

"Fishing? *Pfft.* I haven't seen any real fishermen on Nausset."

"*Nobody* wants seals. Look what happened to the beaches. It's ironic."

I still didn't understand, so she explained. "Seals bring the sharks. No tourist town wants them. Seals bring the white sharks."

Chapter 22

Marsha invited me to watch the fireworks with her. With the dry summer, all fireworks were banned except for these. It was to be a sixteen-thousand-dollar display, firing off a barge they'd anchored in the bay. Marsha found me on the pier just after lunch.

I declined the date. She stepped back slowly. At first she couldn't believe it, but then in one minute she read everything like it was printed on my face.

"Come on," I muttered. "Don't look like that. You didn't want me anymore."

"You are pitiful," she said.

"Come on. I mean if there's one thing I don't need to see again in my life, it's fireworks."

"Do you have any idea what you're doing with her? You don't. You're a newborn."

I was supposed to work the event. Everyone was. I told Chet to keep an eye on my quadrant of the park, and instead I took the cruiser six miles up island, to check on the town clerk.

When would you say I crossed the line into investigation? Right about here. Up to this point, I was working a summer job on a summer island. I tripped around. I didn't know half. What I did know, I was wrong about. At what point do you say, Jim Hawkins started to look into things?

You would have to say that I began to investigate these questions in earnest on Thursday, the Fourth of July.

If you loved Nausset Island and if you wanted others to love it, that holiday was all you could wish for. It was a beach day so fine that first the parents and then the children got off their beach towels and blankets, walked down the wet sand and returned to the ocean. Just like that, everyone was back in the water. No longer was the ocean for me and the bogeyman shark. The day was perfect, crisp toast, and then just when the heat was getting tiresome—smelly and muggy—just then the evening breeze came in across the water like a feather. This weather was why people had started taking their vacations on Nausset Island in the first place.

As I drove east that evening, the sky was light ahead, the last of this perfection. But behind me a storm was coming. In my back mirror the horizon was a solid roll of clouds, dark as something brewed in a volcano. The storm hung there, waiting. At some point it would swoop in with a bang. No telling when. No telling whether or not it would douse the park crowd and those foolish fireworks.

Up island, these weren't summer houses. Many of these were solid places, in ones and twos and clusters, in the thin, scrappy forest, and they had banks of windows instead of porches.

Road signs were few and cryptic—carving, calligraphy, inlay of seashells—but I'd scouted and knew what to do. I drove past Clerk Watterson's place. I had guessed right. He was out for the festivities. His car was gone. I drove past, parked in the trees, and circled back on foot, a quarter mile through the forest.

Clerk Watterson. Town clerk. That sounds even less important than Parking Warden, but apparently Clerk Watterson was the man to see. Megan made a bumper sticker that hated him by name, a whole case of these stickers which had been unopened until I cut the packing tape.

Clerk Watterson. Megan's sticker didn't have me favorably disposed toward the man. However, I reminded myself to withhold judgment. My judgment had proven faulty, even in the recent past. One minute I loved Cunningham, and now was I immediately going to latch onto something else? The greenie dreams of a woman I had barely spoken to? No. I would disregard my own prejudices, and approach the matter with balance and fairness to all parties.

So, earlier in the week, I'd dropped by Watterson's office at the municipal building. His offices dominated the top floor. Judging by the building's outside dimensions, Watterson's area was the size of a ballroom, but this I could never confirm.

I had opened an ancient wooden door to come upon a secretary at her desk. She was positioned as a greeter but seemed amazed when I appeared, as though I was opening doors to random dressing rooms.

She was a spiny little creature. In all ways Watterson's secretary found my visit extraordinary: Who was I again? What was this regarding? The sense she gave was that it was ridiculous to expect an audience, as if I were cold-calling the White House or the Vatican. I gave one careless answer and she pounced: Was the Chief aware of my presence here in the office? When I walked out she was on the phone, trying to raise the Chief out of his iron lung.

Watterson's house was huge, too—long and low—a palace for anyone who called himself a clerk.

For the last approach I came out of the trees and up the road, up the short driveway, in plain sight. Walked tall. Didn't crouch or sneak. Months patrolling the town had given me a healthy regard for spying neighbors. One had to imagine Mrs. Yellow stationed at every window with professional optics, and nothing would light her up like an obvious sneak. But this part of the island was all about privacy. You could watch Watterson's house from this driveway but otherwise it was under cover of the scrubby trees.

I knocked gently. No dog. No nothing. These windows had signs. No Smoking—Oxygen Tanks. Great, another dying old man. I didn't even try the door. I went around the side for a window. I despaired for a moment when I saw a giant air-conditioning unit, but with the tree cover the day had been mild enough that Watterson still cooled his place with open windows. I pried out a screen and was up and in: simple.

What did I learn? It came in bits and pieces. It was definitely a sick man's house. That was the first impression I gathered. There were oxygen tanks. Metal racks and stands. Professional hospital gear. The air was full of disinfectant, not regular cleaning supplies.

I navigated with my work flashlight. I came for papers, but in the study Watterson's personal computer pumped away. He hadn't locked it up with passwords or anything. I'm no hacking master but I could do the obvious. I opened his email and searched for "Cunningham." Not much. Deleted emails in an archive. But it turned out I'd done it wrong, only searching for emails *from* "Cunningham." I tried instead anything that mentioned Cunningham, and three came up.

They were long for an email—screen after screen—and hard to skim. In legalistic language, they described the passing of legal title to a group that included the name Cunningham: "Cunningham, Frobisher, and Trent."

I gradually figured out the context. These emails were written by Watterson, and they were answering inquiries from the Nature Conservancy. Basically the emails said nothing but referred the Nature Conservancy to this group of three, who owned the property. The land in question was the "former federal reservation"—Squab Island, my island.

I skimmed one, two, three, and they were all the same paralegal bullshit. Each time I opened one of these emails, the computer took a few seconds to process the request, which felt like forever, me waiting there with sweat beading on my lip. I was making normal requests on a normal computer, but for some reason these emails were different. A progress bar would come up and gradually fill, making me wait, even if I merely flicked back and forth between the documents.

I was stuck there, so I tried the desk drawers. Nothing much. They contained amber medicine bottles and account statements. One drawer held a little box with passports. I'd never laid eyes on Watterson, so I put my flashlight on his picture. But it wasn't Watterson. It was a girl. So were the other passports. Three passports. Three different girls. They weren't United States passports. One was Polish. The other two were from Ukraine.

Wree-wree-wree. Outside, on the main road, a car idled. I don't know at what point I became aware. It was an island car, so the belts squeaked. The same salt air that eats the houses alive makes the cars groan. Not just belt noise, either. It's organ damage. No part of the car system was completely happy to be on island. Anything that in the original engineering slid or touched, now there was a little rub or scrape. The *wree-wree-wree* sound outside was just the engine idling. When an island car started to roll, the body and struts would complain with their own special noises. This one was holding still.

Flashlight off. I settled to the floor. My scalp blazed. One sensible thing the army trains into soldiers is to fight your instinct to freeze. The training sergeant would say, "Don't lay there and let them decide everything. You're not a rabbit."

I'd made a mess of Watterson's desk. Which passport had

been on top? The dark-haired girl? "Fuck." I slipped the wad of three into my pants pocket. Closed the drawers. Killed the power on the computer. Then with frantic energy I low-crawled across these huge expanses of carpet, toward my window. I got there, up and out.

Wham! I hit the dirt, crouched. A few seconds of silence, with my blood pounding in my ears, and no one challenged me. No lights inside or out. No one on this side of the house. *Wree-wree-wree.*

I tried to make a sober assessment. Behind me was an easy escape through the woods, whenever I wanted that. But in the state I had left things, the house was going to shout "burglary!" The window screen was still lying just inside, bent up at the pins. I'd planned to fix that. And I'd planned to find the electrical box and hammer the circuit breaker back and forth a few times, to confuse any electronics. I'd found the computer turned on, but had shut it down out of panic or habit.

Was there any way to salvage the night? Return the passports, restart the computer, fix the window? Why hadn't the house lights come on yet? Without my blood roaring, I could hear the car still wheezing out front. Wheezing calmly. Why would Watterson idle in his own driveway? On the phone to the cops? Maybe listening to his car radio, for the 1812 Overture to reach the cannon finale?

I went to see. If you don't show a light, it's surprisingly easy to sneak. The car still made plenty of noise, enough that running it seemed like a cruelty. Like somebody's asthmatic mule: Jeez, let her rest. Put her down.

One side of the house had landscaping gravel. The other was dirt. I used the dirt side and stepped around in the shadows of the trees. There stood Malcolm Trent, the owner of the Wharf House. He stood beside the open driver's door of the car and watched Watterson's place. I was close enough to him that if it were daytime, etiquette would call for us to greet one another.

What the hell? Was he visiting? The passenger door of the car hung open.

My wristwatch chose that moment to remind me of my place in the world: *First, do no harm. Second* . . . I quieted it.

Trent stared at me. Ten yards away. Trust the darkness.

A door slammed. Trent dropped into his driver's seat. Movement on my right—I turned to dash—it was another man hurtling to the car. A strange noise rose out of him, a gurgling laugh that turned my head back to the scene.

The passenger door slammed, and abruptly cut off the sound. In his seat, the second man waved thin limbs like a spider, gesticulating. His face was a weird high snout, which was night-vision goggles. Yeah, the same kind I had seen before. The Russian ones, the cheap ones.

Trent backed the car out, then spun away with a rooster tail of gravel. No lights.

What on earth? It was like boys playing a game. Had those two pranked Watterson's doorstep with a sack of shit? Apparently I wasn't the only one using the Fourth of July to visit an empty house.

The weird little guy had slammed the front door of Watterson's house too hard. It had bounced instead of latching, and now drifted open. Everything settled—road dust—quiet settled like a blanket. A few seconds, and again I had the same sensation I had inside, where you become aware of a sound that was always there. Hissing. Hissing like a scuba tank.

I ran for the road. I dove beyond it. Wasn't much of a ditch, but I was down covering my head, with no time to change place or change plan. The house exploded.

Chapter 23

Anna woke to the lightest knock on her door. "Yes?"

"Sasha."

She opened it. Sasha was a slight, pale Russian boy who had known her sister from last summer. When she questioned him earlier, he barely spoke. He answered her with his eyes on Margo, and volunteered nothing. He had seemed shy and also disapproving. Of what? Probably her, but it could be anything: all women, all Ukrainians, her sister.

Maybe Kat kissed him, found these kisses cold, and never informed the young man that he had failed his audition. It wouldn't be the first time she had drawn in these pale, fragile moths. They spent months hovering, tapping on the glass, leaving cat gifts—a single picked flower—making a nuisance. Often they switched their obsession to Anna herself, as a consolation prize.

Now Sasha's light knock. Anna would have guessed he was too bloodless to attempt a midnight seduction. She abruptly opened the door wide enough for her face, confident she could nip this particular silliness with a few brisk words.

Sasha was there. He disarmed Anna by saying nothing. He stood as though reluctantly keeping an appointment, several steps back, his posture bent as a question mark. He could bring his eyes no higher than her waist.

He led her downstairs. Waiting at the kitchen table was an American policeman. A huge brute of a policeman, sprawled back on a chair. Anna turned to Sasha with disbelief, but his mild expression didn't change. This wasn't a surprise betrayal.

"I'm sorry," the policeman said, "for your loss."

"What?" Anna said.

"Your clothes. You're in mourning?" Self-conscious, the man touched the hair behind his ear. His hair was shockingly white, but a wound ran up his neck, a weal that brightened and finally bled, so that behind his ear a patch of the white hair was as orange as a carrot. This ugly wound was fresh and untreated. "I'm sorry," he said to the table. He cleared his throat. "You're wearing mourning clothes?"

"No." Anna looked at her clothes, then back at the man in wonder. "No. Just black clothes. This is a style."

"Sorry." The man blinked and rubbed his forehead. He was nervous or frightened, which did not fit because he was an unreal figure, not a real man but a cartoon version of one, a Nazi Stormtrooper stylized for a rally poster. "Ekaterina Fedorchak?"

"Yes?"

"This is yours."

It was her sister's passport. "Where is she?"

"That's you? Ekaterina Fedorchak."

"This is my sister. This is hers."

"Where is your sister?"

"She worked here sometime, last summer. I came to find her. I'm in this country to locate her."

The policeman took this in. He searched for the right words. "Maybe you should go to the police."

Such a strange thing for a policeman to say . . . For a moment Anna doubted her English.

At once all the alien features of the United States came upon her. The air, the food, the talk, the thinking. It was all unfamiliar, but the differences had seemed harmless.

Instead unfamiliarity had been building up. Now it all came at once and spun her head. Anna found herself sitting. The weight of her sister's passport settled her into a kitchen chair.

"I'm no one," the policeman explained. "A parking cop." He nodded toward Sasha. "I found passports. He was looking them up for me, on his internet service. It turned out you'd met."

Sasha did not nod or acknowledge any part in this. Something obliged him to stand there, and that obligation he would fulfill.

"Okay. You're just a guard?" Anna said. The policeman accepted the justice of that description. Yes, Anna could see it now. His uniform didn't fit, and neither did the authority. He was too shy to command a thing. His chair pressed the wall because he wanted to escape. The confines of this tiny kitchen forced him closer to other people than he wanted to be.

"You police had this passport?"

"No. I found it by accident." He looked down and plucked at his policeman's uniform, as though surprised to discover that he wore it. "I was in a man's house, earlier tonight. It blew up." The cop heard himself and hurried to reassure her: "An empty house. No one was home. Out in the woods."

Anna rested the passport on the table and rested her hands in her lap. The passport opened itself, and the first stamp was for Israel. A boyfriend Kat had met at the junior Olympics. When she traveled there he was married and lived in a commune of all his sixty relatives. More travel stamps. The passport was full. Anna had forgotten about Kat's other trips. Norway. Israel. Saudi Arabia. Her sister was unpredictable. Unstoppable. Uncontrollable. To travel to these places, Kat calculated only the bare price of the airplane or boat. Her job was to set foot on soil; the rest was the obligation of the place.

The policeman still talked to explain. ". . . the explosion. There were oxygen tanks all over the house, because the man is sick. If you light a cigarette around those, I guess they ignite.

Ironic that the guys who need them have already smoked away a chunk of lung . . ."

After he'd continued on a while in this fashion, Anna interrupted. "He was a lover?"

"Of your sister?" The big man shrugged, seemed doubtful. "I haven't met him. He was on supplementary oxygen. Those tanks people haul around the grocery aisles."

"His name? I will speak to him."

"How old are you?" the policeman asked. He allowed himself to study Anna, and she composed herself for his gaze. By this point she understood that he posed no threat to her. He was nothing.

He said, "Tomorrow, we'll go to the man's office together. When it opens. Together, all right?"

"You don't want me to be a nuisance, to this important man."

"No. It's just that you look like you're fourteen. Fourteen years old." He helped himself to Kat's passport. "How old is she?"

"Nineteen," Anna answered. She corrected herself: "She turned twenty."

"How about the other girls?" the cop turned and asked Sasha.

Sasha produced two passports, and mutely examined their fabric covers.

Seeing these booklets, Anna felt suddenly bloodless. She said, "I am very frightened now." Her voice wavered.

They stayed like that until Anna could recover herself. The men were disturbed but had no idea how to offer comfort. Sasha, the Russian, made an expression of distaste, a ticking noise with his tongue. The policeman was simply wide-eyed, as though *he* were fourteen. He was indeed a simpleton.

To compose herself, Anna began to assemble the facts. "It was an accidental explosion?"

"Just a house. No one hurt," the policeman reassured. He

nodded to Sasha. "He can check on his computer, as the news comes in. I can even show you on my police radio." He produced a hand radio from his police belt. "Listen," he said. "Just firefighters talking."

Radio voices spoke back and forth. Several different voices, incomprehensible to Anna. The voices were calm but the situation was confused. Sasha said, knowingly, "They speak their code."

A radio voice said, "We have confirmed, 11-44, 11-44.

"Roger. Is that two? Or one? You said 11-44 twice? A double 11-44?"

"Negative. Single 11-44. Just one."

"What does that mean?" Anna asked the policeman, to allow him a moment of expertise. Then she read her answer off his ashen face.

Chapter 24

At work, right away, Fat Wakin called me in. "Jimbo, am I right, Malcolm Trent is your guy?"

That question dropped my jaw. It was ten hours after Trent had driven away from the clerk's house. Before it exploded.

However, Wakin didn't note my reaction. He had his own concerns. He didn't pause. He read Becky's notes off a stenography pad. "Another vandalism at his restaurant. The big place, the Wharf House. Between midnight and four."

"Last night?"

"Yeah. It says here 'windows' and 'tires.' A vehicle there in the parking lot. Torched it with . . . gasoline. Or part of it at least. Someone shot ball bearings through the glass. Cut the tires."

"Ball bearings?"

Wakin nodded, whistled to his own thoughts. Busy night. He hadn't had much sleep himself. But he sure did appreciate the view from that Chief's chair. He reclined back and forwards and spun a little, like a little boy visiting his dad's office. Maybe Wakin waited his whole career for the Chief to pass him the keys. Who knows what other people dream about. Wakin drummed the desk. "Write it up before you go on traffic."

I said, "Malcolm Trent is in bed with the Chief, right?"

My question made Wakin smile, smirk, scratch his sideburns. Until he saw my face. "Son, you know you look terrible."

"I'm fine. Slept rough. Banged my head on a tree."

"Mr. Trent is a prominent local businessman, and we all owe him our support."

"I owe him, do I?"

The way Wakin watched me, I probed my scalp to see if blood dripped again. My fingers came away pink.

I certainly looked forward to the time when I could figure out what the fuck was going on—just generally, in the world. That would be a relief. But that moment also seemed a long way off. I wiped my fingers on the inside of my pocket. "Trent wants some kind of investigation? Or he just needs a police report to make his insurance claim."

Wakin didn't answer but his face did. Trent just wanted the police report.

"*Pfft.* He's been fucking with that truck for weeks, right out in his parking lot. His biggest truck? He burned it for insurance. I saw him up trying to fix the freezer by himself, with a Swiss army knife. Cheapskate. Beyond belief, really. I'm sure that's what he burned, right, that top freezer unit?"

By this point I had Wakin's full attention. "Should be simple," he mumbled, because that was on his lips. But the long night caught up with him all at once. He rubbed his face, which responded to his touch like he was shaping a mound of loose tofu.

Wakin was not a rude man, so the next few minutes were strange. He simply ignored me. He took a moment for himself. He looked puzzled to find himself in this strange office, and his eyes wandered until they rediscovered the files in front of him on his desk.

The files were just the usual kind. The Chief had thousands, back to the time of kings, and the one confronting Wakin was stuffed with yellow papers. I'd seen Wakin with one of these yellow papers earlier, and I discovered that they were communications from the Chief. The Chief had a yellow pad beside his hospital bed and wrote down whatever occurred to him, little memos of advice and instruction.

While I waited and swayed with exhaustion, Wakin read one of these yellow notes, which meant he had to pick it up and raise it to the window. His massive brow creased, word to word, because the Chief wrote in cursive, with faded ink, from the button pens he stole from banks by the handful.

Finally Wakin spoke again. He said, "This Dr. Harris . . ."

I blew out. "Come on. The doctor didn't slash anyone's tires. Come on. Torching a truck. A Boston doctor."

I stopped because Wakin closed his eyes. However he gave a nod for me to continue. "Dr. Harris only does clever things," I explained. "The dog shit, for example. Then he did the fake menu for the display case. He took out that ad in the tourist newspaper."

"That's right, there was the menu," Wakin granted.

"I've got a copy in my locker. Hilarious. It was the same as the regular Wharf House menu, but he changed each entry slightly. All night the staff left it posted under the hostess's glass display. It sat there until they closed. I wish I could have seen. For the most part the doctor just sourced the food more accurately. So instead of the shrimp being 'wild-caught Atlantic,' they were 'farmed in Thai sewage lagoon. Their succulence derives from being fattened on rich human fecal matter.' Another one he had, it was this lobster cream soup, called a bisque—"

"Jim, Jim." Wakin shook his head gently, against the pain. This wasn't the conversation he wanted. He returned his private attention to the file.

This careful study made me curious about the file, so I went back later and read it. After hours. Do you know, the Chief sent Wakin three different memos to fire me? They were even going to pay me a month's severance. God knows why. The station would just go the rest of the summer season without a Parking Warden.

Of course as I stood there, I didn't know this was a big moment of decision. The yellow papers were on one side of the desk, and I was on the other side—a wreck, no sleep or shower, my hair Mohawked with watery blood, shooting off my mouth.

Wakin made his decision. His head rose slowly, like a granddaddy whale, dragging ten harpoons, seeking one last mighty bellow. "You think that's true?" he asked the air. "Pond catfish, for their bouillabaisse?"

"Jesus," I said. "What do you think? I never ate at Trent's shithole. Give me some credit. No, look, on Friday mornings, I wake up smiling, wondering what the doctor might have done on Thursday night. The doctor is an artist. It's the first experience in my life, anticipating art, appreciating art."

Wakin made a troubled grumble. He didn't like how I talked. Who did? No one. He fingered a "Fire Jim" memo like a totem, sweated it up, blotted the ink, but he never acted on it.

Why? Search me. Pick your reason. Malcolm Trent *was* a dick and a crook. Anyone could see that, from a hundred yards. And the Wharf House—of course Wakin, a man so fat, must respect his food.

It could be that Wakin was a rules boy, frightened I'd raise a lawsuit from the police union. You may imagine how the Chief phrased the "fire him" memo. I do hope I've given you some idea just how bad the Chief was. Though he was at death's door, he sure wasn't going to take responsibility. Not going to be left holding the bag on an actual decision. I forget the exact words, but he wrote as though Wakin had been badgering him and badgering him to let me go (that wasn't the case) and the Chief finally, tiredly, acquiesced to this plea. "If it must be so, you may be able to function with the position unfulfilled, but you can expect no backfill in manning."

I read quite a few of the Chief's memos, going through the files. They were unbelievable. The Chief would rally out of his prescription-drug cloud to insist on some point of vague wisdom ("attitude is of number one importance"), some cryptic command ("always forefront the equipment budget"). If I'd been Wakin, when the first sheaf of those arrived from the hospital by courier, I would have stacked them in the men's room for ass paper.

Actually, as I look back, my best guess . . . I think I misjudged again. Could be. Fat Wakin was a more serious character than I ever credited. I'm not saying Wakin had all of life figured out—he was fat as a planet—but he sat across from me, closed the file decisively, and put on some efficient, black-framed eye glasses. They were combat infantry glasses. They looked terrible on him. That gave me that whiff: Maybe the man wasn't a fool.

"Jim, you know you're a temp. We cut your last paycheck on October 1. I don't imagine you're going to stay on the island after that. You won't be back for us next season."

"Okay. Sure."

"You'll never be a policeman. Anywhere. I don't see how that could happen. But at the same time these complaints against you . . . none of these complaints . . ." He raised his open hands above the file, baffled as though the waiter had just set down in front of him a plate of shit.

At that point at least I understood that the open file was a Jim Hawkins file. A litter of yellow memos. Mixed in had been some white papers, formal complaints from citizens.

Wakin knew all these complaints were bullshit. Now, the world being what it was, he couldn't say that. He couldn't speak the actual words. In fact, he sweated that he'd even *thought* the *thought.* Just the implication, hanging unarticulated in the air, caused him to sweat grease and backtrack. "Any complaint is serious, of course. We take them all seriously . . . Government responds to the citizen . . ." He went on like that for some time.

"Jim," he said, and I tuned in again. "This is my office now. The nonsense with the Wharf House stops today. Whatever the nonsense—Trent? Harris?—this is the last incident I want to hear about. I'll phone the Cambridge police that you're coming. You go. Meet with Dr. Harris on *his* ground, in *his* clinic. See if that doesn't indicate to him that we're serious."

When I was leaving the office, Wakin called after me.

I went back in with a light heart, favorably disposed toward this man. Maybe Wakin had some sense. Maybe he would even listen. What would I tell him? Get up, I'd say. Rise out of the boss chair. That chair is really the electric chair. Straps grow out of the arms and hold your wrists. You may be strong, you may be weak, but we're all susceptible. The boss chair will trap you. Get on your feet, man, and run. Or amble.

But Wakin did not call me for a chat. I didn't reach the threshold of his room. He was already enough of a boss that he wanted to call out a parting shot: "Jim. When you show up at the doctor's office, don't groom yourself. I mean more than you already have. Wear that face. Look exactly like you do now."

CHAPTER 25

On the drive to Boston, Anna took little notice of her cop. This "Jim"—such an American name. He was useless to her. Here, a policeman in his own land, he had fewer friends, connections, and resources than she did. At times he seemed frightened of her, shifting in his car seat to keep distant. At other times he forgot she was there, because he forgot there were other humans on the Earth.

He took the police car onto the ferry. The car's markings made them a subject of interest to the uniformed attendants and other passengers. The cop did not notice this attention.

Once parked, other passengers left their vehicles in order to enjoy the boat ride from the railing, where they could see the ocean. Her cop did not seem to conceive. He shut off the engine and stayed in place, as immobile as a reptile in a terrarium, or a robot without mission, his hands still in place on the steering wheel. He stared through the windshield ahead with such intensity that the ferry attendant didn't dare intrude.

This attendant hovered, returned several times, looked pleadingly to Anna, spoke to the other passengers—"he's taking a local car off island?" After a number of passes, he gave up. Of all this, Anna was convinced, the cop noticed nothing.

He had picked up Anna that morning. They had arranged a plan to visit Watterson, the city official who had kept Kat's passport in a desk at his home. They had made this appointment during their very first conversation, with Sasha hovering. Then came the shock: the 11-44 code, a dead body found amidst the wreckage of Watterson's house. After a few terrible hours, this body was identified as the man Watterson.

Anna and the cop never discussed how this changed their plans. In the morning Anna became aware of her housemates calling nervously, room to room. A police car idled two meters from the house's front door. Anna went downstairs and out. The cop leaned across and called out his open window: "The Russian found one of the ladies in Boston."

"I know," Anna said quietly. The other two passports. One of the women was a student: Valya, another Ukrainian. "She won't be at her college. They have a break for the summer months."

"It's worth a look. The Russian emailed her, but *pfft*, she's not going to respond to a random stranger. Look, I have to go to Boston anyway. I have to drive there this morning. The Russian's stymied. He can't find a phone number."

"The Russian?" Anna asked.

"You know." The cop put out a flat hand to indicate someone short. "I think he gave me his name as 'Sasha.' That seems like a girl's name, so I suspect I got it wrong."

"Sasha is not a girl's name. Sasha." She could not keep the disbelief out of her voice.

With this cop, Anna had the worst sort of bond—with "Jim." He was both cause and witness of the worst hours she had ever spent. He had blundered in with her sister's passport—discovered in a government official's home—and Anna had scarcely started to breathe again when the cop's radio informed them of the dead body. The pattern seemed clear: first Kat's documents found in the house, then, in the house wreckage, her dead sister.

Upon hearing this, Anna promptly vomited a green puddle

onto the floor of the house kitchen. The cop Jim would rather clean that up than find out anything. Anna sat paralyzed, tasting her own bile, for three hours, between when the firefighters discovered a body and when Jim finally confirmed that the corpse was that of a man. During those hours, she did not think anything. She sat in a trance. Over and over, she thought the beginning of the same thoughts. Her sister was . . . Her sister was . . . She caught these thoughts by the tail and pulled them back.

Cop Jim proved himself capable of nothing. Phone calls in which he made shy requests rather than demands. Short trips out into the night where he discovered nothing, and then returned as if she needed him! For his stupid, mute comfort, perhaps. Whoever he questioned on these trips, he didn't learn anything. He didn't dare to insist.

For Anna, in these hours, this strange, rich-man's island revealed its full strangeness. A dead body, yet treated as an afterthought. This wasn't the lead story reported on the news. No one shouted. No sirens. No rush. News of her sister was unimportant, while from every private yard in town, firework rockets rose and exploded to applause and cheers.

Then relief arrived, served in great slabs: the body was a man. This was confirmed. The man was Watterson. Everyone involved had known this all along. His death didn't excite comment. An ailing man died of his ailments. His last careless cigarette had killed him, and then, fallen and smoldering in his carpets, had blown his house to matchsticks.

Near dawn, Sasha returned. More good news. He had discovered one of the other passport girls on the website for a private college. Valya. She was a student. Normal girl, on a normal webpage (updated last week), alive and smiling among the face shots of a hundred others. Sasha had not rushed over to tell her this. He had known for hours. Now he was on his way to his job at the bakery.

Anna came out of her fog. Cop Jim was still there, still impotent on the phone. "Watterson just keeled over?" he asked. "How can we be sure?" Even with the explanation now clear as day, he still could not understand. "I'm just saying we might want to make further inquiry. Six tanks of oxygen and the man lights a smoke? No one is skeptical?"

Cop Jim showed up as they had planned. Anna regarded the police car, breath hissing through her teeth. She agreed to go into the city of Boston. She ran back upstairs for her things, ignoring the frightened, questioning faces of her housemates. In the privacy of her room she strapped her "skin" bag of vitals—money and documents—across her lower back. It was newly stiff with Kat's passport.

She checked her phone. It was off. She had shut it off to sleep. Now as it came alive, it indicated that she had missed a call. Anna checked the number. No number—shielded number. So it was not the debt-collection agency. There was no voice-mail message. Anna made a growl of frustration.

When she returned to the car, she noticed that Cop Jim's headrest dripped water. Because his hair dripped water. Down his shirt and down his seat. It was ocean water. She wondered, of course, but they had already tried and failed at enough conversations.

They did not drive immediately to the ferry terminal. Cop Jim drove past it. "We'll take the ten o'clock boat," he explained cryptically. From the steering wheel, his wristwatch faced Anna. It read 10:20. He noticed and tried to pull his sleeve over the watch face. "Plenty of time. Watch is wrong," he mumbled. The shirt sleeve was short by half the length of his forearm. "Inaccurate. Seventy minutes fast, minimum."

He was embarrassed of his watch and tried to reset it while driving, but the little knob resisted his enormous fingers. As he was doing this for her benefit, Anna turned away and hoped he would concentrate on the road.

Anna also had no way to explain any of this or what happened next. Beside a section of rocky beach, Jim slowed, searching. At a pull-out, he drove up beside a heavy, beaten old car.

He got out. She watched in the mirror as he retrieved a garbage sack from the trunk. An old Asian man came from the other car. A drug dealer? A snitch? The man's stained pants had been taken from a dumpster. No charity organization would offer such pants, dress slacks marked with great smears of putty. He was the poorest man she had seen on the island.

One after another, Jim lifted enormous fish from the garbage sack. The Asian man pointed and commented on each. Jim lifted them high for display. The fish were huge and silver, and blood dropped off in fans and curls, thickened with mucus.

Throughout the exchange, the Asian man moved and gestured. He pointed and jabbed his finger in Jim's face. But this was nothing. When the fish were in his trunk, the men talking, a question ignited him. "Ayee—Ayee—Ayee!" All at once he was incensed, clawing the air. He convulsed backward and forward, bent almost double. His rage was like a patterned dance. "Watt-er-son," the Asian man growled. The name tore his guts. "Watt-er-son."

Amidst the dance, the Asian man delivered a lecture. Cop Jim watched soberly, nodded occasionally. He reached into the other man's trunk. He rinsed his hands with a grab of ice cubes, tossed these aside.

Afterward, they drove to the ferry. Anna said, "Watterson was that man's friend."

Jim was pensive. "The opposite, it looked like to me. You

don't understand any Chinese, do you? I imagine that's what Lee speaks."

"No, I speak no Chinese," she said. She tried again. "He should be happy, because Watterson is dead."

"Uh—" Jim shook his head. "Happiness doesn't really come into play. For Old Lee. Watterson ripped him off. So I gather. Certainly he knew the man."

"Did Watterson sell him fish?" Jim glanced over to see if she were joking. Anna gave up and chose a blunt tool: "He looked in at me. You asked him about Ekaterina?"

"I tried. I mentioned Watterson's name. Old Lee got off on his own thing at that point, and *foom*!" Jim pulled at his cuff. "You saw. It's like prodding a weasel with a stick. I don't think he knew her."

Anna slid and set her jaw. Not a good enough answer. When your sister is missing, that was not a good enough answer. For a few kilometers of empty beach driving, she raged like the Asian man, but her convulsions were inside. When she spoke, it was with cold efficiency: "Tell me the exact words he said to you about Watterson."

Jim shrugged—hadn't listened, didn't care—but her anger pushed relentlessly. To mollify her, he strained to remember the details, pick up the bits where they'd fallen like lunch crumbs. "There is a tax," he said, "a fee. To preserve historical locations. It pays into a fund? There may be federal money in there as well, but all local businesses pay some kind of tax. Mr. Lee wanted the money. He owns places up and down the wharf. He's one of these restaurant guys.

"So, Lee hates this tax. That's a definite. But he also wants some of the payout. Instead payouts always go to the local boys, for their plans and projects."

"Historical locations?" Anna asked.

"Old places," he gestured out of the car. "For the tourists to see. You're from Europe, but for us all this counts as ancient history." Jim completed the loop: "Clerk Watterson distributed these funds. He was in charge of handing out money. So for Lee, you pay your history tax and it goes to put new asphalt shingles on the Wharf House, your competition."

Anna nodded. "Of course he is angry, if Watterson was a thief. A rip-off." Her voice savored the word.

Cop Jim exhaled from the mental exertion. After a moment he heard what she had said. "No. Lee's not mad because it's a rip-off. He's mad because he's not the one who steals the money. It is all a rip-off. All of it." Cop Jim gestured as before, to everything left and right.

Chapter 26

As I drove us back from Boston, Anna talked some about her sister, whatever came to mind. Ekaterina—Kat. As a student, she had always been out beyond her teachers, which they hated and revenged. She was a champion at doing artistic dives off of a board or a platform. Spoke all languages, picked them up on the fly. Had a voice that melted the choir.

The stories were scattered, halves and quarters. They were like the little refresher stories that soldiers tell one another, after you'd already heard the long version a thousand times. With soldiers, you sort of come to refer to these by keyword: tell about the drunk buffalo, tell about the gate at the prison.

Anna loved her sister. Some of Anna's details—coaches' names, rivals—some of this stuff not even a mother would have remembered. Though I gathered that in her family the mother was out of the picture early. Their dad was a famous national athlete, so Kat became the competitive diver and Anna the floor gymnast.

This talk bubbled up from its own spring. It was not a flow I could guide. If I asked a question, Anna would either ignore it or shut up. Five minutes of silence, then she would see something out the window—she liked the Native American words, the place names—and off she would roll again.

"Our church collected the money for the airplane ticket, and then she came over. For the youth festival. In Denver. It was a festival for Catholic youths."

"Last year? Or 2008?" I asked. Nothing. "Did she plan to stay? Was that the plan all along?" Nothing. "Right," I said. "I forgot to tell you, I'm the immigration police. So keep your secrets. Don't tell me anything."

"Why come back to Sevastopol?" Anna said, quietly.

"You spoke to her while she was here?"

"She sent a card."

"If she came over with this religious group, have you talked to the priest?"

Apparently this question was stupid enough to be a show-stopper. This time Anna's silence lasted to the first bridge. She gazed out, from a million miles up.

Too bad, but Anna was one of these people who hated me at first sight. I described this phenomenon. A certain number of people can't stand the cut of my jib, for whatever reason. Like the Chief. The occurrence was perhaps more rare in women, but I hadn't met a lot of European women, and I guessed that was a factor. She hated me down to the air I breathed.

At Dr. Harris's office, earlier, the receptionist had also assumed Anna was in mourning. If Anna and I had been at the level of offering each other advice, I would have told her that she encouraged this misimpression with the hat she wore. Not only did she wear all black, head to toe, but she also wore a black hat, to no purpose. It had no brim. It was like a cup hat, and it looked like it went with a veil, maybe stored up inside like a mosquito net in your helmet liner.

What else can I tell you about my visit with the good doctor? Not much. You meet the artist face to face, there's bound to be disappointment. I assumed he wouldn't even talk with us—I'd leave him a note—but from the back office his voice called, "What-what? Examine room two, room two!"

Anna and I were buzzed back, and we weren't alone thirty seconds before Dr. Harris blew through the door. We sat while he paced the carpet. He ignored his scheduled patients for half an hour. In the waiting room they must have been dying in piles. But the doctor wouldn't let us go. He was giddy with the visit. Finally, finally here was a chance to rub his hands at his own evil genius.

I couldn't even prove he had been back to Nausset Island, could I? That was how carefully he had covered his tracks. What proof did I have? No proof, no proof at all. Ha ha! His eyes twinkled at high candlepower. He opened a line on his speaker phone and called Saul the lawyer, the better to rub it in. Lawyer Saul, at least, was horrified. He told Dr. Harris that he was busy with a client but that he should shut the hell up if he knew what was good for him. Of course Dr. Harris could not contain himself. What's the point of his screwing with someone if they don't know who?

One new development: Dr. Harris wasn't my buddy this time around. When I first met him on the ferry we had a meeting of the minds, because of our common feelings about the Wharf House. But now he wasn't just screwing Malcolm Trent; he was a mastermind criminal outwitting me, law enforcement in general, and all the world! He said, "I think I've demonstrated that you came all this way on a mistaken premise, son."

"Looks like it," I agreed. "Bully for you." I wasn't there to take notes and gather details, just to put the ball on his half of the field, to keep the goalie honest. "As I explained, what's happened now is that Malcolm Trent is making good money off his insurance, because of your pattern of tricks. Maybe he'll send you a Wharf House shirt and gift certificate. You can get the wife out there again. Cleanse your colons.

"There's also a rumor that he hired some guy to wait in the parking lot and kick your ass. If that happens, be sure you give me a call, down at the police station. We'll be very responsive to your needs."

Before Anna and I left, the nurse wanted to clean my head with brown iodine.

Then Anna and I were off for St. Helmett's. Not a huge school, nor an easy place to find. It was outside of Boston, not really in the city, with the same subtle signage as they favored on Nausset Island—maybe a fence post marked, or a special rock, but nothing you could read from a rolling vehicle. We were in among the college buildings and still you couldn't be certain. Nice place, though. Lawns and stone, but none of it straining ten stories into the sky, nothing trying to be the Tower of London.

Anna met with Valya, the Ukrainian girl. I was instructed not to even appear, so I killed time in the library, except when I had to be out re-parking the car. It was summer break. You could have put a car against any curb for a week without troubling a soul, but the campus cops had everything coded by paint color, and with the campus deserted they were dying of boredom. So they chased me around, marking chalk on the tires with a pole they could deploy out the window of a golf cart.

The young guard at the entrance booth never did get over my official car. I told him fifty times, I wasn't there on cop business. When Wakin sent me out in the first place, I think he just assumed I'd take the bus the whole trip to Boston, and now I started to see why, if this blowhard was any indication. One police car out of jurisdiction, and he carried on like a primitive during a solar eclipse.

All the while, I'd loop back, and Anna kept talking to the other Ukrainian girl, who from a distance looked a lot like her. Dark hair, dark clothes, porcelain complexion.

★ ★ ★ ★ ★

At the library, deserted, I also excited personal attention. "May I help you? May I help you?" The librarian was a featherweight. Black guy. All right, sure, I told him. I notice you have stuffed birds under glass. Do you have any heath hens? No? How about plain grouse? I could use a few old feathers. Negative. Well, could I look at a map of Nausset Island?

Unlike the campus cop, this guy quickly became accommodating. He had a special table for maps, and he wasn't content to give me a standard map and leave me to it. He kept bringing more. He was a librarian of antiquities. I barely had one map unrolled before out came another, even older and less accurate. I was only trying to assess my route for when I swam around the entire island.

"I live there," I pointed out. "Squab Island."

"Here it's *Mattaquab.*" He checked the computer at his side. "Wampano word, or at least northern Algonquin. It means 'shark.' "

" 'Shark'? Really? You're kidding me. 'Shark Island.' "

His type was the overly-helpful librarian. He left and returned with several dictionaries of Native American tongues. Neither of us had a use for them, so he returned attention to the top map. "Here it's a federal reserve. You see the coding?"

"They had an old fort there," I explained.

"It's gone?" To answer his own question he flipped to the lower layers on the table, the contemporary maps. The most recent had red cross-hatching. A nature preserve.

"Yeah," I explained. "The fort's all gone. Then for a while some rare birds had the run of the place—the heath hens I was hoping to see. But they seem to have been burnt out. It's just me and the old signs: Heath Hens and Unexploded Ordnance."

"No . . . wait . . . no . . ." He consulted the legend on a middle map. "The fort is gone by 1968. So any explosives would be more than forty years old."

"Right! More than fifty. I swim around down at the footings and it's all cannon balls rusted to half their weight. I've been over the island head to toe and found only one locker, and that was pre–World War II, with maybe three viable shells."

Tiny gave me a new look—didn't believe—thought I was trying to con him—sell him phony war antiques. He began peeling back his oldest, best maps, too precious to risk.

For their talk, the foreign ladies in black sat on the concrete step of the science building. I had imagined this would be the kind of meeting where they would drink coffee at a wire table, but in fact I never saw Anna buy anything to eat, ever, and maybe the other girl was the same. They didn't have any money for special coffees. They got over to America, and if they held on, it was by their fingernails.

The two ladies looked alike, from the same part of the world, but they were not friends. By no means could you say this conversation was friendly. Okay, not every culture was a smile culture; I knew that from my foreign travels with the army. But I don't think I was misreading the hostility in their encounter. They were getting in cuts. What didn't make sense is that they kept talking.

My third time checking, Valya saw me, and she honestly rose to make a run for it. Anna talked her down. I kept my distance but didn't hide. At this point I was pretty sure the campus cop had called a wrecker to tow the car.

In parting, Anna opened her purse, gave the other lady her passport. I would have started with that: Look what I have! Here! But for Anna this handover was not a sure thing. On the other lady's side, the response was similar. She took her passport, but she didn't exclaim with gratitude. Maybe she would take it back; maybe she wouldn't. She didn't like the touch.

When I got Anna in the car, I asked, "Did you get an address?" I figured we would drive right to her sister if she was staying local. The question made Anna sulk behind her bangs, but I waited for an answer because we arrived at the gate intersection. The guard booth was empty. That was worrisome because that guard stationed there had been the most frantic to clear me from the campus.

I stopped. I had to turn east or west. In the center mirror, motion: the campus cops gathered with their fleet of golf carts. I checked the passenger mirror and noticed Anna's hand on the door handle. She was deciding bigger things. Stay or run.

"I can drive you anywhere," I told her. "Really anywhere."

She shook her head in frustration.

I frowned. "Look, I'm going to have to move out here. These bozos . . . But I can drive you to Florida if you want." Anna was silent. I drove and didn't talk again until I started to recognize the roads. "Did you get a phone number for your sister? Anything?"

She spoke quietly. "They had the same boyfriend."

"Yeah?"

"Donald Frobisher."

"Frobisher? I've seen that name."

"Who is he?"

I shrugged. "I saw his name at Watterson's. I don't know, really. I think one of these island lords. Self-declared."

"He pays for the college fees."

"Does he?" I found a sign for the Massachusetts Turnpike. "So how was it that Watterson had her passport?"

"They pass them around, okay?"

"What, the passports? Why?"

"My sister," she said, with scaling hate. "They pass around

the girlfriends." She hated me that much more. For making her say it. And by association.

Chapter 27

Lee had someone watching the ferry. On the beach road, suddenly Lee's dreadnought Chrysler loomed in the center mirror, closing at a speed that would have been shocking even if I had been parked.

He knuckled right up to my bumper, though I waved him off. I certainly hadn't acquired any fucking fish while I was in Boston, and no one wanted to prolong this outing. Anna sat cross-legged on her seat, fizzing like a centrifuge with bad bearings. She held me responsible for the failings of my various citizen groups: all policemen, all dwellers on Nausset, all Americans, and all men.

However, Lee was Lee. He moved his car out of lane and started alongside, suggesting he might nudge me off the road, a maneuver you'd employ on a rival bootlegger. His vehicle wouldn't show the dent, and whatever else you might say about Old Lee, no one could doubt his Mad Max authenticity. Eh. I slowed and parked. Got out. Anna glowered.

"The bluefish are here," Lee pronounced, waddling up in his sticky slacks.

"Bluefish? Oh please Christ."

Lee was already into it like a chainsaw. How many bluefish he wanted. When he wanted them. How prepared. How worthless they were to him, even as bait or chum—a nuisance in his kitchens. He bargained himself from ten dollars a fish to five. Each fish as long as his arm.

"Blues usually aren't that big," I said, holding my wounded head, "and they're hard to spear."

Out of Lee's car came a beautiful Asian girl.

Eighteen? Seventeen? Younger? Whatever her age, the look was illegal. It had never been seen on island. Out of nowhere, it was a touch to the front of your pants. Except that it wasn't out of nowhere. It was out of the backseat of Lee's garbage-mobile.

At that time Mr. Lee presented me with a fresh bluefish, which I took. The fish was proof to refute claims I had made or implied. I held it by the bloody gills. "The bluefish are running," I explained to the Asian beauty. Lee would not accept the return of his fish, unsatisfied by my superficial study of it.

"Finally you are investigating the corrupt Watterson," she said. Lee barked something at her, in angry Chinese. She said, "My father will help you."

"Nah, Watterson is dead."

The girl listened to her father. There was no option on this, Lee was so emphatic. She waited politely until he was finished, then turned to me. "Watterson made a number of contracts that were not in the best interests of the city. My father would like you to study these. Some of these contracts should be declared fraudulent."

"Declared fraudulent?" This had to be a pretty free translation of anything old Lee wanted. Based on tone and gesture I'd guess that he wanted Watterson's corpse disinterred for him to desecrate. "Ma'am. Miss. I think there's a general misunderstanding of the powers of the Parking Warden."

"That's funny. 'Ma'am.' " She smiled. Nothing, blank face, then amused. Back to blank face. A slight shift of her body called attention to the perfection of her slim torso. Her posture alone blew your glands.

How was she dressed? I would tell you that she wore a tee shirt but her garment bore no relation . . . Let me go back to the way she moved. Her moves had a start and stop, like a single move of a game piece. She moved, then she stopped and it was my turn, which I was unprepared to take. I'd never seen a woman like this at all, so to see her emerge from Lee's junker was beyond the plausible.

Lust does not guide my life. In any case my interludes with Sarah left me empty and sexless, without gender. What I describe is an objective phenomenon.

Of course this display was in front of Papa Lee, who had shown himself to be a volatile character. Was Lee a joke or a truly dangerous man? I'd never decided. Some long-time island cops would refer to his criminal connections, like, "Lee, that old gangster."

The daughter told me of her father's grievances. She spoke perfectly of course, in short telegraph notes, after which she would stop and close her lips. Then another telegraph note. It was comparable to how she moved. If she asked a question, she didn't really inflect it as a question, so I didn't have warning that I was to prepare an answer.

At some point I'd had enough watching my own fumbles. I interrupted. "No, no, look, I'm serious, I don't care about mill levies, set-asides, the chamber of commerce . . . At all. Don't care. All bullshit. If you want to play with the machine, get used to its creak, you know? The machine is going to creak."

She did not know. She looked blank.

I said, "Understand that I'm going to do exactly nothing about this."

I might not have spoken. She said, "The balance on the account is eight point two million dollars."

"Eight point two million?" The string around her neck held a computer thumb drive. She removed it with a modest, chaste motion. Because I had still held the fish, she came and placed it around my neck, touching me to do so. "For a preservation fund? I presumed it was a couple thousand, you know, to buy bunting and decorations. Flowers and parade floats."

Lee grumbled a lot. I don't know if it was the liquid sex of his daughter or that he had no share in the conversation. Finally he took the bluefish back, aggressively; it was not mine to keep.

"It's a half-percent sales tax," she said. "On all liquor, food, and novelty."

"That's everything, out here. Eight point two million? That would buy a lot of shingles for the Wharf House."

"Oh, I know that restaurant."

"Really?" A creature so elegant could never go near a place called the Wharf House.

"You can take me."

In context, this was not a reasonable request. These roadside turn-outs were a carpet of bottlecaps, glass fragments, and faded strands of the plastic rope favored by sea communities. The air smelled overwhelmingly of rotten fish. A mad Chinese man grumbled and rumbled and any minute might come over the hood of his car.

She knew. She had a bit of game on her face. Risk was part of the game. "How tall are you?" she asked.

"I don't know. Um. Six foot something."

"The money was going to a developer named Cunningham."

Old Lee was puzzled by the speed with which his daughter spoke, but now, offered that name to chew, he hit it like a pit bull: "Cunningham, oh, oh, Cunningham."

"Cunningham died, too," I said. "So there's a plot or something? I presume there's some plan to steal this pile of cash?"

"No. The funds purchase capital improvements. The money has a hold on it already. So it's already committed to be spent. We don't know to what. We don't know for what." She shrugged happily. She had a slip of paper. "It's my number. It's okay if I give you my telephone number?"

"I'm kind of involved with someone. Thanks."

"I don't care. I was joking."

"If it's really that much money, there probably are police who handle this. Even out here."

"But there is no crime." She was surprised I thought so.

"Agh. Well then it's just business," I said. "Feed the machine. As I said. That's business, by definition. Charge as much as you can. Hope your buyer is desperate; hope he's got a sick child. Give as little as you can in return. If possible, switch the product to something worse."

"Oh. Are you a communist? I'm just asking, just personally."

All the while, Lee offering grunts, repeating important words. He misunderstood that Cunningham was a communist, and that set him off.

The lady watched her father politely for a moment. I took the opportunity to see whether she had written her name on the slip of paper. She hadn't, but there was a phone number. "Now there's blood on it," she noted.

"Fish blood."

"That's okay. I don't mind."

Lee barked something. To his daughter. She bowed her head demurely.

"Bluefish." I nodded to him. So he wouldn't rip the exhaust system off his shit car and beat me with it. "Bluefish."

Chapter 28

Sarah didn't find me until five o'clock that night. I don't know how she found me at all. There was a rental place a few blocks off the park, deserted nine days out of ten, with a family-sized rope hammock between the back oaks, perfectly shaded in the hours of the late afternoon.

Sarah called out something as she came through the gate, so I was opening my eyes when she took hold of one of the frame sticks and flipped the hammock. I hit turf and heard my own breath go out, *POOM,* the sound of a ball flattened by a bus. I rolled under instinctively to protect myself.

From all directions, in all ways, I'd taken a pounding the last twenty-some hours, and Sarah's anger was among the hardest to process. Had I broken a date? Her understanding was that I'd "spent the day in Boston with a maid." Could she be jealous? Rumor networks were abuzz.

No, no, I told her, that was all wrong. The girl was just a girl, a hundred-pound gymnast, and she hated my guts. To say so cost me all my gathered air, and it only made Sarah angrier.

Part of Sarah's theme was that I was difficult to get hold of. This complaint is a symptom of so many people carrying telephones in their pockets.

Finally I hit upon the right thing. I said, "Wakin sent me. Wakin sent me to Boston."

"He sent you? Detective Wakin?"

I lay there, appreciated the quiet time.

"Why?"

"That character who pranks out the Wharf House. He's a Cambridge doctor. I was supposed to ask him questions." I tried to explain.

"What happened to your head?"

"Just now? Or the bandage? They put that on at the doctor's office. Same doctor."

For a moment Sarah stood and breathed, making or weighing resolutions. She saw me watching. "Don't you want this?"

She meant her body. Sweaty from the summer's day. Didn't bother her. She understood what enhanced.

"Of course," I admitted.

"How can you stay away?"

These were serious questions. So perceptive, it was uncanny. Her dark eyes, with their framing of makeup, went through me like an X ray. As it passed, this X ray also left behind its feather touch.

Was I afraid? What of? Silk sheets and indulgence? I said quietly, "It's been twenty-nine hours."

She nodded. The precision of the number mollified her. "Get in the car."

At her apartment, after a while, she said she had things for me. Things? The bed creaked. Vapors rose from skin, tufts of smoke. What kind of things? Clothes. She turned on a light. In forty minutes, we were to attend her grandmother's fete in the park. Grand party. An orchestra came over on the boat.

I've told you I don't get to play much of a hand in my relationships. Instead I wait. I see what I get dealt. What Sarah dealt me was evening clothes cut to fit my particular measurements. A whole suit of clothes. She produced the bag from the closet. On the hanger the getup was heavy as body armor.

The gifting ceremony was quiet. I unzipped and lifted away

the jacket. The dark fabric could appear either blue or black. It was not fabric I was familiar with. "This is a preparation of wool?" I asked. I laid the jacket across my bare legs. The fabric was not army wool, not winter wool, not wool as it existed on a sheep.

How did Sarah know my measurements? I asked. My voice was rusty with disuse. No one knew my measurements, because no one had ever taken them. But Sarah knew. She had measured my body with her hands, and translated that into what the tailor needed to know.

The necktie was silk, Sarah assured me. I turned my attention to that piece, which flashed luminous color like the belly of a snake. I had worn neckties in the past. I thought maybe if I put the two ends in place around my neck, my hands would remember the knot.

The last item was a wristwatch. This arrived in its own display case, like jewelry. The watch was steel and must have been expensive because Sarah looked away modestly when I held it. I was still in bed with the shirt and the pieces of the suit across my legs.

"This is a mistake." I set the case aside on the bed sheets.

"Try it."

"Eh. You can't show me to your grandma. She'll chew her champagne glass." I told Sarah about my final exchange with the old lady. When Megan died, I offered my condolences. After all, Mrs. Yellow and I knew each other. Once or twice a week I came and drank Cokes on her porch. Not anymore, however. When I started talking to Mrs. Yellow about Megan, Mrs. Yellow's face shrank back into itself, in revulsion. She said, "Megan wasn't for servicemen. She wasn't for the Parking Warden."

Sarah listened to this account. She was a realist and didn't apologize, simply explained: "It's different with me. Granny knows I fuck. That's always been the difference between me and

Megan. Put it on."

I cleared my throat. The suit weighed on my legs like a bear skin. I found the watch and extracted it from its display housing. "Looks great," I said.

"Other wrist," she said. "You wear it on the other wrist."

"I've already got one, for my left." I showed her. My watch had once looked expensive, but it hadn't fooled anyone in a long while. Gilt peeled off the individual nodes of the band, so it looked like a smile that was missing teeth. "You see it has a compass." I showed her. "If I'm swimming out in the fog . . ."

I showed her how my other watch was a Mecca watch. It had a bubble compass, so a Muslim could face Mecca when he needed to. Five times a day this watch would ring a bell to remind a Muslim to turn and say his prayers.

"You can't wear two watches to the party."

Now, you may think, Rich Lady! She orders you around like a servant! That wasn't the situation. Yes, Sarah had her ideas about how things should be. This is the trap of money and Sarah wasn't immune. No one is. A lady with extensive property makes a decision every ten minutes—which car? which restaurant? which house?—and the habit becomes a trait. Authority rewires the brain. You forget what people are for. That happens to everyone.

However, resistance intrigued Sarah. Disagreement intrigued her. She raised her head like a dog that caught a radical new scent. I tried to put her off. I held the fresh-cut shirt. "Look. You guessed right on the sleeve. The cuffs cover the wrists."

She wasn't distracted. "You can't wear two wristwatches at one time." She watched me from out of her thick hair, the inner inch dark with sweat. "You are a Muslim?"

"Right," I laughed. "I'm a devout Muslim. No." I explained how the watch was a gift from my army days. I was deployed to western Africa. This deployment happened to be to a gold mining town. Typical me—I chuckled—every other soldier in my unit left town with nuggets and ore. They had socks full of gold ore. My lone souvenir was the wristwatch, gilded with the only fake gold on the continent. "Soon it will give up the ghost." I shook my wrist. "The loose bits? The salt kills the gears. These days the prayer alarm goes off whenever it wants." On my right wrist, the new steel watch clung firm, heavy as a lead sinker. "How wonderful to have a replacement, for when it dies."

We were both still riled from sex. A couple of wolverines, disengaged from a clench, circling. "Your army days. Tell me." She put her hair back but with nothing to hold it, no band or clip. She did it again. It was a beautiful motion. It showed her living shape. "Tell me what you did."

"*Pfft.* So boring."

"But that watch is special to you."

"Special?" I said. "Don't condescend. Don't mistake me for a kindergartener. Special?"

Sarah drew herself away. Her expensive gifts lay all around. I hadn't even thanked her. She drew back and leaned against the closet door. The pose wasn't angry or sexy or contrite or anything, really. It wasn't a pose. Her confident eyes focused on a distance that wasn't there.

I blew out. "It's empty sentiment. I'm aware of that. A man gave me his watch, and then he died. He was a newspaper man, reporter and editor. He ran a newspaper almost by himself. It was better than the island paper here. More substance than the island newspaper, with its fishing forecasts. Its quilting advice."

"This man was your friend?"

I shook my head. "Maybe. It doesn't matter. The watch wasn't a gift. He gave it to me to keep safe. He was getting arrested. They were putting him into a prison. Anomabu was its name." I opened my hands. Years of thought coalesced. "I shouldn't have let it happen."

I listened to my brave words, hanging in the air, and entertained private memories. Probably no harm in communicating these memories, in revisiting them in the tidy parcels that were sentences.

All day, twice an hour, I'd wince. Reminders leapt from behind any random bush. "The man I mentioned was killed. I would have brought the watch to his wife, but she was gone, too. Maybe not dead. Maybe just fled town." I lifted my fingers. "It was a mess."

The newspaper man. I don't want to make him sound like an angel. He'd written articles about a local gang that had refashioned themselves as Islamists. Really they were just the sons of the previous regime, trying to steal back into power. Because they were kids, they wanted attention. Well, declaring themselves Islamists certainly got them attention.

That's why we had come to town, the US Army. Supposed to be a secret but of course everybody knew. The gang wasn't frightened at all by our arrival. They were complimented. They were flattered. The next step, they'd threaten, issue inflammatory statements. And then the next step, they'd have to kill someone or blow something up. The best way to understand these kids is a TV show desperate to keep its ratings. Violence is the only currency they have, and they want to buy themselves some air time.

They're a big deal now, but we could have stopped them in their tracks. Instead of sending in Army Rangers, we should have sent in a Hollywood promoter and signed the boys to do an after-school comedy show (*Runner Bear and Friends!*)—anything to get people watching—We should have signed them to tour the globe as a boy band that danced and clapped in unison.

The newspaper editor was a grown man, so he put their behavior and their threats in context. He knew the boys and talked to them. Wrote stories about them. Our captain used him as his best source for Intel, though the two didn't see eye to eye on the nature of the threat, and this caused friction. Sometimes the way the newspaper man spoke about matters, he sounded like any moment he would chuckle. Ah, those numbskulls! You supervise them yourself, Captain. The impetuosity of young boys! The captain did not compare his troops to the Islamist gang, and he had never chuckled in his life.

"*You* didn't send him to prison," Sarah said, reading my face.

"He handed me the wristwatch."

"But he was under arrest?"

The newspaper man surrounded by grinning guards. Not the kid gang but the local police. He'd pissed them off, too, because they extorted the highest-grade ore from the miners. He wrote about it. He pissed off the government because his newspaper printed stories about girls dying as prostitutes. The girls came to town and caught AIDS, then went back home to their villages. This government worried that this narrative would detract from tourism along their tiny section of coast, where they wanted to have resorts, and the brochures featured local girls wearing shell necklaces instead of tops.

The scene was at a tea shop. I heard the approach of the arrest party but failed to identify it. I failed to identify the sound of leg chains. How was I supposed to know that sound? The guards had found ancient leg chains, two-hundred-year-old museum pieces. I don't know if this was prison policy or the guards' invention to embarrass the older man. They were genuine slave manacles. The men had stripped off his pants and his legs were purple.

I could go on. This particular scene lived in my head more vividly than my hand in front of my face. I could describe those few minutes at any level of detail: the angle of sun—not the earliest—the second phase of the African morning. The smell of old man's liquid shit. The guards' glee and hyena laughter, which was directed at me, because they could show me this, and what could I show them?

I could tell Sarah every word said. Every picture made. What I could not do was listen, if Sarah were to forgive me for taking the wristwatch, sitting on my hands, and letting them march him to Anomabu. I said, "The patterns were there. I was slow to recognize."

"And where did all this occur?"

"What?" Her tone was businesslike. "Doesn't matter."

"Then how is this supposed to make sense to me? I don't even know when this happened. I don't know what country you were in."

"You're going to write my biography? Who cares? Maybe it happened yesterday, down by the ferry terminal."

Until Sarah spoke again, I forgot she was there. She was quiet and contrite. "Are you sure he died?"

"Yes. I found the body."

"You looked for his wife?"

I waved my fingers. Likely she was dead. If she wasn't, contact with me wasn't going to bring rainbows into her life. I said, "I'm not allowed back in that country. Whatever it is. Not really a country anymore. That part of the world. I don't know. I think about it. Soon I will have money for a ticket."

I was in a black mood, during the party, perceiving the world in its broader patterns.

Sarah was right about her grandmother. Mrs. Yellow didn't care that I arrived on the arm of her surviving granddaughter. There was no recognition. Her agate eyes roved near and far. Even when Sarah kissed her she hardly noticed.

For that close work I remained back in the damp grass, a section the orchestra had claimed for their instrument cases, and there I remained as Sarah made her social rounds. The only part of my suit she had measured wrong was the shoes, which gripped like moccasins. I wasn't going to walk without cause. In any case, I was unfit for chatter.

The party was a loose gathering of more than a hundred. Jackets and gowns. The orchestra attracted children and tourists, but an invisible barrier kept them back. They hovered along the edges.

They might have walked over and taken a glass of champagne. Why didn't they? The grass was public. The park was public. No guards walked the perimeter. The tourists nearest to me were three college couples returning from a beer run, clutching paper sacks. They had been lured in and then stunned by our lights, music, and general opulence. They were good looking—better looking than the invited crowd—presumably educated.

To test the invisible barrier, I stepped between the violin cases to the edge of my area. The college kids shuffled back to maintain the distance. They stepped off their sidewalk into the clammy grass.

There was a flow to the party. Most guests came round at some point to speak to Mrs. Yellow, who was settled now. She no longer searched the field. An older guy was at her side, sharing the host duties. He wasn't as decrepit. His handshake involved a little bow. He was slick, dressed in a white suit, with a yellow tie bright as a pennant.

A waiter came by with a plate of quiches. "Hold here," I said. "Right. Thanks. I'll deal with these."

He wouldn't relinquish the tray. I ate methodically, row by row. He put on a face and tried to catch the eye of one of his mates. I didn't see why he cared. He'd been through his rounds, moved all his prawn and chocolate strawberries, and I was doing him a favor by cleaning the least popular items off his tray, these greasy vegetable pies. Besides, it wasn't as if he owned the catering company. He was an older guy, scraggly, hired by the hour. Whatever gravity he was trying to achieve didn't hold up to examination—his gray hair pulled back with a rubber band, his maroon tuxedo fitting him like an organ grinder's monkey.

I finished. He asked, "Did you get your money's worth? There's some kale garnish here that you didn't finish."

"Worth about what I'm paying," I said.

He giggled. "Whatever. Mr. Big." He moved off, adding more as he turned, so I could only catch the tone.

Must have been a slow night in the catering tent, because next thing I know this waiter was back at my elbow. I waved him off—I'd had plenty—but he hadn't even brought his tray. He was there to mutter: Big shot. Big player.

I told him to bug off.

He said, "I'm asking you what you get for your five hundred dollars."

"Five hundred, eh?"

"For five hundred of our American dollars, does the congressman suck you?"

"Congressman? Hope not."

"Fat cats giving money to other fat cats." He nodded at me very seriously to drive this nail home. He was drunk or high or something.

"You're the great proletariat hope?" I said. "You're dressed in a purple tuxedo. You're not just a servant, you're a clown servant. Get back to the van and smoke a peace pipe."

His hands had the jitters. They fussed over his pockets. He wanted a cigarette but wasn't allowed. He was never big but now he went to half size.

I sighed. "So that's the congressman?" I indicated the old guy beside Mrs. Yellow.

My bad guess shocked the waiter. "That's Donald Frobisher,"

he said. He couldn't believe I didn't know. "You paid five hundred dollars and you don't even know where it's going? You're at a fundraiser for Congressman Avon. Do you have any idea how he voted during the recess session? Do you know a single vote—"

"Donald Frobisher. That's Donald Frobisher."

Naming calls. Frobisher looked up. He saw me across the violins and he knew that I was coming for him.

The waiter tried to stop me—"Hey, hey whoa. He's just a citizen now!"

Why did he care? He stopped me. He went to the ground, holding my legs. He didn't give up. He wrapped himself. It was like trying to walk while tangled in an extension cord. "Let go, man."

It quickly became a scene. Over at the drinks table, a young caterer shouted, "Dad? Dad?" Out he came running, in either hand a gin bottle with speed-pourer. Some of the musicians could see, and they lowered their instruments, which was contagious throughout their sections.

"I just need to talk to him," I said to the old waiter on my legs.

"He's out of the game. A citizen. Like you and me, buddy. Whoa whoa." How did this hippie read me immediately? It's true that violence wasn't far from my thoughts. He babbled, "Hate the office, not the man. It's the role, it's a role."

Frobisher moved away into the darkness, already past the grass and into the cars, leaving a wake of people turning after him, puzzled and concerned. The orchestra had ground down to broken silence, and the waiter's son was there speaking sternly—accusations, apologies?

"Jim?" It was Chet, looking lost. Chet—my fellow cop—was at the edge of the party. He hesitated at the invisible barrier. He truly wondered if it was me, because of the fancy suit. "Jim?

Hey. Your girl Anna," he said.

On an emphatic downbeat, the conductor restarted the orchestra on a rousing patriotic number.

"What's wrong?" I disengaged the last tentacle of the waiter.

Chet stepped his way back through people, assuming I would follow.

"What is it?" I caught up.

"You know that Russian girl? Anna?"

"She's from the Ukraine."

"There's some character looking for her. I think maybe her Visa is expiring?"

"Really?"

"Maybe her place doesn't think she can pay her bill?"

"I don't think a Visa is a credit card, in this case. It would be her permission papers. There's an immigration investigator?"

Chet explained how a rumor had come to him through a donut-shop girl he was courting. Not much of it made sense but soon Chet was just repeating himself and evaluating the donut-shop girl. He granted she didn't look like much but Chet thought I would be surprised once I had the details.

Now that we were talking Chet was reluctant to let me go. He kept looking at my new suit. "These ladies of yours, Jim. Where are they coming from? If I can ask. You got the no-kidding bombshell of this island. You've got Bo Derek on one hand. I didn't believe it at first." Chet's voice trembled. "That's your steady. And there was the girl in town who wanted you to lotion her back with sunscreen."

"I just sprayed her out of a can."

"I know. I wanted to say something to you about that. She unstrings her bikini. You had a woman holding her own tits on Slocum Avenue, and you choose to spray her rather than rub her with your hands.

"I didn't understand," Chet said, "but I want to try. I haven't been doing so bad, but this slow-play of yours . . . You've got this Russian girl, or from the USSR, and she is the tender spice. I can say that. She's a change of pace on anyone's dance card."

"She hates me. I'm not having sex with her."

Chet put his lips together—no reason to lie between men—he made no moral judgment. What he had to say here was important, and he got it out at once: "Then today the Chinese girl. Jim. I don't know what else to say. The Chinese girl. Today, she came up to me. I was out directing traffic in the intersection. I turned and holy shit, I blew in my pants.

"No, don't need to be modest. I mean, she talked to me. She came right up and asked about you. Honestly I'm trying to talk but I don't know what liquid is running down my leg, onto the road, if it's sweat or spunk or what. Onto the pavement."

"I didn't—"

"Jim, I couldn't even make love to her in a normal fashion. Like I said, I'm not doing too badly so far." He was pleading. "I don't mean this as a criticism, but I just didn't see it in you. And I wonder, eh, I wonder how, how you do it." His head was down for this. He looked up now, once, with hope. He saw nothing and accepted that as the way of things. "I was wrong, and I regret it. I guess what I'm saying is . . . respect."

Chapter 29

Sloan Jenkins came off the ferry onto Nausset Island, driving his silver Lincoln. He waved two fingers at a lady wearing the windbreaker of the Steamship Authority, a salute ("Keep doing what you're doing," he muttered) and drove slowly into the drowsy town. The loading kid had given him trouble about the length of his Town Car—over 17 feet he wanted to charge for a freight vehicle—but this lady put things right. She put the kid in his place.

All his life, boy to man, people had certain expectations of Sloan Jenkins, because of his big square frame, like Clark Kent, and his big square jaw with a prominent hinge, like a robot bulldog. Only now, past thirty, was Jenkins finally growing into this vision of what others had seen all along. For six years Jenkins had spent his day as a CPB officer at Logan airport, interviewing foreign visitors off the plane from countries whose close relationship with the United States didn't require them to have a formal visa, but whose individual history raised red flags in the computer. Jenkins served as the gatekeeper. He'd take a look, and you'd stay or go depending on whether he liked your face.

These days more than half of the foreigners Jenkins interviewed were Indian men, little guys who liked to look clever whether or not they spoke any English. They were here to scout for a job. Maybe someone in the US wanted to hire them—unbelievable—that wasn't for Jenkins to say. But job hunting was not a legitimate purpose of the I-94. Were they aware of the purpose of the I-94? It didn't seem like they were.

All day of that. Only his last interviewee was worth a look. Some guy's French girlfriend off the two o'clock from Nice. Where did these guys even find women like this? And get them flying over, delivering it right to your doorstep? She had that heavy hair of French women. Coming off an international flight they looked like they had just rolled out of your bed to fetch your coffee. They didn't wash as much but it looked okay. You could really get your hands in there.

This one's problem was that she had come to the States four times in four months, 33 days total. Flag went up in the computer, and Sloan called her in. Did she know how many days she had been over here? Did she? A month? Not a month—no—33 days. He heard her story, okay, he got it, but he wanted to walk her through the details. On each occasion she had stayed where? In this man's Cambridge apartment. She slept there, too? Was she aware of the procedures that governed the marriage of the US citizen to a foreign national, Packet 3? The I-145? Not interested. Not interested? To Jenkins this sounded like a pretty serious relationship, eh? This was not casual. The French lady smiled at the wall, which he hated. That was a slap right to his face.

Jenkins had full authority here. He could send her home by evening flight. He could give her one week. He could give her nine. It was his call completely, but really it depended on her, whether he liked what she said, and whether he liked how she said it. She let slip her boyfriend's name. Her boyfriend was an African? Jenkins consulted his paperwork, quite concerned. Was he even a citizen? Oh, African-American. Natural born, or naturalized? The woman looked away again at the wall and Jenkins snapped: "I'm sorry, are you distracted? You seem distracted."

One requirement for the I-94 was that she had an official return ticket, so Jenkins had that date to play with. Her ticket had her staying in the US for nine days. He thought to himself, *Just a quickie this time, eh?* His face became stone. Sorry, miss, he couldn't allow that to happen. She could have three days. That should be more than enough to contract any personal business.

She was stunned but did not cry. She was tired. She even gave him a wry smile at the inevitable (as he presented it), but too late for smiles. She asked him, would the airlines charge her to change her ticket? Jenkins leaned back as though the question were a surprise. That was between her and the commercial carrier. Did he look like an airline lackey?

After she left the office, Jenkins went over and sat in her chair. French women smelled good. But jeez, Indian men smelled bad enough to soak into the upholstery.

It was easy for Sloan Jenkins to be comfortable in his day job. The people he dealt with had just come from different time zones, exhausted by their international flights. For each of them it was a frightening surprise to be pulled from the cattle lines and seated in a windowless room across from an unsmiling, uniformed official, a man with a real jaw. Whatever their careful, expensive plans might be, these plans were already bending. Bookings had been missed. Airport shuttles. Worried relatives paced around the baggage carousels. Very few of the people Jenkins interviewed had trouble reading the situation and summoning the correct attitude. They were on their best manners.

Years of this had armored Jenkins with a shell of confidence: people behaved toward him a certain way, and he assumed this was because of something intrinsic to himself. He had always looked the part, and now he lived it.

★ ★ ★ ★ ★

Jenkins drove off the ferry behind one delivery van and in front of another, which huffed right on his tail. A young traffic cop directed him impatiently. On every side pedestrians came out into the road like it was a street fair. Jenkins panicked and turned to follow another passenger car. This was a mistake. He found himself driving in a slow-motion parade. It was a one-way street, the one-way street through the center of town. Local kids cruised in open jeeps and shouted to their friends. It was lawless as a third-world country, and Jenkins set his face, deeply unsettled and displeased.

Finally the street darkened and he wasn't hemmed in. He slid the Lincoln into a fat double spot to get his bearings. He engaged the parking brake. He removed his driving gloves. He breathed and felt better. He smelled French fries. He needed to find some cooks.

Jenkins was on Nausset Island to find a Ukrainian girl and put a fright into her. In his office at Logan this task would have been child's play, but here circumstances put him off his stroke. For one thing, this wasn't his job. He was a federal officer, yes, but he was on island as a tourist. For another, her I-94 was still valid. She hadn't been in country even fifty days.

"Bottom line, you're telling me you can't handle a teenage girl, traveling on her own?"—Jenkins's contact for information was a loudmouth named Coburn. Instead of providing aid or clear instructions, Coburn laughed at the difficulties Jenkins suggested.

Jenkins didn't appreciate being talked to in this manner but had no choice. He was over a barrel. His supervisor at the airport was sitting on a red-hot sexual harassment complaint that could not only cost him his federal job but also land him in jail.

Jenkins had rubbed his groin against the face of a girl from

Jakarta. She was flirting with him in her musical English but then she wasn't. She had also seemed penniless and she was—*that* was true—but her brother studied at BU, where student lawyers were clamoring for practice cases. The girl's account interested one of these nightmare indignant Latinas. It didn't help that Jenkins had forced the Jakarta girl to take his home telephone number, which he'd written on the back of his business card.

So all this could go away? With one weekend errand? Jenkins would take that deal any day of the week. He would even listen to this Coburn over the phone: "You can deport for anything, right? You deport them if they badmouth the United States."

"That British couple on TV? The facts didn't bear out the conclusions people were trying to reach. That situation was sensationalized by talk radio. Don't believe talk radio. A special judge will review . . ."

Coburn couldn't stand spineless nitpicking. "So if Anna Fedorchak threatened our country, you are telling me that you are powerless, as an officer of Homeland Security . . . I heard Anna Fedorchak make a threat to our country. To our president, to assassinate. No, actually that would be the greatest boon she could offer our land. I heard Anna Fedorchak express desire to overthrow the capitalist underpinning of our country. Is that enough? Bottom line . . . Or she lies on the form she filled out. She has a crime she didn't report back in Ukranistan. Come on."

"She's a bad seed?" Jenkins got hopeful. "If she has been called to court for a crime, or if she's visibly pregnant, third trimester . . ."

Coburn hung up on him, after a few more "bottom line" pronouncements.

On the drive from Boston and on the ferry ride, Jenkins had tried to make Coburn's fake accusations work. He wanted a clean story that did not require him to produce fake witnesses or forged documentation. None of his attempts were perfect. None gave him the feeling of comfortable power that he was accustomed to in his office. But if this Anna was really some kid here without money or family, okay.

If he could find her. Where did she stay? Coburn couldn't believe the question. He told him to ask some cooks. "Bottom line, get it done."

This cook's advice worked better than Jenkins could believe. He stepped into a pizza joint. It was closing but not with him standing there in uniform. When he walked in, the waitress and hostess and busboy all looked like they'd swallowed their gum.

Jenkins surveyed the room as though he'd interrupted a crime (and that he'd expected no better), then stepped through and washed his hands in the men's room. After that he carried straight on into the kitchen, arriving in the midst of hissed whispers. He had the complete attention of two sullen, Hispanic fellows who both claimed to be from El Salvador. Jenkins rattled out questions in brusque Spanish. He attributed their expressions of wonder to his command of their language, whereas in fact the men were shocked by his lunch-cart accent.

Anna Fedorchak? The fellows shook their head at the name. "She's short?" the dishwasher offered. He indicated with his hand.

Maybe she was, good to know, but Jenkins pressed each of his eyes with the heel of his hand and exhaled toward the wall. He didn't have a *tête à tête* with foreigners he was interrogating. His expression conveyed that at this point he couldn't even stand to look. He'd been lied to so long, so egregiously, that his substantial reserves of patience and goodwill had at last been mined out. The dishwasher glanced at his pal and hung his head, conscious he'd betrayed his caste.

Jenkins liked this dynamic a lot. He hadn't even asked these two for their documents. This was just like home, or even better. "I need you to stay here," he said. "Are you going to do that for me?"

He went out and had the hostess seat him for a meal in the deserted dining room. He ordered a pizza. While he waited he reflected that maybe his job was already done. Coburn had told him to find the girl and frighten her out of the country. But what did Coburn know? He wasn't an officer of Homeland Security. With no real excuse to hassle the girl, the best way to frighten her was to start immigrant rumors and let the girl's imagination run. She would hear something within the hour—God knows what kind of bullshit would trickle down, what with the mishmash of languages.

Jenkins ate complacently. He was deciding about the last slice of pizza when a man in a suit stood over him. The man was someone important, dressed like a mayor's aide. Big white man. "You are trying to locate someone?"

"Eh, nothing official," Jenkins answered, nodding a greeting. He sucked at the ice in his cup. "Sloan Jenkins. I work for Homeland Security. But this is nothing official." He offered his meaty hand. The man was slow to take it but then did—he cradled it in both of his before releasing. Jenkins indicated the empty chair across from him. "Are you local law? It's nothing official, or we would have called your people. But Anna Fedorchak? Any assistance appreciated, any assistance."

The man studied Jenkins. His expression wasn't unfriendly, but it was definitely unsettling. Hard and intense, as though he were preoccupied by a high fever. When Jenkins had indicated the chair, the man didn't follow the gesture but instead the movement of Jenkins's hand.

Jenkins found himself running on: "Not a serious problem. Nothing to sound the alarms. But, I thought, as long as I'm out here for a clam roll . . ."

The man looked pointedly down at the last slice of pizza, orphan on its greasy tray, then resumed his study of Jenkins's face. He wore a hard, mirthless smile. His mouth smiled but no other part of his face cooperated, and his pale eyes attempted no connection.

Jenkins realized that this guy was different—deaf, or demented, or taking drugs. If he went through screening at Logan airport, he would get not only his own room but *two* officers. Finally the man spoke softly: "Why are you looking for this girl?"

"Those two blabbered, eh?" Jenkins said, glancing back toward the kitchen. Though he'd been happy to start threads of rumor, now he implied that the cook and dishwasher would come to regret their treachery, which had in fact been inevitable—who could trust Latino cooks? "It's nothing at all. As I guess I told you."

With raised fingers, Jenkins dismissed the man from his table. But again the man was unable to read the gesture. He leaned closer to the hand as though Jenkins had been trying to call attention to his manicure.

This guy wasn't even a mammal, Jenkins concluded. He was like a chicken or a lizard. "Are you law?" He was skeptical.

"Oh, yes. I am with the Nausset police. Is the girl a criminal?"

"How about I let you know after I talk to her."

"It would be better if you told me right now."

Jenkins shook his head angrily. "Look. She's a visitor to the United States of America. That's a privilege, not a right. We can pull her I-94 at any time, if she violates the conditions of that privilege. If she makes threats to our national security. Other contingencies. We take those things seriously. We have to."

Jenkins's momentum was inevitable. He'd been trying out speeches like this in his head all day. Also, the speech worked.

The crazy guy rose and started to back off like a vampire shown a crucifix. "I'm out here on the island, right? So put it together. I guess there must be something that she's saying. Do you understand? Eh? I'm an officer at Homeland Security. We take it seriously these days. The planes hit the towers. I am not going to forget that. Never." By the time Jenkins drove this last nail, he was standing, speaking very loudly, and the crazy man had left the restaurant.

Jenkins felt pretty good. Lips loose, he shook his head like a giddy horse. Only the hostess was still in the room. "Jesus," he said to her. "Come on then."

She fetched the check. On her return she paused. The man with the suit was back. He was in the doorway. "Is this your car on Slocum Avenue? A white car. There's something on your car."

"There's a parking sticker," Jenkins explained, "but it's for security at Logan airport. I'm not here in an official capacity." His exasperation had run its course and he was almost patient.

"No," the man said.

Jenkins went outside. The picture was hard to process. The items were the common items of the world, but the combination was different. "It's a concrete block," he said numbly. It was. A concrete block was on the hood of his car. It had been dropped. Not from too high, but the block sat flat on the car's curved hood. It had pressed its own rectangle like a treat pressed into a warm cookie. "Jesus Christ. One of those fucking cooks . . . ?"

The man in the suit didn't join in this speculation.

Jenkins couldn't believe. He grabbed the block to hurl it off, but it was heavier than he realized and slid. It wiped an inch of paint. Jenkins used two hands. He dropped the block in the street where it fell as softly as on soil. The dent was deep—maybe deep enough to touch the engine. In sympathy every part of the hood had given up its correct lines.

"You want to get that painted," said the man in the suit. "If you're going to stay on island. This salt air rusts metal lickety-split."

"Are you fucking retarded or something?"

Jenkins repeated this insult, circling his car, holding his head, allowing his anger to build. But eventually he stopped. The man ignored him, but he was not someone you would ever choose to attack or be attacked by. His shape was savage. After a certain amount of silence, the man offered: "Just leave the block there, if it's not yours."

"I'll do that," Jenkins said.

"There is a night boat that departs at eleven."

"Are you telling me to leave the island?"

"There are repair shops here on island, but you'll get screwed, because you're just a tourist. The mechanics know you're a tourist. They have your whole vacation in hostage." In his stillness another thought came to the man: "The girl you were asking about. Anna Fedorchak. Why her in particular?"

"Do you know who she is?" Jenkins didn't have much hope left.

"I asked you why that girl in particular. Someone gave you her name. Who gave you her name?" As the man asked, it dawned on him just what a good question this was.

"Nobody." Jenkins opened his lock with his remote. "I'm not spending the night out here. I don't know why anybody would. The whole island stinks like a port-o-let."

The disappointed tourist act was unconvincing. Both men understood that Jenkins had given himself away. The man in the suit began to track him like a predator. "Now I want to know *your* name."

Jenkins got in and slammed his door. He showed the man his middle finger and pulled his car back recklessly, blindly. The man in the suit faced him for the whole arc, in a diver's posture, slightly crouched and with his shoulders back. At any moment he might dive. Any moment he might launch himself through the windshield.

On the freight boat back to the mainland, Jenkins locked himself in the tiny washroom. He tried on familiar expressions in the mirror, reminding himself who he was. He contemplated his massive jaw both straight and in semi-profile. On the sink, a cup of machine coffee sloshed to and fro.

Jenkins achieved something. He nodded affirmation to himself. He felt better. Though these slim gains were immediately forfeit when the crew began to shout. He understood that the commotion meant more trouble for him.

His car had been the first vehicle aboard. It was parked at the bow, at the tip of the wedge of vehicles. Three crewmen gathered there in uniform windbreakers. When Jenkins approached, an old man rose unsteadily from his knee. "You got a boot on here?"

Yes, Jenkins could see, there was a parking boot. It locked the front left wheel of his Town Car.

"We dock in twenty minutes." The crewman was incredulous. He swept the deck with a gesture. "You're blocking everyone. You're blocking every rig on the boat."

"I didn't . . ." Jenkins shrugged. It was all he had left. "On the island, there was a cop."

Maybe a flicker passed between the three. The old man shook his head emphatically: "Nausset don't use parking boots. Nausset hasn't used parking boots in ten years, fifteen years."

One of the others spoke softly and sadly: "It is an old boot."

"Is it marked? It's all rusty. Nausset don't use parking boots." The older man pointed to an eighteen-wheeler. "You're going to tell him why he has to reverse that off the freight boat."

The four men contemplated the situation. Eventually the sad crewman contributed again: "Your plates are gone."

"Where are your license plates?" The old man's disbelief came afresh. "You got to have license plates to ride the state ferry."

CHAPTER 30

In Anna's search for her vanished sister, the early morning hours were the worst, as her urgency came up against the vacation island's yawning, roll-over start. For three hours she seemed to be the only person awake, and these were the same hours when her little cubicle became unbearable. The sun heated the plywood divider by her head. The old mattress released its dog odors.

Instead of lying there, Anna walked the city like a trapper walking his trapline, checking that her *Missing! Reward!* fliers were still where she'd taped them, on posts and billboards.

This morning the first paper was missing. The absence took her breath. The place was a scrap of fence between buildings, which now was bare, staple-scarred wood. Anna had almost forgotten why she even took this walk, and suddenly she was ecstatic. A development! The only reason for someone to take the flier was so that they would have the telephone number at hand. She checked her phone. (Power on. No calls.) She checked in every direction. The sidewalks were empty.

Her second flier was missing as well. From the post in front of the game store. Anna was unprepared. She carried only one spare in her bag—one of the new kind with her sister decorated and her telephone number hand-written—and no tape. She stepped into the empty street, and from that vantage she could see that her third flier was gone as well, gone from the central kiosk for tourist information. In the blizzard of papers, its spot was flat and bare.

Could she be violating some ordinance, posting without permission? Always she had posted hers among a crowd of others. She checked and she knew these other papers: pet grooming, room rentals, yoga tutoring, fishing trips, band gigs from a month ago, all wilted by the sea air. These bore no permission stamps. Only hers were missing.

The first new thing in days. A puzzle.

Anna had been tireless in her investigations, sometimes afoot for twenty hours a day. She would walk, bus, wait behind the kitchen, wait at the stockroom, and then ambush with her list of questions that had grown tedious even to her: Had he or she known her sister? Where was she living? Was she well? Had she talked about where she might travel? Anna had tracked down and spoken to every worker returning to the island from last season.

And ultimately everything she learned was useless, though Anna persisted, for in addition to being a dogged investigator, she was also a curious younger sister—curious and hurt by silence. She assembled a fairly complete collage of her sister's two months on the island.

Two months. Kat came on the boat as a daytripper—bikini in a knit bag. She came over with a young man delivering soda in a rental van. The man left but she stayed. She had been hired twice—at a coffee shop and at a clothing boutique that had not opened its doors again this year. She had quit both jobs after a week or ten days. During her time on the island she was associated with various men—including "Anglos," which is the term the Brazilians used to mean both the local, permanent boys in the big houses and the (mostly-white) tourists.

This was notable. Most summer workers paired off with each other, found love and friends within their tight, if transitory, community. Unsurprisingly, Kat hadn't found it convenient to so confine herself. Anna got winks and insinuations from some of the macho young dishwashers she interviewed, but to her they seemed wistful. She doubted any were Kat's actual boyfriends. Her questions about an older "Anglo" didn't surprise anyone—Watterson? Frobisher?—but no one could add to the story.

These investigations were not an exercise to lead Anna to admire her sister more. Kat never had a fixed address. Some nights she slept in cheap, windowless rooms like the one Anna had found for herself, but it was just "staying"—Kat never felt obliged to rent, to pay, and apparently no one dared ask her. She was there some nights and then she wasn't. She wouldn't even commit herself to predictable mooching.

How hard and ungenerous Kat seemed. Coworkers spoke of her reverently, stunned by her glamour, but they could only tell tales of what they observed, never of conversations, never of anything Kat shared with them. One young Greek woman from the boutique had folded sweaters side by side with Kat for a week but remained essentially a stranger, and in fact she asked Anna what country Kat came from. She seemed to envy Anna's privileged position as a sister, and would have questioned her all day except that Anna walked out, peevish. While there were many who admired her sister, there were none whom Kat had admired enough to confide in. She was observed and overheard, not spoken to. She moved by whims. She reported to no one. She had no friends.

Kat couldn't have made this harder for Anna if she had tried. And she hadn't tried. Not for a moment had she considered her sister.

Anna rested her hand on the bare wood where the paper picture of her sister had been on display. In her other hand, her phone went off, beeping and buzzing.

She answered without thought: "Yes?"

"Hello. This is Brand Frobisher. I'm trying to help out here. I'm calling about Ekaterina Fedorchak."

"Do you know her? Is she there?"

Bells in the background. "I don't know her," he said. "No. I met her last July. But I called to assist. You're looking for her, correct? She's not here. She's gone."

"Who is this?" The phone displayed "Unidentified Caller."

"I'm Brand Frobisher."

There was a pause for Anna to recognize the name. And Anna did, though not for its blueblood fame. "You were her boyfriend."

"No, I was not. No, not her boyfriend. Did you hear that somewhere? That's a lie. What was the source of that misinformation? May I ask?"

The man's phone manner was difficult for Anna to follow. He rattled out question after question, then stopped on one. The pause went on for heartbeats, but Anna was too far behind to attempt an answer.

Frobisher was Kat's sugar daddy. He was the one man Anna should be speaking to, and here he was. Questions—bitter spit—weeks of private muttering—and Anna found that she had no place to begin. It was so confusing. Was this an old man? He didn't sound like an old man.

Brand Frobisher continued. "Kat was great, the best. She was going to Honduras. She talked about it. So, who are you, searching like this? I bet she's in one of the main cities down there, Tela. There is a capital city but also beach resorts, and that is where you will want to look. I won't even go there unless it's one of the islands, because the mainland is all pigs and dogs, right on the beach. It's beautiful. Tell her hi, for me. Who are you, her sister?"

Anna heard the question. "Yes, her sister."

"What's your name? She was studying Spanish. She had the textbooks and everything."

"Anna," she said. She had done her interview so many times. "Did my sister have any friends? Are there any names you could offer?"

"I really didn't know her. I met her a single time, or two, like parties, group things, but I was not her boyfriend. That's a lie or misinformation. Bad information, and I would appreciate if you didn't pass that on. But I know she talked about Honduras, and that was her certain destination. I don't want you wasting your time. Okay? I thought I would put your mind at ease. If you're searching for her, you know."

"Thank you for calling."

"So, you're what, her sister? How old are you? Younger sister or older?"

"I'm her younger sister, Anna."

"She talked about you. Are you looking for a job? How do you like the island? It's so boring out here, for the young people. Believe me. Where are you staying?"

By now Anna understood how the man talked. When the pause came she answered. "I'm staying in the town. Until I find out enough information."

"She's gone. Honduras, I told you. Do you want to meet? I'm busy but I could meet. Where are you? But you know, maybe Kat sent me a card. I think she did. I can get it to you. Do you want to meet? I'll buy you a drink. Hell, I'll buy you dinner."

Amidst the confusion, Anna recognized the proposition. *This* she had encountered. Men who looked her up and down and began to answer her questions mysteriously. He could tell her everything if she would return after his shift (the kitchen, the stock room). It was all too complicated to explain here and now, but if she came back with him to his room . . .

A bit surprising to hear this, over the phone, from this

American. Usually Anna encountered this proposition from the foreign men. If Americans tried it, it was only the youngest sort of boys—teenagers—and they had no practice at all. It didn't seem to be an American cultural tradition.

"Where are you?" Brand Frobisher asked. "I'll pick you up. I'll take you to breakfast. I'm out. I'm driving. Where are you?" More lies: he waited in silence. No hum of a car engine. Again came the tuneless bells, and this time Anna recognized it: the sound that sailboats made when the wind shook their ropes inside their masts. His lie brought to mind another: He said that Kat studied Spanish out of a textbook. Maybe he didn't know her at all.

"No, thank you," Anna said.

"Don't you want to find her?" He was angry. "All right, then. I thought you were looking for her. This postcard I'm talking about would have the city, and I think it even gives her address. If you don't want to find her . . ."

"Call me, when you find this card," Anna said, even putting a little smile in her voice. To associate this man with Ekaterina made her face tired, as though all day it had been holding false expressions. But Anna knew that her exhaustion changed nothing, and was irrelevant. Even if in the end she had to meet this man, ride in his car, hand on her thigh . . . she had always been aware of the reality of her situation, a young woman alone, without any money, relying on favors.

The first citizens of the morning were coming on to the street. Shopkeepers opening their shops, these shops that sold nothing. First one, then another, they waved to her. She did not know these people.

A balance tipped. Certainly she knew the realities of the world, but she was sick of them. She did not like to hear her sister's name in this man's mouth. With a husky, sweet, deep voice she asked, "Could you spell your name, please?"

"What's that? I'm Brand, Brand Frobisher. Why's that?"

"I'm writing a newspaper story. While I am looking. I am a reporter. For the *Privyet.* It's the paper for our capital. Like your *New York Times.*"

Anna rarely bothered with lies. They never worked on her. That is, others' lies were immediately obvious, and made her impatient at the wasted time—a child's game, twenty guesses, hide and seek . . .

However, she had to be impressed by the impact. Brand barked, incomprehensible, the telephone away from his mouth. Anna thought that perhaps a bad accident was happening to him—a dog bite, a wasp—there among the sailboats. One minute his voice was trying to rub her underwear, the next he had a spiny crab lodged in his throat.

Chapter 31

"He don't sleep. That's one thing about him. He don't sleep."

Coburn knew the caller. Knew the subject.

"You got to watch that about him, because you don't expect it. He hibernates all at once sometimes, like when we were on the boat to Liberia, he hibernated like a damn bear. But you should make sure, you should monitor his sleep, like they do with a trucker, they keep track in a ledger."

Coburn rubbed the sleep out of his face. He had been drinking schnapps. He had been napping at the wheel of his Cadillac. It was a particular challenge to wake not to reality but to Sergeant Martinez's semi-coherent vision of it, in which Coburn had hired Jim Hawkins. The sergeant called to offer Coburn management advice, how to accommodate the idiosyncrasies of this needy employee.

". . . Your soldier needs eight or nine hours to rest or recuperate, keep his mind clear, to keep his decision-making where it's at, up to standards. He don't always get that, for one reason or another, but it's your job, sometimes that's your number-one job . . ."

"Hang on for a minute," Coburn muttered. He lit the dome light of his car so he could be sure of the right phone buttons. He didn't want to disconnect the call, and he was dizzy with the peppermint schnapps. He transferred it to the speaker phone. The Sergeant had never quit talking or even paused and now his tired lisp dropped around Coburn like a voice on the radio.

Coburn listened. He uncapped his bottle, warm from his thighs, and took a nip. Around him in the night flitted the ghosts of *his own* management failures, though for him it was failure to manage events rather than employees. He had failed to manage Brand, set free after decades contained on the island. He had failed to deal with the Ukrainian girl who terrified Frobisher. His vaunted connection at Homeland Security (described as a "hard man") had run away and now wouldn't even answer his phone—if he'd even come to the island. Coburn also felt that he had lost control of the local police, because it couldn't really be just this one man, could it, this Hawkins, crashing around deck like a loose cannon in a storm?

The series of failures was enough to make him philosophical. Whoever even thought it was possible to control events? To shift them off their set course? It was hopeless as trying to redirect an asteroid. You'd bomb and labor and hit it with nuclear strikes and maybe succeed in altering its path by two degrees. It would crash into a bigger city than before.

Old Don Frobisher had been right, essentially, and Coburn had been wrong. Only big moves counted. Not hints. Big moves. Got a bad son? Cut the bridge to the island. Blood evidence? Rub your boat down with toilet acid, until the teak turns black as ebony. Private investigator asks the wrong questions? Break his body and dump it out of an airplane a hundred miles offshore. The pale, meaty, ghastliness of weeping Boco still dominated the sensation in Coburn's hands. At the end, Boco wrestled an arm loose and held the door until his fingers were broken.

". . . You're in your rack, man, you don't know, you're having dreams, but Hawkins makes his way among the indigenous. Living eight whole hours, 'cause he don't sleep, and whatever you told him, he don't hear. Nowhere is off-limits to a guy like that. He starts living a whole life out there and you don't know

. . ." When a soldier left the barracks, the other soldiers didn't snitch. They figured Hawkins had a local girlfriend.

These Martinez monologues were better than radio, more instructive. There were no six-minute commercial breaks because Martinez in fact never ended a sentence or paused for breath. Coburn could identify with this sergeant. At heart they were both plain soldiers. Plus—to be frank—even Marko Mack could start to sound like a nag. His voice pitched the same note of complaint four hours a day—vary it up!—and for Marko the world was always simple. Maybe he should get out here with some real problems. There's no simple answer to problems like this, the real-world problems of the soldier on the ground.

Marko Mack had never acknowledged Coburn's letter to him with the plan for *Bottom Line Time.*

"Martinez," Coburn said to the night around him, to his twin across the continents. He spoke slowly, leaving dead air to show how carefully he regarded what he said, "Sergeant Martinez. I respect your people. I do. You come to this country, and what do you do? You volunteer to serve it. Your people respect what they've been given."

"Like, soldiers?"

"I put it to you, with the history your country has had . . . the only solution is a violent solution. What do you think of that proposition? Bottom line, the only message is a threat. If you look at the problems the United States has, internationally, now . . ."

Sergeant Martinez said nothing. Coburn explained his position further. He took a nip, tried to cap his bottle but the top had disappeared. While he was rooting around he produced a pistol from under his seat.

He rested the schnapps at an angle and worked the slide of the pistol. He ejected the clip. Pressed the bullets against their spring. Spun the top round. In this climate, metal would stick and fall to ruin. He also hoped that Sergeant Martinez would hear these sounds and recognize, one soldier to another. "We sent your boy a message, and I think maybe he finally got it."

Silence passed over the line. Coburn assumed they'd disconnected during his speech. He reached for the button when Martinez's voice came faint: "Hawkins? No. What message did you send?"

Coburn sat back. "He's a vet. I respect that. But there are good and bad vets. You're a good vet. We welcome your kind to our shores. But there are bad vets as well. You accept that proposition?"

"You didn't fuck with him."

"Oh, I think you could say that I did. He's not looking so good. I sent a girl to keep an eye on him. I got his boss to apply the thumbscrews. Then we ran him over with a speedboat. Back and forth. How's that for clear? I'd say we fucked him. No—I don't mean to be vulgar. Vulgarity serves no real purpose. But I had to be clear, and how much clearer can I be? Running him down with a boat."

"Is he dead? Man, Hawkins don't ever look good."

"Not dead. But people *can* die. They die, and maybe he understands that now. Bottom line, your boy and I had what I consider clear communication. You're a soldier. I'm in the communication business. That's the bottom line."

Martinez spoke in response, but his volume had gone way down. Coburn shut off his car's air-conditioning. Suddenly the air in the car was freezing.

Very low, Martinez was muttering, "Man, you never fucked with the White Shark. Love of God, you never fucked with the White Shark. Didn't you ever see him? Didn't you see the man?"

"What?"

"Didn't you never see his eyes?"

Coburn had no response, but Martinez didn't require one.

Martinez was frightened and spoke like a man rocking back and forth at prayer. "Love of God, you never fucked with the White Shark." His voice went to the men beside him in the communications tent. "This guy fucked with the White Shark. Love of God."

CHAPTER 32

I dressed. Sarah was asleep. I know it's not possible that the glow of her body lit the room, but I assure you that it wasn't dark, and that there was no other source of light.

She made an interrogative sound.

"Can't sleep."

"But you didn't *do* anything."

She felt that my failures in Africa explained me. She was wrong. In any case she misunderstood them exactly: I didn't do anything. That was the failure. The guards laughed because they perceived that I would not act.

I stepped outside. The outside air was the exact temperature and heft as the inside air. No incentive to seek it, and the street was empty at this early hour of the morning. Way down by the harbor someone shouted and someone responded, rebel yells, a couple of drunks trying to make up for their low numbers. These were freelance drunks. The bars had been finished for hours. With nothing else, I started in that direction. Then I saw blue light in the window of Sasha's internet shop.

His business was done for the night. He sat at the good computer that always worked. Anna was on the other side of the room making calls on a computer equipped with a microphone. Anger grew in her, and her voice was vicious. She stuck in the knife. Sasha and I watched her.

"Same as you two," I told Sasha. "I can't sleep. A pattern is putting pressure on my head. To resolve itself."

"What do you mean?"

"A pattern. I won't see until all at once. Then it will be too late." His screen showed a newspaper in Russia. "You know it too, don't you? Something is wrong on this island."

"You could get out." He meant escape Nausset.

"Eh? Then I wouldn't have any hope at all. At least I'm close. I may still get lucky."

We were both distracted by what Anna was saying. We had never seen such savagery. She had obtained the home telephone number for the administrators at St. Helmett's. She was pretending to be a newspaper reporter. She had woken the chancellor in her bed: ". . . our story following up on the Interpol report on human trafficking of women and girls. So some questions. Is St. Helmett the patron saint of what? Not the patron saint of human trafficking and prostitution?"

"Yes, human trafficking, forced prostitution of girls and women. Enrolled there by your board of trustees, through direct intercession. He enrolls them in exchange for their prostitution favors. The . . . Frobisher."

Anna's short pauses did not allow the woman to answer more than a few words.

"A source in your admissions office confirms. Are all the trustees involved? We have the names, and are in the process of contacting them tonight, but we have any number of questions. Does the obligation to prostitute continue after enrollment, for the girl student?

"If the woman has a child, is she forced to abort the child, as with most prostitution situations?

"So you offer no comment. That would be fine, but we are printing the article, so this lawyer, she will need to contact me within the hour. I really would answer, in your position.

"Because we are an international paper. A question: Is the Vatican involved with this prostitution arrangement?

"Your professors, what number of them belong to a religious order? How many of them participate in the trafficking of girls, do you have any estimate . . . ?"

Sasha and I huddled at our end of the room. The hostility wasn't directed at us, but the mad dog could snap at any hand. There was venom enough for all.

I spoke to Sasha without looking down. "Did you meet this famous sister?"

Sasha shook his head warily. Not going to be caught in that trap. "I am not that way. I know her sister. I am a Christian."

"I don't know what that means." Though I spoke under my voice, Anna glanced over. Both of us held our breath for a moment. I dropped my voice to Sasha. "You never found signs of the third girl?"

Sasha made a troubled noise. Like me, he didn't move his head, but he opened a bookmark on his computer.

There was a short newspaper article. A human foot had been found in the ocean. Came up in a fishing net off the coast of Connecticut. The date: last October. The police were interested in missing persons, a missing woman.

"The shark?" Sasha asked quietly.

The article said nothing about the condition of the foot, or exactly where it was found. The paper was from Hartford. I was skeptical. "Try some things. Search 'shark sighting.' " I corrected his spelling. Nothing local. Nothing recent. Sasha had a database of all the newspapers in the country. "Sharks don't hide," I said. "They've got no sense of it. People see them. They leave evidence. Dead seals. Dead fish."

Sasha searched "dead seal." "No," he said.

"Bring that back."

He had closed the article. He found it again. Blood surged through my body. The heat started in my limbs and skull.

"Is that close?" Sasha asked, puzzled.

"No." The dead seals were shot. Three dead seals washed up on a beach in Rhode Island. A reward was offered for information. "No, it's not close by," I said. "It's ninety miles away."

"What's this?" Anna asked. She was there and read it over Sasha shoulder. "Have you tracked the money for the Chinese man?"

"Oh no no," I said. I was talking to myself, fitting information into its correct place. A reward. Seals with bullets in them. The newspaper article read like a private letter addressed to me, an invitation to revisit the night I met Megan Palsinger. She was frightened and she was tired of that party.

Anna put her hand over Sasha's on the computer mouse, and opened all the links. She read the article about the girl's foot. She read it once without comment. She politely restored the article about the murdered seals.

"Should I print this?" Sasha asked. My manner made him solicitous.

"I read."

"I could phone this number for the reward," Anna offered, puzzled.

"We're beyond that now," I said.

CHAPTER 33

As he walked into the Life Sciences building, Professor Folger got a strange look from one of these nuisance post-docs, one of the summer visitors who were awarded a thirty-day fellowship and spent every hour of it haunting the lab. He opened his office door and discovered the reason for the man's raised eyebrow. A very young woman—a student worker?—sat at Folger's personal computer, using his personal keyboard. She was very small, dressed all in black with long, black sleeves like a ballerina.

At his entrance, she looked up from the screen, bored. She wasn't lost. She was waiting. "Does your contract with the state allow you to be dismissed for moral turpitude?"

Folger's eyes went to his desk telephone. That was to be his sole act of resistance—a glance at the telephone. The girl's manner said that they knew each other far too well, that they were too far along in this interrogation for a ridiculous claim of innocence. Folger was convinced. Now he just needed to find out what he had done.

Behind him, his office door closed. "You want to tell us about the dead seals," a voice said.

The voice belonged to a very large man in a dark evening suit, exquisitely cut. His coloring was unnatural—his hair platinum white, his eyes light gray, and his face stained with intense emotion. His face was ageless, in that whatever its crags, they came from inner tensions rather than years of wear and gravity.

When Folger had seen the girl, he thought, *No one is here. No one will see. Thank God.* Folger had never touched a student but was familiar with his own imagination. When Folger saw this man in the suit, he thought, *No one is here. No one will see. I will be strangled.* He was familiar with his sins.

The big man's wristwatch began to chime. He shut it off immediately and regarded the floor, sheepishly. "The seals," he said again.

Folger checked his own wristwatch: 9:17. The chill of his deeper nightmares receded.

Now in his fifties, Folger had refined his Boston upbringing into a precise Brahmin manner, almost British. He wore the pomade and bow tie but did not yet carry an umbrella. "I am a marine biologist," he said, "so if you give me a moment to put my lunch in the refrigerator, I can tell you any number of things about seals."

The girl, on her side, actually said, "No, no, no." The man folded his arms and grieved.

Somehow even Folger felt disappointed by this evasion. He did not dare move with his lunch. He reconsidered with a dip of his chin. "The dead seals. Fish and Game handled the reward program. You will want to get in touch with them."

The two visitors said little—waited. The girl climbed onto Folger's desk and sat there, cross-legged, making a nest of the pile of summer mail. Folger tried other drabs of information. He found reassurance in how reasonable he sounded. He was a professor, after all. ". . . But it wasn't my affair. I don't know why they brought the bodies here. I agreed to take a look. Unfortunately, my private notes . . . There was never a formal autopsy, you understand."

"Cause of death is gunshot," the young woman said.

Exhausted, she spoke with a heavy eastern-European accent.

"Yes, I'm afraid that is true. Two of the cases were certainly gunshots. The other case was less certain. One couldn't be certain."

"What caliber weapon?" the girl asked.

"Oh, I don't know that we measured." Folger had gotten comfortable enough that his tone indicated he didn't particularly care.

"Don't do anything yet," said the girl, which puzzled Folger until he realized that she spoke not to him but to the big man. His strange pale eyes did not rise to Frobisher's face, but rather studied his joints like a butcher.

"It was a shotgun," Folger said. "The weapon. Firing a riffled slug."

"You did the dissection?" She indicated the lab room.

Folger licked his lips. "No formal autopsies."

This was the small, stupid truth he often repeated to himself. Saying it aloud, now, he was struck down by weariness. "I have the slugs. I have the bullets."

The big man shivered with pent-up energy, a long spasm of jerks, the machine-gun shudder of a horse's shoulder muscle. Bullets weren't the issue. "Don't waste this golden chance," he said earnestly. "Only those harmed can absolve you of your guilt. That door is closed forever. But you may have the opportunity of redemption. You understand how rare this is." Finally Folger identified the man—he was a priest deeply troubled for the soul of a congregant. "Your decision now will be the concomitant of your every breathing moment."

Folger found this speech more disturbing than a threat of bloody murder. He looked pleadingly to the girl, but found no mercy. She said, "The number in the newspaper is this telephone number." She toed the phone. It moved to the edge of the desk and crashed to the floor.

The strange man spoke as though without interruption. "My father was a professor, like you, a reading man. Recognize the constructs you're caught in. Whatever lies you find yourself repeating. The solace they offer is foolish, is false." He shook his head as if tasting ash.

For his part, Folger nodded more and more vigorously, not out of agreement or understanding. "I offered a reward, hoping to make people think twice." He looked around his office. "Seals are what I study. To shoot them isn't hunting. Okay? You're in a boat, they're in the water, but seals are interested in people. When they look up they don't look at the boat, or the motor. They look up at us, at our faces." Liberated from the professorial mannerisms, decades fell away from Folger. Like his forbears he was a wiry Massachusetts sailor who had spent years of his life on the water. Even an old boating tan rose out on his cheeks. "It's not hunting. The seals don't know what guns do, but if you held one, they would be curious."

The man in the suit closed his eyes. Folger felt relief in waves. "Talk on."

"So I offered a reward, and I received phone calls. Too many phone calls. It turns out it's not a good idea to offer a reward, even a small one. I don't even know why I did it. The reporters were here . . ." Folger felt tempted to continue this digression, but he read disappointment in the lines of the man's mouth. "Someone did call. Eventually. A lady had my home number. Not here." On the floor, the phone had quit protesting with tones and recorded voices. "She called in the dead of the night. Woke me. Unlike everyone else, she knew the bullet, the type of bullet. She knew what kind of weapon was used."

"You took her name," the man said. He had known this all along. "Then someone else phoned."

"Yes." Folger stopped, waited, his lips numb. They had reached his crime. Almost immediately after the woman had rung off, a man called. Again on his home phone. In the conversation that followed, Folger revealed the woman's name: Megan Palsinger. The second caller chuckled to hear it, and with this chuckle Professor Folger understood that he had done wrong. The voice was the voice of an evil child.

Since then, everything had been strategies for Professor Folger to forget, or to forgive himself.

"Who would shoot seals?" This was the young woman.

She did not like him, but Folger considered the interruption a precious gift. He savored his own expertise. "Drunken kids. Fishermen. The damage they cause is exaggerated, but they are carnivores. They do eat fish and they do ruin fishing nets. What can you say? And seals bring with them their predators. Sharks."

Behind Folger the man loomed like an executioner, implacable, his silent presence growing. Folger looked only at the girl. He swallowed dryly. "The seals that came in here had ice crystals in their kidneys. Elsewhere in their viscera. There was extensive ice in two of the specimens. In the viscera."

"Ice?"

"It made no sense. They washed up north of Newport. It was more like a prank." The girl didn't help him so he groped ahead, rushing to tell secrets for the first time. "The seals were *frozen.* Somebody froze them. I mean, put them in a freezer. Brought them here." Folger shook his head. He said, "One of them was tagged. Flipper tag. Flipper tags had been cut away, on another animal. They missed this one. It was ingrown. She had been part of a study undertaken in the 90's."

The man spoke. "Nausset."

"Yes, Nausset Island."

"I need you to bring me the tag," he said. "You need to tell me about the second phone call. We both understand that."

Folger closed his eyes and nodded.

Chapter 34

I asked Sarah to put me in touch with Brand Frobisher. I didn't think she would do so, but I asked as a courtesy because that was her world, and I was going to trample it.

When I said the name, her body stiffened. I hadn't thought it through, and in no way was it courteous to ask while we made love. When our bodies were attached she didn't have her options of response—to pretend she didn't recognize the name, for example.

The feeling of her changed. She stiffened. No rush to it, but we politely disengaged and she spoke to the dark of the ceiling: "Brand Frobisher." Even taking her time, her response was unsettled. "You never need to have anything to do with him," she concluded. "Never. You're here for one summer."

This was news. She was upset and spoke candidly. She and I hadn't discussed my status or my future. I was temporary.

However, I refused to pause on this revelation. What else could I be but a temp hire? I said, "Frobisher can't be that frightening. I saw him, old dude." Sarah rolled over. Her eyes were multicolor misunderstanding. "At your party. I, uh, tried to speak to him."

"He wasn't there," she said. "Brand Frobisher? His father was there."

"There are two of them?"

"Look at me. I can't fathom. I don't understand how I'm not enough for you."

"What do you mean? Of course you are."

"If I asked you to, you wouldn't go away with me."

"Where?"

"Anywhere. Bermuda. Two months in Bermuda. I have a condo there."

"There's no question. I don't understand your question."

"Our sweat mixes well." To dramatize this she traced a line of her belly and sucked her finger.

"Yes."

"You wouldn't leave Nausset Island for me."

"I can't go right now. I can't leave this minute."

"But you want this, don't you?" She meant herself.

"Yes." I motioned to separate the topics. "It's nothing to do with you. It's this island. It's rotting." I explained. "Salt gets in the bones of the concrete. It's settled there. It's like it's waiting there, gnawing on the rebar. The handrails give way in your hand."

Sarah laughed. She had worked herself up, her smell was the whole room. "Corruption, corruption, what's so wrong about corruption?"

Philosophy, mysticism . . . her perspective wasn't without precedent. We examined the matter from all sides and angles. Every so often she would say it: "Corrupt. Corrupt. Corrupt."

At a stopping point, she rolled away decisively. Was I dismissed? That wasn't it. She was trying to decide where to begin.

She began way back: "Donald Frobisher is the most famous man in the state of Massachusetts. He's the former congressman. He served six consecutive terms. He ran for president in the seventies. He owns the eastern quarter of the island, and he owns East Cape, a private island. Years ago it used to be connected to Nausset by bridge."

"Oh." That made sense. There were gated compounds over

there. I had seen the arm of coastal island on the map. I intended to try swimming around Nausset one day soon, the day I left in October. When I'd glanced at maps I wondered whether to include this outer limb. "He must be a bit of a scumbag," I said. "He recruits Ukrainian girlfriends. If they screw him and his friends with enough enthusiasm, he sends them to this little Catholic college he runs. He basically owns it. In Boston."

"He was married to my grandmother."

My turn now, to check out the ceiling, to try and realign some pieces. Mrs. Yellow.

Finally Sarah said, "Donald Frobisher did not pay for my college, if that's what you're wondering. I went to St. Helmett's."

"Oh."

"You've seen Frobisher on television all your life."

"Not sure I have. How do I get to his house?"

"You can't just go to his house."

I set that aside. No advantage in disputing.

"Donald Frobisher doesn't keep prostitutes, whatever you've been told."

"No, I know. I don't mean to call them prostitutes. I met one of these girls. The sister of one of them. They don't have a thousand choices."

I thought about Anna. She stewed in fury because why not? Why not be furious? The way her life started out, all that was in front of her was a set of bad trades she was free to make. Anna herself was okay—a steel contraption—no one's victim. However, that apparently wasn't true of her sister. So Anna could handle this world but someone she loved could not.

I got glimpses of what it must have been like. When we drove back from Boston, after meeting Valya, the other girl, Anna ranted and raved. What destroyed her was not the exchange her sister had made—American college for screwing old guys. Instead, what twisted her guts was that her sister couldn't pull off the bargain. Her sister didn't know how. She wouldn't plan. She would be cheated. She wouldn't have enough sense to nail down the details.

Sarah still talked. She was being offended on behalf of her social class and relations. Any offences committed by Old Frobisher were the sort of wink-wink shit expected of any old guy, like flirting with the waitress in the nursing home.

"So Brand is the kid?" I interrupted. "How old?"

The name, the very thought of this man changed Sarah's face. Her mouth drooped like an old lady's. Her eyes became Megan's—she felt the need to be careful.

"He's not your actual uncle or anything like that, is he?"

She shook her head at the idea. Her throat trembled so that it took her a time to speak. "It was a mistake for them to get married. It wasn't even a divorce. It was an annulment."

"Your grandma and Frobisher?"

"Brand Frobisher. Megan married him. It didn't even last the pregnancy." To be able to speak, Sarah made her voice dull. Years of dragging this anchor. "He raped her when they were kids. Rape. I don't know. He doesn't really ask you for sex.

"It was never clear how many times. Enough to get her pregnant. When that happened, my grandmother persuaded them to marry. To her generation, that was how you solved the problem . . . that problem."

Sarah watched me closely. She wanted to see the news arrive. How it would land. A woman like that, there's always a touch of sadism.

I had not prepared. Sarah read my face, and saw how I loved her sister. Sarah's reaction was equally clear. Hate passed in ugly clenches from her mouth across her eyes. "Megan. The earth mother. Never did her one bit of good. She got fucked, she got pregnant. The punch line is that the father of her child is Brand Frobisher. One of us has a child, and the punch line is that she never gets to see her son."

I wasn't following. Sarah left the bed and went to a drawer. She had manila envelopes, and they were hand-labeled: June, July, August. They were mailed from a company called Rex and Hayworth, addressed to Brand Frobisher.

Only June was open. It was photos of a teenage boy. Young man. They were posed photos, hand in chin, foot on ball, taken in a studio. I didn't know what I was looking at.

Sarah's nakedness was different than usual. It wasn't sexy; it was just naked. "He was adopted, you see. We don't know where, and they're good about keeping it secret, Rex and Hayworth. They're a law firm. Megan got news, if she behaved." Sarah touched her hair and tried a cruel laugh, but for whom? She didn't know. "Earth mother, so what she got was to feel the loss, more than anyone else ever could." Sarah nursed years of mixed grievances. "Whereas me, I fuck anyone, apparently. Anyone, everyone. And no children."

At some point we both understood that I would leave. Just to get out of there I carried my shoes and socks, because she was trying hateful remarks. "Megan always menstruated clouds. The sharks smelled that."

Chapter 35

I only saw Sarah one more time. Surprise, surprise, we didn't go to bed. She did not repeat her offer to whisk me away to tropical paradise.

I was on the porch at Castle Yellow. Sarah answered the door. She thought I'd come to see her and began to pull back her hair and let it fall, which was her habit when caught off guard. "Hello, stranger."

She was pleased at the tribute of my visit. It did my heart good to see, and for a moment she and I could have been a completely different kind of story. But it took her about one breath to realize I was there for business. She laughed in disbelief: "You can't care about real estate development. I know you don't."

"No, not at all," I said. "I think I understand, though. A few characters want to develop Squab Island. Golf courses and whatnot."

"It's not a plot. It's never been a secret."

"Is your grandma around?"

"My grandmother?"

"Doesn't matter." I pushed past Sarah, who didn't understand until I was on the stairs. "I need a map of hers," I said. "I saw it once. The Squab Island plans."

"The sale happened yesterday," Sarah said, her voice quiet with astonishment.

I called back down: "Not yet. Haven't you heard? The government shut down. Shut down for maintenance. Shut down due to the moral reservations of Congress."

September 30th. My last day on the job as Parking Warden of Nausset Island, but I wasn't the only one out of a job. The congress in Washington had decided to "shut down the government" and lay off all employees except themselves.

With the government on vacation, it could not sell Squab Island.

What a novelty! The whole thing. These Congress windbags blab on more or less constantly, I suppose. Maybe for the first time they had an effect on the real world.

Government shutdown! Government shutdown! shouted the newspaper boxes. Can you imagine? The newspapers presumed that with this tasty bait I'd be obliged to buy, in order to read the inside pages, and study the details of Congress's principled stand.

But savor this irony: the government shutdown delayed the sale of Squab Island for two weeks. It was two full weeks before the nation's leaders could salve their consciences. And those two weeks wrecked the entire scheme! If only the congressmen had known! There were billions in free money hanging in the balance! Beach houses! Golf memberships! They would have bellied up like penguins in a conga line.

Jogging a narrow hallway was a novelty, a bobsled track. The upstairs of Castle Yellow was still deserted. Rooms draped with amber dust cloths. The air hadn't moved since first I had visited. It was the same sulfur air.

A few minutes in the map room, I got what I came for. When I emerged, Sarah was right there, looking upset. In my glee I couldn't help but show her the map of Squab Island, where it was divided into building lots and golf courses. I had borrowed other maps, too, and stolen the cock heath hen, which entirely filled my front pocket. From here on, the other specimen would have to dance alone. The one I got was bigger than it looked, like a frying chicken, and the stuffing didn't compress. The little head peeped out of my pocket.

"Is it funny?" Sarah asked. She was familiar with the map and so instead she studied my face.

I showed her. "I just like how they name things. Like would you ever name a beach club after yourself? Especially if your name was Trent?" I had to explain again about the government shutdown. She turned pale while I talked. I said, "No. Come on. Don't tell me you have money with these scum-sucks."

She shook her head at me. Not at my suggestion.

"Argh," I groaned. "I figured your grandma. I was going to chastise her for it. But you? You know these losers. And you're already super rich."

Sarah continued to make me her study. "Why do you hate them all so much?"

I stopped and breathed. "I don't know. 'Hate'? No. That suggests a level of concern, a level of engagement.

"They *did* kill a bunch of people," I said. "They killed Megan. They scared this other guy, by the name of Boco, who was really pretty harmless. Scared him or hurt him, I don't know. Maybe killed him. They killed a girl from overseas, I think at least one. They killed each other, too—killed your ex-husband, and Watterson. Though I suppose that's more like business dealings."

Sarah searched all sides of the empty hallway. "You don't have to be crazy." She didn't know where to start. "Okay. No one murdered anyone else. No one murdered my sister."

"My guess is that it was Brand Frobisher. The kid Frobisher."

"Brand. Frobisher." She pushed the words away. "No. You don't ever need to get near him. You don't need to pronounce his name. He said he wouldn't hurt you. He's not—"

"Hurt me?" I began to understand. "You talk with him, don't you? I saw you together, a long time ago. Creepy guy? You let him into Megan's cottage." I cut off her protest. "No, I have pictures of it."

I considered for a moment. "How well *do* you know these men?" My stomach felt queasy.

"I know I'm not my sister." Sarah chuckled nervously. "I'm sorry. How could I help them, anyway? Who could keep tabs on you?" she asked.

"Keep tabs on me? What? I'm nobody."

"You saw how effective it was. I promise my assistance didn't make them happy."

"Huh." That was the last of our moments of connection. We were connected at a thousand moments. "I'm not kidding, though," I said. "They killed Megan."

Her eyes flared again. "Do you even live in my world? Do you ever stop? Is there any evidence at all?"

"See? Listen to how you frame it, Sarah. You'll hear faulty processing. Either these men did the deed or they didn't, but that's not contingent on whether they left a clear trail."

She did not see.

All emotion is transitory. Whatever intimacy we had, I kept talking and pounded it all away. I said, "I can't tell you the exact scene. I don't know how they ended Megan's life. I'm sure it was terrible. I can't give you the guest list. But the pattern is laid down: Who they are. How they treat others. It coalesces." I said, "You want a fingerprint. That's not going to be there. Why would they leave a fingerprint? As a favor to you and me? You want the story of what happened? Why would they ever tell that story?"

I showed the map again. "Look larger. Megan wanted the island to be a nature preserve."

"That's simply not a realistic vision." As we talked Sarah grew richer and more distant, a lady troubled by a gypsy contractor. "That's a vision from a children's book."

"Sure it could happen. It's federal land. If people voted on what should happen to Squab Island, would it go to ocean seals or would it go to make a handful of rich people richer? Rare birds lived on Squab Island. Remember them? So they had to burn them up. Seals lived on Squab Island, so they had to shoot them. I never knew your sister Megan, but that was the one thing she told me. They were shooting the seals."

Sarah stopped breathing, stunned by a pulse of fright. It was just a moment. Then clouds passed and she went in the more predictable direction. She decided to hate and pity me.

Your pals murdered your sister? To reject this kind of accusation, you have to *reject* it. You had to set your face against it. Not mere disagreement, but fear, hate, and loathing. For months Sarah and I had been lovers. Now—the expression on her face—she wouldn't shake my hand.

However, say this for Sarah, before I never mention her again: She teetered. For a moment. She might have believed if the price hadn't been too high.

She spoke with vicious mockery: "I gave everything to Megan. Those fucking envelopes. Why do you think I was at her cottage? You think that was fun for me? By your pattern, I'm my sister's killer."

"Nah." I brushed past her and went downstairs. I was sick of talking. I had what I came for.

Mrs. Yellow waited at the bottom of the stairs. Her hair was crazy springs. I'd woken her from a nap. She had been listening.

"Don't you hurt him," she threatened.

"Oh brother," I said.

"He's my husband," said Mrs. Yellow. I believe (and hope) she was talking about Old Donald Frobisher. She spun me a theory about great men. It was different for great men. All we could hope was to be of some assistance. I didn't pay perfect attention. She sounded like a girl in love.

"Jeez," I said, "you heard these guys killed your granddaughter! At least you should deny it! Don't justify. Don't assist. You're such a weird old bat, you were probably at the scene."

I brushed past her. She caned after me, across the great room, at a comical pace. "You can't stop his dream."

"Why would I stop it? Jesus Christ. I don't care." I turned, which brought her to a halt, and I blew my stack. "What would I stop? You guys are already dead. You're already dying." I pointed out the door at the park. "Look out there. Where are the kids? Look at this place. This house is built with ten bedrooms, and it's empty.

"Do you look at your old pictures? They show families in the grass. When did you turn these houses into mausoleums? Each with one old lady, sitting in the tower window, leaking into her incontinence pad. You've got five acres of irrigated lawn, and there's not a child on it, not a kite, just half-dogs laying their little turds along the edges.

"You're sick and dying, okay? I just want to get the fuck out of here before I catch your disease."

Chapter 36

"Brand," Coburn called. "Let's go."

Brand got up from the curb on Slocum Avenue and hurried to Coburn's Cadillac. He should have hated Coburn the most—his monitor, his killjoy. He certainly hated his father for being these same things. Instead he worshiped him.

Brand slumped back against the seat, wide-eyed and stunned by how difficult the world had proved. "I cannot locate the reporter," he said.

"*You* can't find her, because you look like shit. Like crap, like crap."

It was too true. Brand was at his worst. His lip curled back from a palsy. A loop of saliva slowly dropped. Brand had quit having seizures, but now it looked like one might be coming on.

Coburn offered a handkerchief. At one point he would have dabbed Brand's mouth, but not anymore. "It's tough," he allowed, assessing the teenagers on the street. "These migrants want the money we give them, but they don't care about this country. In a heartbeat, they'd sell us out, blow us up. They're from the eastern bloc, where human values aren't the same. It's like the mafia."

Brand's eyes studied the paper he held. "If we find her, I'm having her alone." He studied the blotchy photograph of Ekaterina. "I'm having her alone. I don't care what my dad says."

"Your dad. Your dad has flipped his wig," Coburn said,

simply. "He flew guys in. You and I sit tight. He hired some outsiders."

Brand straightened himself to get to his pocket. He pulled out a string bag, a brightly-dyed Indian thing. "You buy some stuff?" Coburn asked.

"No. It's her sister's cheap things. It's like it still stinks from the hippie store. Smell that. It's like incense."

Coburn blinked soundly. He considered his options and drove on. The bag was deadly dangerous evidence. The father scrubbed every protein out of his boat, while the son kept the girl's bag as a souvenir.

At this point, Coburn's options had run out. He had no other play. He needed his money, and the only way to get it was straight ahead. He drove slowly down Slocum, searching the face of each woman and girl. "I told you, your dad brought these guys in. They landed on the grass airstrip in the middle of the night. If we find her, you know it's their job."

"He doesn't care if I fuck her first. I fuck Oxana. He can't but I do. He married her so I'd have someone. He thinks I like the foreign accent. She's like a board, though, and she's stupid. Have you talked to her? She's so dumb. What's that? Stop."

"Just another one of her papers," Coburn said.

"I took them down. She's been here. Stop."

Brand ran out in the sun and retrieved the flier. It was different. It had been colored by marker. Brand made a high, joyful monkey call. He nestled deep into his seat.

"Easy." Coburn thought this was a seizure. "Uh, uh, uh," Brand said, like he was fucking.

Coburn realized that this flier was different. This one listed a street address in the printing.

"Take me there. Can you just find that place?" Brand asked.

Coburn searched Brand for hints. What was the boy asking? Oh, yes. Brand had never lived in the world. Street addresses were mystery science, like magnets and radio waves. "Yeah, I can find it."

"She colored her sister like a coloring book. She's so pretty." Brand rocked back and forth and touched the new paper.

CHAPTER 37

Donald Frobisher was on the phone with Jack, the ferryman. His tone was high migraine. "Brand *will* have a girl. He *does* have a girl. I just told you. That is desirable. That is his job, and he is doing it.

"Coburn? Coburn may not cross the water tonight. He is not invited to my property. How much clearer do I need to be? No one else crosses. Take the shaft off the engine. Unless I'm supposed to walk down there and do the mechanics myself."

Jack asked another question, slow getting it out, but Frobisher turned the handset, located the red button, and disconnected the call.

The sea tonight was a green mess of chop, but thick glass kept out all sound, and echoes of his voice hung in the paneling. Frobisher never doubted his own righteousness, but these words were unusually blunt.

For three decades he tried to cure his son, to make him into a real boy, instead of one carved out of twisted, rotten wood. Now he arranged private time for his son to torture a girl to death. Qualms began to stir. They took the form of irritation. All this had been forced on him by incompetence.

On the granite countertop, a television ran mute. The flickering picture caught his attention, breaking and scattering the early forms of regret. The news channel repeated the same footage as before. Congress was gone, so this was the same old footage. The picture ran a double caption like a stock ticker. The US government was closed for business.

Chapter 38

It was night when I stopped in at Sasha's internet shop. "I need a few satellite pictures."

Sasha sat at his computer. He smirked at me. I didn't understand the expression, coming from him. It made me check the seams of my uniform shirt, that last shirt of mine, to see how I had become a joke. "What's funny?"

"She went with them. They didn't have to grab her. So she's gone, bye bye."

"Anna?"

"Uh huh. She got in the car with them." He regarded this development as a victory. In part the victory was over me. His expression was the mocking expression that the prison guards wore when they dragged the newspaper man to Anomabu, where he would be abused until he died. "She was a slut I guess."

The newspaper man slid his wristwatch off his bony wrist. The guards took him to the hell and squalor of Anomabu. What did I do? I went to report the incident to my chain of command. Pretty bold, eh? Pretty effective. First there was Sergeant Martinez, who was an okay man but weak-headed. He squinted like a blind mouse in a cartoon, and was full to the ears with army blather. If he ever had a thought of his own, it was insane superstition.

He listened, and then he told me about the Tears of Jesus, which I don't believe is part of an actual religion. Martinez or his grandmother made it up. Sometimes out of nowhere you feel a drop of liquid on your skin. Sweat—dew—a raindrop out of an empty sky—or just a ghost perception. Sergeant Martinez called these drops the Tears of Jesus, and they guided his life unpredictably. Because of the name, one would think that a Tear of Jesus would serve as a chastisement. When I told Martinez that our friend had been arrested, the moment before Martinez had apparently experienced a Tear of Jesus. He advised me over and over on its significance, which in this case was fatalism. What was meant to be was meant to be, and Jesus had dropped a tear so that we earthly pilgrims would know that his will was inscrutable.

I went to the captain. The newspaper editor had been our best source of intel. The captain was interested in learning about this development. However, while he appreciated the intelligence source, he had never been happy with the editor's incomplete cooperation. The editor helped us but he didn't *believe*. The forces of freedom faced down an existential threat. A night in Anomabu might make him understand.

I wrecked Sasha's attic and stepped out onto the evening street. Slocum Avenue. As I got in my cruiser, another man slid in the passenger side. He had been waiting, and I did not see him walk up. While we considered each other, a second man also got in. He sat on the bench seat behind me.

"Drive." The passenger nodded ahead. "Simon Boco wants to talk to you."

"Who? Boco?"

Flash in the mirror. The man in the back tapped a gun against my skull. It was a pistol with a very long barrel.

I did as told. I drove. I felt sad because I knew that Boco was dead. Before I had suspected, but now I knew for certain. How cruel to kill that sort of fellow, then to use his name as a stupid trick.

Both men were big, dark Americans. They were very nervous, and having trouble breathing. They had army haircuts, and their sunglasses hid all human expression. At my side, the passenger showed no gun. He checked a massive wristwatch like the one Sarah had given me, flashing huge forearms. Down his head sweat ran in rivulets.

I only glimpsed the man in back. The pistol barrel touched the top button of my spine. That close, the scent of gun oil was oppressive.

The passenger sat awkwardly sideways, ready to reach me with either hand. He also did not fasten his safety belt.

"You guys look like you could use some AC," I said. Among the adjustments I made on the dashboard, I shut off the passenger-side airbag. This feature was for the safety of child riders.

We drove out of the city. They wanted the empty side of the island. We wound into the old trees. Gradually I accelerated to fifty miles an hour, in order that shooting me would be dangerous. Speed limited their options. With the car's soft springs, nobody noticed.

I wished for the man in the back seat to slide out from directly behind me, more toward the center of the bench. To induce him to do so I pointed out sights on the passenger side. "Look at that sign. Can you believe it goes down to twenty miles an hour? Talk about a speed trap. I can't tell you how many customers I get. I bet there's a cop hiding right here. Nope, nobody home. Up here? There are three ideal spots. We can check . . ."

No cop waited in the second good spot. The man behind me did lower his pistol, however. He looked over and even leaned a little. I resettled myself against my door.

I steered us into an oak tree. It had been here, thickening, since before the Mayflower.

We hit at 45 or 50 miles per hour.

Blam! The airbag knocked me silly. When I came aware I was patting at the inflated bag. The impact hurt much worse than I had anticipated. My face scalded from abrasion. I looked to see the damage but the center mirror was gone—vanished—along with the entire windshield. At least my eyes functioned. I unbuckled, discovering new pains.

Next to me my big passenger whimpered and shuddered and tried to restart. Only his huge ass was still in the car. His body had started out onto the hood.

My door was stuck. I climbed out the open window. My face dropped blood, single, fat, audible drops, at about the pace of a clock pendulum. My wrist was numb and wouldn't take pressure. That didn't mean anything. The true extent of the injury would reveal itself in time, and, in fact, later I couldn't recall which wrist had caused me trouble.

Once out, I saw that the car was ruined. I liked the car. I don't even think I was ever supposed to have a car, as Parking Warden. I had more or less claimed it out of the maintenance lot, and now it was a total wreck. As I began to get my thoughts together, I decided that I had to salvage the picture chip from Boco's camera. I rummaged back inside and found it among the garbage of my ash tray. After I held the chip I could think of no reason why I wanted it. Pictures of Sarah.

I experienced a similar confusion regarding the second man. I couldn't find him anywhere. After a search I concluded that I had hallucinated his entire presence, which was horrifying because he was the only one who had threatened me. Then it turned out that he didn't exist and neither did the gun.

You wake from a nightmare, check horrors against reality . . . they may take a surprising amount of time to dismiss. That was my state. I kept blinking. Beads of safety glass glittered a magic trail into the forest, and in due course I realized that the backseat man *did* exist but that he had launched through the windshield, which in fact is what I had intended him to do. What I hadn't anticipated was that he would completely disappear into the greenery like a lost arrow.

Before I got my wits back completely, I entertained one last foolish idea. I decided I should interrogate the two men. I had the standard human desire to know what the fuck was going on. But my car passenger wasn't whining any longer, if indeed he had ever made a sound. Out on the hood his skull lacked its full structural integrity. He was well on his way to being dead, and I was not going to nurse him.

The other guy I finally found in a thicket of poison ivy. He was on his knees and had taken his shirt off, or lost it in flight. His entire back was a tattoo for Operation Desert Storm. He was stone dead. His pistol hadn't achieved anything nearly as dramatic. It lay on the earth between the shattered headlights, and was perfectly functional.

Chapter 39

Sergeant Gilberto Martinez phoned Michael Coburn for the final time. “Hawkins, man, put him on. I want to talk to him. He’s probably right there, eh? Just look outside your car. Heh.”

Coburn checked his mirrors to see if there was, in fact, a man outside the vehicle. He wasn’t feeling strong. The Ukrainian girl was a little bitch, but however he stoked this dislike, it would not justify what was happening to her. What he had done. In Coburn’s weakened state, Sergeant Martinez seemed uncanny—magical; he was across the world and yet he knew that Coburn sat alone in his car!

“When he comes, give him the phone, I want to tell him what a *maricon* . . . Is he there yet? Put him on. I’m not afraid of him.”

“Your boy sure got the goods on us,” Coburn said, exhausted. “He kept at it; I guess you told me he would. He should have stopped, but he didn’t.”

“He don’t stop,” Martinez admitted.

“Some information is meant to stay private.”

“Your information?” Martinez teased. “That don’t sound like the White Shark. You fuck with him, you think he’s going to spread bad rumors? You think the White Shark is going to cut your credit rating?”

Threats and men were better than guilt and teenage girls. Coburn recaptured some of his edge: “You know what, in fact? He’s dead. You see, Sergeant, in the real world, we don’t issue clothes and rations. Don't hold your dick for you when you piss. Sorry. I mean, we don't hold your hand. No USO shows coming around to keep your morale up, all right? Hawkins made us angry? We didn't like it, so we put a kill team right on his ass."

"Kill team?" Martinez tried the term.

Coburn had mixed feelings—"kill team"—hearing it from Martinez, hearing it come out of his own mouth for the first time. What was good? It sounded like a movie. What was bad? Coburn also heard the catastrophic mistake. He had just confessed to capital murder, to a stranger across the world. Had he lost his mind?

This concern was gradually supplanted. Martinez, on his end, couldn't contain his bubbling laughter. "Kill team."

"Oh, believe me. These guys are legit," Coburn said.

Martinez was on the floor. His mirth magnified his accent. "Kill team," came out, pronounced "kee-el team."

"Why don't you call back in an hour. Then I guess we'll see. I'll give you a report."

"Kill team. I told you. I told you. He did Anomabu."

"Anomabu?" This came off Coburn's tongue experimentally, just like "kill team": For years he had heard the word. This was the first time he had pronounced it.

"I told you—"

"Anomabu. The Special Forces took out a prison or something. Some Al Qaeda troublemakers holed up in—"

"No-o." Martinez drew out the word. Could people really misunderstand each other to this extent? "It was *him.* No Special Forces. We were all asleep. There were no Special Forces. There was only Hawkins.

"Some dude handed him a watch. Cheap wristwatch. And then there was a night like you can't believe."

"Yeah." Coburn's disdain didn't carry far.

Through some magic of Earth's atmosphere, their phone line was suddenly clear. All the fuzz, delay, and scratch was gone. The two men could have been sitting beside each other, regarding the night. Ice-clear line. Two American voices.

"Special Forces? It was the White Shark. He's called that, because of how his eyes shut down. It was no mission, man. It wasn't an operation plan except whatever he had in his fucking head. It was him. These *maricons* pissed him off. And then they were all dead.

"We lay there, alarm bells, and outside the guys started running right by the wire. I had to say, don't shoot, because it's a thousand running men. Everyone in the city is running from him.

"What do I do? I look and see his cot, Hawkins's cot. Of course it's empty. Right then I knew better than any court or judge. The court never even believed it, but I knew right then, and I even said it to my corporal, 'Oh fuck, the White Shark is out.' I knew first moment I seen his cot laying there empty." Martinez spoke more and more slowly. "He didn't bring down the walls. Like in the Bible. The walls are still there. But there's not even a country left. Not no more."

"In case you didn't notice, you're calling Massachusetts. United States of America. Not Mexico. This isn't Africa."

"It could be. It will be." Martinez wasn't arguing. No reason to. His voice was sad and slow. "Anomabu wasn't Africa. It wasn't so bad before he started.

"He's like cancer in your body, man. You don't know you're sick. He's already been there. He already took out the generators. *Kaboom!* We woke up, there's no lights in the whole town. There's only the flame from the fuel tank. Super giant tank of fuel. Where did he even get the explosives? The prison had generator devices. *Kaboom!* Not no more they don't. They blow. How? He's got detonators? Who knows. But this city has one thousand of its enemies in one prison. Steel bar doors, and you can hear the locks blowing, so quiet, pop pop. In ten minutes the White Shark sets them all free. In the dark. First he turns off the lights."

"I'm sure he's bad ass," Coburn said. "Ba-aad aa-ss."

Martinez was not listening but instead reliving a private horror. "It was more like ten thousand. A thousand voices can't sound like that. Gunfire is this little nothing. Poppity pop pop. Where's the White Shark? One guy says, we got to go rescue him, get a team together, and the rest of us just look over at this man, this private, because, number one, no one is leaving the wire. Number two, who is it that needs rescue? You know? And White Shark, no one sees him 'til morning."

"Well then. Bottom line time," Coburn said, very sobered. "You say he's stalking me outside my car. I'm looking, and he not there. Okay. I'm looking in my mirror. So fuck you. That's right. Fuck you. Fuck you. Bottom line . . ."

Here Coburn's voice came back to him strangely. He was talking to a brick. His phone was powered and lit, but there was no reception. Checked the screen. No towers. Coburn picked up his other phones—the Love stamp, the Washington, the Kittyhawk. No towers. By the Kittyhawk, he checked more to complete the ritual than anything else.

Chapter 40

Months later—months after my gig as Parking Warden of Nausset Island—I found online obituaries for some of the guys I killed. These articles made it sound like I wiped out the whole book of saints. This one served the United States honorably in a dozen conflicts. This guy left behind a million teary children, dependent wives. This guy framed his certificate of citizenship, more precious to him than any savings bond or stock certificate.

The proud new citizen guarded a little floating dock in Frobisher's harbor. He was a lookalike of the two goons from the car, another bruiser in his mid-forties. He, too, would have worn full-blinder sunglasses if it had been at all practicable, but the night was moonless. Arms crossed. No rifle. He stood guard midway along the dock, which was a very stupid choice of place to stand if he anticipated danger. No kid in a squirt-gun fight would choose that spot.

I came up out of the water, floated around a little, got my bearings. I couldn't believe the man would stand there alone, but his gaze didn't move the way it would have if he had partners in sight. He stood motionless as a Beefeater guard.

I paddled close and put a spear through his calf. The goon looked down, not too concerned, arms still crossed. I yanked the line and *kabloom,* his flab went down hard. The edge of the dock went under, then scooped water into the air.

The goon rolled, crying *"EE EE EE,"* holding his calf, oblivious to the mess he made of the tangled wire. The dock rocked on its floats. "Shut up," I hissed. And for some reason he did—he obeyed me—he shut up. "All right then." We had reached one of these unspoken agreements. Or so I thought, but then I saw a patch of intense darkness, the opposite of a shine. His big arms cradled another of these same pistols, these Glocks with homemade silencers. He was saving that for a surprise.

After that trick I couldn't trust him. His enormous head shifted to locate me in the water. His pork-pie neck could only rotate about five degrees.

I had the pistol from earlier, kept more or less dry in a bread bag. I shot him several times, right through the plastic. He rolled over and his arm flopped in the water. My last two bullets were a waste. I was nervous. It had been so long since I fired a pistol.

That wasn't a bad trick, concealing his weapon, and here's my thought: Use that as his obituary: *He was stupid to stand in plain sight on a boat dock. But he tried to be clever and do his job, even when he'd been surprised by a fishing spear through his calf. Of course, he had it coming to him because he took a violent contract with a shitbag. Whatever the circumstances, we own the work of our hands.*

What the actual article harped on was the man's immigration and his military service. To read it, the guy would be mortified. If you don't know, being a "veteran" is just a ribbon for participation. You don't crow about it. It's embarrassing. As a member of the military you're sent here and there—boredom like a dentist's drill—you do good and bad. All the time, over it all, the army keeps projecting this image that you're a valiant Space Ranger. Oh, man . . . flag folding and merit badges and mawkish guitar . . . such balderdash, it didn't fool an adenoidal homeschooler for more than a month or two.

Then you die, and apparently it's out of your hands! Here comes the brass band. In your write-up someone puffs your silliest credentials. You sound like you spent nights memorizing the lost verses of the national anthem, or embroidering patriotic wall hangings.

When you go about carefully, it's easy to mistake the world as fragile, because people and objects still break, however light your hand. *Crash! Sorry!* You come to think that the world is pricey crystal.

But then you start throwing mugs, fistfight your way across Edinburgh, and you achieve the more complete understanding, which is that damage is also difficult and unpredictable. Things have hidden skeletons. Glass, steel, and flesh—they shatter or hold by their own unknowable system. One rifle bullet passes through a man and pops every organ. He's in tatters. Another rifle bullet passes through and causes nothing worse than indigestion. Apply a band-aid to the hole.

I swam out and climbed the side of Frobisher's motor yacht. The old man was waiting for me, crouched, with a gaff hook. He rose out swinging and hooked under my arm. I took control of the gaff handle and bulled Frobisher forward, until he bent over the lifelines and overbalanced.

A clatter made us both look down. My stolen pistol hit the deck and bounded like a rubber toy into the water. In the struggle it worked loose from my waistband. Then, *Kaplam!* Frobisher back-flopped into the ocean. He surfaced sputtering and indignant but essentially unharmed.

He might be ancient, but he had tagged me worse than I tagged him! His hook hung from the muscles under my shoulder. It was a shark gaff with a four-foot handle. The metal hook rubbed my collarbone.

I prised it out, the full curve. At least gaffs aren't barbed. Frobisher's head bobbed in the water, blowing and complaining. "Shut the fuck up," I said. I whipped the gaff at him. Again his luck was golden—it hit the water and skipped like a stone over his bobbing head.

He started paddling circles around the hull, exclaiming about the water temperature. He called for me to lower the swim ladder.

"Anna?" I scrambled over the yacht, increasingly panicked. Under duress the ferryman had assured me that Frobisher would be here. He was, but no one else. No one else on deck.

Down below? I opened the door and it was an atmosphere of poison gas. "Christ." Powerful poison billowed out in a cloud. Frobisher was stripping the paint down there. The cabin was a dead end, because no one could descend into that dark. Even standing in the pilot house the fumes stripped the mucus from my throat.

"Where's the girl?" I asked Frobisher.

"Over here now. Over here. The ladder."

He presumed I was a public servant, come to save him, or to arrest him, or to advise him of his rights. I still wore my uniform shirt, my last shirt now ripped and bloody at the armpit. The blood flow was nothing. The enormous hook made a little hole like a pencil, and the blood had already stopped.

I sat down with my legs over the side of the yacht. Frobisher did laps. He searched for a place he could hang and rest. He tried the mooring float, but that sank with his weight. He tried to rest with fingers in the through-hulls for the engine coolant water. He slid out and came around again.

"Where is your son?" I said, eyeing the dark island.

Frobisher blabbered about percentages, as though he and I had entered financial negotiations.

"Shut up about your land deal. Where is your son? Where is

the girl he brought out tonight?"

Frobisher reached up and grabbed the cuff of my pants, huffing. "I had no part in any killing," he assured me, looking up with an earnest expression. He gulped and changed hands as his fingers lost grip. "None whatsoever. Categorically. Now, Cunningham tried to steal. He wanted to mine gold in his own fashion, to threaten and blackmail. To build trash, not treasure. But my team wants jobs and overall growth."

"Shhh." I explained to him that he owned the work of his hands. He had a chance at redemption, however. He should grab hold. Grab hold. I made the comparison to his current predicament. His bodily struggles were an accurate metaphor. He was floundering. With his efforts here, he was now too tired to swim to shore.

I was wasting my time. Frobisher was an old man. He had lost the ability to hear. He wouldn't stop panting and talking. In frustration I set my other foot on his face and pushed him under. "Take a lap."

The island loomed huge and warm. On the satellite map it had a dozen roads and twenty buildings. Homes, a lighthouse, boathouses, sheds, woods, and trailers. Unless I got lucky I would search the wrong buildings first.

The bitter taste of failure. I recognized it. It coated my teeth. I was not finished tonight with the panic and the violence. No, I would still blunder through the rest of the hours before the sun rose. When I was spent and exhausted, then I would probably find the innocent body. At some place I should have gone to first.

Once, in eastern Africa, I emptied the entire national prison. The place and the prison were called Anomabu. It held the guilty and the innocent. The rapists and the political prisoners and men who simply bridled against being poor. I blew open the doors and freed a thousand of these men onto their guards and into the night, and brought chaos.

I did all this, and the one man I hoped to free was dead before I started. Before I lit the first match. In the pre-dawn I found him cold and stiff. He had been stomped by men who had taken their time to aim their heels at his eye sockets, methodically, and finally at the temples of his fragile, refined skull.

Frobisher came around. He was fading, turning his mouth skyward, taking tiny waves in the face. "Quit talking," I said. "You're out of breath; quit talking. I told you I don't care. Listen now. I need to find your son. Listen now." I showed him the land. "I am going to burn all your world."

Wham! I slammed forward against the lifeline wire and fell sliding through. I caught myself with both hands on the lifeline, suspended at my chin.

I'd been shot squarely in the back. Without thinking, I pulled myself back up to my same sitting position. Suddenly it was daylight. A glaring sun streaked away. Nothing made sense.

Behind on deck a girl sobbed. She tried to reload a flare gun. She couldn't eject the shell—shrieked and burnt her finger poking in the barrel. The flare itself had bounced off me and gone underwater. Thirty yards away, it burned and bubbled like a witches' brew.

The girl wore a bikini or her underwear. She was very young. She wasn't Anna or Anna's sister or anyone I knew. She was the third girl from the passports. Oxana? She must have been hiding down in the poison fumes of the cabin.

At my attention she gave up on the flare gun. She threw it at me and fled toward the bow of the yacht, making sounds but never a word. "Hey! Don't worry!" I tried to calm her. I lay on deck and stretched. My back ached, totally unproductive pain, every muscle tightened into a cramp. "It's okay you shot me," I called. "I'm all right. I don't mind."

She yanked and struggled hysterically, then *splash*! Into the water she dropped a barrel that was lashed to the deck. It was the life raft. When it hit the water, it opened and started to expand in tubes. It was an enormous orange life raft. She leaped at it, bounced off, and fell into the ocean.

Later I learned that the girl was Frobisher's wife. She saved his life. The last I saw of him, this girl tried to help him over the squishy edge of the inflating raft. Neither had the strength and he cussed her bitterly.

That was later. When she first surfaced, I went forward and called down to her, "Do you know where the other girl is? Another girl, as small as you? Her name is Anna."

She wept. She was brave but she didn't know what she was doing. I cut the tether, so that the raft could float free. "I need to find the Frobisher son. Creepy-looking man. Please, he's got a girl, and I thought she would be here. I thought she was you. Please, I'm out of time."

She understood me, down in the water, but each thing I said made her sob. Each thing I said, she moaned and cried as though I slapped her.

I moaned too—*Yeagh*—bent with rage and frustration. I held my breath and descended into the fumes of the cabin, ripping the louver doors down off their hinges.

Below was a murk of poison gas and wreckage, the upholstery stripped and the hatch covers ajar, everything clammy to the touch, beads of solvent hung wet in the air. I swallowed the burn and threw myself into the forward door. The gilt fastenings blew apart. Nothing. Paint cans and rectangular tins of spirits. I stumbled back. The aft cabin was cleanly stripped. I yanked up the bilge panels over the engines. Nothing. From bow to stern, there was no hiding. The yacht was all old, with precious sizing, no space even for a tiny body.

By the time I got back into night air, snorting and spitting gobs of poison, the yacht had fully revealed itself as a disgusting craft, a site of filth and evil, fraudulent to its skeleton, all the lies of decorative wood. It was easy to see that nothing good had ever happened in its history, however many years it had been afloat.

The keys were dangling in the panel and now I started the engines, to run the boat full on the rocks, crack its prissy hull, and drown its poisons. Screens flickered to life on all sides. There was a map, an autopilot. Okay then, all right. I set a course east. The high seas. England or bust. How fitting—this craft, at least, would have Cunningham's Viking funeral.

It's easy to get in these moods. As I stumbled back from slicing the mooring line, I was giddy enough I even started to laugh. But my wristwatch cut me short with its chime.

First, do no harm. Second, do no harm. Third, do no harm. Fourth, do no harm. Fifth, do no harm.

That was the full run of it. The watch chimed more and more frequently, as the summer wore out, and the salt air corroded its guts. Especially during the day, if I was active, it rang almost hourly.

I'd taken to stopping it, reaching the button without a thought. This time I did not stop it.

All violence was childish. All violence was contemptible. To excite myself, wrecking this worthless trash, when all around, the whole world, stood by waiting to make it again?

The island loomed and chastened, while I wasted my time here with useless gesture. Dozens of buildings and sites, miles of road, acres of dark forest . . . enormous and impervious. In the foreground, Frobisher and his girl bride struggled and groaned to get him into the bouncy-house raft, drifting in the calm bay. Beyond them, unseen in the dark, floated a dead man, tangled in spear-gun wire, his heavy body bleeding into the bay.

Then, on the distant shore, a fan of light. A car turned to park. Its headlights brushed a stand of low trees, and then went out.

CHAPTER 41

Coburn approached Malcolm Trent's parked car, his mood so subdued he couldn't raise his eyes past the door handle. "We need to be out there."

"Eh? It's Thursday night," Trent stage-whispered. He checked left and right that the coast was clear, then lifted the chipped handle of an old, wooden baseball bat. The grip was filthy athletic tape. "My turn tonight, eh? The doctor vandal gets a surprise."

It took a moment for Coburn to understand. It did nothing for his mood. With both hands, he rubbed the thin hair above his ears. "A baseball bat? I need you to grow up. We don't have time. Bottom line, tonight, I can't . . ."

Trent didn't hear Coburn's frustration. Like everyone else, he had been talking to himself a lot, and now he had a speech to deliver. "I figure you did nothing. The cops do nothing. All right. So now it's my turn at the plate. The doctor? Well . . ."

Coburn wasn't listening. He was studying the bushes that surrounded the parking lot. Trent followed his gaze, uncomprehending. "I been smelling gas. Do you smell gas or something?"

Coburn moved his eyes over the bushes. "It's a parking lot."

"What's wrong with you?"

"My car."

Coburn's intense mood drew Trent upright in his seat. "Because the phones are down? They'll come back. Believe me, don't worry. These outages . . ." He got out of his car. "I tell you what I got inside the restaurant, eh? A phone line. A real one. Not those mobiles. Remember back when there were phone wires? You and I remember, right? We're old school."

"I tell you it's down."

"Like it's cut?" Trent wasn't sure whether to smile or not.

Coburn opened his fingers, the most imperceptible shrug: "The lines are cut. My car."

Coburn drove to full speed after every turn, bullying the car's transmission. He didn't seem to hear the abuse, and Trent fell silent. Without taking his eyes from the road, Coburn reached and felt under the passenger seat. He produced a .357 revolver. He set it in Trent's lap and reached under the seat again. Trent chuckled, "Whoa whoa whoa, hey."

"Do you know how to aim and fire a handgun?"

"Heh heh. Man oh man." Trent weighed the pistol inexpertly. He passed it from hand to hand like a ball and sighted it out the windshield.

"Not a smirk," Coburn said. "I need an answer from you."

Trent set the revolver on the floor mat. "All right. Take it easy." He rubbed his chin with his thumbnail—a man with superior knowledge, weighing how many secrets he should share. "Let's just say, okay, that Don Frobisher had a number he could call, and maybe he called it. Right? There are guys in this world who know their way around a firearm. That's their entire business. The best in the world."

Coburn cut him off. "You listen to this? You listen to the police band?" He turned on the radio. The talk was codes and urgency.

Trent frowned at this irritant. "Let's just say, for argument, Frobisher made the phone call, right? And I'm not naming names, but an airplane lands on his landing strip. You know he has a landing strip right out there. That's all I'm saying."

Trent chuckled more. He'd said enough. But Coburn didn't respond. Trent tried again: "This airplane is bringing visitors. Right? Don't fly with lights. No flight plan. This plane exists and it does not exist, you hear me? Right?"

Coburn drove like he was riding a horse to death. Trent was crestfallen. "Frobisher called in some professionals. Heavy-hitters. Yeah, we got professionals in play." In the silence, the radio voices eventually asserted themselves. Trent nodded to the radio. "What are they on about?"

"Fires. The phone towers are gone. The phone tower by the golf course . . . it was blown up."

"Blown up? Right."

Coburn let the cynicism hear itself and die. Then he said, "Men are dead. Unidentified men. They're not even hinting. Which means that they're not local."

They drove to the ferry landing. Police voices broke the silence sporadically. Trent's stomach began to yowl.

The groans were loud. They were notes on the alp horn. "Heh. Something wrong with the pipes," Trent said. "You know, I'm the money man. That's what I am. That's my world. That's why you come to me. I tap into the local money. Believe me, there's a lot of local money, a lot."

Coburn listened to this. Waited. Then spoke. "I'll give you a thought experiment. Imagine Brand Frobisher arrested by a gung-ho policeman. Interrogated. Imagine how that session is going to go. Do you imagine that Brand has the sense to stay quiet? You think he has the moral fiber? You think he'll demand the counsel of his attorneys? Or do you think that Brand will boast?"

Coburn let that sink in. "So imagine how your life is going to change tonight. Your life is changing right now."

"Not for me."

"Yes, for you."

Trent cleared his throat. "You worry too much. That girl you got . . . she's nothing. I get this all the time, these foreigners, with whatever they're doing. This one's just looking for her sister. The sister worked a season out here. That's all it is."

"What girl? What?" Malcolm Trent had said it so quietly, and with so much human sympathy that Coburn turned on him in fright and amazement. "How did you know about the girl?"

In answer Trent rocked his head—a little here, a little there.

Coburn felt that his world was ending. All secrets were out. He thought he'd been careful. Instead he'd left greasy handprints. He shook his head to clear it. "Brand . . . partied too hard with the sister. It was last October. Do you understand me? You understand what I mean?"

Coburn waited. Trent nodded once, sullenly.

"This new sister is not going to stop looking. The new girl. She's not going to stop asking questions. Bottom line, there was one option. We took it. Do you understand?"

"Ok-aay," Trent said. He held the pistol again, and weighed it back and forth between his hands. He would have liked to check the load. He would have liked to work the slide. But the pistol didn't have a slide, and he didn't know what he was doing. Just like that, Malcolm Trent was back to being an imbecile.

Jack did not come out to meet the car. His trailer was dark. Coburn flashed the headlights and Trent got out. "Jack-o? Hey, Jack-o."

Coburn went to the trailer. The door was missing. It was completely absent. He glanced inside. "Gone."

"Jack-o? He's never gone."

"Jack-o! What the fuck happened to his trailer? Did something fall on it? It's all bent."

At that point Coburn quit speaking altogether. There would

be time for that.

For decades he had ridden this ferry. One more time, and he would be done. He pried opened the case of the outboard motor. The stormy channel was at his back, already tugging at the hull. Coburn wound a length of greasy clothesline around the starter wheel.

Chapter 42

"Are you familiar with the term 'gold-digger'? Do you know what kind of girl that is?" Brand asked. He walked Anna along the beach, to the boathouse.

"Yes, sure," Anna answered quickly, and waited for anything more.

Brand was enjoying this date more than any he could remember. No tedious love-lies. No horse-faced girls with bare, hulking shoulders. Instead, from the start, this lively little body scampered at his side, no matter that she was frightened. She was frightened of him and came along anyway.

She had smelled danger before she shut the door of the car. Every step in the sand, she grew more anxious. Yet still she came, lured by the sight of her sister's bag. Brand would show the string bag, whirl it around, and return it to his pocket before she could touch.

This girl was a surprise and delight. She could be no newspaper reporter. She was young for high school! She kept smiling at him. She presumed her smiles earned her something. It must be so among her school friends. Smile and a boy would carry her books! With enough of her sad little smiles, Brand would tell her where her sister was.

"Kat lived here for some weeks, then?" she said.

"Lived here? No."

"It's okay. It's okay she was here. She liked the water."

This girl Anna was forgiving him for fucking her sister. For using her. Unbelievable! Brand teased: "She wasn't such a swimmer, though, was she? Ekaterina."

Anna didn't understand the tone but tried to be friendly. "No. She didn't like her head wet all the way."

"When you're on a date with a young man, what do you bring?" Brand asked her. "What do you bring with you on a date?"

"A date? I don't know. Some money," Anna guessed.

"What do you think of a girl who, the only thing she brings on a date, in her purse, is a pair of stained panties?" Anna stopped. Brand gripped Ekaterina's underpants in his fist, a tiny black handful. He giggled. "That's some lady, wouldn't you say?"

Anna stopped in her tracks, and Brand understood immediately: the underwear in hand broke the rules of their game. Suddenly she knew him.

Silently, gently, Brand offered the whole bait. The bag and underpants. He knew, from experience, that he needed to grab this girl. From here on, she would only understand more and more. Her first move would be hesitant retreat. Straying away. This is the closest she would ever stand again, and distance was incredibly important. If Brand took a single quick step toward her, she could be off like a rabbit. Even the dimmest girl recognized a chase.

Instead of coming closer, Brand shifted up the beach. He crossed their path, the impressions their feet had left in the coarse sand, and put himself between her and the car. She would not yet recognize this as an important consideration. For a few heartbeats she would not recognize the game and the goal.

Anna's eyes rose from Ekaterina's things. Yes. They searched his face for reassurance. Brand imagined the quarrel within her. All her years alive, all her training in the world, told her to distrust her own instincts. Her instincts said to run from this freakish killer.

Now she would talk, blabber. Whatever she said, what she wanted was this same reassurance, for him to tell her that she was mistaken. Of course people don't hurt one another.

Brand was practiced. He shook his head at their misunderstanding. He put Ekaterina's bag in her grasp, and he gently took her wrist.

When Brand took hold of a girl, she would pull away. Like a hooked fish, too late, she would understand and jerk back.

Anna broke this pattern. Instead her free hand came around and she *pushed.* She pushed a pair of craft scissors into the ribs above Brand's heart. The blades snapped like a chocolate bar, with a soft, meaty *click.* She screeched a bird sound and slashed backhand with the broken end. She held almost nothing, only the hinge and plastic handles. The stroke was so vicious she took a pit out of Brand's chin.

"Bitch."

Now she ran. She had her sister's bag. Anna ran. Not for the car but up the beach into patches of roses. Her arms pumped like a machine, as she sprinted. *Pop!* Behind her came a gunshot.

The shot stopped her, astonished—gunfire? A gun? She tripped another unsteady step and raised her hands. She understood. A warning shot. She panted and turned back when Brand fired again. This bullet passed her face with a buzz.

Anna ran again, for her life.

Every child knows the feeling of running exposed. As a girl, Anna had learned it from snowball fights in the winter, and, in the summer, from a game of throwing pinecones. A decade had passed, but as she ran, the familiar sensation flooded back. She felt her million vulnerabilities, the pre-ghost of the actual strike, her slender back as wide as a sign board. Along with the memory came the lesson: How to make yourself a difficult target.

She juked sideways. Brand fired at the same moment. The bullet whined past.

Too late now, a second lesson returned: she had chosen the wrong escape. There was no cover, no hiding spots. The beach roses were brittle and dry. They were barely alive in this summer of drought. The vines scraped down her shins, gathered at her ankles, and tore off. She stumbled but could only sprint forward and present to the man the easiest target. To him she was a solid color, barely wavering, a blouse pinned on a clothesline. Infinitely slowly, her shape would grow smaller, only infinitely slowly.

She had known all this but forgotten. There were no other choices, and no time to alter her choice.

For Brand's part, other than a few birds he had never fired upon anything that dodged. He walked forward, aiming but unconsciously waiting for the expected fair shot. In his life he had never seen an athlete run. With her gymnast sprint and cranking arms Anna *shrank* by the moment. Brand panicked and fired. Anna went down. But she was up again on the bounce.

"Stop. Please stop." A hoarse, desperate call. "Please stop." Brand turned. His eye found a shape, far down the beach, a quarter mile perhaps, clearly outlined by the luminous ocean. The figure shambled. It called out, hurt or drunk, but had no breath. Brand felt a flicker of recognition . . . something of the man, or something of his movement.

Brand's pistol was still raised and aimed. But Anna was gone. The thickets of beach roses jerked, as something struggled among their stalks.

"Please. Stop," the figure croaked.

"Why should I?" Brand asked peevishly, talking aloud to himself. Who was this man? How had he been allowed?

Someone should be here to take him. Where was Michael Coburn? Where was his father?

Light—fire! Beyond the man, the night showed the uneven light of a bonfire. It was the dock burning, or the guest house. Some accident there had hurt the man? And he came stumbling up Brand's beach for help? For aid?

Unbelievable. No. Brand was peevish and puzzled but these feeling were supplanted with a jolt of rage. His shoulders tightened like a spring twisted beyond the limits of the metal, so the spring would seize up, or snap, or lash out wildly and dismiss the whole fucking world. Unbelievable. A minute before, he savored a slow, delectable feast of lust. Now instead, his face was hurt, and what was this? Cleanup? Weeping, wounded, grotesque male flesh . . .

Another light, this one on the water. Two more lights, one of them red. It was the running lights for The *Danube,* his father's yacht. The boat sped away. Not north, not to Boston, but directly away. The orientation of the running lights made no sense, and the speed was wrong. The speed was crazy. There was a white bow wave.

"Is that my dad? He should be here."

The approaching man couldn't hear. Crybaby. He never stopped shuffling.

Brand turned, and was reassured to see the thicket move unnaturally. All was not lost. Fun could still be had.

He turned back to the exhausted panting. A shiny badge glinted. The approaching man wore a uniform. "You're a policeman?"

"Parking Warden. Give me the gun. Where is she? Did you shoot her?"

"Do you see what she did to me?" Brand answered. With the gun acknowledged. Brand held it between them, gradually raising it to aim at the man's feet, and, as his approach changed the angle, at the man's knees. He came on with no regard.

The Parking Warden had made a mistake, allowing the confusing scene to become a clear case of crime, threat, and police. Now, at ten yards, he made a second mistake. Instead of continuing straight, his path veered a bit, up the beach.

No one else would spot this move for what it was, but, of course, Brand knew. The move was to cut Brand off. Brand recognized that immediately. Had he not done the same thing himself, dozens of times? The man moved to put himself between Brand and escape, to herd him toward the water.

Brand did what was simplest: He raised the pistol six inches and shot the policeman.

"Oh, Jesus Christ." The man crumpled.

That done, Brand anxiously turned to search for movement in the rose thickets.

CHAPTER 43

Coburn and Trent approached the boathouse on foot, a path Coburn knew well through the scrubby forest. "Stop lighting your phone," Coburn said. "The tower is down. The tower won't heal itself."

Coburn wondered why he brought Trent. Trent had always been a child, and the tension of the night magnified these traits. He had tucked the .357 revolver through the back of his belt like a pirate. Also, some internal force would not allow him to remain completely silent. "Ye-ah," he kept saying, when nothing else suggested itself.

Why bring him? Whatever happened, he would be part of it. Tonight their conspiracy would change, for the last time. They were just about finished with one another, but all of them—Coburn, Trent, and the Frobishers, young and old—all would need to be together this one last time.

"Hey hey," Coburn whispered. "This looks pretty good." The boathouse showed a single light, though a filthy window. No commotion. No outcry. No girl.

Brand would break the girl but not kill her. He would grow bored before he killed her, and Coburn would have to step in. The trick was to do the obvious, quickly, without thinking about it.

What a nightmare, to imagine a policeman discovering the Ukrainian girl in this damaged state, neither alive nor dead. "Thank God. Thank goodness." Coburn couldn't help himself.

"Brand came through." Cleanup was terrible, but Coburn knew the drill. He'd do the best job of his life. He'd use the airplane. Brand would take care of himself. He would wipe himself with towel after towel, fastidious as a cat. "I can't believe it."

"Didn't I *tell* you no cops were coming?" Trent was bitter from an hour of being frightened and treated like an idiot sidekick. "Frobisher brought in some professionals. Not your amateur hour. Do you even understand that? I mean, what did you think? This cop didn't take the fucking ferry, did he? Did he?"

"He didn't take the ferry."

"So how were you figuring he got here? He's not even fucking alive, okay? That's what was on your radio."

"Could be." Coburn admitted, riding another surge of happiness. Trent's petulance didn't touch him. Relief flowed into his veins so strongly, he would have stayed calm if Trent had attacked him with fists.

"So now you tell me why I'm out here with a cowboy gun. Eh? Because it's fucking amateur night. Yeah, that's what it looks like to me."

As they approached the boathouse, Coburn entertained the question. Why had he panicked? It was those phone conversations with Sergeant Martinez. Those phone calls had poisoned his mind. He'd started to imagine an enemy with magical powers. "Why don't you stay here, Malcolm?" he said, with a gesture of a flat hand. "I'll look inside." However happy he might be, he didn't relish the job. "Look, bottom line, this is my thing. Brand gets keyed up."

"Brand? You're taking me to fucking Brand? No, no. Who I want to talk to is Don. I leverage ten million dollars, cash and assurances. That's not chump change, brother. A lot of guys can talk about seven, eight figures. Not a lot of guys can deliver." Trent huffed. "For my ten million, I get dragged across the water, all hours of the night, on an unsafe craft. The conversation that needs to happen is you, me, and Don. And I don't think you're going to like what's said."

"Sure, sure," Coburn agreed absently. "We'll go over afterward."

"And if you're going in that boat shed, I'm going in that boat shed."

"Okay then." The two figures shuffled down the sand. The world was growing light; Coburn felt chatty, even giddy. "A new day. Even the government has to get back to work sometimes." It was Trent's turn to say nothing. Coburn checked his watch: 2:30. To the east, over the trees, was the aura of dawn. Confused, he asked Trent, "What time do you have?"

Trent turned on his phone to check. There was beeping. "It's not—"

Trent stopped, head up. The sound did not come from his device, and it was not a phone noise. Instead it was the one-note bell, a mechanical chime from a wristwatch.

Side by side, the two men tracked the sound, their heads moving with the same motion. The bell stopped.

Slumped in the shadows beside the door of the boathouse, a policeman watched them. He hugged himself, and the badge on his shirt shone like a salmon flasher. The chime came from him.

Coburn felt disbelief. Realization. "Hey!" He drew his pistol from his armpit holster and dropped to his knee in the rough sand. "Hey!" His mouth couldn't decide what to say.

Beside him, Trent fired, tripping backward. The revolver roared, and Trent let the kick carry the pistol up over his head.

One shot released all the others. Both men fired as fast as they could pull the trigger, an utter tear of bullets, Trent straying backward and Coburn stepping forward with growing confidence.

The policeman hung limp from the start. He jerked but did not fall.

His head slumped, and Coburn recognized the sheen of the hair. "Wait!"

Coburn spun, his hand burning. He discovered that his gun was gone, his gun hand obliterated. Another cough—another faint gunshot. A bullet passed behind him.

"Hold still, gents," a voice said.

Trent had no pistol. He put his empty hands in the air. But at once his control snapped, "Ohh-ohh," and he began to lumber off, building speed to something like a run, farting audibly.

Coburn watched for him to be cut down. Trent ran on and on and Coburn even had a thought that this escape was unfair. He noticed that his own fingers weren't missing but severed at the bones and hidden behind his palm, and the burn of the wound surged.

Chapter 44

Over the beach to the east the false dawn was hungry orange and flickering. It was a low band of smoke lit from its internal flames. "Fire is coming," Anna said, the Ukrainian girl. She disappeared into the boathouse again.

Coburn was relieved that the girl mentioned the oncoming fire. He didn't dare speak himself. Would not speak. The policeman Hawkins regarded him as a nuisance object. When Hawkins first approached, naked to the waist, his torso caked with black blood, he did not talk or look at Coburn. Instead he kicked his legs from under and packaged him with plastic cord. He spun Coburn's entire body over and over in the sand, like a spider wrapping an insect. The expression he wore was not vicious or vengeful but instead empty. By no means was the killing done.

Anna backed out from the creaking door. Her arms were full of stiff rags. "Another bandage," she told Hawkins.

"Do they have oil on them? I'm okay." He wore a bloody cloth tight around his torso, at the bottom of his ribs. "Don't use them if they stink." Coburn felt the loom of Hawkins, who lifted and rolled him sideways, examining his shirt. "This one's already a mess. I could rip maybe six clean inches."

The move left Coburn facing Brand's body, up against the boathouse. It still wore the sodden police uniform. Coburn rasped, "He's dead?"

At being addressed, Hawkins drew back in surprise. He followed Coburn's gaze to Brand, and then looked back to

Coburn, puzzled to understand the question. Back to Brand. "You didn't hit that much. But you didn't miss every single shot."

The sight made Hawkins resentful. "That's my shirt on him. My only good shirt, made out of canvas or something heavy duty. He wouldn't stop squirming, so I tied the arms like a straitjacket, but then you guys came . . ."

Brand's corpse began ringing again. The same chime. The sound came from the body, and it seemed to infuriate Anna, who threw down the rags and went back into the boathouse.

Hawkins explained, sheepish: "I jammed my watch into his mouth, when he was blabbering. He wouldn't shut up. The idea was he needed a more intimate relationship with the truth." Coburn saw that Brand's mouth was gagged with another strip of cloth. "It was stupid, okay. I think he swallowed it."

With conversation opened, Coburn felt licensed to speak. "I know you're a soldier, and an honorable man, and I think we can—"

"Hey. Hey. Just stop talking, okay. I don't have anything for your mouth."

Coburn tried. Swallowed several starts. "You don't want to kill me."

Hawkins considered the plastic rope that bound him, rope from a lobster pot. "It is bad, violence against the helpless. But you think about it, all violence is violence against the helpless. At the moment of its effect. Right? Everyone is helpless at that moment."

Coburn gulped and swallowed. "How bad is my hand?"

Hawkins looked with interest, but was disappointed to find only the obvious. They could both see the destroyed hand clearly. Pulsing sullen blood.

"Malcolm Trent?"

"That scumbag!" Hawkins guffawed. "He's out to sea. I

thought I put enough holes in the pontoons of the ferry, but apparently not. I tried to sink it. There must be flotation foam." Hawkins slapped his knee. "Anyway, I sank the engine. He's on a raft to China, or Nova Scotia. Ha! Plus I burned his shit restaurant."

Which explained why Coburn heard no emergency sirens. The night was silent. Car wrecks, restaurant fires, phone towers blown up . . . the populated side of Nausset had enough to keep itself busy. Coburn coughed and spat. He experienced new difficulty in his lungs. Hawkins was passing along knowledge you would not pass to someone who was going to survive. Coburn tried to focus. "Bottom line, the situation, we're brought together by a very lucrative property deal."

Hawkins waved. This subject was too boring to register. At this same time Anna emerged from the boathouse. She too was bloody. It was the same wound as Hawkins. She too had a tight wrap all the way around her torso. She too seemed to be walking without pain. She regarded the fiery sky severely. "You have to burn everything up?"

She addressed this to Hawkins. In response he gave her the same look Coburn had been getting: Well, that was obvious. Something to add?

This time she carried only her sister's cloth bag, only a fistful. She showed it to Hawkins. Coburn recognized it, but Hawkins didn't understand the significance. Still, after a moment, he understood that it was somehow important.

The two seemed furious with each other. Hawkins, late, went to comfort Anna about the bag, but was rebuffed. Coburn could hear only bits. They cycled through several disagreements, and neither paid as much attention to the burning forest as Coburn would have liked. Ashes floated in the air currents, soaring and dropping in their random way.

Finally, Hawkins broke off and approached, crunching gravel

and sand. Anna followed. Hawkins yanked Coburn to sitting position. He showed him a cell phone, then took it back and manipulated inexpertly, punishing the keys until the screen lit up.

"Service is down." Coburn wanted to be helpful. "I think you'll find that the service is down."

Hawkins ignored him. He covered the microphone with his thumb. "I'm going to ask you a series of questions. Let us communicate clearly. These are things *she* wants to hear about. I myself don't care to hear anything you have to say, and, in fact, regard it as a kind of torture. You understand?"

Coburn nodded on cue.

Hawkins flushed, very angry at his reflexive agreement. "No. You're going to find this impossible. You will consider consequences before you speak. You probably have no access to truth, in the first place, so blinded by constructs. Otherwise you could not behave in the way you have." Hawkins gestured to include the entire world.

"You have no time to learn. So instead, you're considering consequences, you must consider only one consequence." Hawkins did not look but indicated the oncoming fire. If Coburn were left as he was, Coburn would bake like a squab.

"Now, pause a moment, to adjust to this new reality."

Coburn understood. The phone was recording. "Anything you want to hear."

"*No.* No. I was completely clear—"

"Anything. Anything *she* wants to hear."

Hawkins was not wholly mollified. He struggled with a different objection. "I'm also uncomfortable . . . This is not a step toward redemption. This is not the same as a frank acknowledgement of your mistakes, in order that you may attempt to rectify them."

Coburn said nothing. Had no way of knowing what to say.

He eyed the orange fury over the horizon of trees—single embers twisted skyward like rockets missing a fin—forced his eyes away.

Hawkins knelt before Coburn and presented the phone. "Marcus Cunningham?"

"Murdered by Brand Frobisher. With others. With Trent. With Brand's father, I think. I wasn't—"

"Eh. Megan Palsinger had a child with Brand."

"Yes. He got sole custody. Donald. The boy's name."

Hawkins sighed to hear it. "Explain. As succinctly as possible."

Coburn did. Brand's father had the best lawyers in Massachusetts. Megan was thirteen years old and desperate to get out of a marriage that would kill her. Brand did not want the child, of course, but would fight with teeth for any toy. The child went to foster parents in Iowa. Brand doled out pictures and updates when Megan behaved.

"Sarah Palsinger, too?"

"Yes. To help her sister."

"The law firm?"

"Rex and Hayworth."

"How old is the boy?"

"He's eighteen."

"She had him when—"

"She was thirteen. The boy came of age. In April. He was looking for his parents." Coburn swallowed. "There was an agreement that Brand would stay away."

"Uh. I'll need materials on this matter."

Coburn swallowed. Saw no way around the obvious. "I don't know how you'll find them. Rex and Hayworth? Brand may have the papers. In the big house." Now he could look at the fire. Likely the flames had already consumed the place, though the fire lit the sky evenly, with no surge for a burning mansion.

Behind enormous Hawkins, Anna cut in. "Describe the killing of my sister."

Coburn had been involved in the killing of this young woman, or at least the aftermath. He had experienced the intimacy of positioning her broken but still-warm body in an inflatable dingy.

Now Coburn experienced what Hawkins had predicted: his tongue was paralyzed. From a baby's first words, there were reasons to speak: To get a smile. To tell what should be told.

To tell this story, Coburn would condemn himself to flames.

While his head wrestled, his mouth spoke. In a few sentences, he described events. Ekaterina came over and stayed in the small house, kept by Frobisher. She went with him to see Watterson but refused to go a second time because Watterson was old, ugly, and sick. His breath smelled like vomit. Frobisher had shared girlfriends for bribes and blackmail, but Kat was not like the others. She was not controllable. Money, passport, promises—no holds would work.

One night she threw a tantrum and she tried to drive the yacht off of its moorings. Old Frobisher brought his son out to the yacht and left the two alone for the evening. Kat was killed.

As he completed his simple narration, Coburn did feel a weight lift from chest. Whatever Hawkins's skepticism about motives, this was the first time Coburn had spoken clearly about this killing, and he did feel a lifting, a lightening of sorts.

Anna listened without interrupting or making eye contact. When Coburn finished, she considered questions but did not ask them. She had a cell phone, too, and found a button on it. Coburn's voice was recorded forever. Hawkins did the same, or tried to—it wasn't clear his phone functioned.

"I have to go," Hawkins said, eyeing the flames.

Anna answered—words inaudible—something cutting. He shook his head. "Fires have an exaggerated reputation. You can step around them. Anyway," he said, "if there's a kid, I have to find these papers."

Anna followed him a few paces up the beach, and the two conferred again. She knew to speak quietly. Hawkins didn't, or didn't care whether Coburn heard. "Just leave him here."

Anna shook her head, thought the idea foolish.

Hawkins looked east and gauged the burn. "I know it's not perfect. Fear of consequences is not guilt. Still, it allows him twenty minutes of very important time, to come to grips."

Anna cut him with a gesture. That wasn't her objection. The two argued back and forth, increasingly hostile. Hawkins finished, strong and loud. "You're wrong. Right now he'll do anything, because his fingers hurt. But he doesn't have anything you want. Just leave all that. You can't play in their world. You can't visit.

"No. Strike it all down, one last time, or you become one of them." Their roles had reversed. It was Hawkins who was cruelly dismissive. He jogged off toward a skyline of orange fire.

EPILOGUE

Good news! Apparently there's hope for the heath hen, a species indigenous to North America once presumed extinct. Contractors for the Environmental Protection Agency found evidence of the birds in their last known habitat, an island off the coast of Massachusetts that had once housed a federal fort. DNA tests verify: heath hen feathers discovered in the feeder trap.

The island was uninhabited (for the most part) and so perfectly positioned to become a refuge for rare and endangered coastal species.

ABOUT THE AUTHOR

Ross Gresham teaches at the Air Force Academy in Colorado Springs. He is the author of a number of stories and academic works (check out his Amazon author page). He is also fiction editor for the journal *War, Literature, and the Arts.*